Resounding praise for *New York Times bestselling* author

STUART WOODS

and

HEAT

"**S**tuart Woods's *Heat* is another
page-turner."
Providence Journal-Bulletin

"[**A**] mile-a-minute plot. . . . Woods has
concocted a high-octane story filled with
nail-biting suspense and enough unusual
twists to keep even experienced
puzzle-solvers guessing."
Booklist

"**O**ne of the best mystery writers
in the business."
USA Today

"**W**oods is a no-nonsense, slam-bang
storyteller."
Chicago Tribune

"**H**e's so good he cost me several
sleepless nights."
ANNE RIVERS SIDDONS

"**I**n *Heat,* Stuart Woods turns the temperature
up to boil and keeps it steady."
Denver Post

STUART WOODS

HEAT

HARPER

An Imprint of HarperCollins*Publishers*

This is a work of fiction. Names, characters, places, and incidents are products of the author's imagination or are used fictitiously and are not to be construed as real. Any resemblance to actual events, locales, organizations, or persons, living or dead, is entirely coincidental.

HARPER

An Imprint of HarperCollins*Publishers*
10 East 53rd Street
New York, New York 10022-5299

Copyright © 1994 by Stuart Woods
ISBN 978-0-06-201750-5

First Harper premium printing: February 2011
First HarperTorch paperback printing: July 2002
First HarperPaperbacks printing: March 1995
First HarperCollins hardcover printing: June 1994

HarperCollins® and Harper® are registered trademarks of Harper-Collins Publishers.

Printed in the United States of America

Visit Harper paperbacks on the World Wide Web at
www.harpercollins.com

10 9 8 7 6 5 4 3 2

HEAT

1

Atlanta Federal Prison swam slowly out of the smog as the helicopter beat its way south from Fulton County Airport. Kip Fuller was transfixed by the sight.

In his three years in law enforcement Kipling Fuller had never been inside a prison of any sort, and Atlanta held a place in his imagination on a level with Alcatraz and Leavenworth—especially Alcatraz, since that was a prison of the past, as was Atlanta.

Alcatraz was permanently closed, though, while Atlanta had been partly reopened to handle the overflow of federal prisoners. At its peak the prison had held a population of nearly four thousand, but the current number was closer to eight hundred. The prison had been a temporary home to Cuban refugees, Haitian boat people, Colombian drug lords and the occasional special prisoner. It was a special prisoner that Fuller would meet today—or, rather, meet again.

To avoid breaking the FAA regulation prohibiting flights over the prison yard, the pilot made a turn that took him parallel with the wall, a few yards out. They were at five hundred feet now, aiming for the big H painted on the prison roof, and Fuller could see into the yard. As he watched, two figures met in the middle of the open area, and the other prisoners immediately rushed to surround them, leaving a small circle free for the two men, who were now swinging at each other. At the outskirts of the crowd, uniformed guards could be seen trying to push their way to the center, but Fuller thought they weren't trying very hard. He brought the microphone of his headset close to his lips.

"What's going on down there?" he asked the assistant warden sitting next to him.

"That's your man," the official replied.

"What, you mean fighting?"

"That's right. Every time he gets out of solitary, he gets in another fight, and back in he goes."

"How long has this been going on?"

"Fourteen months; the whole time he's been inside."

"Jesus," Fuller said.

Jesse Warden sat on the edge of the examination table and watched through his swollen left eye as the male nurse pulled the thread tight, knotted it and snipped it off with the surgical scissors.

"There you go, Jesse," the man said. "How many stitches is that I've put in you the last year?"

"I've lost count," Warden said in his native hillbilly twang. It hurt when he moved his lips.

"So have I," the nurse said, placing a large Band-Aid over the cut under the eye. "That's it," the nurse said to the guard.

"Let's go, Jesse," the guard said. The guards didn't call him by his last name, as they did the other prisoners; "Warden" was a term of address saved for prison management.

Warden let himself down slowly from the table and preceded the guard through the door, trying not to limp. The guard gave him plenty of room; no guard had touched him since the first fight.

Fuller jumped down from the helicopter and followed the assistant warden across the prison roof toward a door; shortly they were walking down an empty corridor, their footsteps echoing through the nearly empty building.

"It's kind of spooky, isn't it?" Fuller said.

"You get used to it," the AW replied. "In the old days this place would have been full of noise, like any prison, but with the population out in the yard for exercise right now, it's dead quiet."

Fuller followed the man through a door, across a waiting room to another door, where the AW knocked.

"Come in!" a voice called from behind the door.

The AW opened the door, let Fuller in and closed it behind him.

The warden stood up from behind his desk and offered his hand. "J. W. Morris," he said.

"Kip Fuller, from the U.S. Attorney General's office," Fuller replied.

"I've been expecting you, Mr. Fuller. Have a seat; what can I do for you?"

Fuller sat down and took an envelope from his inside pocket. "You have a prisoner named Jesse R. Warden here."

"We do," the warden replied.

Fuller handed the envelope across the desk and waited while Morris read the paper inside.

"This is unusual," the warden said.

"Is it?" Fuller had no idea.

"Normally, when a federal prisoner is released to the custody of the attorney general, it's by court order and a reason is stated—like the prisoner is needed to testify in court."

"Not in this case," said Fuller, who had read the document during his flight from Washington in the Gulfstream government jet.

"Could I see some ID?" the warden asked.

"Certainly," Fuller replied, offering his identification card.

"'Special Task Force,'" the warden read aloud. "What does that mean?"

"Just what it says, sir," Fuller replied. "That's all I'm at liberty to tell you."

The warden nodded. "I see," he said. "I wonder if you'd mind stepping out into my waiting room for a moment?" He didn't return the ID to Fuller.

"Be glad to," he replied. The man was going to

call Washington, and Fuller didn't blame him a bit. He left the room and closed the door behind him. The waiting room walls were bereft of pictures, and there were no magazines lying around. Fuller paced the floor slowly, measuring the dimensions of the little room. About the size of a cell, he guessed. The door opened, and the warden waved him back into the inner office.

"Looks like you've got yourself a prisoner," Morris said. "When do I get him back?"

"The AG's order says 'indefinite custody,'" Fuller replied.

"Does that mean he's not coming back? The man's serving two consecutive life sentences; with the most favorable consideration he's in for twelve, thirteen more years, and his conduct so far has not been such to warrant favorable consideration."

"I'm afraid I can't answer your question, Warden," Fuller said. "I'm just a pickup and delivery man." He was more than that, but the warden didn't need to know.

The warden took a form out of his desk and rolled it into a typewriter at his side. He filled it out, hunting and pecking, then whipped the paper out of the machine and pushed it across the desk with a pen. "I'll need your signature," he said.

Fuller read the form and the paragraph at the bottom:

Received a prisoner, Jesse R. Warden, no. 294304, at the personal order of the Attorney General of the United States, from the Federal Penitentiary at Atlanta, Georgia, this date, for indefinite custody.

Fuller signed and dated the document. "Where is Mr. Warden now?" he asked.

"In solitary confinement," the warden replied, "where he always is."

2

Jesse walked into the punishment cell, and the door was slammed and locked behind him. This time, though, he wasn't alone in the dimly lit room. Just as the door swung shut he caught sight of a man sitting on the bunk, and he wasn't a prison official. Jesse knew him; his name was Charley Bottoms, and he was major trouble. Bottoms was the leader of the Aryan Nation group inside the prison; they were racist, anti-Semitic and extremely violent.

"Come on in, boy, and sit down," Bottoms said.

Bottoms was a biker type, six feet five or six, three hundred pounds and covered in tattoos. Jesse had no intention of sitting on a bunk with him. "I'm all right where I am," he said.

"You know," Bottoms said in a southeastern drawl, "them's the first words I ever heard you say. What kinda accent is that? Where you from?"

No need to be hostile to the man; Jesse wanted to leave this cell alive. "North Georgia," Jesse replied. "Up near the Tennessee border."

"Tennessee was my guess," Bottoms said.

"Yeah, even folks a little farther south in Georgia think my accent's kind of crazy."

"A real hillbilly."

"The real thing." Jesse was a preacher's son and he had three years of college and two of law school, but his childhood country accent had never changed a whit.

"I hear you're heat," Bottoms said.

Now they were on dangerous ground. "Used to be."

"Why ain't you still?"

Jesse thought about it for a moment. Hell, why not? "They found half a million dollars and my dead partner in the trunk of my car."

"You did all that?"

"I couldn't convince them I didn't."

"Come on, boy, I want to know what you did."

"I'm not making any jailhouse confessions; they have a way of turning up later on."

"You think I'd testify in court against another con?"

"Maybe against a con who used to be heat."

Bottoms shook his head. "You got a bad opinion of me."

"Not at all," Jesse said. "I just try to run a tight mouth."

"So you're doin' two big ones, back to back, huh?"

"That's what the judge said."

"How many fights you been in since you got here?"

"A hell of a lot more than I was looking for."

"Yeah, I guess cons just naturally don't like heat," Bottoms said. "You're one tough son of a bitch, though; I'll give you that. You took on some of the hardest guys in this joint, and you're still alive. Don't appear to be punchdrunk, either."

Jesse wondered how long it would be before he was.

"Word in the block is, it's not gonna change," Bottoms said. "Every time you get out of solitary somebody's gonna take you on." He grinned. "There's a long line."

Jesse shrugged. "Nothing I can do about that."

"Sure there is," Bottoms said. "What you need is some friends in this joint."

"Yeah?"

"Yeah. If you're a nigger in the joint, you join up with the niggers; if you're a spic, you join up with the spics. But you're a white man, so you oughta join up with white men. That's us."

"It's real nice of you to think of me, but I don't buy your rules," Jesse said. "Thanks, anyway."

"Just what is it you don't buy?" Bottoms asked.

"I don't hate anybody."

"Shit, man, you gotta hate *somebody* just to live, so we picked niggers and Jews. What's the big deal?"

"Every time I ever hated anybody, even for a little while, it did more damage to me than him. Besides, I know some real good black people and some real good Jews. In fact, in both cases, I've known a lot more good ones than bad ones.

Trouble with you people is, you've got to hate somebody else so you can feel worthwhile. That's what I don't buy."

"Look, Warden," Bottoms said, and he sounded exasperated, "you got a lot of time to pull in this joint, and every time you walk out in the yard, somebody's gonna try and beat the shit out of you, because you used to be heat. Now so far, nobody's been able to do it, but I'll tell you something, my friend, you're not looking so good."

"Well," Jesse said, "I've got thirty days of solitary to rest up."

Bottoms stood up, and his full stature was awe-inspiring. "You're gonna need your rest, buddy, because if I don't hear by the time your solitary hitch is up that you're ready to join up with us, then the next guy you meet in the yard is gonna be me." Bottoms looked him up and down. "What're you, six-three, two-twenty?"

"That's close enough, I guess. It's been a while since I got measured and weighed."

"Most places, that's big. Not in here." Bottoms rapped on the steel door. "You better be in touch, you hear?" The door opened, and Bottoms strode out of the cell, then the door slammed shut again.

Jesse sank onto the bunk and stretched out his aching limbs. The guy he had just fought had kicked him, hard, in the thigh, and it hurt worse than his cut eye. He had another thirty days to do in this cell, and he was looking forward to the rest. Still, with no radio or TV and no reading matter it would be hard. Once again, he was alone with himself, and the company was lousy.

* * *

Whenever Jesse closed his eyes the same picture came back to him: it was the best year of their marriage; Beth was healthy after losing a breast to cancer five years before; Carrie, named after his mother, was nearly four, smart and pretty; they had the little house in Coral Gables, and he was moving up in the Drug Enforcement Agency.

Jesse had never thought of being a cop; he'd had his life all planned. It was college, law school, a few years in an Atlanta firm, then back to north Georgia to set up a practice. Then Beth got pregnant and sick at the same time. Jesse's parents were dead, and Beth's weren't rich; she had to quit her job, and the part-time work he had in the admissions office wasn't enough to support them. There was nothing to do but leave law school and look for a job.

The DEA was recruiting on campus, and they made working for the government look attractive and secure. Beth recovered, the baby was born healthy and things started looking up.

That year was the best—not just because they were comfortable and happy, but because the future looked so bright. Jesse had enrolled, part-time, in law school, and once the degree was his, he could rise to new heights in the Justice Department. His assignment to the South Florida Task Force had been a plum; it was where the action was, where promotions happened and careers were made. He was twenty-eight, smart, hardworking, making big busts on a regular basis, and his superiors, once they got past his hillbilly drawl, thought of him as a comer. Then Beth had gotten sick again.

Her first illness had been covered by her parents' medical insurance, but when they got married, that lapsed. Then, when he had joined the DEA, her cancer was excluded from his insurance as a preexisting condition. Suddenly, all the money was going to doctors, medical laboratories and hospitals. Beth took fourteen months to die, and meanwhile Jesse was left thoroughly in hock, with nearly $400,000 in outstanding medical bills. That was when he had started to think about the cash in the evidence locker.

He was startled by the opening of his cell door; he hadn't expected it to open for another thirty days.

"Jesse, you got a visitor," the guard said.

Jesse sat up and blinked in the bright light. A prisoner in solitary wasn't allowed visitors, and since his lawyer had died a couple of months back, there was nobody left to visit him. He got up and followed the guard.

He was led upstairs, in the direction of the warden's office, and shown into a small conference room. A man who had been sitting at the table stood up. A cardboard box was in front of him on the table.

"Hello, Jess," Fuller said. "You look awful."

Jesse blinked at this apparition. "Hello, Kip," was all he could think to say: Kip Fuller had been with the South Florida Task Force for less than a year when Jesse had been arrested. The young officer and his new wife had been out to the house a couple of times for barbecues, and Jesse had liked them. When Jesse had been arrested, Kip had been sympathetic, had brought him things in jail, had tried to help inside the agency. "Seems like a long time," Jesse said.

"It does, doesn't it?"

Fuller reached into the cardboard box and took out a set of chain restraints, then shoved the box down the table toward Jesse. "Your clothes are in there," he said. "Get dressed; you and I are going to take a helicopter ride."

3

Jesse had trouble climbing the stairs to the roof, because of the chains. Fuller helped him.

"I'm sorry about the rig, but I've got my orders," Fuller said.

As they stepped through the door onto the roof the helicopter started up with a whine, drowning out Jesse's question. Fuller helped him into the machine, fastened his seat belt, then took the facing seat. He clamped a headset on Jesse, then put one on himself.

Jesse reached for the switch that isolated the passenger compartment intercom from the pilot, then adjusted his microphone. "What's going on, Kip?" he asked. The dull whine of the two turboprop engines made conversation noisy, even with the headset on.

"There's not a lot I can tell you," Fuller said. "Barker will explain."

"Dan Barker?" Jesse asked, surprised. Barker had been his last superior on the South Florida

Task Force. They had never liked each other. "What the hell does he want with me?"

"Barker is no longer DEA; he's a deputy assistant attorney general now, and he took me with him to Justice. He's in charge of a new special task force."

"What kind of task force?"

"Barker will explain." Fuller looked out the window; he seemed embarrassed.

"How've you and Arlene been, Kip?"

"We've both been very well," Fuller replied. "Arlene likes living in Washington; she says she needs a place with seasons." Fuller smiled. "There's more good news: Arlene is pregnant."

"That's wonderful, and after trying so long. Always happens when you least expect it."

"Thanks," Fuller said. "I don't think I've ever been so happy." Then he looked embarrassed again. "Jesse, you look like absolute hell. What's been going on?"

"Cons don't like ex-cops," he said.

"The assistant warden said you'd been in a lot of fights."

"I didn't start any of them."

Fuller looked out the window again. "I tried to get them to put you inside under another name, so nobody would know. Barker killed that little effort. I'm sorry, Jesse; I did what I could."

"I appreciate that, Kip," Jesse replied.

"If this thing today doesn't work out, I'll try to get you moved to Leavenworth and work up a new identity. Now that I'm at Justice I have a little more clout, and maybe I can do it without Barker hearing about it."

Jesse leaned forward in his seat. "Kip, was it Barker who hung me out to dry?"

Fuller shook his head. "I honestly don't know, Jesse. I combed through all the paper on your case, all the depositions and testimony, and I couldn't find a thing to hang on him. Certainly, he was in a position to do it, but so were half a dozen other people. I'm damned if I could ever find a motive."

Jesse sat back. "Kip, there's something I never told you, something important."

"What's that, Jesse?"

"I wasn't entirely innocent."

"What do you mean, exactly?"

"I was going to steal the evidence money; Bobby was going to help me. Beth's medical bills were out of sight, and my only other alternative was bankruptcy. I wish I'd taken that route now, but it was something to do with the way my old man brought me up. A man who couldn't pay his bills was worse than dirt to him, and bankruptcy was the worst possible shame. I even went to see a lawyer about it, but I just couldn't do it. Then Bobby, who was the sweetest guy I ever knew, brought up the evidence locker and what was in it."

"That doesn't sound like Bobby Dunn," Fuller said. "He was the straightest arrow I ever saw."

Jesse nodded. "I know he was. And when he brought it up he made it sound, I don't know . . . almost like I was entitled to the money. He even volunteered to move the cash from the locker to the car, while I was upstairs in a meeting. He said nobody would ever suspect him, and he was right; nobody ever did."

"What about the coke and Bobby's death?" Fuller asked.

"I had nothing to do with either one," Jesse replied. "What I think happened is, when Bobby went to the evidence locker for the money, he got caught by somebody and that somebody cleaned everything out of the locker and stuffed some of it into my trunk, then shot Bobby and put him in there. There was about a million and a half more in that locker, and a ton of coke."

"And they nailed you for all of it," Fuller said.

"They did. And somebody walked away with the rest of the money and the drugs and never got caught. I always thought my best chance was that the guy would do something stupid and get nailed. But he didn't; whoever he was he played it very smart. Barker is that smart."

"He is," Fuller said, "but I always thought it was one of the other agents. I never had a line on who, though."

They rode in silence for a few minutes, then Jesse asked the question he had wanted to ask all along. "Did you ever get a line on Carrie?"

Fuller shook his head. "I tried again when I knew I was going to see you, but it was the same as when I wrote to you last year. I got hold of the woman in charge of the adoption agency a couple of days ago, tried to use a little Justice clout, but she wouldn't budge. All she said was that the people were very nice, ideal adoptive parents. She said Carrie was very happy, and that if you knew the people, you'd be pleased. I hope that helps some."

Jesse nodded. "Some. I just wish I could write to her and that she could write to me. There's so much I want to tell her, and if I could hear from her then at least I'd know something about how she was being brought up."

"Carrie's young, Jess, and she'll adapt very quickly. I know it's hard for you, but I really think you should try to put that out of your mind. There's absolutely nothing to be done about it. Believe me, I tried everything."

Jesse looked out the window and saw an airport. "Where are we going, Kip?"

"That's Fulton County Airport; the locals call it Charlie Brown. We're going to a meeting there."

"With Barker?"

Fuller nodded.

"Any advice, Kip?"

Fuller looked uncomfortable, but he seemed to be thinking about it. Finally, he looked up. "Barker needs you pretty bad. You're not in much of a position to negotiate, but you might remember that." He looked out the window again. "I won't be able to help you, Jess; remember that, too."

The helicopter was hovering over the tarmac outside what looked like an office building. Finally it set down, and the pilot cut the engines. Fuller helped Jesse out of the aircraft and across the tarmac to a door at the end of the building, then up a flight of stairs.

Finally, Fuller opened a door and ushered Jesse

into a conference room. A soft drink machine sat in a corner beside a coffee pot. Sitting at the table was the man Jesse held responsible for his incarceration and the loss of his daughter, the man he hated most in the world.

"Hello, Jesse," Barker said.

"Hello, Dan." Barker was the epitome of civil service smoothness, Jesse thought.

"Have a seat. Would you like a cup of coffee or a cold drink?"

"Some coffee, please."

Fuller went to the coffee pot. "Black, as I remember."

"That's right," Jesse replied.

"It's not great coffee," Barker said, "but I expect it's better than what you've been getting."

"I expect."

Fuller handed Jesse the cup, and he raised his cuffed hands to receive it. "You think I could take the restraints off now, Dan?" Fuller asked.

"I think not," Barker replied. "So, Jesse, how are things in prison?"

Jesse had still not sat down. "Dan, I'm not talking to you while I'm wearing this." He held up his cuffed hands. "So you can either get this stuff off me right now or go fuck yourself." Jesse knew he was flirting with a trip back to prison, but he was angry.

Barker waited a beat before he turned to Fuller. "Kip, get this piece of shit back to the pen."

Jesse turned and hobbled toward the door.

Fuller caught up with him in the hallway. "That was a mistake, Jesse."

"The hell with him," Jesse said.

Barker's voice came down the hall after them. "All right, all right, come on back in here and let's talk."

Jesse turned and held his hands out to Fuller, who began unlocking. First the handcuffs came off, then the leather belt that buckled in back, then the chain that connected the cuffs to the leg irons and, finally, the leg irons. Jesse walked slowly back into the conference room, rubbing his wrists and stretching his legs, then he sat down. There were some pencils on the table; Jesse wondered whether he could plunge one into Barker's neck before either he or Fuller could shoot him.

4

Barker took a seat at the opposite end of the table. "How would you like to get out of prison?" he asked.

"I'm already out of prison," Jesse said. "Now why don't you just cut to the chase and tell me what I have to do to stay out?"

Barker nodded at Fuller and the younger man placed a briefcase on the table, opened it, took out an eight-by-ten photograph and put it in front of Jesse.

Jesse saw a head and chest shot of a young man in the uniform and green beret of the Army Special Forces. He was rail thin, handsome, deeply tanned, square-jawed and his chest displayed many ribbons. Master sergeant's stripes adorned his sleeves.

Barker opened his own briefcase and took out some papers, glancing at them as he spoke. "This man's name is Jack Gene Coldwater; that photograph was taken in 1972, and, as far as we know, it was the last picture ever taken of him. Christ only knows what he looks like now. He was born in Ship Rock, New Mexico, in 1949, to a Navaho father and a white mother; he attended the local public schools, played football and was good at it. He turned down a football scholarship when he graduated from high school; instead, he joined the army; he was good at that, too. He was big, smart and tough as nails, and Special Forces got hold of him right out of boot camp. His service record says he was a natural. He pulled *four tours* in Vietnam and led missions all over the country, north and south, in Cambodia and Laos, mostly infiltration with only a few men; he rose to the rank of master sergeant faster than it should have been possible, and by the time the war ended he was the practical equivalent of a company commander. There were bird colonels who were scared shitless of him, and his commanding officers, his platoon leaders and company commanders, *always* did what he told them to. He won just about every decoration the army had to offer, except a Medal of Honor, and he was recommended for that. Word is, his regimental commander—one of those colonels who was scared shitless of him—blocked it; I wasn't able to find out why.

"Coldwater didn't want the Vietnam war to end, and when Saigon fell, he passed up a seat on the last chopper out, then fought a rear guard action for another week. He finished up at Vung Tau, southeast of Saigon, with his back to the sea and two men left. Then he stole a boat and sailed it down the South China Sea, past the mouth of the Mekong River, fighting a running battle with Vietnamese craft, around the cape called Mui Ca Mau, then northeast along the Cambodian coast to Trat, in Thailand, right on the Cambodian border.

"From there he and his merry band took a bus to Bangkok and reported to the military attaché at the American Embassy, who got them onto a plane back to the States before anybody knew they were there. Once home, he took discharge, and that was the last we heard of him until a couple of years ago."

"So what's he doing now?" Jesse asked. "Dealing drugs?"

"The DEA can be happy he's not," Barker said. "The truth is, we're not exactly sure *what* the hell he's doing, but we think it involves a lot of weapons. He's living in the Idaho panhandle, on a mountain just south of the Coeur d'Alene Indian reservation, next to a little town called St. Clair; he has at least four wives, numerous children and no visible means of support. He's the titular head of something registered as an official religion in the state, called the Church of the Aryan Universe."

"Funny," Jesse said, "I had a meeting with a fellow from Aryan Nation just this morning."

"This isn't Aryan Nation; it's an entirely separate organization. Aryan Nation is mostly made up of convicts and ex-convicts. The people around Coldwater are apparently model citizens. They do seem to share a view of the world with Aryan

Nation, though—the idea that the white man is God's supreme creation and that everybody else is inferior."

"Sound like a delightful bunch of people," Jesse said.

"Yeah. A couple of years ago the Bureau of Alcohol, Tobacco and Firearms began to get reports of somebody buying large amounts of small arms on the West Coast; then the reports got to be of bigger stuff—anti-tank weapons, recoilless rifles, that sort of thing. They put a couple of men on it; one of them got close and got a bullet in the brain for his trouble, then the trail went cold.

"About fourteen months ago—just about the time you went away—we got a snitch who said that Coldwater was the guy buying the weapons. ATF sent two men up there, undercover. One went in as a life insurance salesman—they actually trained him to sell insurance. The other got a job as a shoe salesman. Both of them simply vanished."

"Did they report anything before they went up in smoke?" Jesse asked.

"Only what I've told you; that's everything we know up to now. When the new administration came into office, some people at Justice began to take an interest in cults and white supremacist groups, and somebody at ATF, which was backing away from this real fast, passed on the Coldwater file, such as it was, to us. All of it is in Fuller's briefcase; you can memorize it at your leisure, then destroy it. A special task force was autho-

rized to investigate cults in general and Coldwater's in particular, and I was picked to form it
and lead it."

"And naturally," Jesse said, "the first person
you wanted aboard was good ol' Jesse Warden."

Barker managed a tight smile. "The last person,
actually. But I didn't want to follow the ATF ex-
ample of bureaucratic stupidity and lose a couple
more men."

"So you decided to lose me?"

"Christ knows you're expendable, Jesse, but
you also have something to gain from all this."

"I was hoping we'd get to that," Jesse said.
"Just what do I have to gain?"

"Your freedom, if you bring off the assignment.
We're talking about a presidential pardon."

"Oh, I love that," Jesse said. "I suppose you
have a letter from the president in your briefcase,
confirming all this."

"Of course not," Barker said irritably. "You'll
have to take my word for it."

Jesse leaned forward. "Dan, before we go any
farther there's something you'd better understand: I'll go back to prison before I'll take *your*
word for a goddamned thing. Now let's stop wasting time; you tell me what you want done, and
I'll tell you what you have to give me to do it. If
we can't agree, then the hell with it."

The hell with it, indeed. Jesse figured he could
disable Kip, kill Barker and disappear before
anybody knew it. The two of them probably had
enough money on them to get him started, and
he no longer resembled any existing photograph

of himself. He'd have a better chance than he would back inside Atlanta Federal Prison.

"All right, let's get down to brass tacks," Barker said. "As you'll see when you read the ATF reports, Coldwater appears to have two principal lieutenants: their names are Casey and Ruger, both ex–Special Forces. Both were on that boat with Coldwater, and a distillation of both their service records is in Fuller's briefcase. I want to know what this organization is doing, where they're getting their funding and what other organizations they're connected with. And I want hard evidence for at least one serious felony conviction—I'm talking twenty-five to life—for each of the three top men—Coldwater, Casey and Ruger. I intend to break up this outfit, and when you get the evidence, I want to *personally* make the arrests."

"All right," Jesse replied, "and here's what I want: I want a written agreement that guarantees me, first: an unconditional recommendation by the attorney general for a presidential pardon for *any* crime committed up to the actual date of the pardon; second: I want a hundred thousand dollars in cash; third: I want a completely new identity, tailored to *my* specifications and entry into the Justice Department's witness protection program; and finally: I want a package delivered to the adoptive parents of my daughter, *immediately*, which will contain a letter from me to my daughter, and you will secure their written agreement to give it to her no later than her twenty-first birthday. The agreement is to be *personally* endorsed, *in writing*, by the attorney general herself, and my obligations will be satisfied when Coldwater, Casey and Ruger are either dead or indicted for a serious felony."

"Why dead?" Barker asked.

"So that, if you try to take these guys and you kill one or all of them, you won't be able to weasel out."

Barker looked at Fuller. "Can we do this thing about the letter to his daughter?"

"I've spoken with the head of the adoption agency," Fuller said. "I think she would be amenable to passing the package to the parents, but I don't think there's anything in the world we could do to force them to give the girl the letter. They might, but they might not."

"All right," Jesse said, "I'll settle for a letter from the head of the adoption agency swearing that she has passed the package to the adoptive parents."

"I think I can get that," Fuller said.

"And I can swing the rest," Barker replied. "It's going to take me a couple of days, though, and you'll have to go back into the joint while I work things out."

"No deal," Jesse said vehemently. "There's a hotel in this city called the Ritz-Carlton Buckhead; Fuller and I will wait there in a suite, and I want my own bedroom."

Fuller chimed in. "Dan, it'll give me a chance to brief Jesse on the new background we've got worked out for him, and that'll save us time."

Barker turned back to Jesse. "I used to think of

you as an honorable man. Will you give me your word that you will remain in Fuller's custody until I get back from Washington?"

"I give you my word on that," Jesse said. "But no more chains." There would be time enough later to kill Barker if he came back from Washington empty-handed.

"All right, you've got a deal," Barker said. "But I'm damned if I'll shake your hand on it."

That was just fine with Jesse.

5

Jesse sat at the dining table of a twelfth-floor suite at the Ritz-Carlton in Buckhead and polished off a large cut of prime rib. Elsewhere on the table were the remains of a loaded baked potato, a Caesar salad and a bottle of Mondavi Cabernet Sauvignon (the reserve). He took another swig of the wine, then turned his attention to a large dish of macadamia brittle ice cream.

"Prison hasn't improved your table manners," Kip Fuller said from across the table.

"You'll have to forgive me, Kip, but it's been a while since anybody cared." The ice cream was sensational. "Why aren't you eating?"

"Because it's three o'clock in the afternoon, and I had lunch," Fuller replied. "Are you sober enough after all that wine to start absorbing some detail?"

"Shoot."

"Ordinarily, I'd just build you a legend for this job, but last week I got lucky." He handed a large newspaper clipping across the table.

Jesse picked it up; it was from the Toccoa, Georgia, newspaper: LOCAL BUILDER'S FAMILY WIPED OUT IN DUI CRASH.

He read a few paragraphs, then looked up at Fuller. "Okay, so the guy's name is Jesse; what else?"

"His wife and three daughters were killed in a head-on car crash."

"I read that much."

"What's not in the article is that the husband, one Jesse Barron, lived through the crash and was hospitalized with head injuries. When he recovered enough, he checked himself out of the hospital and disappeared. I talked to the local sheriff, who knew the man well, and he reckons he's a suicide; they just haven't found the body yet."

"What else do you know about him?"

Fuller took a file folder from his briefcase and opened it. "Born in a place called Young Harris."

"I know the town; not far from where I was born."

"He's two years older than you are; went to North Georgia College, in Dahlonega, flunked out the first year. Single for a time, then married in his early thirties to one Sally Terrell, had three kids close together—daughters, Margie, Becky and Sherry, ages seven, five and four. The guy worked in construction in Atlanta for half a dozen companies, then moved to Toccoa a little over a year ago and started his own business. He was having a tough time of it, apparently—on the verge of bankruptcy, so the loss of his family wasn't his only reason for suicide."

"He could have just taken a hike," Jesse said.

"The sheriff doesn't think so. Barron had been drinking heavily, was depressed and had talked about suicide before the accident."

"Sounds good. Anything unusual about the guy?"

"Very little. A high school football knee injury kept him out of the military, and he was too young for Vietnam, anyway. There is one delicious little detail, though; something we'd have been hard put to invent."

"What's that?"

"He was arrested nine years ago in a fight; he was one of a group of hecklers who were badgering a black couple who had bought a house in a white neighborhood."

"I like it," Jesse said. "A nice little credential. Was he a member of the Klan or anything?"

"I checked with the FBI—they've got a man in just about every Klan organization. He was actually on a list of people approached about joining, but he never did. It shows that the guy must have had a reputation for bad talk around town."

"Good. What did he look like?"

Fuller handed over a small color photograph. "This was his driver's license picture. A little smaller than you, and fatter, but you could be him after a car crash."

Jesse nodded. "Does he have any family?"

"A grandfather in a county nursing home—in his nineties and ga-ga. That's it."

"How'd you come across this guy? You don't read the Toccoa, Georgia, newspaper."

"No, but researchers at Justice do; they keep an eye out for identities that could be used in the witness protection program. I've also got a name from Alabama, but he's not nearly as good—too many relatives. The nice thing about Jesse Barron is that he's from your part of the state, so your accents are probably similar."

"If he's from Young Harris, they certainly are. What happens if Barron's body turns up?"

"The sheriff has agreed to keep it quiet," Fuller said. "There's nobody to notify, no heirs, nothing to leave them if there were any. The guy was living in a rented trailer." He pushed the file across the table to Jesse.

Jesse looked through it; it was complete down to Barron's failing grades his first and only year in college. "Sold," he said. "Now let's talk about this town in Idaho. What was it called?"

"St. Clair. It's a one-industry town—a chipboard manufacturing company called St. Clair Wood Products. Family-owned, employs around four hundred people. We've been subscribing to the local weekly newspaper, the *Standard*, for a while and, apart from jobs in the local stores, county government, the sheriff's office, that sort of thing, Wood Products is about it."

"Any black people in town?"

"None. A few Indians."

"If this guy Coldwater is half Indian, what's he doing as head of something called Aryan Universe?"

"Apparently, they consider the Indians as some sort of racially pure strain; I know, it's bizarre."

"What sort of ideas have you got about infil-trating?" Jesse asked.

"Maybe you, as Barron, could set up some sort of small business, maybe remodeling of houses, like Barron? You had some construction experi-ence in your past, didn't you?"

"I worked summers at house building when I was in high school and college. I'm fairly handy, but God help the person whose house I tried to remodel."

"Well, then."

"I don't like it; two guys have already gone in there in regular middle-class jobs. If Coldwater is recruiting, I doubt it's from that bunch. He's likely to want a more disappointed kind of recruit, I would think; somebody who's pissed off at the world. Certainly Barron, if he were alive, would have a lot to be pissed off about—he's lost his family and his business. Tell me, was the drunk who hit his family black?"

"I'll find out. I think you've got a good idea about the guy being disappointed. How would you infiltrate?"

"Maybe just drift in there, look for work, drink at the local beer joint, see who's who around St. Clair. If Barron suddenly turned up, would the local cops want to talk to him about anything? Did he do anything illegal?"

"Nothing like that in the record."

"So I could use Barron's name with no fear of his name ringing alarms if he got busted for speed-ing or something?"

"Why not? That way, if somebody did some

checking on him, we'd know exactly what they'd find. He's got a social security number and that's helpful, if you're going to look for work—and we could have a word with some of Barron's former construction employers in Atlanta, alert them for requests for references."

"Okay, let's do it that way. What about a driver's license and credit cards? I'd like to have one working credit card in my pocket."

Fuller looked through some papers. "His credit report says he's got a Visa, but it's tapped out and way overdue. I'll fix something up with the bank and have them issue a new card. As for the driver's license, I can get one made up with your picture on it. Hang on, I've got a Polaroid camera in my luggage." Fuller got up and went to his bedroom.

Jesse wiped off the hefty steak knife the Ritz-Carlton had furnished with the prime rib, slipped it under his belt in the small of his back and tucked his shirttail in over it. He had still to hear from Dan Barker, and he meant to be ready if he didn't like what he heard.

6

Jesse stood at the bathroom sink and looked at himself in the mirror. The face that stared back at him was still unfamiliar; there had been no mirror in the solitary confinement cell where he had spent so much of his prison stay.

The nose was the worst; it had been broken twice and badly repaired in the prison infirmary. It was flat across the bridge and distorted at the tip, but at least he could breathe through it properly. There was scar tissue around the eyes, and the right ear had begun to cauliflower at the top. He looked like nothing so much as a punchdrunk fighter. The face would scare anybody; it certainly scared him.

The doorbell of the suite rang, and Fuller knocked on the bathroom door. "Barker's here," he said. They had been in the suite for three nights.

"Be right there," Jesse said. He tightened the knot of his tie, slipped into his jacket and looked at himself. The suit and shirt had been finely cleaned by the hotel, and, except that his clothes were a bit loose on him, he thought he looked quite well. He wrapped the blade of the sharp steak knife in two sheets of hotel stationery, making a kind of scabbard, then tucked it into his belt at the small of his back. In a few minutes, he knew, he would either have preserved his freedom or stolen it by killing Barker. He hoped Kip would not force his own death by resisting. Since the day he had been arrested Kip had been the only person who had treated him decently.

Jesse buttoned his jacket and walked into the living room. Barker sat at the dining table, and a catalog case rested on the floor beside him. "Sit down, Jesse," he said.

Jesse took a chair two down from Barker, so he could reach him easily.

Barker took a sheaf of papers from an inside pocket and handed them to Jesse. "See if that's what you want," he said.

To Jesse's surprise, it was, including the letter signed by the attorney general. "It looks just fine," Jesse said.

Barker reached into the case and removed an automatic pistol and a box of ammunition. "I wouldn't send anybody, even you, up there unarmed," he said. "It's a brand new, Hechler & Koch 9mm automatic; takes fifteen in the clip and one in the chamber. It was bought this morning at an Atlanta gun shop in the name of Jesse Barron, and all the proper forms were filled out, so it can't be traced to any government agency."

Jesse nodded and removed the weapon from its holster.

"No need to load it now." Barker handed him a card. "Here's an eight hundred number; memorize it; Kip will be on the other end of it."

Jesse glanced at the number, committed it to memory and returned the card to Barker. "I'm not going to report in every day," he said. "I don't want people noticing the calls."

Barker reached into his magic case again and produced a small cellular phone in a leather pouch. "This is a very special cellular phone," he said. "Press this button and your conversation is scrambled. Hide it somewhere. The eight hundred number is programmed in already; just hit zero-one and S-E-N-D. The cellular coverage in the St. Clair area is good."

Jesse accepted the phone and its recharging accessories. "Anything else?"

"Yes. Remember that you have absolutely no law enforcement authority. Whatever happens, this is not going to be your bust. I want you to work this so that you get evidence, then call us in for the climax, is that clear?"

"Perfectly."

Barker handed him a well-worn wallet; inside were a driver's license, a credit card, social security card and some business cards from Jesse Barron's business.

"These look good," Jesse said, shoving the wallet into his hip pocket.

"Kip tells me you've got your cover down pat,

and I've arranged to have Barron's name put on your fingerprint record, so if you get printed for any reason, you're okay."

"It sounds like we're all buttoned up, then," Jesse said. "Except I'm going to need a good bit of cash."

"How much?"

"I'm going to need a vehicle and a little nest egg; say, thirty thousand?"

Barker turned to Fuller. "Get him twenty-five, and get a receipt."

"I've got that much now," Fuller said.

"Give it to him."

Fuller produced some banded stacks of bills from his briefcase and handed them to Jesse; he wrote out a receipt, and Jesse signed it.

"I want you on a plane to Boise today," Barker said, "and in St. Clair tomorrow."

Jesse shook his head. "I'm going to buy a vehicle here, register it in Barron's name and drive across country, picking up motel receipts and buying stuff I need. I'll be in St. Clair in a week or ten days."

Barker leaned forward and put his elbows on the table. "I guess you think I'm just turning you loose," he said. "I guess you must think I'm a blithering idiot."

Jesse smiled. "That's pretty close to my personal opinion of you, Dan, but I know very well you wouldn't let me out except on a leash."

"I've got better than a leash," Barker said. "You're to report to Kip daily on your way to St.

Clair and every chance you get once you're there. If you go too long without reporting in, I'll fall on you from a great height."

"Sure, Dan."

"Get something straight, Jesse; you haven't been paroled; you're still serving your sentence. You're just going to be doing your time in St. Clair."

"Right up until you get your indictments," Jesse said.

"That's right, pal; right up until the president signs your pardon. Until that day, you're nothing but an escaped federal prisoner. You got that?"

"Sure, Dan."

"I can press a button, and there's a nationwide manhunt for you in full swing; the Immigration and Naturalization Service already has you down for arrest if you try to cross any border, so don't get it in your mind to tool on up to Canada or down to Mexico, got it?"

"Sure, Dan."

"And something else you'd better know, boy; if this doesn't work out—for *any* reason—if I don't get good busts on those three men, then you're going back to Atlanta, and you'll *never* see the light of day again. If the cons don't kill you, then you'll never make parole; I'll *personally* see to that."

"I know you will, Dan," Jesse replied. He stood up and turned to Fuller. "I'll need a ride to a used car lot," he said.

Barker stood up and turned to Fuller. "Call me when he's on his way." He picked up his catalog case and walked out of the room.

Fuller sighed. "I'm glad that's over," he said.

"Let's get moving," Jesse replied.

"Jesse," Fuller said, "you've got a gun now; can I have the steak knife, please? The hotel would just charge it to my bill."

7

Jesse found what he wanted at the third car lot; it was a two-year-old Ford pickup with four-wheel drive and a camper box filling the truck's bed. He made the deal and counted out ninety-six hundred dollars. When he had the paperwork, Kip walked back to the vehicle with him.

"Are you driving West now?" Kip asked.

"I've got a few things to pick up—the license tag, some clothes, a sleeping bag. No need to come with me; I'll be on my way by tomorrow."

"Call me when you're on your way," Kip said. He looked embarrassed again. "I wish I could have done more for you, Jess. I wish I could have fixed it for you to be with Beth when she died. I know it must have been hell, locked up at a time like that."

"You've done a lot more than anybody else, Kip, and I'll always be grateful to you."

"You understand that Barker thinks what you're about to try to do can't be done," the agent said.

"Sure, I understand that; he always underestimated me, though."

"That he did," Kip said, smiling.

Jesse started to offer his hand, then surprised himself by hugging Kip.

"You take care of yourself, Jess," Kip said. He handed over a card. "This is my home number; if you can't reach me at the office, don't hesitate to call."

Jesse handed Kip a thick Ritz-Carlton envelope. "You'll see that this gets to the adoption agency?"

"I'll FedEx it before the day's over."

"I'll be seeing you," Jesse said, climbing up into the truck.

"I hope so," Kip replied, waving as Jesse pulled out into traffic.

Jesse went first to the courthouse and got a tag for the truck, then, making several detours to be sure he wasn't being followed, he drove to Hartsfield International Airport, parked the pickup in the short-term lot, went into the terminal and bought a round-trip ticket for Miami, with a two-hour wait before the return flight.

On the flight down, he went into the men's room, opened the lining of his suit and removed a key that was sewn in place, then he had lunch and slept like a baby. In Miami he took a cab to the bank and told the driver to wait. He signed in at the safety deposit desk and an attendant took him into the vault; using his own key and Jesse's, the man unlocked a large box. Jesse took the box into a private booth and opened it.

He removed a small satchel containing forty thousand dollars that he had stolen from a bust the week before he was arrested, then he returned the empty box to the attendant and turned in his key. He had a snack and a beer at the airport, then flew back to Atlanta.

It was too late to do anything else that day, so he checked into a hotel near the airport, had dinner and watched TV in his room. Television was wonderful, he thought.

Next morning, he was at an office supply store when it opened. He bought a small safe, the kind meant to fit between a building's studs; then he found an army surplus store, where he bought a sleeping bag and some work clothes. He sold his suit to the man behind the counter for twenty bucks, then he rode around Southwest Atlanta until he found a small, independent car repair shop.

A mechanic slid out from under a car. "What can I do for you?"

"How much to rent some space, your welding equipment and some tools for half an hour?"

"I don't know, man; there's liability problems, you know?"

"I know how to use it; how's a hundred bucks?"

The man smiled.

Jesse began by drilling a quarter-inch hole in the back of the little safe; he then wired into a spare fuse, then ran it to the cellular telephone charger inside the safe. He put the truck on the shop's hoist, found a space in the frame and welded the safe in place. When he was sure the mechanic wasn't looking, he counted out a thousand dollars, stuffed it in his pocket, then put his own forty thousand and the fourteen thousand he had left of the government's money into the safe, along with the cellular telephone, which would be constantly on charge when the engine was running. He loaded the pistol and put that and the spare ammunition inside, then locked the safe and let the vehicle down. He memorized the combination, then threw away the paperwork.

"That's it," he said to the mechanic, handing over the money. Then he got into the truck and drove west on the interstate. When he had crossed the Alabama line, he stopped and called the 800 number, tapped in the extension and got a recording. "I'm on my way," he said. "Calling from eastern Alabama; I'll check in again tomorrow."

He drove west, marveling at the light and the open spaces. Occasionally, he left the interstate and drove through small towns, grinning at their filling stations and fast-food joints. He'd thought he'd never again have a fast-food hamburger, and he wolfed them down joyously.

He reveled in driving the pickup, in charge, master of his own fate, sort of. No guard sat beside him; no wall barred his way; no citizen wanted to beat him to death. He was a free man again.

He stopped in Mississippi for the night, sleeping

in the camper box, and called in again the follow-ing morning. He drove on, astonished at what a big country it was, trying to forget the oppression of a six-by-eight cell. He stopped feeling panic at the sight of a police car, setting the cruise control at sixty-five, enjoying the slow ride. He spent one night in Amarillo, and he kept waking up, think-ing about Mexico, a day's drive to the south. He lay there, pondering total escape. He had fifty-four thousand dollars and a used pickup truck, but that wouldn't get him far. He didn't want to be a bum in Mexico; he wanted to be a free man, able to go wherever the hell he wanted to go, and he had a chance of pulling it off in Idaho. He went back to sleep.

He spent a night in Santa Fe and another in Denver, alternating between motels and the camper. He stopped in Jackson Hole, Wyoming, and allowed himself half a day to look around Grand Teton National Park. It was early autumn and the changing leaves were magnificent.

The following day at sunset he reached the city limits of St. Clair, Idaho, and checked into the town's only motel. He gorged himself once more on pizza and television and slept soundly. The next morning was clear and frosty as he left the motel.

Fun was over; it was time to go to work.

8

Jesse walked down the main street in the early morning light and took note of St. Clair. Low clouds hung over the town and the dim light made it seem earlier than it was. There was only a single block of Main Street—a couple of dozen stores, two filling stations, newspaper office, doctor's office, veterinarian. The buildings were mostly red brick, with tin awnings out front—looked as if they'd been built around the turn of the century. The place was like a lot of small Georgia towns Jesse had seen. One difference, though: outside the police station, a modern building, there were five squad cars parked. As he walked past, four uniformed men came out of the building, got into the cars and drove off. Must be the early shift, Jesse thought. He also thought that five squad cars were a lot for a town this size.

He stopped and peered through the window of something called Nora's Café. A woman was busy behind the counter, and she was alone in the place. He tried the front door; it was locked, but when the woman saw him she came and let him in.

"Morning," she said.

"Did I get here too early?" Jesse asked.

"Seven on the dot," she replied, looking at her watch. "Coffee?"

"Thanks, yes."

"Take your pick," she said, waving at a row of booths along the wall.

A boy walked in with a stack of newspapers and put them on the counter. Jesse picked one up, left some change on the counter and sat down in a booth.

The woman came over with his coffee. "New in town?"

"Brand new; just passing through, really."

"I'm Nora; I run the joint."

"I'm Jesse. How you doing?"

"I'm okay. You're not from around here, are you? Not with that accent."

"Naw, I'm a hillbilly, from Georgia."

"They got hills in Georgia?"

"They got mountains; not like the ones around here, though."

"What do you feel like for breakfast, Jesse?"

"Two scrambled, bacon . . . I don't guess you've got grits?"

Nora laughed aloud. "You're a long way from home, Jesse; we got hash browns."

"That'll do."

"Toast? English muffin?"

"English muffin."

"Juice?"

"Orange."

"Good choice; I squeeze it myself." She left him with his newspaper.

Jesse read through the paper carefully; it was as good an introduction to the town as anything. There was a problem with the sewage treatment plant, and it looked like property taxes might go up; a main-street merchant had died at sixty-eight; the high school football team had won its first game; and St. Clair Wood Products had gotten a big order for plywood and chipboard from a company building a new ski resort near Park City, Utah. An unsigned editorial blasted a gun control bill now in the state legislature; letters to the editor dealt with the need for new playground equipment at the grammar school, a complaint about drunk drivers in the county and a yard sale at the First Church on Saturday.

Jesse sipped his coffee and watched half a dozen customers wander in and take booths or stools at the counter. The sound of bacon sizzling was pleasant to the ear, and nobody put any money in the jukebox across the room, for which he was thankful. He was not fond of rock and roll or country music.

Nora came with his breakfast, and he forced himself to eat slowly. He had lost a lot of weight in prison, and he thought he'd better watch his eating, or he'd gain it all back. He'd finished his breakfast and had accepted a second cup of coffee when a man in a policeman's uniform entered the café and took a stool at the counter. He and Nora exchanged pleasantries, and she poured him a cup of coffee. There was another, quieter exchange between the two that Jesse caught in his peripheral vision, then the cop walked over to Jesse's booth, carrying his coffee.

"Morning," he said to Jesse.

Jesse looked up. "Good morning to you," he replied.

"Mind if I join you?"

"Take a pew," Jesse said.

The cop eased into the booth opposite Jesse and set down his coffee. He stuck a hand across the table. "I'm Pat Casey," he said. "I'm the law around these parts."

The name registered from his briefing; this was one of Jack Gene Coldwater's top two men, one of the ones he was going to nail. "Jesse Barron," Jesse replied, shaking the man's hand.

"Don't recall seeing you before," Casey said.

"Naw, I just rolled in last night," Jesse replied. "Probably move on tomorrow, the next day. Thought I'd take a rest from the road; I've been driving for a week."

"Where you headed?"

Jesse leaned back in the booth and sighed. "I was thinking about Oregon. Hear that's nice country."

"It is; I've been there."

"Pretty nice around here, too."

"We like it. I can't place your accent."

"Georgia, north Georgia. Town called Toccoa, up in the mountains. Hillbilly country."

"I thought that was Tennessee and Kentucky."

"Us hillbillies are all over."

Casey grinned. "You're a long way from home, boy."

Jesse let himself look a little sad. "Boy, I guess I am."

"What caused you to up and leave Georgia?"

Jesse shrugged. "Hard times, I guess. I had a little business went under."

"What kind of business?"

"Construction. Remodeling and additions mostly. Folks weren't spending their money like they used to; I guess it's the recession."

"Got any family back there?"

"Not anymore," Jesse said, gazing into the middle distance. "Oh, I got a granddaddy, but he's in a home. He doesn't know anybody anymore, not even me."

"How'd you travel in here, Jesse?"

"I got a pickup over at the motel."

"You got any means of support, Jesse?"

Jesse looked up from his eggs. "Well, I haven't done any work for a few weeks, but I put a little by."

"How little?"

"I guess I could get by two or three months, if I stretched it. You're not looking to get me for vagrancy, are you?"

Casey grinned. "Not at the moment. I wouldn't want you to become a drain on the public purse, though."

Jesse changed his tone just a little. "Listen, Pat, I've never been a drain on nobody in my life; I worked since I was twelve, and I haven't given it up yet."

"You got some ID, Jesse?"

Jesse produced a wallet and tossed it onto the table between them. "I guess you're the welcoming committee in St. Clair, huh?"

Casey went through the wallet carefully, looking at the driver's license, credit card and bits of paper. Jesse had put that package together very carefully.

"Looks like your license expires five years from last week," Casey said.

"I just renewed it."

Casey nodded. "You ever been in jail, Jesse?"

"Not to speak of."

"Now, what does that mean?"

"I had a little conversation with the sheriff when I was eighteen or nineteen. We haven't spoken much since."

Casey nodded. "Well, I guess I can't hold your youth against you." He peered closely at Jesse's face. "Looks like you've been roughed up a little."

"Car wreck," Jesse said. "I spent a few days in the hospital."

"Were you drunk?"

"Nope; the other guy was though, the nigger."

"That's not a politically correct word these days," Casey said.

"Well, I'm sorry if I offended you," Jesse said, reaching into his pocket for some money. He left five dollars on the table and got up.

"Rushing off?"

"I sort of get the idea that I'm not too welcome around here. I guess I'll have a look at Oregon."

"Aw, sit down, Jesse; I'm just doing my job. C'mon, sit down."

Jesse sat down.

"Let me buy you a cup of coffee."

"Thanks, I've already had two."

Casey nodded at the newspaper on the table. "You read the *Standard*?"

"Yep."

"You see any reports of crime in there? Juvenile delinquency? Drug busts?"

"Nope."

"That'll give you an idea of the sort of town we got here. Our last drug bust was nearly four years ago."

"Sounds like a real safe place," Jesse said.

"Exactly," Casey said, "and I mean to keep it that way. That's why I'm so inquisitive; I like to know who's in town and what they're doing here."

"That's reasonable, I guess," Jesse said, sounding mollified.

"Take your time in St. Clair; have a look around; there are worse places to settle."

"Any work around here?"

"Most of the work's down at Wood Products. The place is humming right now; you might find something there."

"Thanks, maybe I'll take a look at it."

"You do that. If you decide to stay a while, come see me down at the station. I'll see if I can't help you settle in."

"Thanks, Pat, I appreciate it."

Casey got up and stuck out his hand again. "Well, I got to do my rounds. Good talking to you."

Jesse shook the man's hand again. "See you around."

Casey picked up Jesse's plate, cup and glass. "I'll take these over for Nora; save her a trip."

Jesse nodded. "Thanks." He took a deep breath and let it out. That went pretty well, he thought. He watched as the policeman walked to the lunch counter and set down the dishes. Casey turned and left, and Jesse saw that his orange juice glass wasn't on the counter with the plate and the cup.

"Well, Pat," Jesse muttered to himself, "you sneaky bastard, you."

9

Pat Casey strolled into the police station, walked over to the desk where a young, uniformed man sat and gingerly handed him the orange juice glass. "Pull the prints on this and run 'em, Rick," he said. "Nora's are on there, too, but it's the other ones I want."

"Right, Chief," Rick replied. He took the glass, one finger at the top and one at the bottom, and went into a back room.

Casey went into his office, sat down at his desk and picked up the phone. He looked up the area code for Georgia, dialed information and asked for the number of the sheriff's office in Toccoa, Georgia. He wrote down the number, then dialed it.

"Hello, this is Chief of Police Pat Casey in St. Clair, Idaho. I'd like to speak to the sheriff."

"Yes, sir, I'll connect you."

There was a click. "This is Tom Calley, Chief Casey. Was that Idaho you said?"

"Yessir. I just want a little information, if you can help me."

"Do my best."

"You know a fellow named Jesse Barron?"

"Sure do. Where'd *you* run across him?"

"Right here in St. Clair. He's down the street at the café drinking coffee."

"Well, I'm glad to hear it. Tell you the truth, I thought Jesse was dead."

Casey's grip tightened on the phone. "Oh? Why's that?"

"He didn't tell you what happened to him?"

"Said something about a car wreck."

"That's right. A bad one."

"Would you tell me about it?"

"Well, Jesse and his wife and three little girls were coming home from a movie out at the shopping center, and a drunk, a colored fellow, ran head on into their car. Jesse—"

"Can you hang on a minute, Sheriff?" Casey interrupted. One of his officers had just entered the station, and Casey waved him into his office. He punched the hold button. "Jim, you see if our man is out of the way, and if he is, go down to the motel and turn over his room and his truck— and do it *neat*, you hear?"

"Yessir, Chief."

Casey punched another button on the phone. "Sorry, Sheriff, you were saying?"

"I was about to tell you that Sally and the girls were killed in the wreck, and Jesse was busted up pretty good. When he was able to get out of the hospital, he went out to the cemetery and looked at the graves, then he went downtown and got on a bus to Atlanta, and that was the last anybody saw of him around here. Tell you the truth, I thought he'd gone out and put a bullet in his head. I'm glad he's all right, though; I always liked him."

"Can you describe him for me?" Casey asked.

"Sure, I guess he's six-one or six-two, about two hundred pounds, brown hair, going gray and receding, blue eyes. He had some injuries around his head and face; I'm not sure just what he'd look like after those heal."

"That's our man," Casey said.

"Has he broken the law up there?"

"No, sir; I just wanted to be sure he's who he says he is. How long you known him?"

"Most of his life, I guess; his family moved here from Young Harris when he was in grammar school."

"Was he ever in any kind of trouble?"

"Nothing serious. The summer after he got out of high school I had to pull him and a couple of other young fellows in."

"What was the charge?"

"Well, a colored family moved into a house down the road, and a lot of folks around here didn't take kindly to it. The boys broke a few windows, that sort of thing. Justice of the Peace gave 'em three days and expunged the record, because of their youth. I never had any more trouble with Jesse."

"When would that have been?"

"Oh, early seventies, I guess; around there."

"What sort of a fellow is Jesse?"

"Solid, hardworking. Wasn't his fault his construction business went under; just wasn't enough work around here. I'd have made Jesse a deputy, if I'd had an opening. He's on the quiet side, but he's real smart."

"Do you think you might be able to get hold of a photograph of Jesse for me?"

"I might be able to. Chamber of Commerce might have one."

Casey gave the sheriff his fax number. "I'd appreciate it if you'd fax it to me, if you can find one."

"Glad to; I'll send somebody down there right now."

"Sheriff, I appreciate your help."

"You see Jesse again, you tell him I said we miss him around here."

"I'll do that." Casey hung up and swung around to the computer terminal next to his desk and began typing. Early seventies; the closest newspaper with a computerized database was probably Atlanta. He found a listing for the *Atlanta Journal-Constitution* and dialed the number. Shortly he was connected and called up the index. A few more keystrokes and he had a list of stories containing the name Barron between 1970 and '75. He got the right one on the second try: TOCCOA YOUTHS ARRESTED IN RACIAL ATTACK. It was brief and as the sheriff had described the incident. Jesse Barron was one of the boys named.

Rick stuck his head in the door. "Chief, I've got the record on screen two."

Casey cleared the screen and typed more keystrokes; the record came up. The photograph wasn't great, but it was nearly two decades old. Jesse Adam Barron had no known criminal record. He had been fingerprinted when he had tried to enlist in the marines; rejected because of a knee injury resulting from high school football.

He typed more keystrokes, and the printer at his side disgorged the record and the photograph. Casey looked at the picture more closely. He was younger, skinnier, had more hair, hadn't been in a car crash. Casey thought he'd have had a hard time putting together the face he had just met at Nora's with the face in the photograph if he hadn't known the man, but it was a match. The prints matched; that was the important thing. Casey sat back and waited for Jim to return from the motel.

"I did it like you said, Chief," the officer said, easing into a chair opposite Casey.

"What did you find?"

"A couple of old suitcases, some clothes, the usual toiletries, some books, mostly old novels, and what looked like a family picture."

"Tell me about the picture."

"Just a snapshot in a frame; a woman and three children, girls."

"Any ID documents?"

"Nossir, I guess he must have 'em on him."

"Any weapons?"

"Nossir."

"What about the truck?"

"Some tapes and a bill of sale in the glove compartment. He bought the pickup in Atlanta ten days ago."

Casey sat back and thought about this. The man seemed what he said he was, but two things bothered him: his driver's license was new, and so was the truck, both acquired about the same time. Still, Barron had said he had the license renewed, and the sheriff had said that he had left Toccoa on a bus. It made sense that in a wreck that had killed three people, Barron's car would have been totaled. "Hang on a minute," Casey said.

He turned back to the computer and spent a minute and a half getting connected to the Georgia Motor Vehicles Bureau in Atlanta. In another moment, he had the driver's license he had just seen up on his screen. He printed that out, then moved down a couple of screens to the historical record. It showed that Barron's old license would have expired before the month was out. He went into vehicle registration and found that two pickup trucks were currently registered to Barron, the one at the motel and another, larger truck, the kind with a back seat. That would have been the one in the wreck, he thought. Nobody had canceled the registration yet. He printed out the record.

"Jim, anything strike you as odd about this man's stuff? Anything at all?"

Jim shook his head. "Looked real ordinary to me, Chief. Except—"

"Except what?"

"Well, it's a little thing, but the tapes in his glove compartment—"

"What about them?"

"They were classical stuff. You know, symphonies, and like that?"

Casey nodded. "You'd think a guy in a pickup would be listening to country music, wouldn't you?"

"Yessir, I guess I would."

"Well," Casey said, "it takes all kinds, I guess."

"I guess."

"Thanks, Jim, that'll be all for now."

The officer left, and Casey sat and thought about what he had on Jesse Barron. He had been expecting another undercover man from the ATF for weeks and, after what had happened to the last two, he expected one with a good cover. Still, Barron's background seemed too good to be just cover. It was the sheriff who had made the difference. He'd gotten the information, one cop to another, and that made it right.

Casey heard the fax machine ring in the outer office. He got up and walked to the machine and waited. A moment later it disgorged a sheet of paper. Casey picked it up and looked at the photograph. He was four or five years younger, dressed in a business suit, hair neatly cropped and combed; the hairline hadn't yet started to recede. He looked a lot less beat up than the man Casey had just met, but he was the same man, no doubt about it. The picture was clipped from some sort of business directory. Underneath it, set in type, were a few lines of copy:

> Jesse A. Barron, president, Barron Construction, specialists in additions, renovations and remodeling. Mr. Barron takes pride in finishing jobs on time and on budget. Free Estimates. Member of the Chamber since 1981.

Casey walked back to his desk, picked up the phone and dialed a number.

"Yes?"

"Hi, it's Pat. I don't think he's who we're expecting."

"What makes you so sure?"

"He checks out to a tee—background, paperwork, everything." Casey told him about Barron's history.

"Wouldn't you expect him to check out?"

"Yeah, but it's more than that. First of all, I talked to a local sheriff in Georgia who's known him since he was a boy. It was all good, and get this—as a kid he got arrested for trying to run some niggers out of his neighborhood. I checked the back newspaper editions and found a confirming story."

"How do you know this guy is the guy the sheriff is talking about?"

"He faxed me a photograph. It's the same man."

"I don't know . . ."

"One more thing: I've known a lot of cops, and I can usually spot 'em a mile away. This guy is less like a cop than anybody I ever knew. If I'd had to guess I'd have said he was an ex-con, but I guess that's because the injuries make him so rough looking. St. Clair didn't seem to be his destination, either; said he was on his way to Oregon."

"Well, if he decides to stay don't hassle him; make it easy for him, but keep tabs on everything he does."

"Of course. If he's real, he sounds like he might be our kind of guy."

"We'll see." He hung up.

In Toccoa, Georgia, Sheriff Tom Calley dialed an 800 number.

"This is Fuller."

"Mr. Fuller, this is Tom Calley, in Toccoa, Georgia."

"Yes, Sheriff?"

"The call came, like you said it would."

"Everything go okay?"

"Seemed like it. He asked for a picture, so I faxed the thing you fixed up."

"That's good, Sheriff; thanks for your help."

"Not at all."

"And you'll let me know if the real Barron turns up?"

"Yessir, I will."

"And I'd like to hear about it if anybody else calls about Barron—anybody at all."

"Sure thing."

* * *

Jesse closed the door to his motel room and looked around. His things were, if anything, more neatly arranged than when he had left. So far, so good.

10

Jesse strolled down Main Street, taking stock of the town. The place was still overcast, but the light was becoming brighter; the clouds would burn off soon.

His first impression of Main Street was of something out of the twenties or thirties, and for a while, he couldn't figure out why. Certainly, it was very clean and neat, with every storefront looking freshly painted, but that wasn't it. Finally, it struck him. Although it was daylight, he saw that there were no electric signs, just the old-fashioned, hand-lettered kind. It was as though the business district was constructed and maintained to some very strict, but out-of-date design code.

He stopped in front of a small shop. The windows were soaped over, and above, on the facade, there were holes in the brickwork where a sign had been removed. He had noticed it because it was the only vacant storefront on the street, and at a time when most small town businesses were struggling to stay open, competing with the new malls. Some lettering on the glass front door caught his eye: "J. Goldman, Jeweler and Watchmaker," it read.

Jesse continued his walk, stopping in the drug-store for a Boise newspaper. To his surprise, there was a soda fountain taking up one wall of the store. He hadn't seen one since high school. A wave of nostalgia washed over him, a memory of sharing a strawberry soda with a teenaged girl— two straws. And even in those days the soda fountain had been mostly an anachronism.

"Good morning," the druggist said as he rang up Jesse's quarter.

"Good morning," Jesse replied.

"New in town?" The man stuck out his hand. "I'm Norm Parsons."

Jesse shook the man's hand. "Jesse Barron. I'm so new I might not even be here tomorrow."

"Sorry to hear it," the druggist said. "We need new blood all the time. Fine place to live, raise a family, St. Clair."

"I can believe it," Jesse said, waving goodbye with his newspaper. He took a right at the corner and walked through a residential neighborhood. The houses were mostly Victorian or that most American of houses in the middle third of the twentieth century, bungalows. A new house was going up on the corner, and that, too, was an old-fashioned bungalow.

"Time warp," Jesse said aloud. Each house was neatly painted, and its front lawn was closely clipped. He couldn't spot a weed in a flower bed, not anywhere. He stopped on the corner and looked up and down Elm Street. "Jesus Christ," he said aloud to himself. "Isn't this where Andy Hardy used to live?"

Back on Main Street Jesse was waiting to cross at what was apparently the town's only traffic light when a patrol car pulled up next to him, and Pat Casey got out. "How's it going, Jesse?"

"Not bad. This is a real pretty town you've got here."

"Glad you think so. Thinking of sticking around?"

"I don't know," Jesse replied, looking up and down the street. "You sure this isn't a movie set?"

Casey laughed. "We like it that way. You stick around, and you'll get to like it, too."

"I sure like the soda fountain down at the drugstore," Jesse said. "I haven't seen one since I was a kid."

"Yeah, and Norm whips up a mean milk shake or banana split."

"Mmmmm," Jesse moaned.

"I spoke to your sheriff back in Toccoa, Georgia," Casey said.

Jesse let his eyebrows rise. "You're a thorough man, Pat."

"I am that."

"How is old Tom?" Jesse asked.

"He seemed well. Had a good opinion of you."

"He sort of spanked me once, a long time ago. We got along pretty good after that."

"That's what he said. You interested in some work?"

"Might be."

"You make up your mind, you drive out the road there about a mile, and you'll come to St. Clair Wood Products, our local industry. Ask for Herman Muller; tell him I sent you."

"Thanks, Pat, I'll keep it in mind."

Casey took a small notebook from his shirt pocket, scribbled something on a page and tore it out. "The motel gets expensive after a while. If you want a nice room and home cooking, try this lady, and—"

"Tell her you sent me?" Jesse laughed.

"Just part of the service," Casey said, then got back into his car and drove away.

Jesse read the notebook page. "Mrs. Weatherby, 11 Elm Street," it said. The street where Andy Hardy used to live.

Jesse pulled the pickup into a large parking lot, got out and surveyed St. Clair Wood Products. A long, low building sat fifty yards from the highway, and the noise of machinery could be heard from inside. Jesse found an entrance that said "Offices" and went in.

"Can I help you?" a middle-aged woman behind a desk asked.

"I wonder if I could see Mr. Herman Muller?" Jesse asked. "It's about a job. Chief Casey sent me."

She looked at him a moment without reacting,

then said, "Have a seat; I'll see if Mr. Muller's available."

Jesse sat down and watched as she walked into an adjoining, glass-enclosed office and spoke to an elderly man who was sitting at a large, rolltop desk. He nodded and said something to her, then she returned.

She took a sheet of paper from her desk and handed it to Jesse with a pen. "Fill this out, please, then Mr. Muller will see you."

Jesse filled out the application, taking time to describe his new job background, then he was shown into Herman Muller's office.

Muller stood up to greet him, a lean, tan seventy-year-old, Jesse figured. Muller shook his hand and waved him to a sturdy oak chair. He took the application and read it slowly before he spoke. "Nice to meet you, Jesse," he said when he had finished.

"Thank you, sir," Jesse replied. "It's nice to meet you. Pat Casey said there might be some work going here."

"Might be," Muller replied. "I see you've been in the construction business."

"That's right," Jesse said. "Had my own business until the recession came along."

"We've been lucky around here; in fact, we just got a nice new contract for chipboard."

"I read about it in the local paper," Jesse said.

"Were you good at running a business?" Muller asked.

"I think I was," Jesse said. "I never could seem to get together enough capital to bid on the big jobs, but I had a lot of happy customers on the little ones."

"How many people worked for you?"

"I only had three, full time, but if we got a nice job I'd have a dozen or so at work, plus the sub-contractors."

"How'd you get along with them?"

"Nobody ever quit me, except for more money than I could pay."

Muller glanced down at Jesse's hands. "Looks like you've done some hard work before."

Jesse looked at his own hands and saw what Muller meant. They were gnarled and scarred, and Muller didn't know that they'd gotten that way from beating up other men. "I guess I've done my share," he said. "I started working for my daddy when I was twelve, and I never stopped. In fact, right now is the only time I've ever been out of a job."

"You got any family?"

"I lost my family in a car wreck," Jesse said, avoiding Muller's eyes.

"I'm sorry to hear it," Muller said. "I'm a widower myself, and I lost my only grandson not long ago." He rubbed a hand quickly over his eyes. "Let me tell you how we work around here. Everybody starts at the bottom. I've got a force of five hundred and two people, and everybody started at the bottom. I've never hired a manager or a foreman; I've always promoted from within. I'll offer you the worst job I've got around here, feeding the chipper; pays seven dollars an hour. You give me a day's work for a day's pay, and I'll give you something better to do before long. How's that sound?"

"It sounds all right to me," Jesse said, managing a smile.

"Good. Let me take you down to the floor and I'll introduce you to Harley Waters; he'll be your foreman." Muller rose and started for the door, then stopped. Two men had just come into his outer office, men wearing suits; one of them was carrying a briefcase. "Uh, oh, looks like I'll have to talk to these gentlemen," he said. He opened the door. "Agnes, this is Jesse Barron, he's going to work on the chipper. Will you call Harley and ask him to come up here and get Jesse?"

"Yes, sir, Mr. Muller," Agnes said. She turned to Jesse. "Have a seat; Harley'll be here in a minute." She picked up a phone and tapped in a four-digit number.

Herman Muller waved the two men into his office, followed them in and shut the door.

Jesse noticed he didn't shake their hands. He watched as the two men sat down, and one of them opened his briefcase. He removed a thick sheaf of paper and handed it to Muller, who took it and began reading. The second man offered Muller a pen, which the old man ignored. Muller opened a desk drawer, dropped the papers into it and turned back to the men.

"I'll think about it," Jesse thought he said.

The two men sat, staring at Muller, saying nothing. One of them said something briefly, then they got up and left Muller's office.

"Good morning to you, Mr. Ruger," Agnes said as they passed her desk.

"Morning," Ruger replied, and then they were gone.

A man in a hard hat walked into the office from the direction of the factory.

"This is Jesse Barron, Harley," Agnes said. "Jesse, this is Harley Waters."

Jesse shook the man's hand.

"Follow me," Waters said. "I'll show you around."

"That would be fine," Jesse replied.

"When can you start?"

"How about tomorrow?"

"That's good; I can use you."

Ruger, Jesse thought. That's Coldwater's other right-hand man, and Herman Muller didn't seem too pleased to see him.

The machinery was noisy, and Jesse was given ear protectors, a kind of headset without electronics. Harley Waters started at the beginning of the chipboard production line and walked him through to the end, shouting comments over the noise, while Jesse nodded his understanding.

When they were finished, Waters walked him to the car park exit. "This is a good place to work," he said, "because Herman Muller is a good man to work for. He built this business from nothing, designed a lot of the equipment himself, picked every man who works here. He must have liked you, or he wouldn't have hired you, not even when he needs people bad, because of this new contract."

"I liked him, too," Jesse said.

"Good; I'll see you in the morning," Waters replied. "We work seven to five Monday through Thursday, and we take Friday off. It's a good deal."

"Sounds fine to me," Jesse said. "See you tomorrow."

He got into the pickup and drove back to town, wondering what this man, Ruger, was up to with Herman Muller. As he drove back into town, the sun broke through. On Main Street, Jesse stopped the truck, got out and looked up. Right behind the business district, a sheer mountain wall rose a good five hundred feet. It looked as if it might fall on the town.

Wow, Jesse said to himself. With the sky overcast, he had never known it was there.

11

Jesse pulled up in front of the house and gave it a good look. A two-story Victorian with a beautiful lawn and flower beds, a wide front porch and gingerbread everywhere. It looked old but was in perfect condition. He got out of the pickup, walked up the front walk, climbed the steps to the porch and rang the doorbell. He reckoned on a long wait, while Mrs. Weatherby made it to the front door with her walker.

He had turned and was admiring the flowers when a low voice behind him said, "Good morning." He turned to find a much younger woman than he had expected. Mrs. Weatherby's nurse, no doubt.

"Good morning," he replied. "My name is Jesse Barron. May I speak with Mrs. Weatherby?"

She rewarded him with a quizzical smile. "I'm Mrs. Weatherby," she said, opening the screen door. "Please come in." She turned and walked toward the rear of the house, expecting him to follow.

Jesse followed. "Forgive me, I suppose I was expecting a nice little old lady—the widow Weatherby," he said to her back.

"I am the widow Weatherby," she said without turning, and there was amusement in her voice. She led him into a large kitchen and indicated a chair at the breakfast table. "I was just making some tea; would you like some?"

He sat down and looked at her again. She was nearly as tall as he, slim, in her mid-thirties, he guessed, with gray streaks in her light brown hair. She wore a simple cotton dress that emphasized her small waist and full breasts.

"Would you like some tea?" she repeated, and as if on cue, the kettle began to sing.

"Oh, yes, I'm sorry. My mind was wandering, I guess."

"Milk?"

"Just lemon, if you have it."

She poured the tea and set it before him with a wedge of lemon on the saucer. "Sugar's there on the table," she said as she poured herself a cup. She set down her tea and pulled up a chair.

Her nose was slim and straight, her large eyes wide apart and her mouth broad, revealing large teeth when she opened it. She sipped her tea tentatively and gazed at him in a direct manner.

"Pat Casey said you might have a room to rent," he said, trying not to seem unsettled.

"Jesse, you said?"

"That's right."

"You look like a pretty tough guy, Jesse."

"I was in an accident; I used to look a little more respectable."

"I'm sorry," she said, and a hint of a blush ran up her cheeks. "It's just that I'm particular about who comes into my house, even if Pat Casey did recommend him."

"That's understandable," Jesse said. "I don't blame you a bit."

"I have a little girl, you see; she's at school right now."

"How old?"

"Six. She's in first grade."

Jesse looked away, a move that was becoming more natural as he perfected his performance. "I had three girls, once," he said.

"Are you divorced?"

"Widowed. My wife and daughters were killed in the car wreck that made me look like this."

Her face fell. "Oh, I am sorry. I can only imagine what it must be like to lose a child, let alone three."

"Thank you; I'm living with it."

"Was the accident your fault?"

"No, thank God. I don't think I could have lived with that."

Slowly, methodically, she extracted his story from him, leaving nothing unexamined. Jesse gave her what she wanted, a little at a time.

"Thank you for telling me all this," she said finally.

"Not at all. But you've told me nothing about yourself." He smiled. "I'm particular whose house I live in."

She laughed. "All right, I'm a local girl, married in my late twenties, lost my husband in my early thirties, in an automobile accident."

"I'm sorry. That's your whole story?"

"Just about. I dote on my daughter, I help out at the local library, do some volunteer work."

"No regular job?"

"My husband provided for us."

"It's a lovely house," he said.

"Thank you. I have the time to work on it." She set down her tea cup. "Come, I'll show you the room." She got up and led the way down the hall and up the stairs. "Carey's room is straight ahead," she said, when they had reached the top of the stairs. "And—"

"What did you say?" The name was an arrow through his heart.

"It's my daughter's room; Carey's."

"How do you spell the name?"

She spelled it.

"I used to know a little girl named Carrie," he said, spelling it.

"Oh. Well, my room is to the right, and the spare room is to the left, here." She led the way into a large, sunny bedroom, comfortably furnished with a double bed, a chest of drawers and a comfortable chair. "The bath's over there."

"It's very nice," he said.

"I'd be happy to have you here, if you want it," she replied. "The rent is fifty dollars a week and another fifty with three meals a day. I cook well."

"I'm sure you do," Jesse replied. "I'll take the

room and the meals. Is a month in advance all right?" He counted out eight fifty-dollar bills.

"Thank you, yes, and you should open a bank account, Mr. Barron. That's a lot of money to be carrying around."

"Good idea, and will you please call me Jesse, or Jess, if you like?"

"Sure. My name is Jenny." She held out her hand for the first time.

He took it and didn't want to let go. "I'm starting at the Wood Products plant tomorrow morning," he said.

"Then you'll want an early breakfast. That's all right, we rise early here. Go to bed early, too."

"That's fine by me."

"Cereal or eggs?"

"Eggs, please, scrambled?"

"I can manage that. I'll put lunch in a bag for you. When would you like to move in?"

"I'll go back to the motel and get my things and be back in half an hour."

"Fine."

"May I have a door key?"

She laughed. "Oh, we don't lock our doors in St. Clair," she said. "No burglar would dare operate in our town."

Jesse pointed the pickup toward the motel and reflected on his good fortune. A very handsome landlady, and a little girl in the house, to boot. He would have to be very careful not to sweep her into his arms when he saw her. The daughter, he meant, chuckling to himself.

On Main Street he passed the Bank of St. Clair, and, on impulse, pulled into a parking spot. He might as well start getting respectable, he thought. He got out of the truck and walked toward the building. He opened the front door, stepped in and immediately knew something was wrong. A young man was backing toward him and, across the marble floor, a guard stood, a riot shotgun held tensely at port arms. He'd never seen a bank guard with a shotgun before, he thought, as the man continued to back toward him, apparently oblivious of his presence. Before Jesse could move, the man bumped into him.

The younger man spun around, his face full of surprise, and Jesse saw the pistol coming around. Instinctively, he grabbed the man's wrist, made the gun point toward the ceiling and twisted hard. The gun came away in his hand. At that moment, all hell seemed to break loose. Jesse saw the guard's shotgun swing toward the robber and, flinching, he turned his body away. The shotgun went off at exactly the moment that the front window of the bank caved in.

The robber flew toward Jesse, knocking him off his feet, then there was another shotgun blast. Jesse thought it was the third. He looked out onto the street and saw another young man, looking frightened, standing next to a pickup truck and yelling.

"Come on, Dan, get out of there!" he screamed.

Dan was lying on top of Jesse, and he wasn't going anywhere. The young man outside suddenly figured this out and leapt into the pickup.

As he did, a police car suddenly appeared, skidding sideways into the truck, and another squad car rammed the pickup from behind. The driver started out the truck's door, but before both his feet had made the ground there were half a dozen gunshots, and the young man was lying on his face in the street.

Jesse pushed the robber's body off him and started to get up, but he was pushed back onto the floor by a large foot. The bank guard was standing over him, pumping the shotgun.

"Hold it, Frank!" somebody shouted from the street, and the guard stepped back, still pointing the weapon at Jesse.

"I don't think he's one of them," the voice said, and then Pat Casey was helping Jesse to his feet.

"Well hello, Pat," Jesse said. "I was just coming in to open an account. Does this happen every day in St. Clair?"

Casey laughed. "Put down the shotgun, Frank; this is a customer."

The bank was suddenly filled with policemen, and Jesse was herded off to one side. Eventually, somebody took his particulars, accepted his money and gave him a temporary checkbook. The man called Ruger watched from an office and talked with Casey, occasionally nodding at Jesse.

Jesse finished his business and left for the motel, to collect his things. On the way he reflected on the bungled robbery, and it occurred to him that at least one of the robbers, the one he'd taken the gun from, had been shot unnecessarily, after Jesse had the pistol. The other one had been shot down very quickly, too, but Jesse hadn't seen that as clearly.

He remembered Jenny Weatherby's comment that no one would dare commit a burglary in St. Clair. Now he knew why. He bet himself that there were no prisoners in the city jail.

12

Jesse packed his things, then checked out of the motel and drove up Main Street. He parked in front of police headquarters, went inside and asked for Pat Casey. Casey, who was sitting in a glass-enclosed cubicle, waved him into his office and into a chair.

"What can I do you for, Jess?"

"I just wanted to thank you, Pat. I arrived in this town less than twenty-four hours ago, a complete stranger, and now I have a job and a very nice place to live and you to thank for all of it."

"I'm glad to be of help. I'm grateful for your help, too. It seems you disarmed one of the bank robbers."

"It seemed like a good idea at the time."

Casey laughed. "It certainly was."

"I'm a little overwhelmed, I guess," Jesse said. "Since I got out of the hospital I've been sort of numb, just going through the motions, wandering across the country. Now, all of a sudden, I seem to have some sort of life again. I just want you to know I appreciate your help, and I hope I'll be able to find a way to repay you some day."

Casey shrugged. "Who knows? One of these days you might be able to do something for me. I'll let you know. In the meantime, just settle into St. Clair and be one of us."

Jesse stood up. "That, I'll do." He shook Casey's hand and left the station.

Jesse carried his bags up the front steps of Jenny Weatherby's house and was met at the door by a somber little girl with hair so blonde it was nearly white.

"Hello," Jesse said to her. "I'll bet you're Carey."

"How did you know?" the little girl asked.

"Oh, I know all about you. You're six years old and in the first grade."

She smiled shyly. "Mama told you."

"That's right, she did."

"Are you going to live with us?"

"I sure am, and I hope you and I are going to be good friends."

"That depends," Carey said. "Do you like niggers?"

Jesse was brought up short. "Why do you ask that?" he asked.

"Because at school they told us we're not supposed to be friends with nigger lovers."

Jesse set his bags down at the bottom of the stairs, struggling for a way to continue this conversation. "And where do you go to school?" he asked lamely.

"At the First Church school," Carey replied. "Everybody goes there."

"And do you like school?"

"Oh, yes," she said. "We get to learn lots of stuff."

"Well, I want to hear all about that," Jesse said, "just as soon as I take my things upstairs."

"Carey!" her mother called from the kitchen. "Who's that out there?"

She turned to him. "What's your name?"

"Jesse."

"It's Jesse, Mama," she called out. "I'm helping him take his stuff upstairs."

Jesse handed her his small bag and followed her up the stairs to his room.

"Do you like this room?" Carey asked. The phone rang downstairs.

"I like it very much," he said, sitting on the bed. "And I think I like you very much, too."

The little girl giggled and ran out of the room and down the stairs.

Jesse was stretched out on his bed, dozing, when there was a soft rap at the door.

"Come in."

Jenny opened the door. "Seems you're the local hero," she said.

"You've heard already?"

"It's a small town."

"I'm lucky I didn't get my head blown off."

"Luckier than you know," she said. "Supper's in half an hour; would you like something to drink before? I've got some gin and some bourbon and some beer."

"I'd love a bourbon on the rocks," Jesse said, swinging his feet over the edge of the bed and standing up. "But room and board can't include liquor. I'll buy my own."

She smiled. "Tonight you're my guest."

"Carey's gorgeous," Jesse said. "She comes by it naturally."

The little blush again. "Come on downstairs, and I'll fix your drink."

Jesse splashed some water on his face, brushed his teeth and went down to the kitchen. Jenny handed him a large drink. "What time does the evening news come on in Idaho?"

"You mean on TV?"

"Right."

"We don't have much TV," she said. "Not in St. Clair. Oh, they've got a satellite dish at Harry's Place, where the fellows go to watch football, and down at the motel, I guess, but TV is sort of frowned on around here."

"Oh," Jesse said, nonplussed. Never in his life had he been to a place that didn't have much TV. He sat down at the kitchen table and raised his drink. "Will you join me?"

"Sure," she said, and poured herself a bourbon and water. She peeked under a pot lid, then sat down and sipped her drink. "You think we're missing anything by not having TV?"

"Well, I guess you're missing the news and some movies and a few good programs," he replied. "But you're missing a hell of a lot of junk, too, and, on balance, I'd guess Carey might be better off without it."

"That's sort of what I thought," she said.

"When I was a kid we didn't have a TV for a long time," Jesse said, then stopped himself. He was about to start talking about Jesse Warden instead of Jesse Barron, and he couldn't have that.

"Strict father?"

"That's it."

"I had one of those, too. If he could see me now, sitting in my kitchen with a strange man who's just moved into my house, sipping whiskey with him, he'd roll over in his grave."

"You've always lived in St. Clair?"

She nodded. "Always."

"Have you traveled much? Seen any of the country?"

"I've been to Boise half a dozen times," she said, "and once I went to Seattle to visit my mother's sister. That's about it."

"Is your mother still alive?"

"No, she died before my father did, when I was fifteen."

"What did your father do?"

"He worked out at Wood Products, like everybody else."

"That's been here a long time, has it?"

"Sure has; all of my life and before. Herman Muller's daddy came here from Germany to farm, and when he died, Herman sold the farm and started that business. It's grown and grown.

Soaked up just about all the farm boys around here." She talked while gazing out the window into the middle distance.

Jesse took in her fine profile and the gray in her hair, and he wanted her. "Girls as beautiful as you are don't usually stay in small towns," he said.

"Why, thank you sir," she said, raising her glass to him. "I haven't heard anything that nice for a long while." She sighed. "Once, when I was twenty-one or twenty-two, I was putting some gas in my car and a fellow in a Mercedes pulled into the filling station, got out and gave me his card. He was with Paramount Pictures, he said, and he wanted to put me in the movies."

"That doesn't surprise me in the least," Jesse said. "What did you say to him?"

"Shoot, I didn't say anything. I just paid for my gas and got out of there!"

Jesse laughed aloud, and it suddenly occurred to him that he had not laughed in at least two years. A rush of well-being came with the laugh.

"I think I've still got his card somewhere," she said, blushing.

Jesse laughed again.

"I like the way you talk," she said.

"You mean, my hillbilly accent?"

"Yes. There's nothing like it in St. Clair. Everything has a sort of sameness about it around here."

"Seems like a beautiful part of the country."

"I guess it is. You tend not to notice when it's all you've seen all your life. What's it like where you come from?"

"We've got mountains, too, but smaller ones, with lots of pine trees."

"How about the town?"

"Not very different from this one, but not so neat. I think most American small towns are alike."

She started to say something, but stopped.

They ate in the dining room—roast beef, Idaho potatoes and fresh green beans. Jesse and Jenny both had another drink with their dinner. Afterward, she put Carey to bed, and then they went into the living room, where Jesse was surprised to find a piano, and even more surprised to hear her play it well. She played a Chopin etude without referring to the music and something else she said was Mendelssohn that he had never heard before.

"Where did you learn to play so well?" he asked.

"My mother was the piano teacher," she said. "It would have looked bad for her if I hadn't learned to play. I always enjoyed it, and I still don't let a day go by without playing."

His mother had taught piano, too, but he couldn't mention that.

She fixed them another bourbon, then switched on the record player and sat down in a chair facing his. Symphonic strains filled the room.

"Beethoven's Sixth," Jesse said. "The Pastoral Symphony."

"It's my favorite," she said.

"I have it on tape in my truck; listened to it all

the way across the country. It seemed to fit the landscape."

"I can't think of a landscape it wouldn't fit," she said, then laughed. "Even if I've never seen much landscape."

"One of these days," Jesse said, and he found himself meaning it.

She finished off her drink. "One of these days."

She seemed to mean it, too, or was that his imagination. Jesse finished his drink, and they walked upstairs, pausing on the landing.

"It was a wonderful dinner," he said. "A fine welcome to St. Clair."

Again she started to speak, then stopped.

"What?"

"I'm glad you enjoyed it," she said. "Good night, Jesse."

"Good night, Jenny."

Jesse lay in bed and tried to sleep, but couldn't. He replayed every part of the evening in his head—the bourbon, the beef, the little girl and, most of all, Jenny. It had been like having a date, and he had given up hope that he would ever again have an evening like that. His breathing was shallow, and his heartbeat rapid. In his whole life, so far, he had slept with only one woman: Beth. Certainly, he was no seducer, but an hour before, on the landing, he had thought for a moment she might say something that would allow him to take her in his arms. A presumptuous, foolish thought. An arrogant thought. This was not a perfect world, he knew that.

There was a tiny creak, and the door to his room opened. He lifted his head from the pillow and looked, but the darkness was too thick, he could see nothing. He could hear, though, and feel.

A rustle of fabric and the covers were pulled back, and she was in bed beside him, in his arms. They kissed eagerly, then struggled from their night clothes.

There was no foreplay, just the immediate, ecstatic joining of two hungry human beings, taking each other quickly and, astonishing to him, because he was so quick, finishing together, muffling their cries so as not to wake Carey.

They lay together, panting. Jesse turned to her. "Jenny, I—"

"I guess you think I'm pretty bold," she said, interrupting.

"Bolder than I am, anyway," he said, laughing.

"I got the impression that if I'd waited for you to make the first move it might have been months."

He laughed again. "You read me well."

"I don't know what made me do it," she said. "I guess I was lonely and thought that you were, too. I may be brazen, but it seemed like the right thing to do. You won't hold it against me, will you?"

He lay back and hugged her to him. "I'll just hold *you* against me."

"Mmmm," she moaned. "I like it here."

"I like it here, too." He had been in St. Clair for little more than twenty-four hours. What a difference a day made!

13

When Jesse woke there was a gray light in the room, and she was gone. For a moment he was sure he had dreamed too well, but her scent was still in the sheets, arousing him again. He heard her bedroom door open and close and her steps on the stairs; it was five-thirty A.M. by his bedside clock.

Jesse rose, showered, shaved, dressed in work clothes and went downstairs, not knowing what to expect from her. All seemed normal; Carey was eating her cereal while reading a schoolbook, and Jenny was at the stove, her back to him.

"Good morning," he said.

"Good morning, Jesse," Carey said. "Mama's fixing your breakfast."

Jenny did not speak, but turned and looked at him, and there was uncertainty in her face.

"Good morning, Jenny," he said with the warmest smile he could muster.

She blushed, then smiled. "Good morning,

Jesse. You're timing's good; your eggs will be ready in ten seconds."

A glass of freshly squeezed orange juice awaited him, and he sat down and drank it. The eggs were perfectly cooked, and the sausage was wonderful. "The sausage must be local," he said.

She nodded, eating her own eggs. "I get it from one of our few remaining farmers."

He finished his eggs, then glanced at his watch. "I think I should be a little early on my first day," he said. "Can I drop Carey at school?"

Jenny shook her head. "She's not due there until eight, and it's close enough for her to walk."

"That's nice. See you later, then, Carey."

"Goodbye, Jesse, have a nice day," the little girl said.

He winked at Jenny, then left the table and started for the front door, grabbing his jacket from the coatrack in the hall.

"Jesse," Jenny said. She had come out of the kitchen and into the hall.

Jesse looked to be sure Carey was still in the kitchen. He smiled.

"Don't say anything," she said, raising a hand. "Not yet." Then she smiled broadly at him. "I just wanted you to know that I'm not feeling the least guilty this morning."

He laughed. "Neither am I."

"Go safely."

In the truck he shoved the Pastoral tape into the player and hummed along with it. The morning was spectacular—chilly, crisp, with sparkling sunshine. He thought his heart would leap from his chest.

The Wood Products factory was quiet when he arrived, but the employees' door was open, and Harley Waters was there before him.

"Morning, Jesse."

"Morning, Harley."

"Come on, I'll show you the drill."

Jesse followed him to the back of the building and watched as Harley hit a button and the truck entrance clattered noisily open. They climbed a few steps to a wooden platform. Harley pointed. "It's real simple," he said. "The trucks back in there, through the doors, and dump their loads. Further down there, they're unloading cordwood, but here, at your station, it's the remnants, and everything has to be fed into the hopper, there, by hand." He handed Jesse a hardhat, some ear protectors and a pair of heavy gloves. "Don't fall behind. Herman doesn't like it when the trucks have to wait." He took off his hardhat and scratched his head. "I think you're smart enough to see that there's nothing but your good sense to keep you from falling into that hopper yourself, Jesse, and if you do fall in, this machinery will make chipboard out of you."

"I got you," Jesse said, glancing at his watch. Ten minutes to go. "Have I got time to use the john?"

"If you hurry." Harley walked away, and Jesse headed for the men's room. He was back in time to see the first truck backing in.

The truck dumped a load of odd-sized pieces of wood, branches and trimmings, a real mess, Jesse thought. The machinery was turned on, and he began to grab stuff and throw it into the hopper.

At nine-fifteen, a bell rang, and the machinery stopped. Jesse thought he would faint with relief. His face, arms and body were covered in scratches from the logs and branches he had manhandled into the hopper. He walked stiffly to the men's room to pee and to throw some water on his face. Harley Waters came in and assigned him a locker, and he drank some coffee from the thermos Jenny had prepared for him.

"How you like it so far, boy?" Harley laughed.

"It's just swell," Jesse replied.

When the bell rang again at five o'clock, Jesse could hardly walk to his truck. His body ached from one end to the other, and the only thing that kept him going was the knowledge that when he got home, Jenny and Carey would be waiting for him. He turned out to be half right.

When he walked through the front door, Carey appeared from the living room. "Mom's upstairs getting dressed," she said.

"I see," Jesse replied. "Well, I think I'll have a bath and change clothes. He trudged up the stairs to his room and peeled off his work clothes while the water ran in the tub. When it was full he climbed stiffly into it and sank under the water with a groan. He had, he reckoned, just done the hardest day's work of his life. Herman Muller hadn't been kidding when he said it was the worst job in the plant.

Jesse was wakened slowly by the cooling water. He climbed out of the tub, feeling half-human again, got dressed and started downstairs, glancing at his watch. He had been in the tub for more than an hour. The doorbell rang.

There was a man at the door, wearing a suit and looking as though he didn't often wear it. Jesse walked to the door and opened it. "Evening, can I help you?"

The man stared at him. "I'm expected," he said. "Who are you?"

Jesse opened the door and offered his hand. "I'm Jesse Barron; I'm boarding here."

"Fred Patrick," the man said shortly, shaking Jesse's hand.

Carey appeared from the kitchen. "Oh, hello, Mr. Patrick," she said, "Mama will be down in a minute."

As if on cue, Jenny came out of her room and down the stairs. "Hello, Fred," she said to the man, pecking him on the cheek. "Oh, Hello, Jesse."

"Hi," he replied.

"Fred and I are going to a dinner out at the Legion Hall," she explained.

Jesse's heart fell. He had been looking forward to seeing her. "I see. I'll be happy to take care of Carey."

"That won't be necessary," Jenny replied. "She's staying with a friend for the night."

"For the night?" Jesse said dully.

"Yes, I won't be back until late. I left you a plate in the oven."

"Thanks," he managed to say. "You folks have a nice evening."

"Let's go, Fred," Jenny said.

Jesse watched them to the door. As they went out, Fred Patrick shot a suspicious glance at Jesse.

Jesse didn't blame him a bit. He went into the kitchen, retrieved the warm plate from the oven and sat down disconsolately to eat it.

It wasn't the evening he'd had in mind.

14

Jesse washed his dishes, dried them and put them away. The food had revived his exhausted body and made him able to think again, but he didn't want to think. He was experiencing some sort of strange emotion, and he didn't like it.

He slipped on his coat and walked out the back door toward the garage; there his pickup truck rested beside Jenny's sedan. He wriggled under the truck, worked the combination on the safe and took out the cellular telephone, stuffing the pistol and the money back inside the steel box. He got into the truck and, resisting the temptation to start the engine for warmth, switched on the phone and waited for signal strength. He glanced at his watch; it would be nearly ten o'clock in Washington, so there was no point in calling the 800 number. He dredged up Kip Fuller's home number from his memory and dialed it.

There was the expected ringing, then a click and a squawk from the handset, followed by a series of beeps, then Kip's voice.

"This is Fuller."

"It's Jesse. How openly can I talk on this thing?"

"It's an encrypted unit; my phones, both at the office and at home can read it, so we're very secure. How's it going, Jess?"

"Better than I could possibly have hoped," Jesse said. He gave a detailed account of the past two days.

"Doesn't it bother you a little that it's going so well?"

"I don't know," Jesse said. "I mean, they could hardly be expecting me."

"They're expecting *somebody*," Kip said. "After all, they've already had two agents up there and dealt with them both. They can't think the government is going to just give up."

"Well, sure, I've got to be careful for a while, but I get the impression they need people, that they're recruiting. I think I'm just their kind of guy."

"I hope so. I didn't expect you to see Casey and Ruger the first day. Any sign of Jack Gene Coldwater?"

"No, and no word of him, either."

"For Christ's sake, don't ever mention his name to anybody; wait for them to mention it to you."

"Don't worry."

"How are you feeling, Jesse, I mean, really feeling?" Kip sounded concerned.

"A hell of a lot better than I was a couple of weeks ago," Jesse replied. "I'm still a little numb in some ways, but I'm getting used to the idea of being a free man."

"Don't get too used to it," Kip said. "Remember, there's somebody who'd love to see you back inside, if he could get what he wants from you first."

"I'll remember."

"I've had word from the lady at the adoption agency. She says that the adoptive parents have your letter, and they'll think about what to do. It'll be a long time, of course."

"I understand. I just want her to know that her mother and I didn't deliberately abandon her."

Kip was quiet for a moment. "That phone uses more juice than an ordinary cellular phone; you've only got about four minutes talk time between charges."

"I'd better sign off, then."

"Keep me posted; if I don't hear from you at least twice a week, I'll get worried."

"Okay, take care."

"You too." Kip hung up.

Jesse returned the phone to the safe under the truck, plugged it into the charger and locked up. Back outside, he discovered he didn't want to go back into the empty house. He wandered in the direction of Main Street, only a couple of blocks away.

The shops were closed now, their windows mostly dark. Only one lighted sign remained on the street: Harry's. Jesse ambled into the place and stopped inside the front door.

The smell of stale beer and tobacco smoke reached his nostrils, and the sound of pool balls clicking together came from the rear of the long room. Country music was playing on the jukebox. He'd never liked country music. Fifteen or twenty customers, all men, were scattered about the place, some of them watching a sports program on a silent television set above the bar. It was the sort of place he'd avoided all his life.

Jesse walked to the bar and took a stool a little away from anybody else. A man wearing an apron approached.

"Get you something?" he asked.

"A draft," Jesse said.

The man pulled the beer and set it in front of Jesse. "Passing through?"

"I guess not. I went to work out at Wood Products this morning."

The man stuck out his hand. "I'm Harry Donner; this is my place."

Jesse took the hand. "Jesse Barron." Harry seemed friendly enough.

"Where you bunking?"

"I'm boarding over at Mrs. Weatherby's."

"Nice lady."

"Seems to be." Jesse sipped his beer. "How long you been in business, Harry?"

"Nineteen years," Harry replied. "Before that I tended bar in Boise. I come up here and took a job doing the same thing, and a couple years later the boss died, and I bought the joint from his widow. Yours isn't a local accent; where you from?"

"North Georgia, up in the mountains. I was wandering West, headed more or less toward Seattle, when I happened on St. Clair."

"You coulda done worse. How'd you end up at Wood Products?"

"I ran into Pat Casey, and he recommended it."

"Herman Muller's a good man; he'll treat you right."

Jesse laughed. "Well, he just about killed me today."

Harry smiled. "They put you on the hopper?"

"That's right."

"They do that to everybody; stick it out, and Herman'll find you something better."

"I'll do it, if I live."

Another customer sat down at the bar, and Harry moved to serve him, leaving Jesse alone.

This is what he had never wanted, he thought, sitting in a saloon somewhere crying into his beer. It was just the sort of place his father would have figured him to end up in, he knew, and the thought made the evening even more painful.

Suddenly, he identified the emotion he had been dodging all evening: it was jealousy.

Jesse had known Beth all his life, and since high school he'd never had anything to do with any other woman. She'd been his from the ninth grade on, and he'd never given a moment's thought to her running off with somebody else. Now Beth was gone, another woman had crawled into his bed and made him happy, and she was out this evening with another man.

What the hell, he thought, he had only just entered her life; she might have had that date for a long time. Why should she break it just for him? Still, that was what he would have wanted her to do.

This jealousy was powerful stuff, he realized, made up of equal parts of anger, pain and depression. He finished his beer and trudged back toward Jenny's house.

She wasn't home when he got there, and he turned in quickly. Exhausted, he didn't hear her when she came home.

15

Jesse barely made it to work on time. He'd over-slept, then had to make his own breakfast. Jenny still hadn't surfaced by the time he left for work.

He faced the first of the day's many truckloads of scrap lumber and branches, and occasionally he got a tree limb so big he had to trim it with a brancher, a hooked steel cutting implement fixed to a long handle. He looked upon that work as a welcome break from the monotony of feeding the hopper.

He got through the morning, then at lunch-time discovered that he had nothing to eat; he'd forgotten to fix himself a sandwich. He sat down on a bench in the locker room, too tired and numb to do anything about it.

Harley Waters came in and sat down beside him. "Aren't you eating anything, Jesse?"

Jesse shook his head. "Forgot to bring some-thing. In a minute, when I get up the strength, I'll ride into town and pick up a burger."

Harley handed him a thick, carefully wrapped

sandwich. "Take this; my wife always makes me too much."

"You sure? I can pick up something in town."

"I'm sure; I still have to deal with a piece of pie."

Jesse got a cold drink from the machine and sat back down next to Harley.

"Where you from, Jesse?"

Jesse told his story yet again. It came so naturally now that he hardly remembered his real background. "How about you?"

"Been here all my life," Harley replied. "My grandad worked for Herman Muller's old man, on his farm. That was a long time ago."

"You've known Herman a long time, then?"

"Oh, sure; I went to work for him right out of high school."

"Has the business changed much since then?"

"It's gotten bigger, I guess; Herman's built it up practically with his own hands. Once in a while he gets an offer from one of the big companies, like Georgia Pacific, but he's hung onto it. Tell you the truth, after that boy died, I thought he'd sell out."

"His boy?"

"James, his name was; his grandson, really. Car accident."

"That's bad."

"It was a mess, I'll tell you. Nobody's ever figured out who killed him."

Jesse looked up from his sandwich. "Somebody killed him? An accident, you mean?"

"Well, Pat Casey said it was an accident, but I didn't like the look of it. He ran off the road coming down the mountain."

"The one that sort of hangs over Main Street?"

"That's the one. Kill Hill, they call it; Herman's boy wasn't the only one to run off that road. Real steep."

"This happen recently?" Careful, don't ask too many questions, he told himself.

"Four, five months ago. Herman was real broke up about it. I thought he'd sell."

"He's had a lot of offers, huh?"

"Three or four. Latest one was . . ." Harley looked up to see another workman walk in. "Well," he said, standing up. "I'll see you."

"Thanks for the sandwich," Jesse said. He watched as the other man sat down on a bench across the room. He was a big one, six-four, maybe six-five, heavy-set.

"You're the new fella," the man said.

"That's right. Name's Jesse Barron."

"Good for you."

What the hell did that mean? Jesse wondered. He munched on his sandwich and sipped his drink.

"How you like it on the hopper?"

" 'Bout the most fun I ever had," Jesse replied.

"First time I ever heard anybody say that."

"It was kind of a joke," Jesse said.

"I guess I don't have much of a sense of humor," the man said.

Jesse knew this man, in a way; there had been one in every schoolyard in every town his father had preached in. Big guy, bad attitude, didn't like newcomers, especially preachers' boys. "I didn't get your name," Jesse said.

"Phil Partain," the man said, lighting a cigarette. "Cigarette smoke bother you?"

"It's your lungs," Jesse said.

"That's lucky for you," Partain said, blowing a cloud in Jesse's direction, " 'cause I'm not putting it out. So if you're one of them antismoking types, I guess you'll just have to put up with it."

Jesse was one of those antismoking types, he guessed, and he had learned in every one of a dozen schoolyards how to put a stop to this. He got up, walked over to where Partain sat, plucked the cigarette from his fingers, dropped it on the floor and stepped on it.

Partain looked astonished for about a second, then anger flashed across his face and he started to stand up.

Jesse, who was standing no more than a foot from Partain, reached out, put a hand on his shoulder and sat him back down. "Listen to me, Phil," he said before the man could try again to get up. "Let's you and me concentrate on safety in the workplace. Neither one of us wants to get fired for fighting in the locker room; I know I don't, and that's just what Mr. Muller would do to both of us, don't you reckon?"

"Fuck Muller," Partain said, starting to rise again.

Jesse pushed him back down onto the bench. "Let me give you some good advice, Phil," he said quietly. "Never pick a fight with a stranger. You never know what you're getting into."

"That's advice you might take yourself," Partain said, looking up at him.

"Oh, I don't want you to get the wrong idea," Jesse replied, smiling. "I'm not picking a fight, I'm nipping one in the bud. In fact, I'm going to make a real effort to get along with you, just as long as you don't blow cigarette smoke at me, and I hope you'll make an effort to get along with me. Life's going to be a whole lot sweeter that way."

"Oh, yeah? Sweeter for who?" Partain asked.

"Why for both of us, Phil," Jesse said in the friendliest tone he could muster. "We're both all grown up now, and when grown men get into fights, somebody gets hurt, likely as not, and I don't want it to be me. I mean, you're a big fella."

"You noticed that, did you?"

"Couldn't miss it," Jesse laughed, slapping Partain solidly on the shoulder. He looked at his watch. "Well, I'd better get back to work." He turned and strolled out of the locker room, back toward the waiting hopper. Phil Partain remained seated on the bench.

Jesse took a deep breath and thought about his pulse. Back in the schoolyard, his heart would have been hammering after an encounter like that, but now it beat right along, just the way it was supposed to. In the yard at Atlanta Federal Prison he had learned to fight without being angry and to avoid fights when he was angry, and the experience was serving him well. He hadn't felt the need to prove anything to Phil Partain; he'd done all his proving back in Atlanta.

He faced the hopper once more.

16

As Jesse walked up the front steps of the house he was struck by a scent from his past, an aroma of small-town Georgia, of the inadequate kitchens of parsonages in the mountains, of his mother making do and doing wonderfully. Somebody was frying chicken.

As he opened the door Carey ran out of the kitchen toward him. "Mama says you get your bath right now," the little girl said. "Supper's in half an hour."

Jesse trudged up the stairs, trying to deal with the emotions that the smell of fried chicken were causing to well up in him. He shaved, then soaked in the tub for fifteen minutes, then got dressed and went downstairs. The table was set, and Jenny's back was to him; she was dishing something up from the stove.

"Hey there," she said, turning toward him. "That's perfect timing; have a seat."

Jesse held a chair for Carey, who beamed up at him as she sat down, then he took a seat. Jenny set a platter of chicken before him, next to a bowl of green beans and another of corn, plus a plate of biscuits.

"You being a Southerner, I thought I'd whip up something Southern," she said, placing an open bottle of beer and a glass on the table, then opening one for herself.

"I started smelling the chicken about halfway home," Jesse said, spearing himself some white meat. "I can't tell you how long it's been since I had some." He wasn't lying; the last time was before Beth had gotten sick. Two years? Three? They hadn't served fried chicken in prison.

"I'm glad you like it," she said, watching him tear into the food.

"The beans and corn are what my mother used to make. The biscuits, too."

"I'm a good guesser, then."

"You certainly are."

The three of them consumed their dinner, and when they had finished, Jenny produced a hot peach cobbler from the oven, and Jesse thought he had died and gone to heaven. It was different from wishing he had.

"About last night," Jenny said when they were comfortable in the living room. Carey was doing the dishes.

"You don't owe me any explanations," Jesse said, and he hoped she didn't believe him.

"Fred and I have been out a few times. There's nothing there—not for me, anyway; he's just okay, no more. We met some other people at the Legion

Hall for a dance, and I had a lot to drink, mostly because I wasn't where I wanted to be, which was with you."

Jesse flushed, and it felt wonderful.

"I was hungover, I guess, and I overslept. I'm sorry I wasn't up to get your breakfast."

"It's okay," he said, patting her knee.

"I told Fred Patrick last night that I wasn't available anymore," she said. "Maybe you think that's rushing things, but it was the way I felt. Still do."

"I'm glad you told him that," Jesse said, and I'm glad you feel that way.

She reached over and kissed him lightly. "Carey'll be in bed in half an hour," she said. "I'll come to you."

As he climbed the stairs to his room Jesse was overcome with the feeling that he was now Jesse Barron, not Warden; that he had become the man he pretended to be. Reality was no longer the Atlanta pen and Kip Fuller and Dan Barker. Reality was St. Clair Wood Products and Jenny Weatherby and her little girl and fried chicken on the table. By the time he had crawled into bed the past was receding from him at the speed of light, and when Jenny opened his door and climbed into bed with him and pressed her naked body against his, he sloughed off the broken man called Jesse Warden like a dirty shirt.

17

Pat Casey got out of his car and walked toward the church, nervous at the prospect of the meeting. He had known Jack Gene Coldwater for more than twenty years, and he could not remember a relaxed moment in his presence. There was something in the man that kept Casey on edge, but also something that made him want to please his leader.

Kurt Ruger was waiting in the anteroom and stood as Casey entered. They walked together to the office door and knocked.

"Come," a deep voice replied.

The two men entered the room and took seats opposite the man who sat at the desk. Casey saw Coldwater only once a month, unless there was some special reason, and this was the regular monthly meeting.

Coldwater was bent over the desk, reading a document, and the sunlight through the window fell on his white hair, which was long and tied at the nape of the neck. The effect was nearly that of a halo, and Casey wondered if the man had planned it that way.

"Good morning, gentlemen," Jack Gene Coldwater said in his rumbling voice.

"Morning, Jack Gene," Casey said in unison with Ruger. They were the only ones who were allowed to call him that, in memory of their early days together in Vietnam.

"Let's hear from finance first," Coldwater said, nodding at Ruger. "Kurt?"

"You've seen the monthly financial statement," Ruger said, indicating the document on Coldwater's desk. "We're in pretty good shape, if a little cash poor."

"Did you talk to Schooner?"

Ruger nodded. "He poor-mouthed me; said the stock was down, and there's a threat of an antitrust suit from the Justice Department over the acquisition of Security Software."

"I told him to expect that," Coldwater said. "It's winnable."

"I tried to buck him up, but he's shaky. I think maybe you should consider talking to him."

Coldwater swiveled in his chair and gazed out at the mountains, offering Ruger and Casey his Indian profile. "Perhaps it's time we had Schooner up here for a little retreat; get his mind concentrated."

"Excellent idea, Jack Gene," Ruger said. "Shall I call him?"

"I'll call him myself," Coldwater said. "What else do you have for me?"

"Collections are coming in well, except for Herman Muller, of course."

"Of course. He turned down our latest offer?"

"He did."

"How much do you think he'll take?"

"Jack Gene, it's my feeling about Muller that he just won't sell. He doesn't need the money—I mean, the man's an elderly, childless widower who lives like a monk; the business keeps him alive, and he knows it."

"Maybe it's time just to remove Muller from the scene," Coldwater said. "He's beginning to annoy me."

"I'm not sure that's wise," Ruger said. "He's childless, but he has relatives out of state. We don't know who would inherit, and we could just be opening a big can of worms."

Coldwater nodded, then turned back to face his two subordinates. "Let's hear from security. Pat?"

Casey sat up a little straighter. "All's well, Chief."

"That's it? 'All's well'?"

"Everything is running as smoothly as we could want. There's no threat from any quarter. It's what we've planned for all these years."

"What about the new boy? I hear he did well during the bank robbery."

"That's true, although Frank damn near shot him. Barron's settled down at the hopper, working his ass off. Settled in at home, too, from all appearances."

"Good. He could still be a cop or a fed, though."

"Possible, of course, but, in my judgment, very unlikely."

"I've always trusted your judgment, Pat," Coldwater said. "You're a hard man to fool; you've proved it over the years."

"Thanks, Chief."

"But we're entering a critical time."

"I know that, Jack Gene, and that's why I've been so careful with him. I've checked him every which way, and he adds up."

"If the feds were putting in a new man, they'd have an airtight background for him, wouldn't they?"

"It's not just his background, though that certainly checks out. It's the kind of man he is. I've known one hell of a lot of cops, and, believe me, he doesn't fit the mold. I've nudged him a little, and—"

"Nudged him? How?"

"I let Phil Partain push him, just to see how he'd react."

"And how did he react?"

"He didn't take the bait, but he didn't back down, either. I think Partain's a little scared of him."

"Partain's a bully; he's scared of anybody who stands up to him," Coldwater said.

"That's true," Casey agreed, "and it would take a pretty sharp guy to figure that out right off the bat. Partain's got a real mean streak; Barron could have walked into a buzz saw, but he didn't. Partain was impressed; so was I, when I heard about it."

Coldwater gazed off into the middle distance. "Doesn't fight, but doesn't back down; I like it. That's how I chose you, Pat; did you know that?"

Casey blinked. "No, I didn't."

"The first time I laid eyes on you was some godawful bar in Saigon. There was a drunk marine raising hell, and he tried to take you on. I liked the way you handled him; you didn't fight him, but you didn't back down."

"I remember that," Casey said. "It was quite a while before we met."

"I marked you down on the spot," Coldwater said. "Later on, I got you transferred." He winked at Ruger. "I picked Kurt, here, for different reasons."

"Partain says Barron's foreman likes him, that he'll recommend to Muller to move him to the line, when a vacancy comes. Partain doesn't like that, figures he's in line first."

"Tell you what," Coldwater said. "Let Barron stew on the hopper for a couple of weeks more, then make a vacancy."

"One of our people?" Casey asked.

"Certainly not," Coldwater replied. "One of Muller's."

"Consider it done."

"I know you'll do it subtly, Pat; you usually do."

"I will."

"Don't come between Barron and Muller; let them build a relationship, then we'll see how he reacts when we bring Muller down."

Ruger sat up straight. "We going to bring Muller down?"

"Somehow. I don't see any other way, do you?"

Ruger shook his head. "No, but it's going to be tricky; we certainly can't let it get around that we had anything to do with it. He's awfully popular, and there are still questions around town about the grandson."

"I'm aware of the affection in which most of the town holds Muller. I'm not about to do anything precipitous."

"You never do, Chief," Ruger said. "I'll look forward to seeing how you handle it."

"I'll handle it simply," Coldwater said. "Simple is always best."

"I'll get Barron promoted," Casey said.

"Good," Coldwater replied. "And when Phil Partain finds out about it, don't get in his way. I want to know what will happen when the two butt heads."

"Partain will kill him, if he gets the chance."

Coldwater shrugged. "If Phil Partain can kill him, then Barron's not for us, is he?"

18

Jesse had been at St. Clair Wood Products for nearly a month when Harley Waters approached him just as the workday began. Another man was with him.

"Hey, Jesse, Herman wants to see you in the office. This guy's going to spell you."

"Okay, Harley," Jesse replied. He dusted off the shavings that clung to his clothes and walked upstairs to Herman Muller's office. The secretary showed him in.

Muller stood up and shook his hand. "Morning, Jesse."

"Morning, Mr. Muller."

"My folks all call me Herman," Muller said. "Have a seat."

Jesse took a chair, wondering what was going on.

Muller leaned back in his chair. "Jesse, I'm real proud of the way you've worked on the hopper; so is Harley. I'm promoting you."

"Well, thanks, Mr. . . . ah, Herman."

"No thanks due; you've earned it. I'm putting you further up the production line, on the pressing equipment. The pay's nine dollars an hour, and when you've learned the equipment, I'll raise it to ten. I don't think it'll take you long to get the hang of it, but remember, that machinery has to be run right, and right every time. The quality of every sheet of chipboard that comes out of this plant depends on this job being done right. You understand me?"

"Yessir, I sure do. I promise you, I'll do a good job."

Muller stood up. "That's good enough for me, Jesse. Harley's down showing your replacement the ropes; when he's done, he'll take you up the line and get you started."

Jesse shook the man's hand and went back to the plant floor. His replacement was stoking the hopper with a truckload of scrap timber, under the watchful eye of Harley Waters. Poor bastard, Jesse thought.

Harley waved him to follow, and Jesse bade a sweet goodbye to the hopper. He followed Harley through a door into another room of the plant, and the noise subsided a bit. Harley led him up a ladder to a glass booth ten feet above the production line. He slapped a worker on the back. "Take a break, Bob." Harley took over operation of the machinery. "Okay, Jesse, I'm going to run a few sheets, and you follow me as I work the controls.

Jesse became aware that somebody was watching him from below. He looked down and saw Phil Partain dumping a bin of wood chips onto a conveyer belt that led to the press. Partain was spending more time watching him than doing his work.

Jesse watched Harley Waters operate the machinery for a while, then took over himself, operating under Harley's sharp eye. It was pleasant to be doing something that took some skill and coordination; he hadn't liked being a laborer. By the time the noon whistle blew, chipboard was emerging smoothly from the press, under Jesse's operation.

"Go get your lunch," Harley said. "I'll stay on with you the rest of the day, and then I think you'll have it down pat. I've got a new job for the man you replaced."

Jesse went back to the locker room, retrieved his lunch and walked out back of the plant. It was a clear, chilly autumn day and the aspens were a bright gold on the mountains behind the factory. Jesse sat down under a tree, ate his sandwiches and drank his soft drink. After that, he rested his head against the tree and dozed.

He was awakened suddenly as someone sharply kicked the soles of his shoes. He opened his eyes and looked up to find Phil Partain standing over him.

"Get on your feet, Barron," Partain said.

"What do you want, Phil?" Jesse asked laconically.

"I want to kick your ass," Partain replied, then kicked Jesse's feet again.

Jesse guessed it was time. He got slowly to his

feet. "Phil, I gave you some real good advice the last time we talked. Remember that?"

"You keep your fucking advice to yourself, you bastard," Partain said, circling Jesse to his right. "I was in line to operate that machine, but I guess you've been sucking Harley's cock real regular."

"Phil, Phil," Jesse said wearily, "I'm going to have to ask you to shut your mouth."

"Shit," Partain said, "you're going to be sucking *my* cock in just a minute." He feinted with his right, then came around with a left hook. Jesse stepped back, and the punch grazed his cheek. He stepped into Partain and planted a short left in the man's considerable gut.

Partain grunted, but he kept coming. That gut had been pretty solid, Jesse thought. He ducked under Partain's right and landed a stiff punch in the ribs. Partain still kept coming, and now he had a knife in his right hand.

I wonder, Jesse thought, how Phil feels about the sight of his own blood? As Partain swung the knife, Jesse stepped inside the swing and struck the man's wrist hard with the edge of his hand, then he knocked back Partain's head with a pair of left jabs, and the bigger man's nose started to bleed.

Partain wiped his face with his sleeve and looked at it. "You goddamned son of a bitch!" he roared.

Jesse kept his guard up. The sight of his own blood apparently made Partain steaming mad. Jesse dodged as the man rushed him and landed a hard right to a kidney as he passed. Partain went down on one knee with a cry of pain, and Jesse punched him in the side of the neck. Partain hit the ground, rolled over and got to his feet again.

Jesse began to use everything he had learned in the yard at Atlanta, kicking a shin, punching under the heart and landing teeth-rattling punches to the jaw. Partain landed a few shots, mostly on Jesse's arms and shoulders. He seemed unaccustomed to fighting somebody who knew how to fight back.

Jesse wore the big man down, hurting him, but leaving him on his feet until he seemed ready to go down. Finally, he doubled Partain over with a left to the solar plexus, then straightened him up with an uppercut. Partain's knees buckled, and he went backward like a felled tree.

There were some shouts, and Jesse looked up to find that a small crowd of workers had gathered. The whistle blew, and Jesse walked back to the plant, leaving Partain where he lay. Nobody, he noticed, went to the man's aid.

Partain didn't come back to work after lunch, and the following morning, he was replaced by a new man. Jesse heard later that Herman Muller had fired Phil Partain.

19

Jesse sat on the hood of his truck, which was parked in deep woods outside St. Clair, and talked to Kip Fuller on the scrambled cellular phone.

"I'm moving up in the world," Jesse said. "Making nine bucks an hour, now, and I expect to get raised to ten any day." He told Kip about the promotion.

"Glad to hear it, Jess."

"Not everybody is as happy as you are about my advancement," Jesse replied. "Fellow called Partain took exception."

"And what did you do about it?" Kip asked, sounding worried.

"I hit him until he got over it," Jesse replied.

"Listen, Jess, I know you're good at that sort of thing, but it can only draw attention to you. I hope you stayed away from anything they taught us at Quantico."

"I did that; I wasn't anxious to look like a federal cop in a fight."

"Good."

"I think it was a setup."

"Oh, shit."

"It's natural that they'd be very wary. I think they wanted to see how I'd react."

"So you reacted by beating the shit out of the guy?"

"Not at first; I let him push me some, first. From the reaction of my coworkers at the plant, I gather he wasn't the most popular guy around."

"So you won a few admirers?"

"Maybe."

"Has there been any reaction from the opposition since this happened?"

"Not so far; it's been a couple of weeks, so I wonder if they're going to react at all."

"I hope you're not going to make a habit of this, Jess."

"Depends on whether they make a habit of it."

"You getting any ideas about where Coldwater is getting his money?"

"I gather the church has a piece of a few businesses around town. He's apparently tried to hustle Herman Muller into selling out, but so far, Herman is standing pat. I hope he goes on doing that; it's hard not to root for the guy."

"No evidence of big money behind Coldwater, though?"

"Nope. It's hard to see how any big money could get generated around here. It's not a big place, and Muller's business has got to be the important earner in town. So far, I can't see that Coldwater is spending any big money, either."

"Let's not make that judgment, yet," Kip said. "You haven't really had a chance to look around, have you?"

"I've deliberately not done any looking around, just traveling where my life here leads me. Snooping could get me burnt."

"I'm glad you see it that way; I don't want you burnt."

"That's sweet of you, Kip; I know Dan feels that way, too."

Kip laughed. "You always did have a sense of humor, Jess."

"Well, I'd better get back to town. I'm supposed to be running an errand for Jenny, and I shouldn't be gone too long."

"No need to call me too often, until something happens," Kip said. "Next week will do."

"Right, see you then." Jesse broke the connection and crawled under the truck to put the phone away. As he closed the safe, he heard another vehicle approaching down the dirt track. He crawled out from under the truck in time to see a police car pull to a stop and Pat Casey get out.

"Hey, Pat," he said, brushing off his clothes.

"Howdy, Jesse." The chief of police watched him warily. "What are you doing out here?"

"I turned down this road to take a leak, to tell you the truth, and what with the bumps, I thought my muffler was loose. I went under there to have a look at it."

"You should have taken it down to the filling station and put it on the rack."

"Not while I'm making nine bucks an hour, I won't," Jesse replied.

Casey grinned. "Guess not. How's it going out at Wood Products?"

"Pretty good; I got promoted. I'm running a press, now."

"That means Herman likes you, I guess."

"I guess."

"I hear you and Phil Partain had a little rumble."

"A little one."

"I'm impressed you came out of it with your ears on your head," Casey said. "Partain's messed up more than one fellow around here."

"Partain's a schoolyard bully, that's all."

"I guess that's true, but he can be dangerous, especially if you've made a fool of him, like you have. I'd watch my back."

"I'll keep it in mind."

"I wouldn't take it hard if you killed the son of a bitch," Casey said.

"I'm not out to kill anybody, but I'm not going to let him kill me," Jesse said.

"That's a reasonable attitude," Casey said.

"Well, I've got to go to the drugstore for my landlady," Jesse said, digging for his keys.

"You do that; never keep a woman waiting."

Jesse got the truck started, turned it around and headed back toward the highway. He glanced in his rearview mirror and saw Casey starting to look around the clearing where he'd been parked. He was going to have to find a better place to use the telephone.

* * *

Jesse stood at the magazine rack in the drugstore and waited for Jenny's prescription to be filled. He flipped through a home improvement magazine, taking care not to be seen reading the *New Yorker* or *Esquire*. He had been there only a moment, when a tall, thin man wearing glasses and a full beard walked into the store and past him. Jesse tensed, but tried not to show it. He knew that man, but he couldn't remember from where, and he hoped to hell the man didn't recognize him. Who was he? Jesse racked his brain.

"Jesse, your prescription is ready," the druggist called out.

"Thanks, Mike," Jesse called back, returning the magazine to the rack and keeping his back to the visitor. Then, as he was about to turn toward the counter, a computer magazine caught his eye; the cover photograph was of the same man who had just entered the store. Melvin Schooner, Jesse realized. Head of one of the fastest-growing software companies in the world. Jesse had read about him half a dozen times in the business section of various newspapers. Schooner departed the prescription counter as Jesse approached, and Jesse got another good look at him. No doubt about who he was.

"There you go, Jesse," Mike said. "I put it on Jenny's account."

"Thanks, Mike. Say, that fellow who just left looks familiar."

"Sure, that's Mel Schooner, the computer guy; hometown boy, he is."

"Oh, yeah, I've seen him on TV, or somewhere."

"Mel's done real well, but he still has time to come home and see his mother," Mike said. "Real nice fellow; belongs to the church here. Been real generous with local contributions."

"That's nice. Take care, Mike."

Jesse went back to his truck with a new thought in mind. Just which contributions had Schooner been so generous with? He got into the cab, and peeked into the bag at Jenny's prescription. Was she ill? He smiled. Nope. Birth control pills. He was glad to know she was taking those.

He drove back toward the house, wondering about Melvin Schooner and his software company. The papers said he was fast gaining on Bill Gates at Microsoft. The guy wasn't forty yet, and he was supposedly a multibillionaire. He wondered if Schooner was acquainted with Jack Gene Coldwater.

As he drove toward home, it began to snow, and Jesse, who had spent nearly all of his life in the South, felt excited, like a schoolboy. The snow was one more indication of how far from Atlanta Federal Penitentiary he had come.

20

Almost as soon as Jesse had begun to operate the press, he was made foreman of his section. He was startled, and then, looking around, he realized that Herman Muller was no fool; he could look at a crew and know who the best man was. And Herman, Harley Waters explained, wasn't one to stand on any such ceremony as seniority. He was suddenly making fifteen dollars an hour, and it amused him that it seemed to be big money.

Then, the week before Thanksgiving, Jesse got the shock of his life. Herman Muller summoned him to his office, sat him in a chair and regarded him solemnly.

"Jesse," Herman said, "I'm not getting any younger."

"I hadn't noticed, Herman," Jesse replied.

"Oh, I'm not getting all that much older, either, I guess, but yesterday my doctor put me on some medicine for arthritis, and it kind of shook me up. I mean, in all my life I never took any medicine for something that wasn't likely to go away pretty fast."

"Arthritis isn't all that much of a problem these days, is it?"

Muller shrugged. "I guess not; it was just the notion of having a chronic ailment that got me thinking."

"I wouldn't worry about it, Herman; you'll bury most of us."

"I expect to," Herman said, allowing himself a small smile, "but I guess it wouldn't hurt for me to have some help upstairs, here."

Jesse didn't reply, since he had no idea what Muller was talking about.

"I told you when you came here, not so very long ago, that it's my policy to promote from within."

"That's right, you did, and I guess I've benefitted from that policy."

"Well, this morning I sat down and I went through my list of foremen. There's six of you fellows, and you've all got different qualities to recommend you. None of you has a lot of education, but some of you are smarter than others, and I think you're the smartest of the lot."

"Why thank you, Herman."

"I was looking back over your employment application and remembering our first conversation, and it appears that you're the only one of my foremen who's ever run a business."

"I am?"

"Yessir, and even though you went bust, I don't think it was your fault; it was the times, is my guess."

"That's what I'd like to think myself," Jesse said.

"Anyway, you've had some experience running a business, keeping costs down and volume up; you've handled men, I can tell from the way you do your present job."

"I guess I have."

"Well, I've decided that I need a . . . well, a kind of assistant manager, I guess; somebody who can learn the business from my perspective and who can keep the place going if I'm out with the flu for a few days."

"I see," Jesse replied.

"You're my man, Jesse; I've looked 'em all over, and even though you're the newest foreman, you're the best, and the job's yours, if you want it."

"Herman, I sure do want it, I'll tell you that," Jesse said, not without feeling.

"You'd have to wear a white shirt and a tie every day, like me," Muller said.

"I guess I can handle that."

"You'd have to learn the computer bookkeeping system."

"I can handle that, too, even though my wife took care of that part of my old business."

"You'll have to learn to buy materials, and I mean *negotiate*. You'll have to hire and fire—with my consent, of course—and you'll have to order machine parts and keep an eye on the salespeople. I've only got three, and they're all in the West. One of these days I'll have a shot at some Eastern markets, I guess."

"I'll give it my best, Herman," Jesse said.

"All right, you can start by picking out a fore-man from your crew. Watch him for as long as you think necessary, and when you think he's ready, you put on that white shirt and tie and come on up here."

Jesse stood up and stuck out his hand. "I really appreciate your confidence, Herman. I won't let you down."

Muller shook his hand. "I don't believe you will, Jesse."

Jesse turned to go.

"Oh, I guess we'd better talk money," Muller said. "How's seven-fifty a week, to start?"

"That's fine with me, Herman."

"Do a good job, and you'll get more."

"Thank you, sir."

"Go on, get back to work. Your crew will be messing up, without you there."

Jesse stopped on Main Street and bought a suit and some shirts before going home to Jenny. When he told her the news of his promotion she threw her arms around him and kissed him on the neck.

"Good Lord! You're setting records at Wood Products! Assistant manager!"

Jesse hugged her and savored the moment. He pushed away his past and tried to believe that he was just an honest working stiff who'd gotten a promotion.

"Why don't I take you and Carey out to din-ner? We'll celebrate."

"We'd love to! You wait, and I'll change my clothes and get Carey dressed up. We'll go to the Steak Shack, is that all right?"

"Fine with me," he laughed. "I love a good steak."

He watched her run up the stairs like a happy schoolgirl, and he felt happy himself.

21

Kurt Ruger picked up Melvin Schooner at the motel and drove him toward the mountain. Schooner, he thought, looked nervous, but that was understandable. Everybody was a little nervous around Jack Gene Coldwater.

"Why does he want to see me?" Schooner asked, dabbing at his forehead with a shirtsleeve.

"I think he just wants to say hello, Mel. He knew you were home visiting your mother, of course."

"It's about the money, isn't it?"

"Don't worry about it, Mel. Jack Gene's not mad at you." He turned at the church and started up the mountain.

"He just doesn't understand the cash flow," Schooner said. "We've spent the past two years updating our word processing product and that cost us a bundle. You can't imagine how much cash is soaked up by three or four hundred programmers sitting there, day after day, writing code."

"Jack Gene will understand," Ruger replied soothingly. "If there's anything he understands, it's cash flow."

"Yeah," Schooner said disconsolately.

The road steepened, and they climbed past houses tucked back into the trees, houses occupied by the elite of the church. Near the top of the mountain Ruger turned into a driveway, then stopped in front of a small television camera and waited until he was recognized and the wrought-iron gates were electronically opened.

"We're going to his house?" Schooner asked, sounding almost alarmed.

"Yes. He wanted to see you here."

"I've never been to his house. Jesus Christ."

"Just about," Ruger replied.

Jack Gene Coldwater received them in the garden, which was English in style, planted with many flowers and perennials. This time of year, Ruger noted, the place was still green, even though the flowers were not in bloom and patches of snow appeared here and there on the grass. Two of Coldwater's wives were gardening, working away, crouched or kneeling, doing their master's work.

"Have a seat here," Ruger said, indicating a stone bench. The two men sat on the cold granite and pulled their coats closer around them. They had only a moment to wait before Jack Gene himself appeared from around a corner of the garden path, striding toward them, his breath coming in clouds of mist. Ruger and Schooner stood to meet him. He shook both their hands and sat down on one end of the bench, placing Schooner between Ruger and himself.

"Mel, how are you?" Coldwater asked.

"I'm just fine, sir," Schooner said, like a schoolboy called into the principal's office.

"I'm glad to hear it. How's the work coming on the new release of the WordPlay software?"

"We're just finishing up the beta testing; I'm planning to release the first of the year."

"Good, good. I know what a drain on resources such a huge project can be."

"Yes, sir, it certainly has been a drain."

"What sort of acceptance of the new version do you anticipate?"

"Well, the feedback from the beta testing has just been phenomenal. My marketing people think we will ship two million copies the first forty-five days; most of them upgrades, of course."

"Sounds as though I should buy some more Schooner stock," Coldwater said, rewarding Schooner with a broad smile.

"Oh, God," Schooner moaned, "let's not get into any insider-trading problems with the SEC. I'm already worried about the antitrust division of the Justice Department; they're breathing down our necks on the acquisition."

"Don't worry, Mel, I'll be discreet; I'll buy through third parties, and I'll spread the buys around—some in Texas, some in New York, some in California."

"I'd appreciate that, sir," Schooner said, sounding relieved.

Coldwater gazed off into the distance. The

view was spectacular from so high up, and he seemed to drink it in for a full minute of silence. Then he spoke. "Mel, I'm concerned about your spiritual state."

Schooner looked alarmed. "Oh, sir, I'm certainly working to keep straight."

"I know you are, Mel; you always have." He turned and looked at Schooner. "It's what I've come to expect from you," he said slowly.

Perspiration appeared on Schooner's forehead. "Thank you, sir," he said.

"But I want to see a manifestation of your spiritual state," Coldwater said, keeping his eyes on Schooner's. "I want more than words; God wants material evidence of your continuing commitment to the church." He paused. "So do I."

"Sir, right now ten million dollars is difficult," Schooner said, his voice trembling.

"Ten million?" Coldwater asked, his eyes widening slightly. "Is that what Kurt has asked you for?"

"Yes, sir; that was the figure he mentioned."

"I think, say, five million dollars would satisfactorily demonstrate your faith," Coldwater said.

Schooner seemed almost to swoon with relief. "Oh, I can manage that, sir. I'll have it in the church account by Monday."

"In my own account," Coldwater said. "The Cayman Islands account."

"Whatever you say, sir."

"You said you'd ship two million copies of the new WordPlay the first forty-five days?"

"That's what we anticipate, sir."

"Good. You can send the other five million the middle of February, to the church account."

Schooner gulped. "I should be able to do that by then, sir."

"You won't disappoint me?" Coldwater asked, placing a fatherly hand on the younger man's shoulder.

"Oh, no sir," Schooner blurted. "Of course not."

Coldwater clapped Schooner sharply on the back. "Good man! Your church can always depend on you!"

"Thank you, sir," Schooner said, managing a smile.

"You have a very fine soul," Coldwater said, his gaze boring into Schooner. "Go with God." He stood up and walked back up the garden path.

Schooner and Ruger stood as he left.

"Mel, would you mind waiting in the car for a moment?" Ruger asked.

"Sure," Schooner replied, and turned back toward the house.

Ruger walked up the path and rounded a curve. Coldwater was standing beside an iron deer, gazing out over the view.

"Jack Gene?"

Coldwater turned and looked at Ruger.

"There's something I thought you'd want to know."

"What is it?"

"Herman Muller has made Jesse Barron the assistant manager at Wood Products."

"*What?*"

"I know, it's entirely unexpected."

"Barron hasn't been there eight weeks yet, has he?"

"Just about that."

"Herman has never let anybody help him manage that place."

"It occurred to me that it might be some sort of defensive move."

"That's possible, I suppose. We haven't entirely co-opted Barron, yet. Maybe Herman thinks of him as an ally against us."

"I think that must be it."

Coldwater turned and looked out over the mountains again. "Still, eight weeks on the job, starting on the hopper like everybody else. That's *very* impressive."

"I suppose it is," Ruger replied.

"Kurt, I think it's about time I met Jesse Barron."

"I'll see to it, Jack Gene."

"Let's keep it subtle; I just want to get the feel of him."

"Consider it done."

Coldwater's attention seemed to drift back to the landscape. "Thank you, Kurt."

Ruger backed away, then went to join Schooner.

22

Jesse stood by the truck and looked at the First Church of St. Clair. It was medium-sized, as churches go, prosperous looking, a Greek facade topped by a soaring steeple. The building sat on a broad lawn, now covered by snow, at the base of the mountain that loomed over the town. It was a respectable-looking church, Jesse thought.

Jenny took Carey to church faithfully, every Sunday morning, but she had never asked Jesse to come. Then, that morning, she had snuggled up to him in bed, pressed her naked breasts against his back and said, "There's a communal Thanksgiving dinner at the church today. Carey and I would like you to come."

"I'd like that," he had responded, relieved that she had finally given him an excuse to see the congregation up close.

Jenny led him into the auditorium, and Jesse was stopped in his tracks at the sight of the place. It was not very different from the more prosperous churches where his father had preached, with one exception: at the rear of the church, looming over the choir loft, was a large stained-glass window depicting Jesus Christ, who was holding in his hand, not a dove, but a pair of lightning bolts. Jesse's attention was drawn to the face; something about it was odd. As Jesse followed Jenny down a side aisle, the face seemed to change slightly, until another face was revealed. It recalled the optician's billboard in *The Great Gatsby*; the eyes seemed to follow him as the face changed.

He followed Jenny down a flight of stairs, and they emerged into a large basement room with a table that stretched nearly the length of the church. There was a great bustle as women set the table and streamed from the kitchen with platters of food, while others stood to one side of the room with their children. Carey ran over to a small group and greeted two other little girls.

On the other side of the table, standing in threes and fours, the men waited, chatting idly and watching the progress of food from the kitchen.

Jenny tugged at his sleeve. "Why don't you go over there and introduce yourself to some of the men?" she asked. Then, without waiting for a reply, she followed Carey to the clutch of women.

Feeling abandoned, Jesse walked around the long table and approached the men. He was relieved to see somebody he knew.

"Hey there, Jesse," Pat Casey said, extending his hand. "Let me introduce you to some fellows. This is Luther Williams, that's Paul Carter, and over there is Hank Twomy."

Jesse shook their hands and sensed a reserve

among the men. They had stopped talking as he approached.

"I'm glad to see you here," Casey said. "We should have gotten you to church a long time ago."

"Thanks, Pat; I'm glad to be here."

"Congratulations on your promotion. You're moving right up at Wood Products."

"Thanks," Jesse said quietly.

"Herman Muller must think highly of you."

Jesse shrugged. "I'm glad to make a little more money. I appreciate you sending me down there. I don't know where I'd be if you hadn't been nice enough to do that."

"Glad to be of help, and I'm glad to see you settling into our town so well. It's starting to seem like you've always been here."

"It seems like that to me, too," Jesse replied, truthfully. "If you'd have told me three months ago that I'd be where I am now, I'd have thought you were crazy." That was the truth, too. In fact, he had expected to be dead by this time.

There was the sound of movement in the crowd and Jesse turned to see Jenny beckoning to him from the table. He went forward with the other men and took a seat opposite her and Carey, all the men on his side and all the women and children on the other. Then, as if at some secret signal, the room fell suddenly quiet, and Jesse followed Jenny's gaze to the head of the table. There stood a tall man dressed in white trousers and a white silk shirt, open at the throat. His skin was bronzed and his long hair was entirely white, and Jesse thought he looked like nothing less than an apparition. His face was just recognizable as that of the young man in uniform that Jesse had seen in the photograph at his briefing in Atlanta; moreover it was recognizable as the face that had alternated with the face of Jesus in the stained-glass window upstairs.

The sound of a door slamming caused Jesse to look toward Coldwater's right. There, staggering drunk and making his way toward the minister, was Phil Partain. The two men seated nearest Coldwater, one of them Kurt Ruger, jumped up and intercepted Partain, steered him from the room. The minister seemed not to notice.

Jack Gene Coldwater raised his hands wide and his voice was like the rumble of thunder. "We thank our God for this day; for the lives we lead together; for the love we share; and, most of all, for the purity of the consecrated blood that flows in our veins."

Jesse suddenly realized that his was the only face turned toward the speaker. Every other head was bowed, yet he was unable to wrest his gaze from Coldwater.

"We thank our God for the new world that awaits us, just beyond our sight; for his choosing of us from all the people of the earth, to do his final will; for the lightning from heaven that awaits our enemies. We thank our God for this food, this plenty afforded to those who follow his new word. Amen."

"Amen!" the group said in chorus, startling Jesse.

He leaned across the table toward Jenny. "Who is that?" he asked.

"That's our pastor, Jack Gene Coldwater," she replied, then began to eat. She didn't seem anxious to continue about Coldwater, so Jesse began to eat, too.

Pat Casey spoke up from beside him. "He is a very remarkable man, Jesse. You will get to know that."

The dinner was over, and people were making their goodbyes as the dishes were taken away. Jesse stood with Jenny and Carey, ready to leave, but Jenny seemed to be waiting for something. Shortly, Pat Casey tapped Jesse on the shoulder from behind.

He turned to see the police chief standing with Jack Gene Coldwater, who was gazing expectantly at Jesse.

"Jack Gene, I want to introduce you to Jesse Barron, a new member of our community. Jesse, this is Jack Gene Coldwater, our pastor."

Jesse's hand was enveloped in Coldwater's, which was large and surprisingly soft.

"Jesse," Coldwater said, "I want to welcome you to our church. This is the first of many visits, I hope." He did not let go of Jesse's hand.

Jesse stood, fixed in Coldwater's gaze, suddenly seized with the feeling that the man could see inside him, see who he really was and why he was there. "Thank you, pastor," he managed to say. "It was a very fine dinner."

"Those who dine at my table never want for anything," Coldwater replied. "Anything," he repeated.

Jesse didn't know how to respond to that, so he said nothing.

Coldwater continued to clasp Jesse's hand. "Come and see me Monday, after work," he said. He gave Jesse's hand a final shake, then turned and walked away without acknowledging Jenny or Carey.

"Come around to the station when you get off," Casey said. "I'll take you up there to see him."

"All right," Jesse replied. There didn't seem to be anything else to say.

"Let's go home," Jenny said, taking his arm.

On the drive home she said nothing.

"You're very quiet," he said. "For you, I mean."

She smiled up at him. "I'm just full," she said. "Eating that much always makes me sleepy."

"I'd better get you home to bed," he said.

"I guess you'd better," she said, then winked at him.

Jesse drove home, looking forward to bed, looking forward to the weekend off and looking forward to his appointed meeting with Jack Gene Coldwater.

23

The four men arrived separately in Seattle: two at Seattle-Tacoma International airport on different flights from different destinations. The third arrived by Greyhound bus a little after nine in the evening, and inside an hour had stolen an anonymous van and changed its license plates with those of a Toyota Corolla parked nearby. He then picked up the two men at Seattle-Tacoma airport.

After midnight, the fourth man landed a light airplane, a fixed-gear Cessna 182, at Tacoma Narrows, a small, general-aviation airport on one of the many islands in the area. He taxied to a remote end of the tie-down area and cut the engine. Immediately, the van pulled up to the airplane, and its contents were quickly transferred to the vehicle. Two of the men refilled the airplane's fuel tanks from jerry cans stowed in the luggage compartment. Not a word was spoken. The men got into the van and drove toward Seattle.

The four men were named, for the occasion, Black, Gray, Brown and White. Black, who had piloted the Cessna, held a flashlight to a map of the city and gave monosyllabic instructions to Brown, who drove, while Gray and White quietly slipped into boiler suits in the back of the van. It was nearly 2 A.M. when the van arrived at its destination.

"Around the block at twenty-five miles an hour," Black said. As they turned the first corner, a police car passed them going in the opposite direction.

Brown stiffened at the wheel, but Black put a hand on his arm. "It's all right; in fact it's good. Better now than in half an hour." He began climbing into a boiler suit. "Stop there and change," he said, pointing to the curb. When Brown had donned his suit, he drove back toward their destination.

Black pointed to the parking lot of a printing company across the street, and Brown pulled into a parking place. Two small canvas duffles were handed forward from the rear of the van, and the occupants got out. Wordlessly, the four men crossed the street and walked at a moderate pace down the sidewalk along a high hedge, each carrying an identical canvas bag. Black was counting paces under his breath.

He raised a hand, and his companions stopped. Gray and White plunged their arms into the hedge and parted it, while Black and Brown stepped through; then Gray and White followed them. The hedge closed behind them.

Quickly now, Black led them to the rear door of the building. Each man unzipped his canvas bag and removed a pistol with a silencer affixed. Black produced a key, unlocked the door, and the four men stepped inside, then their leader went to a security keypad just inside the door and tapped in a four-digit code. A soft beep sounded. Black turned to his companions and shone his flashlight on his wristwatch. He held up three fingers, for three minutes. His companions nodded, and on a hand signal from Black they spread out into the building.

Black found room number one, sat cross-legged on the floor under the central table and laid his pistol on the floor beside him. He took a small packet from his canvas bag and taped it to the table pedestal, making sure to leave a six-inch length of aerial wire exposed. He went back into the hallway and to the rear door, where he was joined by his three companions. He took another packet from his bag and taped it to the rear door. Glancing at his wristwatch, he tapped a number into a keypad on the unit, then looked at the others and nodded.

Black opened the rear door. To his astonishment he was staring down the barrel of a .38 caliber pistol.

"Freeze! All of you!" The uniformed man cried.

Black did not hesitate; he swung his canvas bag at the man's weapon and felt a round blow past his head. He fired one shot into the middle of the man's face, then stepped over his body and waved the others to follow.

"Jesus Christ," White said.

"Shut up," Black barked. "Nothing has changed."

He looked carefully through the parted hedge, up and down the street. It was deserted, but he saw a light come on in a house across the street. "Don't run, walk," Black growled at the others. They made their way toward the van, and Black heard a door open and voices. "Walk!" he said again.

They reached the van and got in. Brown started the engine, and Black put a hand on his shoulder. "Twenty-five miles an hour, no more," he said. He switched on his flashlight and started to give instructions again. From the distance came the sound of a police siren.

"Jesus Christ!" Brown shouted, then floored the accelerator.

"Slow down!" Black yelled. "Twenty-five; no more!"

"People came out of that house," Brown said. "They had to get a look at the van."

At that moment a huge explosion erupted behind them, and the interior of the van was lit with a fiery light. The two men in the rear of the van cheered.

"Shut up," Black said to them. "We can't return the van to where you stole it," he said to Brown. "We go to Plan B. Right at the next intersection; we'll stay off the big streets and go through neighborhoods to the Plan B rendezvous. We've got a local contact waiting there for us, just in case. Now left at the corner. And slow down!" He turned and looked over his shoulder at the two men in back. "Listen to me carefully. If a cop car gets on our tail, we won't run. Brown will slow down;

you kick open the back doors and pour everything into their windshield."

"We've already killed one cop," Brown said.

"That was a security guard, and anyway, we've already bought the death penalty if they get us, so another cop or two won't matter."

Brown set his jaw and drove.

"Two rights, now." In a moment they were approaching a school. "Turn in here; drive around back." As they came around the corner of the building the van's headlights picked up a Lincoln Town Car parked near a dumpster. "That's our ride," Black said. "Make sure everything is out of the van. Everybody still wearing gloves?"

Affirmative noises came from all three men.

Black got out and rapped on the driver's window of the Lincoln, and as it came down he found himself looking into the face of a plump, pretty blonde woman. "Hit your trunk release," he said. He turned to his companions. "I want all three of you in the trunk."

"What?" Brown asked, incredulous.

"They're looking for four men in a van, not a woman and a man in a Lincoln. Don't worry, it's a big trunk."

The three men got out of their boiler suits and arranged themselves in the trunk; Black tossed his suit into the trunk along with his bag, tucked his pistol into his waistband and closed the lid. He got into the passenger seat and fastened his seat belt. "All right, let's go," he said. "I'll give you directions."

The woman turned toward him. "Did everything go all right?"

"Shut up and look straight ahead," Black said. "Have you forgotten your instructions?"

The woman snapped her head around. "I'm sorry."

"Let's move it, then! Don't turn your lights on yet; drive to the corner of the building and stop."

The woman obeyed, sitting quietly while he looked up and down the street.

"All right, turn right out of the parking lot; twenty-five miles an hour, no more."

The woman followed his instructions. "I thought you weren't coming," she said. "I was about to leave."

"I'm not going to tell you again to shut up," Black said. "If you speak again, I'll throw you out of the car. Do you have your story straight if we're stopped? Nod your head."

She nodded.

He finally seemed to have gotten through to her. He began to concentrate on giving her directions.

Half an hour later they crossed a bridge to the island and immediately turned left at a sign for the airport. "Stop here," he said. He opened the glove compartment and pressed the trunk release button, then got out of the car. His three companions were extricating themselves from their cramped positions and stretching their limbs. One of them took their equipment from the trunk.

"Hey, we made it!" White said, seeing the airport sign. "Good going, Chief Casey!"

Casey opened his mouth to yell at the man; then he saw the woman. She had gotten out of the car and was standing at the rear bumper, looking at them. "Partain," he said, "you are one stupid son of a bitch." He pulled the pistol from his belt and raked the woman across the head with the silencer. She went down with no more than a sigh.

"What did you do that for?" Gray asked.

"I did it because she was stupid enough to see all of our faces, and because Partain, here, stupid as he is, told her my name! Now get that bitch into the front seat of the car."

"What are we going to do with her?" Partain asked.

"What do you think?" Casey said. "Get behind the wheel. You two guys wait here." He got into the backseat. "Drive back down to the bridge and stop just before you get to it."

Partain did as he was told. Casey got out and pulled the limp woman into the driver's position. He turned the steering wheel to the right, put on the emergency brake and put the transmission in drive. He moved the woman's right leg until her foot rested on the accelerator, pressing lightly on the petal. The car revved slightly and strained against the parking brake. He turned to Partain. "Come here."

Partain walked over. "Yeah?"

"Release the parking brake," Casey said.

Partain scratched his head, stepped forward

and, after a moment's hesitation, pulled the control that released the brake. The car jerked forward and began to move toward the side of the road.

As it passed, Casey slammed the driver's door. The car left the road, gaining speed, and started down the slope of the bridge approach, knocking down small pine trees as it went. At the bottom of the incline the car went over a small cliff and flew through the air toward the narrows. There was a loud splash and white foam spread across the black water.

Casey stood and watched as the waters quieted. Then the Lincoln popped to the surface, or nearly so. The roof could be seen as the car drifted away from the bridge with the current.

"It's not going to sink!" Partain cried.

"It's going to sink," Casey said. "If not here, then down a little ways. The farther from the bridge, the better." As he watched, bubbles spilled from the cabin, and the car slowly sank from sight. "There," he said. "They won't find her for a while."

The two men trudged back up the hill and joined their two companions. It was a few minutes' walk to the airport. They skirted the building where the night attendant was and boarded the Cessna, tossing their bags into the luggage compartment with the empty jerry cans. Casey worked his way through the checklist deliberately; he could not allow himself to rush. The engine started quickly, and Casey taxied onto the runway, turning upwind. He pushed the throttle all the way forward; the airplane started its roll, and in a moment, they were airborne.

As they climbed away from the field the lights of Seattle appeared in the distance. Near the center of the city, Casey could see a large fire burning.

"Wow, look at that," Partain said from the backseat. "We must have ignited a gas main."

Casey stayed under a thousand feet until they were clear of the Seattle Terminal Control Area, then he began his climb and pointed the Cessna east, toward Idaho. All that remained for him to do on arrival was to remove the taped-on, fake registration number from the side of the airplane and reapply the original numbers.

That, and beat the shit out of Partain, he mused.

24

Jesse left work on Monday afternoon and drove into town. He parked his truck, picked up a Boise paper at the drugstore and walked down to the police station. A young officer was manning the reception desk.

"Hi, I'm Jesse Barron," he said to the officer. "Chief Casey is expecting me; will you tell him I'm here?"

Pat Casey gave him a wave from his glass-enclosed office, took his hat from a hook and walked into the reception area. "How you doing, Jesse?" he asked shaking his guest's hand. "Ready for your meeting?"

"Sure," Jesse said. He followed Casey outside and into a patrol car. Casey backed out and drove toward the church.

"You know, Pat, that's a real impressive station you've got there. Not what you'd expect to see in a small town."

"You're right about that, pal; we've got all the

latest computer stuff, and we can plug into any of half a dozen law enforcement networks with a few keystrokes. My squad cars have got computer equipment, too. You know, Jesse, I ran a check on you the day you hit town."

Jesse tried to look surprised. "No kidding? You're a careful man, Pat."

"I try to be."

"And what did you find out?"

"That you're not a liar. You know, I thought about offering you a job on the force, but you moved up so fast at Wood Products that I couldn't afford you now."

"You think I'd make a cop?" Jesse asked.

"I think so. You're a smart guy, and you've got guts; you showed that when you took on a guy the size of Phil Partain."

Jesse shrugged and unfolded his newspaper. "What's in the news?"

"Looks like somebody took out another abortion clinic," Jesse replied, scanning the story. "That's the fourth one in a month, and it's okay with me." He could feel Casey's gaze on him.

"You against abortion?"

"Murdering babies? Damn straight, I am. I had three girls, you know, and the second two were big surprises. I wouldn't have stopped either one of them for anything."

"I'm with you, pal," Casey said, swinging past the church and starting up the mountain.

"We're not going to the church?"

"The pastor wants to see you in his home. That's a rare honor, believe me."

"I'm flattered." Jesse glanced down at the bottom of the newspaper's front page. SEATTLE ANTI-ABORTION ACTIVIST DEAD IN PUGET SOUND PLUNGE, it read.

"What's that piece?" Casey asked.

Jesse read aloud: " 'The body of Martha Terrell Peary, a prominent member of Seattle's pro-life movement, was found in her car near the Tacoma Narrows bridge yesterday, the victim of an apparent accident. Raymond Peary, her husband, said his wife often took late-night drives and that she must have lost control of her car. Mrs. Peary had taken a leading part in many demonstrations against family planning clinics in the Northwest over the past four years, and it seemed ironic to her friends that she should have died on the night of the firebombing of the Parsons Street Clinic, in Seattle, by unknown perpetrators.' That's it."

"Well," said Casey, "win some, lose some."

Jack Gene Coldwater's house was situated at the end of a long drive, very near the top of the mountain. It was a solid-looking stone structure, with elaborate plantings along the drive and in the turnaround at the front door. Jesse thought it looked like something out of an architectural magazine. This impression was reinforced when they were let inside by a pretty young woman and shown to the pastor's study.

Coldwater sat in a leather armchair, his striking profile toward the door, apparently lost in a book. The room was paneled in walnut and lined with bookcases. Books were everywhere, on a sofa, on a coffee table, on the floor and on the limestone mantelpiece. A cheerful log fire burned in the grate.

"Pastor," the woman said softly, "your guests are here."

Coldwater looked up and smiled. "Jesse, how are you?"

"Fine, sir."

"Miss Betty," Casey said to the young woman, "do you think you could find me something to nibble on in the kitchen?"

"Of course, Chief," she replied, and led the way. Casey closed the door behind them.

"Come and sit down," Coldwater said, indicating a matching chair facing his own.

Jesse sat down.

"I believe the sun is over the yardarm," Coldwater said, looking out the window at the winter twilight. "May I offer you something to warm you up?"

"Thank you sir, maybe a bourbon."

Coldwater went to a drinks trolley and poured them both a stiff drink, handed Jesse his, sat down and raised his glass. "To a better day."

Jesse raised his glass and drank. It was excellent.

Coldwater took a small sip, then set his glass down on a side table. "What do you know about us here, Jesse?"

"About the town?" He set his drink down.

"About the church; about me."

"Not very much, I guess. The Thanksgiving dinner was my first visit to the church."

"No gossip around town?"

"I've been spending most of my time at home, when I'm not working."

Coldwater nodded. "At Jenny Weatherby's. A fine young woman, Jenny; fellow could do a lot worse. Nice little girl, too."

"I've grown fond of them both."

"Good. A man needs the affection of a woman."

They sat silently for a moment, and Jesse elected not to speak first. After all he had been summoned here.

"I want to tell you something of the background of this place," Coldwater said. "I came here some twenty years ago, fresh out of the army and the Vietnam war. I came with a couple of thousand dollars in back pay and two friends, Pat Casey and Kurt Ruger. Pat, you know; have you met Kurt?"

"No, sir."

"A financial wizard. One of the best minds for money in the country. On Kurt's advice, we pooled our funds and made a down payment on land that includes this mountain. We built a log church on the site where the First Church now rests, lived in it, worshiped in it, conducted our lives in that building for years. We worked hard, marshaled our resources and attracted others to our way of life. We multiplied and prospered." He stopped and looked at Jesse. "Are you a religious man, Jesse?"

"My father"—he stopped himself; he had

nearly said that his father was a minister—"kind of rammed it down my throat, I guess. I didn't feel close to the church at home, but I . . . I guess I sort of carved out my own religion from all of what was thrown at me as a boy. I believe in God, I really do."

"Do you believe that some people are chosen *personally* by God?"

"Yes, sir, I believe that. I've never known what he wanted me to do, though."

"Jesse, I believe God has brought you here, to us. Do you believe that God can do that?"

"I believe God can do *anything*," Jesse said, nodding vigorously.

"Good man. Do you believe that God speaks directly to some people?"

"I'm sure he must," Jesse said. He looked into the fire for effect. "Sometimes I wish he'd speak to me."

"Do you believe God chooses some groups of people over others?"

"Well, the Israelites were the chosen people of the Bible, weren't they?"

"Yes, until they renounced and murdered his son," Coldwater replied softly. "God has never forgiven them for that; they are, each of them, cursed. God has a new chosen people now." He leaned forward and bored his gaze into Jesse's eyes. "They are here, in this community, and God has chosen *me* to lead them to him."

Jesse let his eyes widen slightly and his jaw drop.

"Do you believe that is possible?" Coldwater asked.

"Yes, sir, I do."

"Do you think I am insane, Jesse?"

"No, sir; you seem very sane to me."

"People to whom God speaks are often thought to be insane. Some of them are, I suppose, but I assure you, I am not."

Coldwater suddenly sat up straight and pressed his back against his chair. "Jesse," he said, and his voice seemed to waver, "Jesse, sometimes God gives me to know about people, and he is speaking to me of you at this moment."

Jesse leaned forward. "About *me?*"

"You have had a great tragedy in your life," Coldwater intoned, closing his eyes. "You have lost those dearest to you in the most violent way."

"Yes," Jesse said, "it's true."

"There are three little girls and a lovely woman; they are with God."

"Yes," Jesse said again, allowing his voice to waver. I'll match you con for con, he thought.

"They are happy, but they are worried about you," Coldwater said. "They want you to have a new life."

"Can you see them?" Jesse asked.

"God can see them. God has chosen this moment to heal your wound, to make you whole again."

"Oh, God," Jesse moaned. He was actually enjoying this. The guy was some salesman, and this was some pitch.

Coldwater opened his eyes and looked at Jesse, then closed them again and his brow furrowed. "There is someone else," he said.

"Sir?"

"Another little girl, younger than the three."

A chill ran through Jesse. What was going on here?

"She was torn from you, but she has not forgotten her love for you."

Tears sprang involuntarily to Jesse's eyes. *"Sir?"*

"She is far from here, but with kind strangers."

"Who?" Jesse demanded. "Who is she with?"

"A young couple in a sunny place."

Miami, Jesse thought, she's still in Miami. What the hell is going on here?

Coldwater opened his eyes again, then reached out, took Jesse's hand and pulled him to his knees. "Will you pray with me?"

"Oh, yes, sir!"

Coldwater pressed a palm onto the top of Jesse's head. "God, Jesse and I have heard you. He is with us now, his wound healed. Give him the strength to go forward with us!" Coldwater released Jesse and sank back into his chair. The spell seemed broken.

Jesse struggled to his feet and sat down. He grabbed his drink, took a large swig and tried to slow his breathing.

"I'm sorry if I frightened you, Jesse," Coldwater said. "I have these . . . visitations from time to time, when I am told things. Did it all make sense to you?"

"Yes, sir; I had a wife and three little girls, and they were killed in a car accident."

"What about the fourth child?"

"I don't know about that, sir; it didn't make any sense to me, unless it was really one of my girls."

"Yes, that must have been it." Coldwater stood. "Our time is up for today. Will you come and see me again?"

"I'd like that, sir," Jesse said, rising.

Coldwater took Jesse's arm and steered him toward the door. "Jesse, God has work for you to do here with us. Will you join us? Will you do His will?"

"Yes, sir; I want to be with you," Jesse said earnestly. "You just tell me what to do."

"I'll have something for you soon," Coldwater said. Then he pulled Jesse to him and embraced him in a bear hug.

Jesse had the breath crushed from him. He put his arms around Coldwater, feeling small. The muscles in the man's back were as hard as nails.

Coldwater held him at arm's length. "Goodbye, my good friend. I will see you again soon."

"Goodbye, Pastor," Jesse said, and allowed himself to be shown out of the study.

Pat Casey was waiting for him and led him to the squad car, saying nothing.

Jesse sat in the passenger seat of the car, staring out the windshield. What had happened back there? Had Coldwater, in the middle of that *spiel*, somehow tapped into his soul for that moment?

Carrie still remembered him, Coldwater had said. He hoped to God the man was right. Casey silently delivered him to his truck, then said goodnight. Jesse drove home slowly, thinking of Carrie. She was never far from his mind.

25

"He's made you," Kip Fuller said.

"I don't think so," Jesse replied. He was in the woods behind the Wood Products plant, on his lunch hour. "I've thought about it, and I don't think so."

"He couldn't just pull something like that out of a hat, for Christ's sake. How could he possibly know about your daughter? I'm pulling you out of there."

"No, no, Kip; listen to me. It's just possible that he could have broken the Jesse Barron cover; I don't know how, but since I'm not Barron, it's possible. What's not possible is that he could figure out who I really am. There's just no way he could do that."

"You have a point," Kip admitted.

"No, I think it was something real, just for a minute there. He used what Casey had told him about Barron, and then he just . . . I don't know, he read some part of me."

"Now, that's *really* scary."

"There are people who can do that, you know, and I suspect that Coldwater is a very intuitive guy. That's the mark of any good con man, knowing how to read his mark."

"But you think you're in now?"

"I think so. I've had a formal invitation from the man himself, and I've accepted. Let's see what happens next."

"I want to know about it if Coldwater comes up with any more stuff about your past life, do you hear me?"

"I hear you, Kip."

"I mean, sometimes it helps to have another valuation of what's going on, not to just trust your own perceptions."

"I have a feeling I told you that when you were a rookie."

Kip laughed. "You probably did."

"I've got to get back to work; I'll call you when I can."

"Don't keep me waiting," Kip said.

Jesse cut the connection, folded the phone and put it into the false bottom he had made in his lunch box. He would transfer it later to the safe under the truck for charging.

Back in his office he found Herman Muller waiting for him.

"I was looking for you, Jesse," the old man said.

"Sorry, Herman; I walked back up in the woods a ways to have my lunch."

"Jesse, I'm going to ask you to do one of those things that I don't want to do anymore."

"What's that?"

"I want you to go to New York for me next week. I've bid on a good-sized job—chipboard and plywood for a new hotel that's building next year, and the architects want to see somebody from Wood Products up close. It's the sort of job that could lead to others, but to tell you the truth, I just hate New York City. I swear, I think it's hell on earth, and it just scares me to death."

Jesse did not share Herman's feelings about the city. "I'd be glad to go, Herman," he said, trying not to sound too happy about it.

"You're sure you don't mind?"

"Not at all. What do I have to do?"

"They want to know about our plant and our production facilities—capacity, quality, reliability. I'd send one of my salesmen, but to tell you the truth, they're more comfortable talking to lumberyards than architects, and I think you'd handle yourself better."

"Well, thank you, Herman; that's high praise."

"I want you to take some pictures of our plant and equipment and write up a little history of the company and some of the jobs we've handled, like the ski resort in Park City. Do whatever you think will make up a good presentation."

"I'll get right on it, Herman."

Muller nodded and went back to his own office. Jesse leaned back in his chair and took a deep breath. New York! He hadn't been there in years. He'd take Jenny, and they'd have a good dinner or two, maybe see a show. The phone rang.

"Jesse Barron."

"Jesse, it's Pat Casey."

"Hi, Pat."

"Listen, can you stop by the station for about an hour on your way home tonight?"

"Sure, what's up?"

"I'll tell you when you get here."

"Sure. I'll see you a little after six." He hung up the phone. Maybe he was about to be let inside at last. He picked up the phone and called Jenny.

"How'd you like a weekend in New York?" he asked gleefully.

There was a shocked silence for a moment. "I don't know," she replied.

"What do you mean, you don't know? Herman's sending me on business. We'd have a terrific time."

"Can we talk about it when you get home?"

"Sure we can. Oh, I've got to make a stop on the way. I should be there around seven or seven-thirty."

"I'll make dinner for seven-thirty, then."

"Perfect; maybe I'll pick up a bottle of wine on the way."

"Sounds good."

"Bye."

"Bye."

He was disappointed in her reaction to the possibility of a New York trip; he'd thought she'd be dying to go, to get out of this little town for a change.

*   *   *

Jesse stopped at the liquor store and chose an extra-good bottle of California Cabernet, then he drove over to the police station.

The place was quiet, with only one officer on duty. Pat Casey met him in reception. "Hey, Jesse. Come on back here with me." Casey led him down a corridor to the rear of the station. He opened a door with a four-digit combination, and showed Jesse inside.

Jesse was careful to memorize the combination. You never knew. But something he saw in the room nearly made him forget the numbers. Sitting on a table in the center of the room was something he had not seen for a long time, and the sight of it made his blood run cold.

"Have a seat, Jesse," Casey said. He motioned to a chair next to the table, then pulled up a chair for himself. "Something we have to get out of the way, just a formality."

"Yeah?" Jesse asked, trying not to sound nervous.

"Yeah. Jack Gene wants you to take a polygraph test."

"A what?"

"A lie detector test."

26

Jesse sat and stared at the machine. He remembered a conversation he'd had with an FBI polygraph operator whom his unit in Miami had borrowed from time to time. "You can't beat the machine," the man had said. "Not if the operator's good. An experienced man will pick up the lies every time. There's only one way you can beat it, and that's by believing your own lies."

"Excuse me a minute," Casey said, "I've got to get another roll of paper for this thing."

What did the machine measure? Respiration and pulse and something to do with skin reactions: sweat? It was cool enough in the room, but he slipped off his jacket and hung it on the back of his chair. How could he handle the respiration and pulse changes? Yoga. He didn't know much about it, but his wife, Beth, had bought a book on the subject once, and she had read to him about a breathing exercise that he had tried. He could hear Casey in conversation with someone out in the hallway.

Jesse got as comfortable as he could and began the relaxation exercise he'd learned. He took slow, deep breaths, counting to ten as he did so, and released them to the same count. After ten of those, he began holding his breath for a count of ten before releasing. Casey continued to talk outside.

I've got to believe myself, he thought. Don't think about what will happen if I fail this test; think about Jesse Barron, *be* Jesse Barron. Nobody else exists in this body; the other guy is dead. He started as Casey reentered the room.

"Sorry, didn't mean to scare you," Casey said.

Jesse breathed less deeply, but kept the rhythm. He relaxed his toes, his arches, his calves and thighs, then his stomach muscles, arms, neck and shoulders. While the chief connected him to the apparatus he thought of his new life, of Jenny, of his coming trip to New York. He breathed and let his mind wander over his existence. He thought of Jenny in bed with him, of Carey laughing at his jokes, of dinner by candlelight with Jenny in New York.

"Okay," Casey said, "I'm going to start asking you questions, and all you have to do is answer them truthfully by saying yes or no. Got that?"

Jesse nodded.

"Say yes."

"Yes."

"Is your name Jesse?"

"Yes." Easy first question.

"Are you fifty-five years old?"

"No."

"Do you live in St. Clair, Idaho?"

"Yes."

"Are you six feet five inches tall?"

"No." He began to pick up a kind of rhythm in the questioning.

"Have you ever been convicted of a crime?"

Jesse felt his pulse lurch. "Yes."

"Do you know how to drive a car?"

"Yes." He slowed his breathing, tried to calm down.

"Are you a police officer?"

"No." God's truth.

"Do you work at St. Clair Wood Products?"

"Yes." Jenny was nuzzling his ear.

"Did anyone send you to St. Clair?"

"No."

"Do you know Jack Gene Coldwater?"

"Yes."

"Do you drive a Cadillac?"

"No."

"Had you ever heard of Jack Gene Coldwater before coming to St. Clair?"

"No."

"Are you a Christian?"

"Yes." Sort of.

"Do you believe everything you read in the Bible?"

"No."

"Do you live in the home of Jennifer Weatherby?"

"Yes."

"Do you sleep with Jennifer Weatherby?"

He hesitated.

"Answer all questions immediately. Do you sleep with Jennifer Weatherby?"

"Yes." He felt Jenny's body next to his.

"Do you like your work?"

"Yes." Breathe slowly.

"Have you ever lied to me?"

"No."

"Were you born in North Georgia?"

"Yes."

"Did you grow up in North Georgia?"

"Yes."

"Have you ever been married?"

"Yes."

"Do you like spaghetti and meatballs?"

"No." Another lie. Maybe a few lies to inconsequential questions would help scramble the results.

"Have you ever had any children?"

"Yes."

"Do you go to church regularly?"

"No."

"Is your wife living?"

"No."

"Have you ever fired a gun?"

"Yes."

"Have you ever had any weapons training?"

"Yes."

"Are your children living?"

Jesse managed something like a wince. "No."

"Did you love your wife?"

"Yes."

"Do you prefer the company of white people to the company of blacks?"

Be Jesse Barron! "Yes."

"Do you believe white people are superior to other races?"

"Yes."

"Have you ever had sex with a black woman?"

"No."

"Do you like your steak cooked rare?"

"No."

"Have you ever had sex with a man?"

"No."

"Have you ever been in prison?"

"Yes."

"Do you like apple pie?"

"Yes."

"Have you ever been addicted to alcohol or drugs?"

"No."

"Are you an escaped convict?"

"No."

"Do you believe you could kill in defense of your own life?"

"Yes."

"Do you like ice cream?"

"Yes."

"Have you ever killed another person?"

"No."

"Have you ever stolen anything?"

"Yes."

"Do you sometimes drive too fast?"

"Yes."

"Are you opposed to abortion?"

"Yes."

"Do you believe in God?"

"Yes."

"Are you a police officer working undercover?"

"No."

"Do you like sports?"

"Yes." This was a lie.

"Are you employed by a federal law enforcement agency?"

"No." He breathed the word.

"Have you told any lies during this examination?"

"No."

"Are you wearing socks?"

"Yes."

"Is your true name Jesse Barron?"

"Yes."

"Is your shirt red?"

"No."

"Before St. Clair, did you live in Toccoa, Georgia?"

"Yes."

"Okay, that's it," Casey said. He switched off the machine.

Jesse had tried to keep count; he had lied nine or ten times, he thought. "How'd I do?" he asked. If he got the wrong answer, his plan was to grab the pistol Pat was wearing, walk him out of the police station, then make a run for it.

"You lied three times," Casey said.

Jesse tried not to look relieved.

"No, I didn't."

"You never stole anything," Casey said, looking at the tape.

"I stole five dollars when I was treasurer of the agriculture club in high school."

"You said yes to being a Christian."

"Well, if I could have, I'd have said I was sort of a Christian."

"The other one is funny. I got a reaction when you said no to being an escaped convict."

Jesse couldn't help but laugh.

"You said yes to having been in prison."

"Well, in jail, once, in Toccoa, when I was a kid."

"Oh. But you're not an escaped convict?"

"Nope."

"Actually, Jesse, you did better than most. What I was looking for was a pattern of lies, and that didn't show up."

Jesse could feel the sweat under his arms. "I swear, I didn't tell you a single lie."

"Well, if I were a more expert operator, I might not have called the three I did. Mostly, Jesse, I wanted to know if you are a cop."

Jesse tried looking amazed. "Why on earth would you think I'm a cop?"

Casey slapped him on the back. "Never mind, it's not important. You better get on home for dinner."

"Okay, see you later."

"Goodnight, Jesse."

Jesse walked out of the station into the cool night air, breathing deeply. He got into his truck and started for home, nearly limp with relief. Then he had a disturbing thought: what if Pat Casey were a better polygraph operator than he'd let on?

When Jesse had left the station, Casey called Jack Gene Coldwater.

"How'd it go?" Coldwater asked.

"There were two anomalies that might be important," Casey replied. "First, I got a reaction when I asked if he were an escaped convict, but judging from his other answers, I think that was a fluke. No ex-con would have a sheriff in his hometown vouching for him."

"And the other?"

"I think maybe he once killed somebody."

"Natural enough to lie about that," Coldwater said. "Is he who he says he is?"

"The polygraph says yes. Oh, and he admitted to sleeping with Jenny."

Coldwater laughed. "Well, at least we know he's not queer."

27

Jesse stood at the kitchen counter opening the wine while Jenny put dinner on the table. He poured a little wine into a glass and tasted it.

"Where'd you learn to do that?" she asked.

"Oh, I've been to a good restaurant or two, you know."

"You have? Where?"

"Atlanta, mostly, and, of course, New York."

Her eyes widened. "You've been to New York?"

"I've been around."

"Why in the world would you have gone to New York?"

Jesse thought fast. "I went to a builder's show at the Coliseum, once. Spent nearly a week up there."

"What's it like?"

"Why don't you find out for yourself?"

She put her arms around his waist and hugged him. "I'd love to."

"You mean it?"

"I do."

"Shall we take Carey?"

"No, not if it means missing school."

"It would, I'm afraid." He wasn't afraid at all; he looked forward to having her all to himself in the big city.

"The school frowns on kids missing a day for *any* reason."

"Can she stay with a friend?"

"I'm sure she can. Come on, let's eat." She called Carey to dinner and sat down. She had cooked steaks, his favorite.

Jesse tore into his dinner.

"Can I have some wine?" Carey asked.

Jenny looked shocked. "Certainly not, young lady. Not until you're twenty-one!"

"Aw . . ."

"Carey, would you like to stay with Harriet Twomy for a few days next week? I'll call her mother."

"Sure, but why?"

"Jesse and I are going to New York City for a short vacation."

"Why can't I go?" the child wailed.

"You know very well you can't miss school."

"And who gave you permission to go?" Carey demanded.

Jenny reddened. "I don't need anyone's permission."

"You'll get in trouble," Carey said.

"That's enough, young lady; eat your dinner."

Jesse drove to Coeur d'Alene the following morning and bought a 35mm camera. As his

purchase was being wrapped he spotted a Polaroid instant camera, and he bought that, too. On
the way back to St. Clair he pulled over at a rest
stop and retrieved his cellular phone from his
lunchbox.

"This is Fuller."

"It's Jesse."

"How's it going, buddy?"

"More and more interesting. Pat Casey gave
me a polygraph examination last night."

"Oh, holy shit!"

"Looks like I passed."

"How could you beat a polygraph?"

"A combination of a little yoga breathing, and,
I suspect, Casey is either a green operator or a
piss-poor one."

"Are you sure you're in the clear?"

"I'm still alive. The acid test will come next
week, when I go to New York."

"New York? What are you talking about?"

"My employer is sending me to make a pitch to
an architectural firm. If Coldwater lets me get
out of town, then I figure he trusts me."

"How long will you be there?"

"Going Thursday, coming back Monday."

"Where are you staying?"

"I haven't figured that out yet."

"You're staying at the Roosevelt, at Madison
and Forty-seventh Street."

"Why?"

"I think it would be good for you and I to meet
and have a talk."

"Okay, sure."

"Call the hotel direct and make the reservation. I'll take care of the rest."

"How will I contact you?"

"I'll contact you."

Jesse put the phone away and drove back to St. Clair. He had one errand to run for Jenny; he parked in front of the courthouse and went to the county registrar's office.

"Can I help you?" a woman asked.

"Yes, Mrs. Jenny Weatherby would like a copy of her daughter's birth certificate," he said. "It's for school; apparently the principal's office says her records are incomplete. Her name is Carey Weatherby."

"It'll just be a minute," the woman said.

He watched as she went to a long row of filing cabinets and looked for the certificate. She plucked it from the file, went to a copying machine and made the copy, then returned the original to the file cabinet. Then she took a rubber stamp from a desk drawer, stamped the certificate and signed it. "There you are," she said, handing him the paper. "All certified. That'll be two dollars."

He paid her and left. As he was folding the certificate he glanced at it and saw something that mystified him. In the block for the mother's name, Jenny's name appeared, but in the block for the father's name there was only a blank space. He put the certificate in his pocket and thought no more about it. He did, however, think about what he had just seen in the courthouse, and he remembered it.

28

Jesse spent an entire day photographing the Wood Products plant, machinery and employees for his presentation and working on the text, and when the factory closed for the day he stayed on, explaining to Herman Muller that he wanted shots of the machinery bays with no people in them.

When he was sure that he was alone in the factory, he walked down to the machine shop and turned on the lights. He went to the storeroom and found a package of replacement hacksaw blades and moved to a small electric grinder. He took a pair of heavy shears, cut a blade into several smaller pieces, then donned safety glasses, switched on the grinder and began work on the thin ribbons of steel. First, he ground off the saw-teeth, then he began grinding each strip of metal into a particular shape. An hour later he had what he wanted. He closed up and went home.

After dinner, Jesse produced his new Polaroid camera and insisted on photographing both Jenny and Carey repeatedly, then asked Jenny to photograph him. He wanted the pictures for his wallet, he told them.

Some time after 2 A.M. Jesse woke and gingerly got out of bed. Jenny always slept deeply, and she never stirred. He dressed in his dark dress trousers and a dark blue shirt; downstairs he slipped into a coat and went to the garage. There was a bit of a slope, and he allowed the truck to coast down to the street before starting it. He drove into town and parked the truck in an alley near the courthouse, then walked the rest of the way.

He skirted the square stone building until he saw what he was looking for—a door on the side of the building that housed the county registrar's office. After looking carefully around the street to be sure it was still deserted, he went to the door and took out his wallet. He knelt and, using a small flashlight, examined the lock. It was an ordinary Yale deadbolt and, from the strips of steel he had machined earlier in the day, he selected two picks. He was rusty, but he still had the door open in under two minutes. He closed it softly behind him and found himself in a narrow rear hallway. He listened carefully. The building was made of stone and marble and any sound would echo through the halls. Hearing nothing, he slipped off his shoes and padded around the building, making sure there was no night watchman.

When he was sure he was alone in the building, he went to the registrar's office and began work on the lock. This one was unfamiliar and very frustrating. He tried three sets of picks before he got the hang of it. Finally, the door swung open, and he had the place to himself. His eyes had become accustomed to the darkness, and he could see quite well without resorting to the flashlight. There, on the opposite wall, was a lucky break. He walked across the large room and examined the steel cabinet closely; the lock was nothing more than a common desk lock, and he had it open in seconds. Arrayed before him on hooks, clearly labeled, were the keys to every filing cabinet, desk and cupboard in the office.

He started with the filing cabinets. Switching on his little flashlight, he opened drawers until he had found both Jenny's and Carey's birth certificates. He took them to the desk of the clerk who had helped him the day before, then worked on the desk lock. Soon he had the certification stamp she had used on the copy of Carey's certificate.

Now he needed something else, and rifling the clerk's desk didn't produce it. He began a systematic search and finally found what he was looking for in a bank of pigeonholes that held office stationery. He went back to the desk and switched on the electric typewriter that sat on a wing.

He needed names, names that were new, but close enough to their real ones. He rolled the first form into the machine and, under the space for a name, typed Jeffrey Warren. He invented names for parents close to those of his own, chose a birth date a year later and shortly he had a brand new birth certificate.

Then, working from the original forms, he cre-

ated new certificates for Jenny and Carey. He carefully forged the necessary signatures of the doctor
and recording clerk, then went to the copying machine and made two copies of each certificate. He
then applied the certification stamp and forged the
illegible signature of the clerk. All that remained
was to file the new certificates in the proper place
in the filing drawers, and it was as if these three
brand new people had always existed.

He was about to leave, when he had another
thought. He located the files for marriage certificates, found the proper form, made copies and
filed the new certificate in the proper place. No
one would ever suspect.

He put everything back in its place, locked the
key cabinet, the desk and the door and he was
about to leave the building when he had an in-
spiration. Directly across the hall was a door
painted with the legend, "Idaho State Police,
Licensing Division."

He got the door open and entered the room.
There were benches lined up for the waiting public and there, on the high desktop separating the
public from the workers, was the machine, the
one that photographed, laminated and recorded
driver's licenses.

He sat on the stool behind the machine and
tried to figure it out. There weren't a lot of controls,
but none of them made sense. This was too good
an opportunity to pass up, though, and he began a
search. Shortly he had found the instructions for
the machine, nicely printed on a single sheet of
paper and laminated. After that, it was simple. He

typed out the license application, stood himself before the machine, took his own picture, flinching at the flash, then waited while the thing hummed and worked and produced a laminated Idaho driver's license in the name of Jeffrey Warren. He put everything back in its place, and, as a final touch, added his completed application to a stack waiting to be entered into the state's computer network. Tomorrow some clerk would do his job, and Jeffrey Warren would exist with the state, as well as with the county.

He had just let himself out and locked the door behind him, when there was the loud bang of a door closing.

Jesse grabbed his shoes and ran soundlessly down the hallway. At the end he stopped and saw the beam of a flashlight from around the corner. He took refuge behind the nearest door—the ladies' room, as luck had it. He ran the length of the room and ducked into the last stall, stood on the toilet seat, crouched and waited, breathing deeply to get his pulse and respiration down. He could hear the footsteps of the searcher, hear each door as it opened and closed. When the ladies' room door opened, Jesse stopped breathing.

"All right, you son of a bitch," a male voice said. "You come out of here right now, because if I have to look in those stalls I'm going to shoot whatever I see."

Jesse squatted on the toilet seat, put his hands on the walls to either side and got ready to spring. He'd have to overpower the guy and hope he didn't get shot while doing it.

"Last chance," the man said, and took a step, his shoe leather ringing on the marble floor.

Then the floor under Jesse was illuminated as a strong flashlight searched for feet in the stalls.

"Shit," the man said. There were more steps, and the door closed behind him.

Jesse tried to make himself comfortable; he was not going to move until his muscles forced him to, and he figured he could last a while. He waited and listened as the cop radioed in; the voice was faint from the hall, but he could make out the words.

"It's Prentice," the cop said. "Call somebody who has the keys to the courthouse and get him over here. I found a side door unlocked."

There was a rasp and an unintelligible squawk as the reply came.

"I thought I saw a flash of light from inside the building, so I investigated," the cop said back. "But everything seems okay, except the open door. I'll stick around until somebody comes and locks it. Ten-four."

His footsteps echoed down the hallway, and Jesse heard the side door open and close. Painfully, he straightened up, then sat down on the toilet seat to wait. Half an hour passed before somebody showed up with the keys and locked the door. Jesse waited another fifteen minutes before letting himself out of the building and heading for the truck.

The first light of dawn was in the sky before he crept back into bed with Jenny.

29

As Jesse was loading Jenny's car for the trip to the Spokane airport, Kurt Ruger drove up and got out, carrying a briefcase.

"You're up early, Kurt," Jesse said. It was not daylight yet.

"Jack Gene sent me, Jesse," Ruger said. "He'd appreciate it if you'd do him a favor while you're in New York."

Jesse wasn't sure how Coldwater could know that he was going to New York, but he smiled. "Sure, glad to."

Ruger handed him the briefcase. "He'd like you to deliver this to an address in midtown Manhattan at eleven o'clock tomorrow morning." He handed Jesse a card with the address typed on it. 666 Fifth Avenue, suite 7019, and a name, Mr. Enzberg.

"I can do that; my appointment isn't until tomorrow afternoon."

"Jesse, the contents are very important; you're not to let the case out of your sight, not even to put it in the overhead luggage rack on the airplane. Keep your hands on it at all times. When you arrive in New York tonight, put it in the hotel safe and get a receipt."

"All right, I'll do as you say."

Ruger nodded, got into his car and drove away. Jesse looked at the briefcase. It was black aluminum, the sort of thing that might usually hold cameras, and there were two combination locks, one for each clasp. He hefted the case; heavy, something solid inside.

The airplane set down at La Guardia in a light rain, and by the time it had taxied to the ramp Jesse was practically having to hold Jenny in her seat.

"I'm sorry," she said, trying to be patient, "but I've never been this excited before."

"La Guardia is the least exciting part of this trip, believe me," Jesse said, laughing.

They got their luggage and a cab, and as they approached the Midtown Tunnel, the lights of the skyscrapers swam out of the fog.

"I've never seen anything so beautiful," Jenny sighed.

"Not even the mountains of Idaho?"

"I never want to go back. I want to live in one of those buildings."

They were at the hotel by six and, as they approached registration, Jesse saw Kip Fuller. He was behind the front desk, pretending to use a computer.

"My name is Barron; I have a reservation," he said to Kip.

"Yes, Mr. Barron; just a moment." Kip tapped a few computer keys. "Here we are; a room with a view. How did you wish to pay?"

Jesse handed him his credit card, and Kip produced two room keys. "Bellman!" he snapped, and a uniformed man appeared at Jesse's elbow. "Please take Mr. and Mrs. Barron up to their room." He handed the keys to the man.

"Oh, by the way," Jesse said, "I'd like to put this case in your safe." He waited for the receipt.

As they made their way to the elevator Jenny tugged at Jesse's sleeve. "They must know you here, the way they're treating you," she said.

Jesse laughed all the way up.

The room was large and sported views of both the Chrysler and Empire State buildings. Jesse tipped the bellman generously and began unpacking, while Jenny inspected everything in the room and read all the information in the hotel's information packet.

"You can have dinner in your room!" she exclaimed.

"We're not going to do that," he said. "I'm taking you someplace fancy."

"Where, where?"

"A place called Café des Artistes." He had booked the table a week before. The phone rang, and Jesse picked it up.

"Out your door and to the left," Kip said. "First door; it'll be ajar." He hung up.

"I'll be right down," Jesse said into the dead telephone.

"Where are you going?"

"They didn't get a proper imprint of my credit card, so I have to go back to the front desk for a minute. Why don't you get into a tub? Dinner's at eight."

Jenny began removing clothes from her luggage.

Jesse left the room and went next door. He pushed open the door and closed it behind him. Kip Fuller stood up, smiling, and offered Jesse his hand.

"Jesus, it's good to see you," he exclaimed, clapping Jesse on the back.

Jesse smiled back. "You too, Kip."

Kip turned and indicated another man. "This is Ted Manners, from our office. Ted, this is Jesse Barron."

Jesse noted that Kip had used his cover name.

"Ted, will you excuse us?" Kip said.

Manners nodded and left the room.

"I wanted him to get a good look at you," Kip said. "He's going to be following you while you're here."

"Following me?"

"Or maybe I should say, following the man who's following you."

Jesse blinked. "Somebody followed me here?"

"About thirty-five, five-nine, a hundred and sixty pounds, dark hair, gray suit and a gray felt hat. He was on your flight."

"I guess they're not taking any chances," Jesse said.

"What's in the briefcase you checked downstairs?"

"I don't know, but I suspect that's why I'm being followed. I guess they want to see if I'll do as I'm told."

"It was pretty heavy," Kip said. "Felt like a lot of money, to me."

"Why would they send me to New York with a lot of money?"

"Where are you supposed to take it?"

Jesse produced the card, and Kip made a note of the address. "We'll check it out. Listen, I want you to make time for a serious debriefing while you're here. When's good?"

Jesse shook his head. "Not if I'm being followed. I'm not taking any chances on getting busted, not at this stage of the game. Anyway, you know everything that's happened so far."

"I didn't know about the woman," Kip said. "She's lovely."

"My landlady. Well, that's how it started out, anyway. Things developed."

"I see. What will you be doing while you're here?"

"I've got an appointment at an architect's office at Fifty-seventh and Fifth tomorrow at two. There's a chance I could have to see them again on Monday. I'm to drop off the briefcase at eleven tomorrow morning."

Kip nodded. "What will you do with the rest of your time?"

"Show Jenny the town, I guess, maybe do some Christmas shopping."

"Your tail will probably drop off after you've

delivered the briefcase. If that happens, I'll pull Manners off, too."

"Thanks, I'd appreciate that. I don't want to spend the weekend looking over my shoulder."

"We'll have a look at the briefcase overnight."

"Be very careful, Kip; I don't want any marks or scratches on the thing. It might even be alarmed or have a dye bomb inside."

"We'll X-ray it; don't worry, I'll handle it with kid gloves."

Jesse glanced at his watch. "I've got to get back; anything else?"

Kip shook his head. "Nothing. If you need to reach me, there'll always be somebody in this room. Just ask the operator to ring extension two-zero-four-six."

Jesse looked at Kip narrowly. "Is my room bugged?"

"Behind the mirror over the chest of drawers."

"Is there a two-way mirror?"

"Nope. We'll respect your privacy."

"Thanks." He started for the door.

"Let me take a look first." Kip opened the door and looked up and down the hall. "Okay, go."

Jesse slipped out of the room and let himself in next door. He could hear the bath water running.

"Jesse?" she called.

"It's me."

"I'm going to smell great tonight," she said. "There's wonderful bath oil here."

"You always smell great. We have to leave here in an hour."

"I'll be ready."

Jesse stretched out on the bed and looked at the ceiling. With two men following him it was going to be a lot harder to accomplish what he had planned for New York City.

They had barely sat down at the restaurant when Jenny looked around and said, "There are naked ladies on the wall here."

"I know. They were done by a famous illustrator of the thirties named Howard Chandler Christy."

"How do you know that? How do you know this place come to that?"

"On my trip to the convention, a supplier brought me here and told me all about it. Do the naked ladies make you uncomfortable?"

She looked around the room. "They have different faces, but they all seem to have the same body."

"He must have had a favorite model," Jesse said, laughing.

"They don't make me uncomfortable, exactly," she said. "They make me want to see you naked."

"Order some dinner," he said, "and I'll see what I can do."

They swept back into the hotel room, full of good food and wine, stripping off clothes as they went.

"Just a minute," she said, "I've got to go to the bathroom."

Jesse made sure she was gone before he lifted the corner of the mirror, located the hidden microphone and held it to his lips. "Fuck you, Kip," he said, "and the horse you rode in on."

He found a pair of nail scissors, snipped off the microphone and dropped it behind the chest of drawers.

Jenny came running to him.

30

Jesse left the hotel at eight o'clock the following morning, the briefcase in his hand, and walked uptown on Madison Avenue. Jenny had still been in the tub when he'd left, and she had a morning of sightseeing planned. The street was full of other men and women, most carrying briefcases, hurrying to their jobs, and he felt anonymous among them, until he caught sight of his tail in a shop window.

He had to be somewhere at nine; that gave him an hour to lose both his followers. He walked up to Fifty-seventh and Madison, cut over to Fifth Avenue and headed for the park. He walked as far as the zoo, then exited the park and headed down Fifth at a leisurely pace, doing a lot of window shopping and making a point of not looking at his watch, taking in the available clocks on the street and in the shops to keep his schedule.

He made Rockefeller Center by a quarter to nine, and he stood for a moment and looked down into the ice rink. Then, still playing the tourist, he walked into 30 Rockefeller Plaza and found the nonstop elevator to the roof. On reaching the top he immediately got onto a down elevator. Back in the lobby he walked quickly to Fifth Avenue and north a block, skirting behind the statue of Atlas and into the building. A quick glance at the directory gave him the floor for the United States State Department. He walked up and down the lobby twice to make sure he had shaken his tail before taking the elevator.

His timing was good; the doors were just being unlocked and a line of a dozen people was being let in. He waited a few minutes for a vacant window, set the briefcase between his legs and pulled a thick envelope from his inside pocket. "I'd like to apply for passports for my family and myself," he said, removing the documents and handing them to the woman behind the counter. "We're flying to London tomorrow, and I understand a one-day service is available here."

"That's correct," the woman said, looking through the papers. "Let's see, you have three birth certificates and a marriage certificate?"

"That's right," he replied. "Here are the photographs of my wife and daughter. Are they all right? We took them ourselves."

"They meet the specifications," she said, handing him a set of forms. "Please fill out these applications; you can sign for your wife and daughter."

Jesse sat down on a bench and quickly filled out the forms, inventing what information he didn't have. He returned to the window.

"These seem to be complete," she said. "There's

a fifty-five dollar charge for each passport, plus twenty-five dollars each for the one-day service, a total of two hundred and forty dollars."

Jesse paid her in cash.

"And I'll need to see some form of identification," the woman said.

He produced his brand new Idaho license in the name of Jeffrey Warren.

"Thank you, Mr. Warren; you can pick up your passports after three o'clock."

Jesse thanked the woman and left. They would certainly check with the county seat on the authenticity of the birth certificates, but that would not be a problem, since the originals were in the county registrar's files.

He had been in the office about half an hour. He went back downstairs and resumed his stroll downtown. At Forty-eighth Street he spotted a very worried young man in a gray suit and hat and looked away before he was seen. A pity, he thought; he would have liked to see the expression on the man's face.

He walked downtown to Forty-Second Street, crossed to the east side of Fifth and strolled back uptown. He reached Sak's Fifth Avenue at Forty-ninth Street exactly at ten o'clock, and he spent the next forty-five minutes Christmas shopping. He found a beautiful negligee for Jenny and a very pretty winter coat for Carey that he hoped was the right size, and he bought some neckties for himself. He took the neckties with him and had the gifts sent to St. Clair.

At quarter to ten he started up Fifth Avenue

again toward number 666. He reached the seventieth floor one minute before the appointed time and quickly found the suite. There was only a number on the door, and although the reception room was luxuriously appointed, there was no company name visible.

"May I help you?" the woman behind the reception desk said.

"My name is Jesse Barron. May I see Mr. Enzberg, please? I believe he's expecting me."

"Just one moment, please." She picked up a phone, tapped in a number, spoke briefly in German and hung up. "He will be right with you," she said to Jesse.

Shortly a beautifully dressed man in his forties appeared. "Mr. Barron? Will you come with me, please?"

Jesse followed the man to a small, clinically furnished office, where he was asked to wait. "May I have the case, please?"

Jesse handed it over.

"I will return shortly," Enzberg said. He left the room. Ten minutes later, he returned and handed the briefcase to Jesse. "A receipt is inside," he said.

"Thank you, Mr. Enzberg," Jesse said, and left. He was followed into the elevator by the young man in the gray suit.

"I'm from Pat Casey," he said.

"Oh?"

"You may give me the briefcase now."

"I wasn't given any such instruction," Jesse said.

"You have your instructions now."

The elevator reached the ground floor. "Come with me," Jesse said to the man. He walked to a bank of public telephones and telephoned Pat Casey. "Hi, Pat," he said. "I've made the delivery Kurt Ruger asked me to, and now there's a guy who says he's from you and wants the briefcase."

"It's okay, Jesse," Casey said. "Give it to him, and thanks for your help. Have a good time in New York."

Jesse handed over the briefcase. "There you are," he said, "and have a nice day."

The man took the case and left the building.

Jesse walked slowly back down Fifth Avenue, thinking. He'd had occasion in Miami to see large sums of cash displayed from time to time—once an even ten million dollars in hundred-dollar bills. He thought about the bulk that had represented and he figured that the briefcase had held two million. He got a cab back to the Roosevelt, picked up his presentation materials from his room, put on one of his new neckties then knocked on the door of the next room. Kip opened the door.

"Everything go smoothly?"

"No problem."

"Manners lost you for half an hour; where were you?"

"Doing some sightseeing. Couldn't he keep up?"

"No, and neither could your other tail."

"Their problem, not mine."

"We X-rayed the briefcase last night, but no joy. The technician reckoned it was lined in lead foil. However, the office you delivered it to is the New York branch of a small, very private Swiss bank."

"I reckon it was two million," Jesse said, explaining his reasoning. "My tail approached me in the elevator and asked for the case. Enzberg said there was a receipt inside."

"Very interesting," Kip said. "We now know Coldwater is not short of a few bucks, not if he's sending millions outside the country."

"I've got a theory about the source," Jesse said. "Mind you, it's only a guess."

"Tell me."

"St. Clair is the hometown of one Melvin Schooner; ring a bell?"

"The software billionaire?"

"One and the same. I spotted him in the local drugstore."

"What makes you think he's funding Coldwater?"

"Like I said, I'm only guessing, but one of the richest men in the country has a St. Clair connection."

"You could have something there," Kip said.

"Now don't put the IRS on him or anything; let's not muddy the waters."

"Right. Do what you can to develop your theory."

"If I've learned anything on this assignment, it's not to develop anything, but to let them do the developing. So far, they can't say that I've so much as asked an untoward question, and I'm going to keep it that way."

"Do it your way."

Jesse looked at his watch. "I've got a lunch date with Jenny at the skating rink at Rockefeller

Center, and my business appointment is at two. I'd better get going."

"Okay, looks like we're all finished here. I'll pack up and go; you and your lady have a good weekend. And you take care of yourself, Jess."

They shook hands, and Jesse left. He walked to Rockefeller Center and found Jenny gazing up at the huge Christmas tree.

"Isn't it the most spectacular thing you've ever seen?" she asked.

"It certainly is. You hungry?"

"Starved."

They found a table at the skating rink restaurant, and Jesse heard the story of her morning. He kept his appointment at two, and left with assurances that orders for chipboard and plywood would be placed almost immediately.

Back at Rockefeller Center, he made sure he wasn't still being followed, then went back to the State Department office. He walked back down Fifth Avenue toward his hotel, the new passports in his pocket, regretting that he couldn't have taken the two million dollars and Jenny on the next plane to South America. At least, now, he had an out that included the two people in the world who were most important to him.

As that thought came to him he stopped dead in his tracks. A woman and a little girl were just turning into a shop. He watched them through the window for a moment and convinced himself that the child was not his own Carrie; she was too tall and her hair was too long. The woman looked oddly familiar, though. He walked back to the hotel, remembering that there was a third person, somewhere, who was terribly important to him, and that his chances of ever seeing her again were just about nil.

31

Pat Casey sat in Kurt Ruger's office at the bank and watched the young man on the sofa. He had trained the man himself, and he felt proud.

"The two subjects made the plane on schedule," the young man, whose name was Ken Willis, said. "At La Guardia they got their luggage and took a cab to the Hotel Roosevelt and checked in. Barron put the briefcase in the hotel safe, just as you said he would. He and the woman stayed in their room until dinnertime, then left the hotel and went to a restaurant on West Sixty-Seventh Street. They were back at the hotel and in their room by eleven o'clock."

"Tell me about the next day," Ruger said.

"Barron was earlier than I'd expected," Willis said, glancing at a notebook. "He picked up the briefcase at the front desk at eight o'clock and walked uptown. He seemed to be on a sort of sightseeing trip."

"What sort of a sightseeing trip?" Casey asked.

"He walked uptown to Central Park and

through the zoo, then he started down Fifth Avenue. At Rockefeller Center he watched the skaters for a couple of minutes, then he went into the NBC building and took the elevator to the roof."

"Good place for a meet," Ruger said. "Did he speak to anybody?"

"No, sir."

"Did he bump into anybody, even look at anybody?"

"No, sir; he seemed preoccupied with sightseeing."

"Then what?"

"He did some more walking; went into Sak's and bought some things, apparently for the woman and a little girl, also some neckties. Then he walked up Fifth to number 666 and arrived at the office exactly on time. I waited in the hallway, and when he came out I asked him for the briefcase. He insisted on calling the chief before he'd give it to me."

"From the time Barron picked up the briefcase at eight o'clock until he turned it over to you, was he ever out of your sight? Even for a few seconds?"

"No, sir," Willis lied solemnly.

"Did you follow him anymore after that?"

"No, sir; I went straight to the airport, as I was instructed to do."

Casey spoke up. "I only wanted to be sure he delivered the case; I saw no point in any further surveillance. If he'd done something untoward, we'd have heard about it."

Ruger nodded. "Let me have the briefcase," he said to Willis.

The young man placed the aluminum case on the desk.

Ruger worked the two combination locks, opened the case and removed two sheets of papers. "The receipt is in order," he said, then he examined the other sheet. "Enzberg says that Barron behaved correctly and expressed no curiosity about the transaction." He looked at Casey. "Pat, do you have any other questions for Ken?"

"Nope," Casey replied.

"That'll be all, Ken," Ruger said. "You did a good job."

"Thank you, sir," Willis said, and left the office.

"Are you pleased, Pat?" Ruger asked.

"I certainly am," Casey replied. "He did as he was asked to do, and I'm particularly pleased that he wouldn't give Willis the briefcase until he'd called me."

"Yes, I agree that was kind of a bonus. Shows he's both a thinker and that he's of a cautious nature."

"I think Jesse Barron is quality material," Casey said.

"What is Jack Gene's take on him?"

"You know Jack Gene; he relies more on intuition than judgment."

"And what did his intuition tell him?"

"That Jesse is covering up something."

Ruger chuckled. "Who isn't? Did you pick up anything like that on the polygraph?"

"Not really."

"What does that mean?"

"Well, I got the impression that he lied about a couple of things there was no need to lie about. He could have been planting a lie or two to cover a real lie."

Ruger frowned. "If he actually did that, then we have something to worry about."

"I know. Nobody of Jesse's background—his stated background—is going to know anything about defeating a polygraph."

"Pat, if you were Jesse and you were a fed, how would you have played the New York delivery?"

"I'd have tried to find out what was in the briefcase," Casey replied. "But there's no indication that he tried, and there's no indication that he even contacted anybody before he delivered the case."

"But if you were a cop trying to gain our confidence, might you just do as you were told?"

Casey shook his head. "Maybe, but I think the briefcase would be too much of a temptation."

Ruger took a magnifying glass from a desk drawer and began examining the case closely. Casey joined him, switching on the desk lamp. "You see any sign of attempted entry?"

"Nope, not a thing."

"Could they have X-rayed it?"

"The lead foil lining would have obscured the contents, and the combination has to be reset after the case has been opened twice. If they'd cracked it, you wouldn't have been able to open it with the same combination."

"What do you think our recommendation to Jack Gene should be?"

"Well, Jesse has had as much or more scrutiny as anybody else who's joined us, and he's passed with flying colors so far. Still, as long as Jack Gene has doubts, I don't think we want to go the whole hog."

"I agree. What should we do then?"

"I've already done it." He explained his action to Ruger. "All we have to do is wait."

32

Jesse had been back from New York a week when Pat Casey called and invited him to do some shooting on a Saturday morning. Jesse wasn't sure what Casey meant by shooting, but he accepted.

Casey picked him up mid-morning and drove toward the mountain. They passed the church and started to climb and, near the top of the mountain, shortly after passing Coldwater's house, they turned right onto a dirt road. They emerged from the trees into a clearing that had, apparently, been scraped into the side of the mountain by a bulldozer. To Jesse's left, some one hundred feet away, was the exposed side of the mountain, with many pockmarks and a rail system for transporting targets to and fro. They got out of the squad car, and Casey went to the trunk.

"You done much shooting in your time?" Casey asked.

"A good bit."

"What with?"

"I've owned a twelve-gauge shotgun for birds and a thirty-ought-six for deer."

"Handguns?"

"Somebody gave me a World War Two–vintage forty-five automatic once. I could never hit anything with it."

Casey was rummaging in the trunk. "A formidable weapon at close range, but a pig otherwise. The newer stuff is a lot easier to handle. Give me a hand, will you? Grab that ammunition box." Casey walked away from the car with a cased rifle under his arm and a canvas hold-all in the other hand.

Jesse picked up the ammunition box, and it was a lot heavier than he'd expected. As he closed the trunk lid a Mercedes sedan drove into the clearing, and Jack Gene Coldwater got out.

"Good morning, Pastor," Jesse said.

"Good morning, Jesse; glad you could join us."

"I didn't know you'd be here."

"Shooting is a hobby of mine." Coldwater took a large bag that looked as though it might hold skis from the backseat of his car.

Casey removed an assault rifle from his gun case. "Come over here, Jesse, and try this."

Jesse accepted the weapon and looked it over as if he'd never seen one.

"It's an AR-fifteen that's been converted to an M-sixteen," Casey said. "Only takes a few legally obtained parts and it becomes fully automatic." He showed Jesse how to operate the weapon, then attached a paper target to a metal rack and pulled a rope until the target was against the bank a hundred feet away. "Try a few rounds."

Jesse brought the rifle up and fired carelessly in the direction of the target. He was expert in this, but he certainly didn't want to appear so. Holes appeared in the top right-hand quadrant of the target.

"You're pulling the trigger," Casey said. "Do it more slowly and squeeze."

Jesse fired more rounds and brought them closer to the center of the target.

"Looking good," Casey said.

Coldwater stepped up to the firing line, shoved a clip into his own rifle and emptied it quickly. The bull's-eye became one large hole.

"That's very fine shooting," Jesse said.

"My country taught me well," Coldwater replied. "A little practice, and you'll do well, too."

"Try the prone position," Casey said, spreading a blanket. He helped Jesse arrange his body into the proper position.

Jesse fired more carefully prone, then moved into a sitting position, then into a kneeling position. With each clip his accuracy improved.

"I believe you're a natural, Jesse," Coldwater said. "Draw a finer bead; you're still a little high."

Jesse followed instructions, and his target no longer had a center.

"Let's try a handgun," Casey said, removing a pistol from his hold-all. "This is a Heckler and Koch nine-millimeter automatic." He instructed Jesse on loading and firing, then stepped back.

Jesse turned his shoulder toward the target

and fired a round. It went high and wide of the target. "Not so good," he said. "I haven't had much experience with handguns."

"Turn your body square to the target," Casey said, "and support your shooting hand with your left. Again, squeeze off your rounds."

Jesse obeyed, and his shots began to hit the target, although erratically. He concentrated on seeming to concentrate, but he didn't allow himself to improve much.

Coldwater stepped up. "Watch me," he said. He assumed a firing position and emptied a clip into his target. Again, the bull's-eye disappeared.

"You look a lot more relaxed than I do," Jesse said.

"That's right. You were much too tense."

Jesse rolled his head around and shook his arms to loosen up. "Keep both eyes open this time," Coldwater said. "Don't draw a bead, just point where your eyes fall on the target."

Jesse squeezed off a round and clipped a corner of the bull's-eye.

"Much better. Now use up the clip, but do it slowly, one at a time."

Jesse kept firing, and put everything near, but not in, the bull's-eye.

"A little off, but a nice grouping," Casey said, taking Jesse's pistol and reloading it.

"If your target had been a man, he'd be very dead," Coldwater said. He shoved a new clip into the pistol and handed it to Jesse.

"That's what you're going to be, Jack Gene," a strange voice said. "Very dead."

Jesse was already in the firing position, and he swiveled his head to the left to see what was going on. Phil Partain, his face very red, stood ten yards beyond Coldwater, a heavy revolver in his hand. It was pointed at the pastor's middle.

"I've had enough," Partain said. "You won't give me any responsibility; you give me shit work to do, and there's no respect for me in this crowd." He thumbed the hammer back.

Jesse realized he was the only other person with a firearm. Without moving his feet, he turned his upper body toward Partain and put a round into the man's right shoulder. Partain's weapon fired wild, but he held onto it; he spun around and fell face-down, the pistol still in his hand. He began struggling to get up.

Coldwater reached out and took Jesse's pistol. He walked the few paces to where Partain lay and stepped on his gun hand. "Well, Phil, you've made a big mistake, haven't you?"

"Please, Jack Gene," Partain squealed, "don't hurt me. I'll do good, I'll do right by you. I'll do whatever you want."

"I want you to die, Phil," Coldwater said, then fired one round into the back of the man's head. Partain convulsed, then lay still.

"Jesus," Jesse said. He had shot to wound, but Coldwater had simply executed the man.

"That was a nice shot, Jesse," Coldwater said calmly, turning away from Partain's corpse. "Where were you aiming?"

"At his bellybutton, I think," Jesse replied. "I hardly thought about it, I just fired."

"You were high and to the left, but of course, you weren't in position, and you didn't have much time. I thank you." He clapped Jesse on the back.

"Is he dead?" Jesse asked.

Casey walked over to the body and looked at it. "You bet he is." He bent over, picked up Partain's pistol and wiped the dirt from it. "It's just as well; Phil was at the end of his usefulness."

"Well, I guess we don't have to call the cops," Jesse said.

Coldwater laughed aloud. "I guess not. Pat, get rid of that," he said, nodding at Partain's body.

"Toss me that blanket, Jesse," Casey said.

Jesse picked up the blanket he'd been firing from and took it to Casey.

"Open the trunk, there, will you?"

Jesse opened the trunk, then watched as Casey rolled Partain's body into the blanket.

"Give me a hand?"

He helped Casey lift the corpse into the trunk of Casey's car.

Casey closed the lid and turned to Jesse. "No need to mention this to anybody," he said.

"Just forget it happened," Coldwater chimed in. "You've removed a nuisance from our midst, not to mention saving our lives, and I'm grateful to you, Jesse."

Jesse couldn't think of anything to say.

"Well, I think that's enough shooting for one morning," Coldwater said, stretching and yawning. "You fellows want some lunch?"

"Sure, Jack Gene," Casey said. "You hungry, Jesse?"

"I'm not sure," Jesse replied.

He and Casey got into Casey's car and followed Coldwater up the mountain to his house.

It was as if they had been expected; the kitchen table was set, and food prepared. Jesse sat down with the two men and had some soup, while they talked of hunting, but he could not forget that Phil Partain's dead body was outside, in the trunk of Pat Casey's car. It came home to Jesse, as never before, that if he made a mistake with these people he would be dead very quickly.

On the way home he could not get over the feeling that the incident had been orchestrated to test him and that he had passed.

33

Jesse had been regularly attending Sunday morning services at the First Church, and Jack Gene Coldwater's sermons had become more and more apocalyptic. He noticed, too, that outsiders never heard these sermons, because guards, in the person of ushers, were posted at the doors and around the building. On one occasion he had seen a man using electronic debugging equipment around the pulpit before a service.

Coldwater's references were, increasingly, indicating a siege mentality, along with a strong suspicion of any stranger in town. Nobody that Jesse knew of had come to live in the town from outside since his own arrival. The plant had not employed any new people, though he was quite certain that Coldwater had had nothing to do with that—Herman Muller was far too independent to let anyone dictate any policy to him.

On the Sunday before Christmas Coldwater seemed very disturbed during his sermon, and he made repeated references to "last days" and quoted extensively from Revelations. His audience was more than rapt; they were, literally, on the edge of their seats, and Jesse tried to exhibit the same concentration.

When the service ended, Pat Casey approached him. "Jesse, Jack Gene would like you to have Sunday lunch with him." He turned to Jenny. "You and the girl go on home; I'll bring Jesse later."

Jesse turned to see if that was all right with Jenny, but she had already headed toward her car, Carey in tow. "Sure, Pat, I'd be honored," he said. He followed Casey around the corner of the building and found Coldwater waiting for them in his Mercedes.

Lunch was roast beef, Yorkshire pudding, fresh vegetables and apple pie, accompanied by a bottle of California red wine that Jesse reckoned was expensive, called Opus One. He enjoyed the food, but only the most perfunctory conversation took place, with Coldwater rambling on about the weather and Casey trying, unsuccessfully, to start a conversation about college football.

When they had finished lunch, Coldwater stood. "Jesse, you're one of us, now, and it's time you knew some things. Come with me." The three men got back into the Mercedes, and Coldwater drove to the top of the mountain.

It was the first time Jesse had been there, and he was surprised at what he saw. They passed through solid-looking gates and a maze of concrete forms that required a car to make three ninety-degree turns before entering what turned out to be a sort of compound at the mountaintop. There were a number of small buildings scattered about four or five acres of quite flat land, and several pieces of heavy construction equipment were scattered about. One very large stone building had an official air about it, like a government building. Coldwater parked in front of this building and motioned for Jesse to follow him.

Jesse got out of the car and took in the facade. It was built of rectangular slabs of cut stone and had high, narrow windows along its front and sides.

Coldwater spoke up. "What you see here is the last refuge of my people and me," he said solemnly. "The world is against us, we know that; our activities are commissioned by God himself, but the government of this country is opposed to our beliefs. Government money, raised from exorbitant taxes, is spent on abortions for our African-American and Hispanic friends." His descriptions of these groups were sarcastic. "They send agents to spy on us, to try and learn the source of our funds and our various activities. We have dealt with these people before, and, no doubt, we will again. Of course, we mean to survive, but should we have to fight we will make a stand like no one has ever seen in this country." He turned to Jesse. "You were in the construction business, weren't you?"

"Yes, sir," Jesse replied.

"Then I think you will find this structure interesting. Come inside." Coldwater led the way to the front doors and let them inside with a large key, then went to a switchbox and flipped several switches.

Jesse found himself in an entrance hall, oddly narrow and ending only a few feet away in a concrete wall. As his eyes became accustomed to the light, he put a hand on the wall next to him. It was made of long blocks of concrete, and he suddenly understood that what he had thought was an exterior of cut stone was really the ends of these blocks. He was stunned. This meant that the walls of this building consisted of an eight-foot thickness of reinforced concrete.

"Jesus Christ," he murmured.

"Indeed," Coldwater said. "I see you have grasped something of the construction already."

"I've never seen anything like it," Jesse said truthfully.

"Neither has anybody else," Coldwater replied, smiling. "Not the Maginot Line, not the Germans' defenses in Normandy, not even Hitler's bunker itself was constructed as heavily as this. There are a number of government installations, I am given to believe, that have been constructed to withstand a direct hit by a large nuclear device. Only those structures are stronger than this, but then the government would never use a nuclear bomb in a populated area of this country."

"I certainly hope not," Jesse said.

"You may count on that. Come, let me show you more." Coldwater led the way to the end of the entrance hall, then turned left. They were faced with a heavy steel door. Coldwater tapped a code into a keypad, and the door slid noisily aside.

Ahead of them lay a long hallway with doors on either side. Coldwater began opening them.

On the left were rooms containing heavy weapons, not all of which Jesse recognized. There were certainly antitank weapons and some sort of recoilless rifles, and they were aimed out the narrow windows he had seen from outside.

"First line of defense," Coldwater said, leading him down the hall. They turned a corner to the right and he opened more doors, revealing huge amounts of ammunition and explosives. They descended a flight of stairs and came to what appeared to be an enormous dormitory. Rows of bunk beds disappeared into the distance; crates of food and bottled water were stacked in piles among the bunks. Coldwater showed him three large and well-equipped kitchens and two infirmaries, each of which looked like the emergency room of a large hospital. Here and there among the bunks were television sets and speakers were everywhere.

"I can communicate with any part of the structure instantly from my quarters," Coldwater said. "Come, I'll show you." He led the way downstairs to yet another floor and toward the rear of the building. Double doors opened into an extensive suite of rooms, filled with computers, fax machines, telephones and every manner of office equipment. Finally, Coldwater showed him to another set of steel doors, behind which lay another suite. "I can live and work here for years, if necessary," he said, waving an arm around a large living room lined with books and showing Jesse an apartment with every comfort.

"It's breathtaking," Jesse said.

"Questions?" Coldwater asked.

"How is it ventilated?"

"There are three discrete ventilation systems, each of which is more than enough to put fresh, filtered air anywhere in the structure."

"Electric power?"

"Again, three systems: first, we have hydroelectric power from a small plant down the mountain, which has its own extensive defenses; second, we have two twenty-five-thousand-gallon tanks of gasoline stored far underground to operate generators; third, we have an extensive solar collector system that can supply eighty percent of our needs all by itself. It is inconceivable that even a very large force could deprive us of electricity."

"I am astounded," Jesse said, and he truly was. "What did this cost?"

"If we had built it in the conventional way, perhaps twenty-five million dollars," Coldwater said. "But by doing it with our own people over a period of years, we've done it for half that. Not including armaments, of course."

"Where on earth did the money—"

"Don't ask," Casey said, speaking for the first time.

Coldwater glanced at his wristwatch. "It's later than I thought; let's get Jesse home to his family."

Jesse followed Coldwater as he retraced his steps. He counted his paces as he went, trying to get some idea of the size of the place; he memorized everything about it he could. As the front doors opened, he blinked in the sunlight, glad to be above ground again.

Coldwater pointed at the other, much smaller buildings on the mountaintop. "Those contain other defensive systems to deal with aircraft or an invading force."

Jesse pointed in the direction of the town. "Can you see the town from here?"

"Yes, have a look."

Jesse walked a hundred yards and found himself looking over a precipice at the bottom of which lay Main Street. He also noted defensive positions dug into the rock near where he stood. He returned to Coldwater and Casey. "This is absolutely fantastic," he said with enthusiasm.

"I thought you might think so," Coldwater said.

"An army couldn't take it," Jesse gushed.

"You are quite right."

Coldwater drove them down the hill and toward the town. "I've shown you this, Jesse, because there is no faster way to impress upon you the seriousness of our purpose here."

"You've certainly done that, sir," Jesse replied, although Coldwater had said nothing of his purpose.

34

Jesse thought for several days about what he had seen before making any attempt to report it. In his mind he wandered through Coldwater's redoubt, making new discoveries each time; he sat at his desk and used a calculator to translate his pacing into area; he tried to figure out what the hell it all meant, and he could not fathom it.

On Christmas Eve he and Jenny stayed up late arranging Carey's gifts for the following morning, and, long after Jenny had fallen into an exhausted sleep, he crept from the bed, went to the garage and retrieved his scrambled telephone.

"Jesus Christ, what time is it?" Kip asked blearily.

"It's very late, but it's very important, too," Jesse replied.

"Wait a minute while I go to another phone."

Jesse waited on hold until Kip was away from his no-doubt sleeping wife.

Kip picked up another extension. "All right, what's so important?" he demanded.

"I hardly know where to begin," Jesse said. "The whole thing is so unbelievable."

"What's unbelievable?" Kip was awake, now.

"Last Sunday, I think I was finally fully accepted by Coldwater," he said.

"That's certainly good news, but couldn't it wait until after the holidays?"

"I wanted you to have the holidays to think about what I'm going to tell you, Kip, because you're going to have to figure out a way to make Barker and the attorney general believe you—or rather, me."

"It sounds as though you've finally figured out what Coldwater is up to."

"No, I haven't. But I think I can safely say that, whatever it is, he expects to fail at it."

"You're not making any sense, Jesse."

"I know, and I'm sorry; but what I saw on Sunday doesn't make any sense unless Coldwater expects to go out in a blaze of glory."

"What did you see on Sunday?"

"He invited me to lunch with Casey, and when we had finished, he drove me to the top of the mountain that rises above the town."

"Did he show you all the earth and offer it to you on a platter?"

"No, I think what he offered me was the opportunity to die with him."

"Go on."

"Coldwater and his people have, over a period of years, I'm not sure how many, constructed a series of defensive positions on the sides and top of the mountain that probably isn't like anything else on earth."

"What sort of defensive positions?"

"A long list of various types of heavy weapon, well dug in and placed strategically to repel any invader—antitank weapons, probably anti-aircraft weapons—more hardware than exists anywhere in this country outside a military base."

"What else?"

"He's constructed what I can only describe as a cross between the White House Situation Room and Hitler's Berlin bunker."

"How big?"

"At a conservative estimate, something in excess of sixty thousand square feet."

"*What?*"

"And that's only the beginning of it. The exterior walls are a good eight feet of reinforced concrete."

"*Eight feet?* What's he expecting?"

"Armageddon, apparently. Let me go on. The place is on three levels, only one of which is above ground, and the thickness of the floors seems equal to the outside walls. There are weapon emplacements on the top, or ground, level on all four sides, and he has amassed an extraordinary amount of munitions to support them. There are living quarters for, I don't know, in excess of a thousand people, maybe a lot more—kitchens, infirmaries, entertainment facilities, and food and medical supplies stacked to the ceilings. On the lower level, Coldwater has a suite of offices, completely equipped, and an apartment for himself. It looks as though he could take his people inside and remain for years, and I'm not exaggerating."

"What sort of force do you think would be required to take it?" Kip asked, still sounding skeptical.

"Kip, I'm no military genius, but my guess is it couldn't be taken—at least, not without wildly unacceptable losses on the part of the attacking force."

"Jesse, there can't be any such thing as a civilian installation that can't be taken by a military force."

"It isn't a civilian installation, Kip; it's an unbelievably fortified military defensive position. It sits on top of a mountain that has about a twelve-hundred-foot sheer wall on the south side and very steep sides on the other three. Mountain goats might be able to make it to the top, but infantry couldn't and neither could tanks. There's only one road to the top, and that must be heavily defended. They could simply blow the road and bar all access to the top of the mountain."

"What about aircraft—helicopters with assault troops?"

"Any slow-flying aircraft would be shot to pieces before it could even land, and even if it could land, its troops would be cut up the minute they were on the ground. There's simply no cover. You could bomb the site with high explosives, but you'd probably destroy the town in the process; you'd certainly have to evacuate thousands of people. Coldwater says only a nuclear weapon would have any effect, and he's right when he says the government would never use it. I swear, you could spend a year attacking the place at a cost of thousands of casualties, and you might not even make a dent."

"He's got to have some sort of outside support," Kip said. "He couldn't exist inside a mountain without it. What about power, water and air?"

"He's got it all, and in triplicate."

"Jesse, this just doesn't make any sense."

"I know it doesn't, but it's real, I promise you that. And I'll tell you this, I don't think Coldwater would have built it if he didn't intend to use it."

There was a long silence from Kip's end of the line. "I don't know what to say," he said finally.

"Neither do I, except you'd better report this as soon as you can, and you'd better see that all knowledge of it is absolutely secure. If Coldwater had the slightest notion that the government knew about it, he'd go in there right now and zip it up behind him. And God only knows what he'd do before he went inside."

"When can you call again?"

"When do you want me to call?"

"I need to think about this before I spring it on my people. I'll do that on the first day of business of the New Year. Try to call me around that time—during office hours, if possible. They may want to pass instructions to you."

"All right, I'll try to do that."

"I'm certainly not going to sleep tonight," Kip said forlornly.

Jesse laughed. "Well, if I can't, why should you?"

"Oh, go to hell," Kip grumbled, then hung up.

Jesse put away the phone and went back to the house. As he let himself in the back door, Jenny came out of the kitchen.

"Where on earth have you been?" she demanded.

35

Jesse gulped. "I went outside for a while," he said. "What are you doing up at this time of night?"

"I had to go to the bathroom, and you weren't in bed. I was frantic."

"There's no need to be upset," he said soothingly, taking her in his arms. "I just couldn't sleep, and I thought some fresh air might do me good."

She pushed away. "But what were you doing in the garage? I was at the kitchen window, and I saw you come out of there."

"I was looking for my spare key to the truck, and I thought it might be in the glove compartment."

"It's upstairs in that little tray where you keep change and things," she said.

"Oh. I don't know why that crossed my mind, it just did."

"Jesse, is something wrong? Is there something I should know about?"

He put a hand on her cheek. "No, of course

not; everything's fine. I couldn't imagine things being any finer."

She stepped closer and looked up at him. "Jesse, do you love me?"

"Of course I do; haven't I told you often enough?" He put his arms around her again.

"Sure, after making love. But I want to know if you love me *all* the time."

He turned her face up. "*All* the time," he said. "At the dinner table, at the breakfast table, at work, in bed—everywhere, all the time."

She relaxed in his arms. "Oh, I'm so glad to hear that."

"I can't believe you doubted it," he said, rubbing her neck.

"Maybe it's going to be all right after all," she said, sighing.

"It's going to be all right. I'll make it all right."

"Do we have a future together?" she asked.

"I certainly hope so. That's what I'm counting on."

"Because, if we don't, I'll just make a trip to Spokane and take care of it there. I won't do it their way anymore."

"Jenny, sweetheart, I don't have the faintest idea what you're talking about. What's this about Spokane?"

"Well, they've got a clinic there that hasn't been bombed yet."

He held her at arm's length and looked at her closely. "What do you—"

"I'm pregnant," she said. "I'm going to have your baby."

He pulled her to him again so that she wouldn't see his face. God in heaven, he thought, what have I gotten this girl into? "How long have you known?" he asked.

"I guessed a few days ago. This afternoon I used one of those home pregnancy tests."

"And it was positive?"

"It was positive. Jesse, is this all right? Do you want this baby?"

He tried to quell the panic inside him. What was he going to do? Here he was, undercover, his life in danger at every moment, Jack Gene Coldwater waiting for him in one direction, the federal government and its prison system waiting in the other. Was he going to get this girl killed or just banished from her community? "Yes," he heard himself saying, and he knew it was true. "Yes, I want this baby and you and Carey. I want to take care of you all forever. Let's get married tomorrow, Jenny, or as soon as it can be done in this state. Will you marry me?"

"Oh, yes, yes!" she cried, then began sobbing.

He stroked her hair, said soothing words, held her close and after a while she stopped crying. "I'm sorry I doubted you, Jesse; I should have known you would make it right; I should have trusted you."

"Trust me now and from here on," he said. "I promise I'll never let you down." It was a promise he knew he might not be able to keep, but he was goddamned well going to try.

"I will trust you," she said. "I'll never keep anything from you again."

"You should have told me when you first suspected," he said.

"That's not what I mean," she replied, and started to cry again.

The birth certificate, he thought. She wasn't married to Carey's father and the secret must have been eating at her. "Don't worry," he said. "And don't talk about it now. You're exhausted." He took her hand and led her toward the stairs. "Let's get some sleep."

Upstairs, she snuggled next to him, and he wiped away her tears. "Sleep," he said. "Tomorrow's Christmas Day, and we'll have a wonderful time with Carey. Don't think about anything else for now."

"All right," she said, moving closer.

I won't think about anything now, either, he thought. I'll sleep, and when I wake up I'll have an answer for us. He had a question of his own, too.

In the middle of the night he got out of bed, tiptoed across the room then crossed the hall and entered Jenny's bedroom. In her bathroom he silently opened the medicine chest and found what he was looking for. Only three of the birth-control pills had been removed since he had delivered the package, and that had been more than a month before.

Jesse replaced the pills in the medicine chest and padded back across the hall. He did not sleep again that Christmas Eve night; he was wide awake when Carey came to tug them from bed.

36

They went to a Christmas morning service at the church and watched a children's nativity pageant in which Carey took part. Coldwater's sermon was mercifully brief and free of his usual cant. When the service ended, Jesse and Jenny approached the pastor.

"Good morning, Jesse, Jenny," Coldwater boomed. "Merry Christmas to you."

"And to you, Pastor," Jesse said.

"I thought Carey looked very pretty as the Virgin Mary," Coldwater said.

"Thank you, Pastor," Jenny replied.

"Pastor," Jesse said, "Jenny and I have decided to be married, and we would be honored if you would perform the ceremony."

"Well, congratulations to you both," Coldwater said, beaming at them. "When would you like to hold the service?"

"We thought Sunday, just after the regular service. We'd like to keep it as small and quiet as possible," Jenny replied.

"I'll put it on my calendar. Will you have a honeymoon?"

"We hadn't gotten that far," Jesse said. "I'll have to talk to Herman Muller about getting some time off when he can spare me."

"Good, good. I'll see you on Sunday." Coldwater wheeled and walked out of the auditorium.

Jenny was unusually quiet on the way home and during Christmas dinner. It was not until Carey had gone out to show her friends her presents that Jesse spoke up.

"Jenny, what's the matter? And what were you talking about last night, about keeping things from me?"

She beckoned for him to follow her, then led him out of the house. He found an old broom and brushed the snow off a picnic table, then they sat down. It was cold and clear, and they wouldn't be comfortable for long.

"First of all," she began, "I want you to know that I wanted to get pregnant; I did it deliberately. Does that make you feel trapped?"

"No, it doesn't. I think that if you'd asked me I'd have wanted to wait for a while, but that doesn't matter now. I learned last night that you haven't been taking the birth-control pills, and I thought about it a lot, and I decided it was all right with me. I'm curious, though; why did you do it that way?"

"Because that's what Jack Gene wanted."

Jesse stopped breathing for a moment. "How's that again?"

"Pat Casey came to see me and said that Jack Gene wanted me to get pregnant. You're new in the community, and I think they wanted to test you, see how you'd react."

"And you were willing to do that for them?"

"No, not exactly; I love you, and I wanted a child; but I wasn't in a position to say no to them."

"I don't understand."

"When you went to the courthouse to get Carey's birth certificate, did you look at it?"

"Yes."

"So you saw that there was no father listed?"

"Yes, but it didn't matter to me."

"I sent you to get the certificate so you'd see that and ask me about it. I was surprised when you didn't."

"Like I said, it doesn't matter."

"Do you understand why there's no father listed?"

"I assume you weren't married."

"I was married, in a way."

"Then why wasn't the father's name on the certificate?"

"Because I can't be certain who the father was."

"I'm sorry, but this is very confusing. Why don't you just tell me the whole story?"

"All right," she said. "I'll tell you from the beginning. I was a little girl when Jack Gene Coldwater came to St. Clair, along with Pat Casey and Kurt Ruger. My parents became his followers, and they lived by his every word. When I was fifteen our house caught on fire. My bedroom was downstairs, and I managed to get out, but they didn't."

"I'm sorry, I never knew."

"I was alone in the world, and Jack Gene took me in." She paused and a tear ran down her cheek. "He married me."

Jesse gulped. "At fifteen?"

"Yes. It wasn't a real marriage in the usual sense. He performed a kind of ceremony, and I became one of them."

"One of who?"

"One of his wives."

"How many did he have?"

"I was one of five at the time. There've been more at times and less at others."

"And Jack Gene fathered Carey?"

"I think so, but I'm not sure."

Jesse was becoming very uncomfortable with this conversation, but if she was willing to talk about this, he was willing to listen. "Tell me why you're not sure."

"I didn't get pregnant at first. I tried not to. And after a while, Jack Gene began to get impatient. He wanted children, a lot of them, and he hadn't much use for those of us who couldn't give them to him. We were separated from the other women, those of us who couldn't get pregnant, or who had girls. Jack Gene wanted boys, you see."

Jesse was at a loss for words.

"So he put us aside—there were three other women—and sometimes, if he got bored with the wives who were living in his house, he would come to visit us. And he would bring Pat Casey and Kurt Ruger."

In spite of the cold Jesse began to sweat inside his coat.

"And it was during one of these . . . visits . . . that I got pregnant."

"All three of them?" Jesse asked quietly.

"All three," she said, and the tears flooded down her face.

He reached for her, but she pushed him away.

"I want to finish this," she said. "When Carey turned out to be a girl, they put me out of the inner circle, which was all right with me. I was nineteen; they put me in this house and gave me an allowance. I wanted to leave town, but Jack Gene wouldn't allow it. They made me send Carey to that awful school, and if I had tried to teach her different from what they did, she was trained to tell them. They would have taken her from me and . . . I don't know what would have happened to me. Sometimes people just disappear from this town. I had no money, no education, no skills. There were no relatives I could go to, nobody at all. The only place I existed was here, and it was at the whim of Jack Gene. He seemed to forget about me for a long time, but when you came to town I heard from Pat Casey."

"He told you to take me in?"

"Yes."

"He told you to get into my bed?"

"Yes."

Jesse laughed ruefully. "And I thought it was because I was so irresistible."

"I'm sorry; it's so difficult to tell you all this, but I felt I had to."

"Why?"

"Because I fell in love with you that first night, and I don't want us to go any farther on false pretenses. If, having heard all this, you want to forget about marriage, I'll understand."

He took her shoulders and turned her toward him. "I'm glad you told me all this," he said. "None of it matters, but I'm glad you had the courage to tell me."

"You don't mind about . . . my background?"

"I'd change it if I could, but I want you the way you are, no matter how you got to be you."

She snuggled her face into the hollow of his neck. "Oh, I love you so much, Jesse. Even more, now, I think." Then she jerked away from him. "We can't stay here after what I've told you," she said.

"I don't want to stay here, but I have to for a while. Can you stand it a little longer?"

"How much longer?"

"I'm not sure."

"I have to get Carey away from that school and these people. She's Jack Gene's child, I'm as sure of that as I can be, and he'll want to keep an eye on her. He'll use her as he used me; marry her off to one of his cronies, or just put her into a house of women, as he did with me. I'll kill him before I'll let that happen."

"I understand, and I want to take you away from here, but I can't just yet."

"Why not? What is there to keep us here?"

"Did Pat Casey ask you to pass on information about me?"

"Yes, he calls once or twice a week. I brought you out in the yard, because I thought he might have some way of listening to us in the house."

"What have you told him?"

"Whatever he wanted to know. I don't know anything about you that he would think derogatory. If I had, I wouldn't have told him."

"I'll take you away from here, Jenny, you and Carey, I promise; but I have to stay on for a while, and I can't tell you why. I don't want to put you in the position of knowing about me and having to lie to Casey."

"What I don't know, I can't tell him, is that it?"

"It's for your protection. I'd trust you with my life, but you and Carey are safer knowing only what you know now, that I love you, and I'll take care of you both."

"I guess that's good enough for me," she said.

"Good. You have to go on living your life as usual, for a while. You can't say anything at all to Carey. We have to let Coldwater do this ceremony; I'll give you a better one later. And one of these days I'll say to you, 'Let's get out of here,' and—"

"And I'll go with you the second you say it," she said, and put her arms around him.

Jesse's mind was elsewhere. He was having fantasies of castrating Jack Gene Coldwater.

37

They were married on the Sunday after Christmas, in a brief, entirely conventional ceremony performed by Jack Gene Coldwater. Jesse had trouble with the occasion. Up until Christmas Day, he had not hated Jack Gene or Casey or Ruger; now he did, for what they had done to Jenny. His best chance of bringing revenge to all of them lay in calling in the feds, and he could not wait to talk to Kip Fuller again.

Eight days passed before the first business day of the new year, and they were difficult for Jesse. He was glad to be married to Jenny, but nervous about the possibility of the house being bugged. Coldwater's people stayed away from him, and for that he was grateful.

On Monday, the fourth, he took his telephone into the woods behind the plant and called Kip Fuller.

"Jesse, I've been waiting to hear from you."

"What kind of reaction did you get from Barker?"

"You're not going to like it."

"They don't believe me?"

"Something like that."

"Kip, my deal is that I get Coldwater on a felony indictment, and I'm out of here. Well, I've got him; it's a felony to buy or possess the kind of armament he's got stashed up on that mountain."

"That's Barker's point," Kip said. "He thinks you're making this up to get out."

"Well, I'm prepared to prove it; all he has to do is to bust Coldwater, Casey and Ruger, then search the place. What's the big deal?"

"It's too fantastic, that's all. You're going to have to get proof of your allegations."

"Jesus Christ! What are you, a judge of the federal court? Act on my information and you'll have your proof."

"The proof has to come first."

"What do you expect me to do? Walk in there with a camcorder and tape Coldwater posing with a lot of munitions?"

"Not exactly; you'll have to use something a little more subtle than a camcorder. I can take care of that."

"Kip, I don't know if I'll ever be allowed into that place again. It was a fluke that I saw it at all. How am I supposed to get back in?"

"That's up to you," Kip replied, and he didn't sound happy about it. "We've got to find a way to get a small camera to you."

"This is insane; I'll never be able to do it."

"What about some other way, some other felony?"

"I think they may be bombing abortion clinics, but I don't have a shred of evidence to back that up."

"Get them to take you along, then."

"They haven't asked me to do anything illegal, so far. Oh, I did shoot a guy, and Coldwater finished him off."

"Tell me about it."

"We were target shooting with M-sixteens and handguns, and a guy named Partain appeared out of nowhere and tried to waste Coldwater. I hit him in a shoulder, and Coldwater, cool as ice, took my pistol and put one into the back of his head. Casey was there; does murder count in our deal?"

"You got any other witnesses?"

"Just Coldwater, Casey and me."

"Then it's your word against theirs, and I'll be willing to bet it would be hard to prove this guy Partain ever even existed. Also, Ruger wasn't there, and we've got to have him, too. Come to think of it, he wasn't at the fort with Coldwater and Casey, was he?"

"That's right."

"Well, then, you've got to tie all three of them in a neat bundle, or your deal's no good."

"Ruger runs the local bank; I'd be willing to bet that a stiff audit would turn up all sorts of stuff. There's the money I took to the Swiss bank in New York, for instance."

"You want me to call in the bank examiners while you're there in the middle? That might make them suspicious, since you're the new boy."

"You have a point."

"Listen, the fort is your best chance. Can you find an excuse to go to Coeur d'Alene this week?"

"There's no office supply store in St. Clair, and we're low on some things at the plant. I might be able to manage it."

"What day?"

"Let's try for tomorrow."

"Okay, on the outskirts of town—you'll pass it on your right driving from St. Clair—is an old-fashioned hamburger joint called Mack's. What time will you go?"

"I should be there by ten, if all goes well."

"Okay, from ten to eleven, there'll be a guy at the counter drinking coffee and reading a Seattle newspaper. He's six-four, two-fifty, and he'll be wearing a checkered shirt and a down vest and a New York Yankees baseball cap. You sit next to him, have a cup of coffee, and when he has a chance he'll pass you a package. There'll be a camera inside a Zippo cigarette lighter; it'll be loaded with thirty-six exposures of a special, low-light color film, and it will shoot in anything but total darkness, if you brace it against something to hold it still. There'll be typed directions inside; memorize them and burn them—the lighter works. The guy will leave first; you finish your coffee, then go on your way. When you get your shots, FedEx them to me, care of the Justice Department, and don't get caught doing it."

"Okay, but I can't guarantee that I can get back inside the fort."

"Then nail them on something else; make them take you on an abortion clinic raid."

"But if I participate, will my testimony be any good?"

"As long as you can make a case for duress, it will. Are you going to stick it out, Jess?"

"Do I have a choice?"

"Not that I see."

"Then I'll stick it out." He hung up.

Jess walked back to his office deep in thought. By the time he was at his desk he had made up his mind. He knocked on Herman Muller's door. "Herman, I've got some news; Jenny Weatherby and I got married a week ago Sunday."

"That's wonderful, Jesse; congratulations," Muller replied, bestowing a rare smile.

"I wondered if I could get a few days off for a honeymoon sometime soon."

Muller turned to his calendar. "Let's see; we're starting the New York plywood order this week. If things go smoothly, I should think you could take off the week after next."

"I haven't been here long, Herman; I'd be happy to take it without pay."

"Call it a wedding present," Muller said, and smiled again.

"Thank you, Herman; that's very generous. Oh, we're running low on a bunch of things in the office; I thought I'd run up to Coeur d'Alene in the morning."

"Sure, go ahead."

Jesse went back to his desk. He had the passports; he had, what, something over fifty thousand dollars in his safe under the truck. It wouldn't last long on the run, but it was better than nothing. San Francisco, that sounded good for a honeymoon, and it offered flights to half a dozen Far Eastern countries.

The more he thought about it, the more he knew his fifty thousand wasn't enough. He'd have to put his mind to finding more over the next couple of weeks.

38

Jesse spent an hour at the office, making a list of needed supplies, then left for Coeur d'Alene. As soon as he left the plant's parking lot, he noticed the car behind him, and it stayed there all the way through town and up the road to the city. This must mean that the office was bugged. In the countryside it kept a car or two between them, but it was always there. Jesse was tempted to pass up the meet at the hamburger joint, but the camera offered at least one possible way out, and he couldn't pass it up. Mack's restaurant hove into view, and he pulled into the parking lot and got out.

There was a variety of vehicles parked out front, everything from a UPS van to a couple of eighteen-wheelers. Jesse wondered what his contact was driving. Inside the door he put some change into a machine and got a copy of *U.S.A. Today*, while looking over half a dozen men seated at the counter. None of them fit the description of his man.

He glanced at his watch; ten past ten; his contact was late.

Jesse took a stool at the end of the counter, away from the other customers and with a pair of empty stools next to it. He ordered a cup of coffee and a doughnut and glanced into the mirror behind the counter. A young man, very like the one who had followed him in New York, came through the front door, looked around, then, spotting him, took a stool near the center of the counter and ordered coffee.

Jesse took his time over the coffee and the newspaper, but he couldn't be seen to tarry, and his contact didn't show. Finally, when he'd been there for twenty-five minutes, he paid his check and got up to leave. As he approached the door, a man fitting the description of his contact walked into the place and headed for the counter. Jesse prevented himself from even pausing and continued on out of the restaurant.

Cursing the man's tardiness for screwing up the meet, Jesse got into his truck and started the engine, then looked down and saw a package of Bicycle playing cards on the front seat beside him, and they didn't belong to him. He waited until he got to cruising speed before opening the package; inside was the Zippo lighter and a tightly folded sheet of instructions. He glanced in his mirror and saw that his tail was one car back, then he held the sheet against the steering wheel and read it carefully, alternating with watching the road. If he started a fire in the truck it might be noticed, so he wadded up the paper and slipped it into a pocket; he'd deal with that later.

At the huge office supply store he got a shopping cart and began to fill it from his list. Halfway through the store he caught sight of his tail, pushing a cart and pretending to shop. Then, as he was about to approach the checkout counter, he saw exactly what he needed. A pretty young woman was demonstrating, of all things, a shredder. He stopped and, keeping his back to his tail, removed the wad of paper from his pocket and opened it up. "Can you shred this for me?" he asked the woman.

"Just shred, or would you like to see our burn feature, too?" she asked.

"I'd just love to see the burn feature," Jesse replied, handing her the folded sheet of paper. He watched as she fed it into the machine, and he followed it with the playing card package. A puff of smoke rose from the bin as the paper was converted to ash. "That's very impressive," he said.

"Can I order a machine for your company?"

"I'll have to ask my boss," Jesse replied. He smiled at her and continued to the checkout desk. He noticed that his tail preceded him from the building and was waiting in his car.

Jesse loaded the supplies into the back of the pickup, got in and drove back toward St. Clair, occasionally glancing in the rearview mirror to be sure his tail was in position. He drove straight through the town and back to the plant and, as he was unloading the supplies, he saw the tail's car make a U-turn and head back toward the town.

The young man would have nothing to report, Jesse thought, with some satisfaction. It was clear, though, that someone—Coldwater or Casey— didn't yet entirely trust him.

At supper, he broached the subject of San Francisco. "Herman says I can have the week after next off."

"That sounds wonderful," Jenny said, glancing worriedly at Carey. "I don't think Carey could miss school, though."

"Well, it is a honeymoon, after all; I thought maybe she could come just for the first weekend. We could fly from Spokane on Friday night, then send her back on Sunday afternoon. Do you think we could get someone to meet her at the airport?"

"Oh, please, mommy, I want to go to San Francisco," the little girl said.

"Well," Jenny said, reluctance in her voice, "Let's see what we can do. I'm not promising, though."

The little girl was practically jumping up and down with excitement.

"I'm sure we can work it out," Jesse said, reassuringly. Carey beamed at him.

After dinner, when Carey was absorbed in her homework, Jesse put down his newspaper. "Want to take a stroll around the neighborhood?" he asked Jenny. "It's a starry night."

"Sure," she replied. "I'll get our coats."

When they were away from the house and Jesse was reasonably sure they were not being watched, he spoke up. "I have some things to tell you," he said. "First of all, we're talking about a lot more than a honeymoon."

"I was hoping you'd say that," she said, slipping her hand into his.

"I don't want you to ask any questions about this, but I have three valid passports with yours, Carey's and my photograph in them. I also have enough money to get us out of the country."

She squeezed his hand. "I've never been out of the country," she said excitedly. "Where would we go?"

"Maybe Hong Kong, as a first stop. There are excellent airline connections from there to points all over the world. I want to give some more thought to where we might end up on a more permanent basis. Where would you like to live?"

"Anywhere you say is fine with me," she replied. "I mean that; Carey and I will go *anywhere* with you."

"Here's what we'll do, then; we'll drive to Spokane and leave the truck there, then fly to San Francisco. We'll check into a hotel, the three of us, and stay until Sunday. When time comes to take Carey to the airport for her flight back to Spokane, we'll simply get onto another flight. I'll have to check the schedules and see what our best bet is, and we'll have to go with only the clothes on our backs. We won't even check out of the hotel. Carey will have some things with her, of course, but that will be all we can take."

"There's nothing here that I can't live without," Jenny said. "Not one damned thing."

"My, my, I've never heard you use strong language, ma'am."

She laughed. "I guess I must feel pretty strongly about it."

"Something I have to know about," Jesse said, serious again. "Carey. Just how firm a grip does the church and school have on her?"

"I know this isn't a very good answer, but it's hard to say. You've heard her spout the racial stuff they're taught there, and as I've said before, they insist that she never miss a day's school, unless she's certifiably ill. The children are also taught to report any derogatory remarks their parents make about the church or Jack Gene; I think they use them as a sort of early warning system against parents who seem to be straying from the fold."

"Have there ever been consequences for those people?"

"As I said before, people have been known to disappear."

"Are there ever any questions asked about these disappearances?"

"People are afraid to ask questions. Sometimes there's a story that they've been expelled from church and are ashamed to show their faces in St. Clair; sometimes they're just gone."

Jesse nodded. "We're going to have to be very careful with Carey. It's important that she not have the slightest idea of what we're planning. Answer her questions about the San Francisco trip, but don't overdo it; tell her we'll visit Fisherman's Wharf and the Golden Gate Bridge and see all the other sights. We'll do that on her weekend with us. I don't want her to know that anything at all has changed until the last possible moment, when we're at the airport, and you're going to have to figure out what to tell her to be sure that she's not upset by the change in plans."

"I understand."

"Also, talk with her about things beyond the San Francisco trip, things at school or at church. Make the trip seem like just one event in the coming months. That way, if anybody questions her, she'll have the right answers."

"I think the best way to handle things at the airport is to tell her that Jack Gene is sending us on a trip, a secret trip, maybe, to do something or other for him or the church."

"Good. You'll have to build our name change into the story, too."

"What is our new name going to be?"

"Warren. I'm Jeffrey, you're Jillian, Carey is Katherine."

"I like the sound of them," Jenny said. "Jeff, Jilly, and Kathy, the all-American family."

"That's us," Jesse said. "Something else: I've got enough money to keep us for a while, if we're careful, but we could certainly use more."

"I rarely have more than a hundred dollars in the bank at any one time, after I've paid the bills," she replied.

"That's not what I was thinking of," Jesse said. "When you lived with Jack Gene, did you live in the house he's in now?"

"Yes. He'd just built it when I went to live there."

"Did he keep large amounts of money in the house or in the church?"

"There was a big safe in his study," Jenny said, holding out a hand at waist level. "This high, at least. I watched them install it, but I never saw what was in it. Jack Gene always seemed to have a lot of cash in his pockets, though, and it could have come from the safe."

"Where in the study was it?"

"Opposite the fireplace, behind a bookcase that swung out. Jesse, you're not thinking of trying to rob Jack Gene, are you?"

"I will, if I get the chance."

"This is what I think," she said. "I think that if we just disappear, he might not take the trouble to look for us much, especially if we've left the country. We won't be able to hurt him in any way, after all. But Jack Gene has a monumental temper, and in the past he's gotten maddest when somebody stole from him. If we take his money, he'll never stop looking for us."

"You're right," Jesse said. "We'll manage on the money we've got." But, he thought to himself, after what Jack Gene has shown me up on the mountain, he'll never stop looking for us, anyway, so what the hell?

39

Jesse was leaving his office on Wednesday, two days before the beginning of his honeymoon, when Pat Casey pulled into the parking lot in his squad car.

"Hey, Jesse," Casey said.

"Evening, Pat."

"Jack Gene wants us up at his house for a meeting."

"When?"

"Right now."

"Let me go back inside and call Jenny; I don't want her to worry."

"Forget about that; get in."

Jesse got into the patrol car. "What's up?"

"You don't ever ask that when Jack Gene calls a meeting; you just go."

"Glad to," Jesse said mildly. He did not speak again on the trip.

They were greeted at the door by an attractive young woman, not the same one Jesse had seen on his last visit to the house, and shown to Coldwater's study. Coldwater and Kurt Ruger were already seated on a sofa before the fireplace, and Coldwater indicated that Jesse and Casey should sit opposite them.

"How's married life, Jesse?" Coldwater asked.

"Couldn't be better," Jesse replied, smiling.

"Good, good, glad to hear it. Jesse, it's time we had a talk about something that's been going on for some time, and it concerns you."

Jesse nodded. He didn't like the sound of this.

"You've been accepted into our midst, Jesse, but I've never really talked to you about what that means, have I?"

"Not specifically," Jesse replied.

"In order to keep the coherence of our group, I require a very high degree of loyalty from my congregation."

Jesse said nothing.

"Have I ever told you what loyalty means to me?" Coldwater asked.

"No, sir, not in so many words, but I've had the strong impression that you would not have told and shown me the things you have unless you felt I was capable of loyalty."

"You're quite right, Jesse; I always seem to be underestimating you. You've understood from the beginning without my spelling it out for you." Coldwater rewarded him with a large smile.

"Maybe you'd better spell it out," Kurt Ruger said suddenly. "That's the only way of being sure."

"Of course, Kurt," Coldwater said smoothly, but he seemed miffed by the interruption. "First of all, Jesse, I don't think I have made it clear to you the sort of rewards that are available to the people who are loyal to me."

"I've never asked for any reward," Jesse said.

Ruger interrupted again. "But you knew there was something in it for you, didn't you, Barron?"

Jesse turned and looked directly at Ruger. "Kurt, when I came to this town only a few months ago, I was at rock bottom. I had lost my wife and children and my business, and I thought I might go crazy. Since I've been in St. Clair I've come to have good work, a wonderful wife and little girl and the friendship of the people of the First Church. My life has been transformed, and I just don't know what more reward than that I could ask for."

"Don't get sanctimonious with me, you—" Ruger began.

Coldwater cut him off. "That's enough, Kurt. You apparently don't recognize gratitude when you see it."

"Jack Gene, I only meant that—"

"I said, that's enough."

Ruger stopped talking and looked at the floor.

Coldwater turned back to Jesse. "Jesse, you've proven to me that you want to be a part of what we have here, and I think you're ready to play a more important role in our community."

"Thank you, sir," Jesse replied.

"From today, you are going to be a part of, shall we say, management. There are three divisions of our group; Pat, here, is charged with protecting us from outsiders who might harm what we stand for. Kurt is the financial director of our organization;

nominally, he is president of the Bank of St. Clair, but what he does is far more important than that. Kurt marshals our resources, invests in income-producing ventures and, through what you might call sub-managers, directs, in a broad sense, the operation of those ventures we own. I am the third and higher arm of the organization. In general, I administer our affairs, and I take a great interest in what both Pat and Kurt do in their daily work."

"I see," Jesse said.

"Good. Now, ever since the three of us came to St. Clair, an essential part of the financial structure of this community has eluded us, and the time has come when we can no longer tolerate that."

Jesse knew what he was getting at now, and he was both relieved that there was no new suspicion of him and worried about what was about to be said.

"The only business of any size in this town that we do not control is St. Clair Wood Products," Coldwater said. "We have made repeated offers to Herman Muller for the business, but he has always rejected them, and my patience is wearing thin."

Ruger spoke up again. "Did you know about this? Has Muller ever mentioned this to you?"

"Herman has never mentioned it, but on the day I went to work out there, you and another man were in his office, and I got the impression that you had made him some sort of offer that he hadn't accepted."

"Did you hear what was said?"

"No, I was sitting in the waiting area, and

Herman's office is glassed in. It was pretty obvious what was happening."

"I see," Ruger said, then was quiet again.

Coldwater spoke up again. "Eventually, we will control Wood Products, and when we do, I want us to be able to operate it efficiently. Are you getting an overview of how the business is run?"

Jesse nodded. "Yes, sir. That's what Herman has said he wants me to do. Before he promoted me, he seemed to run every aspect of the business personally, and he still does; but he seems to feel that he needs some backup. I have to tell you, though, that I don't see how anybody could run that business more efficiently than Herman does. There isn't an ounce of fat in that company, and I'm sure its profit margins must be much higher than for most businesses of the same kind."

"Has he revealed any of the financial operations to you?" Ruger asked.

"No; he takes care of that himself. He signs every paycheck, every purchase order, makes every decision to do with money."

"So you have no real idea of the financial condition of the company?"

"I don't see how it could be anything but very healthy. Herman has never hesitated to order new equipment when we need it, and he pays every bill the day it comes in. You must have some idea of his financial condition, since you're the only bank in town."

"He doesn't bank with me, except for a small account; he banks in Coeur d'Alene."

"I didn't know that," Jesse admitted.

"Where does he keep the books?" Ruger demanded.

"He does it on computer. I've never seen a ledger in the office."

"Do you use the computer?"

"I do for word processing, that sort of thing. Once I wanted to see if a particular bill had been paid, but when I tried to access the check register I was barred. Herman apparently uses some sort of password to get into the bookkeeping software. And I've never seen any ledger printouts."

"You don't know the password?"

"No."

"Could you find out what it is?"

Jesse shrugged. "I don't know. Herman sits in a corner of his office, and the computer screen faces the corner."

"Jesse," Coldwater said, "I would be very grateful to you if you could learn what that password is."

Jesse thought fast. He was being asked to betray Herman Muller, and he didn't like that. On the other hand, if he resisted doing so, Coldwater would be unhappy with him, and he might lose much of the good will he had built up. "I'd be glad to try," he said.

Coldwater smiled broadly. "Thank you, Jesse. Now, as I said before, I'm elevating you to a management level with us, and you will find there are many benefits at this level of trust. First of all, you will be put on a salary of ten thousand dollars a month."

Jesse had no trouble looking stunned.

"It will be paid to you by Kurt in cash each

month, so there will be no need to mention it to the Internal Revenue Service."

"Why, that's wonderful, Pastor," Jesse managed to say.

"In addition, any medical treatment you or your family may require will be made available to you, free of charge, at our own clinic in town, and you will find there will be other benefits."

"I hardly know what to say, sir," Jesse said.

"Say nothing, but I will count on your help in acquiring Wood Products."

"I have a lot of respect for Herman Muller," Jesse said. "I hope that he will be treated fairly."

"More than fairly," Coldwater said, standing to indicate that the meeting was at an end. He stood for a moment, making small talk with Ruger and Casey.

Jesse now had an opportunity to look at the bookcase opposite the fireplace. He had not noticed it on his first visit, but the books in the lower part now seemed to be only spines. He wondered how to get at the safe. Something else caught his eye, too: at one end of the bookcase was a compartment that held a couple of dozen rolled-up blueprints. There were too many for just a house; they must be for some larger structure.

"Have you thought any more about a honeymoon, Jesse?" Coldwater asked suddenly.

Jesse started. "Yes, sir. We're going to San Francisco for a week starting Friday."

"Good, good. Where are you staying?"

"I don't really know; I thought we'd find a room when we got there."

Coldwater turned to Ruger. "Kurt, arrange a nice suite at the Ritz-Carlton for Jesse and Jenny, and have the bill sent to you. And be sure that Jesse gets his first month's salary before he leaves on Friday."

"That's extremely kind of you, sir," Jesse said. Certainly, he could use the ten thousand dollars.

"Don't mention it," Coldwater said. "A couple needs to get away alone when they've just been married. What will you do with the child?"

"She's going to spend the first weekend with us, but she'll fly back on Sunday, so that she'll be in school the next day. We didn't want her to miss school."

"Yes, yes, quite right," Coldwater said. "I'm surprised you'd want a child on your honeymoon."

"Carey and I get along very well, and we didn't want her to feel excluded," Jesse explained.

"I see. Well, thank you for coming today. I'll look forward to your reports on Herman Muller and his business."

He shook Jesse's hand, then Casey drove him back to the plant.

As Jesse got into his truck he made a note to have a serious conversation with Herman Muller before he left. After Friday, he wouldn't be around to help the old man, and he felt sorry about that.

40

Jesse woke up feeling elated. It was his last day in St. Clair, and he couldn't wait to get out of the town with Jenny and Carey. Jenny was no less excited than he; he could see her restraining herself at breakfast, talking casually with Carey about the sights of San Francisco.

"When is your science project due?" Jesse asked Carey.

"In two weeks," the child replied.

"We'll be back in plenty of time for me to help you, then," Jesse said.

"We're not supposed to have any help," Carey said.

"Oops, sorry."

"Well, maybe you could help a little," she said, smiling.

"You work on it next week, and if you have any questions, make a list and I'll answer them when we come back."

"Okay, Jesse."

* * *

At lunchtime Jesse put on his coat and boots and took his periodic walk in the woods, the telephone hidden in the bottom of his lunchbox. He took a fork in the path that went along the mountainside; there was a steep drop off to a stream two hundred feet below, and he kept to the inside of the narrow path. The skies were low with heavy cloud; it looked like snow before the day was over. He ate his sandwich slowly, thinking about what was ahead. He knew a life on the run was not going to be easy for any of them. The telephone weighed heavily in his pocket; he had one more call to make to Kip Fuller, and the single purpose of that call was to buy time.

"This is Fuller."

"It's Jesse."

"Did you get the camera all right? Our man said he couldn't make a straight pass at the restaurant."

"I got it, but I haven't had an opportunity to use it."

"What else is happening?"

"I've been promoted to management."

"At the factory?"

"No, in Coldwater's organization. He likes me, but Ruger doesn't."

"What's the problem with Ruger?"

"I don't know. Certainly I'm too far down the pecking order to be any sort of threat to him. It may have something to do with the fact that Herman Muller trusts me, and he'll barely speak to Ruger. Coldwater wants Wood Products, and he's going to use me to get it."

"How?"

"Right now all he wants is information about the business. It's wholly owned by Muller, and he plays his cards very close to his chest. He even banks in Coeur d'Alene to avoid dealing with Ruger."

"What are you going to do?"

"Play along, for now. If I don't, Coldwater might move a lot faster, and Muller could get hurt. It's possible that they took out the man's grandson a while back."

"Have you learned anything new about Coldwater's organization?"

"No, but I'm in a better position to do that, now. If I can get Wood Products for him, he'll think I hung the moon. The man likes me, that much I can tell."

"Do you like him?"

Jesse hesitated, thinking about what Coldwater had done to Jenny. "He's a likeable fellow; every con man is."

"I've got some news; Arlene had a baby boy yesterday; nine pounds, one ounce."

"Kip, congratulations; that's wonderful news! You've waited a long time."

"We're thrilled, of course. I had almost given up."

"Now that you know you can do it, you'll have to have some more kids."

"I think one more will do me. Listen, Jess, you've got to get back into that building somehow. My people here are really on my back about this."

"I was at Coldwater's the day before yesterday,

and I noticed a lot of blueprints in his study. If you bust him, then you ought to make his house your first target, get in there and clean it out. Those plans would tell you a lot about the fortifications."

"Good idea, but I'm not going to get to bust anybody until you get me those photographs."

"Kip, I can't just ask to go back in there and have a look around. I've got to wait until Coldwater feels the need to take me back inside there, and you're just going to have to be patient. Unless, of course, you want to just pour in here and nail the lot of them right now."

"You know I can't do that, Jess."

"Kip, if this ends badly, I want you to remember that I did what I was ordered to do; that I got you everything you need to indict."

"Jesse, you know goddamned well that, if it were up to me, I'd be in there today with a dozen swat teams, the army, if necessary. But I answer to other people."

"You make sure Barker remembers what I said," Jesse said hotly.

"That I'll do."

"Listen, Kip, I'm not going to be able to call for a while. I'm under a lot of scrutiny right now, especially with Ruger's attitude being what it is. Every time I leave town there's somebody on my tail, and the house may be bugged, too."

"You've been leaving town?"

"Just to go to Coeur d'Alene on business."

"Jesse, if you go any farther afield, I want to know about it, you hear?"

"Sure, Kip. I'd better go now; I'm due back at the plant. You give my best to Arlene and the new baby."

"I'll do that, Jess. You call me as soon as you can."

Jesse broke the connection and put the phone back in his pocket. It had started to snow, and he turned to retrace his steps to the plant. As he did, he found himself looking down the barrel of an automatic pistol, maybe six feet away.

"Just hold it right there," the man said. "I heard all of that; I'll take the phone." It was the young man who had followed him to Coeur d'Alene on his last trip.

"What's going on?" Jesse asked.

"I said, I'll take the phone. Toss it over here."

"Why do you want my phone?" Jesse asked.

"If you don't throw it over here right now, I'm going to shoot you someplace painful. Nothing fatal, just painful. You have a lot of questions to answer, my friend."

"You want the phone, you can have it," Jesse said. "Just don't get careless with the gun. When I've had a chance to talk to Coldwater you're going to see this in a different light, and it would go a lot better for you if there weren't any holes in me."

"The phone," the man said.

Jesse pointed to his pocket. "It's in here."

"Take it out very slowly and toss it to me."

Jesse slowly removed the telephone from his pocket, and, holding it in two gloved fingers, tossed it high and to the right of the man. As he had hoped, the man's gun hand swung around in the direction of the phone. Jesse took two running steps and dived at that hand.

The two men hit the ground together, dangerously close to the outer edge of the path. If they went off together, Jesse thought, he hoped the other guy would be on the bottom. He doubled his grip on the man's wrist and twisted outward. The pistol fell into the snow. Jesse got the man's arm behind him and shoved his wrist up between his shoulder blades.

The man screamed.

"Shut up, or I'll break it off. What the hell are you doing following me with a gun?"

"You'd better let me go, if you know what's good for you."

Jesse twisted the wrist again. "I asked you a question, and if you want to live through this little meeting, you'd better start talking."

"Ruger sent me," the man grunted.

"Not Casey?" Jesse asked, surprised. Casey handled security.

"It was Ruger; I've been following you for a couple of weeks. Now do the right thing; let me go, and let's go see Ruger."

Jesse didn't have to think about that for very long. There was only one possible result of this meeting, and it wasn't seeing Ruger. He grabbed the pistol, then got to his feet still holding on to the man's wrist. "All right," he said, "we'll go see Ruger, but not with a gun in my back, agreed?"

"All right, agreed," the man said. "Just ease off on my arm, okay?"

"Which pocket do you keep the pistol in?"

"Shoulder holster, left side," the man said.

Jesse reached inside the man's coat, found the holster, wiped the snow off the gun and shoved it into the holster. He also found a leather tab and snapped it across the trigger guard. "All right, do I have your word you won't draw that again?"

"Yeah, yeah," the man said. "Now, *please let go of my arm*."

"Sure," Jesse said. First he turned the man so that his back was to the steep slope, then he let go of the arm. Then Jesse hit him once, in the gut. He made himself watch as the man left the path and started down. There was one short scream that ended when his head struck a boulder, then the limp body ricocheted down the slope and free fell the last hundred feet to the stream below. The man ended up face down in the stream, wedged between two rocks.

Jesse sat down for a minute and tried to restore his breathing and his thinking to normal. The man was dead, that was sure; either the blow to the head had done it, or he would drown in the stream. He found it strange how easy it was to kill somebody when his own life was in danger. He looked around him; the snow, now falling heavily, was already obliterating signs of a scuffle. In ten minutes the whole area would be covered. Jesse waited the ten minutes before going back to the plant. He had two choices: say nothing and get on that plane tonight; it might be days before they found the man; or play innocent and try to carry it off.

He ran the last two hundred yards; he had to be out of breath when he reached his office and telephoned Pat Casey.

41

Pat Casey stood on the path and looked down into the ravine. "Who is he?" he asked.

"I don't know," Jesse replied. "I was sitting on a rock up there a few yards. I had just finished my lunch when I heard somebody shout, or maybe it was more of a scream."

"Did you see him go over?"

"No, in fact I almost didn't see him at all. I walked back down the path to about here and looked around, but it had begun to snow, and I didn't see anything at first. Then the red jacket caught my eye."

"Did you try to help him?"

"Are you kidding? How the hell was I going to get down there? I'm not a mountain goat." Jesse looked down the path and saw half a dozen people coming; two carried a stretcher, the others had rope and equipment.

"Okay, you guys," Casey called out, "he's right down there; go to it." He turned back to Jesse. "What were you doing up here, Jesse?"

"I come up here once or twice a week to eat my lunch."

"You were eating lunch outdoors in this snow?"

"It hadn't started when I got here; it had only just begun when I heard the sound."

"You're going on your honeymoon tonight, aren't you?"

"We're getting a nine o'clock plane from Spokane."

Casey nodded noncommittally. "Merv, don't you fall down there with him! Be careful!" he yelled at the rescue party, who were halfway down the incline. "Maybe you better wait a few days before you go, Jesse."

"I can't do that, Pat; we've got a big order for plywood, and we have to start on it the week after next. We'll be on it well into the spring, and I promised Jenny and Carey San Francisco." He looked down the path and saw Kurt Ruger walking toward them through the snow. In his suit, tie and overcoat he looked distinctly out of place.

"Hey, Kurt," Casey said.

"What's going on, Pat?" Ruger asked.

"We got a guy all the way down there in the creek; don't know who it is yet."

Ruger nodded, and he was looking straight at Jesse. "Did you throw him down there?"

"Don't be ridiculous," Jesse said. "I don't even know who the guy is; why would I want to throw him down there?"

Casey spoke up. "Jesse says he was having lunch up there a ways, and he heard the fellow holler. Could be he slipped right about here; the path's narrow, and it slopes that way."

"Barron did it," Ruger said.

Jesse squared toward Ruger. "Now you wait just a goddamned minute before you start accusing me of murdering people. Do you know who that guy is? Do you know something about this?"

Ruger looked down the incline to where a stretcher was being hauled up, but he said nothing.

"Now we'll get a look at him," Casey said, grabbing a rope and helping to haul the stretcher onto the path. He pulled back the blanket. "It's George Little," he said to Ruger. "He works for you; what was he doing up here?"

"See if he has his gun," Ruger said.

Casey pulled open the man's coat. "Right there in its holster; the safety tab is still on. Doesn't look like he was about to use it."

"Your pal Jesse killed him," Ruger said. "I suggest you lock him up while I tell Jack Gene about this."

"Lock me up?" Jesse said, outraged. "I don't even know the man. Just what the hell are you talking about?"

"Come with me, Kurt," Casey said, walking farther up the path. Ruger followed him, and they spent five minutes arguing and gesturing at each other. They came back to where Jesse stood. "You come on with me, Jesse; we're going to see Jack Gene." He glanced at Ruger, then back at Jesse. "Bring your truck; you can follow me up there."

Ruger glowered at Jesse.

* * *

Coldwater seated the three in his study and looked at them. "All right, what's happened?"

"George Little is dead," Ruger said. "Barron threw him off a mountain."

"I don't even know George Little," Jesse said.

Ruger started to speak, but Coldwater held up a hand. "One at a time; you first, Jesse."

"I went up on the mountain behind the plant to eat my lunch; I do that every so often; there's a nice view. I had just finished eating when I heard somebody yell or scream. I looked down the path, but there was nobody there. It had started to snow about that time, and it took me some time looking before I saw a man in the creek, about two hundred feet down the mountain. I ran back to the plant and called Pat and told him to bring some men, then I waited there for him to arrive."

"Pat?" Coldwater said.

"I've got no reason to contradict Jesse," Casey said. "George was wearing a gun, but it was still in his holster and strapped in. I think it's true that Jesse didn't know him."

Coldwater looked at Ruger. "All right, Kurt, let's have it all."

Ruger looked embarrassed. "I've had George following Jesse for a while."

"Why?"

"Because I don't trust him, and I don't think you should either. There's something wrong about him, and I want to know what it is."

"Jesse, did you know somebody was following you?"

"News to me; I didn't have a clue."

"Let's get it all in the open right now, Kurt. Tell me exactly what's bothering you about Jesse."

"He's gotten in too fast," Ruger said. "What is it, three or four months? We haven't had time to check him out thoroughly."

Casey spoke up. "Checking him out is my job, Kurt, and he has been *very* thoroughly checked."

"It's happened too fast, Pat," Ruger said. "You're getting sloppy."

"There was *nothing* sloppy in my investigation of Jesse," Casey said. "I think you know that, Jack Gene."

Coldwater turned to Ruger again. "All right, Kurt, tell me specifically what you know that Pat doesn't."

Ruger sat very still and didn't speak for a moment. "I don't have any hard evidence; it's just a suspicion."

"Have you confided this suspicion to Pat before now?"

"No, I haven't."

"Kurt, you know how we work here; if you had a problem with security on Jesse, you should have gone to Pat with it, or at least come to me."

"I didn't have anything definite," Kurt said. "Not until now."

"And what do you have now?" Coldwater asked.

"He killed George, that's what."

Jesse spoke up. "Pastor, this is ridiculous. I didn't know the man, had never laid eyes on him. Why would I kill him?"

"Because he caught you at something," Ruger said.

"Caught me at *what?*"

"I don't know, do I? What were you doing up that mountain?"

"Eating my lunch; I already told you that."

Coldwater spoke up again. "Jesse, please wait outside for a moment, would you?"

"Yes, sir," Jesse replied. He got up and went into the hall, closing the door behind him, and sat on a bench. He could hear nothing from inside the study. This could not have happened at a worse time, he thought; a few more hours and he would have been on his way. Why the hell hadn't he watched his back more carefully? The door to the study opened, and Casey waved him inside. Jesse resumed his seat and waited.

Coldwater looked at Ruger. "Kurt, I believe you have something to say to Jesse."

Ruger turned toward him. "Jesse, I'm sorry; my suspicions were unfounded, and I now believe the death of George Little to have been an accident."

"Thank you, Kurt," Jesse said. He turned to Coldwater. "I'm sorry I couldn't be more helpful in this, but I honestly had never seen the man before."

"I know that, Jesse," Coldwater said. "You go on to San Francisco; you deserve a good honeymoon. This matter is closed." He rose, and the others stood with him.

Jesse eyed the bookcase that concealed the

safe. If he'd just had more time, he thought, he might have gotten inside it.

Back at the plant he told his story to Herman Muller. "I'm sorry to have been away all afternoon, Herman, but—"

Muller held up a hand. "Of course, I understand, Jesse." He glanced at his watch. "If you're going to make your plane to San Francisco, you'd better get going. You and Jenny have yourselves a nice honeymoon."

Jesse couldn't leave yet. "Herman, you've been very kind to me, and I want you to know I'm grateful."

"Don't mention it; you're doing a fine job for me."

"Herman, I've gotten the impression that Kurt Ruger has been trying to buy the business from you. I know it's none of my affair, but I'm concerned about it."

"Don't you worry; I'm going to die running this business," Muller said.

"I hope you do, sir. I just think you ought to be real careful with Ruger. It would be better to sell than to get into a fight with him, I think."

Muller regarded him through half-lidded eyes. "Jesse, I believe you've been listening to rumors around here about my grandson."

"It's been mentioned," Jesse said. "I'm just worried that if Ruger wants the business bad enough, well—"

"The thought has crossed my mind," Muller said, "and I've taken precautions. Don't you worry about it. You go to San Francisco and have a wonderful time, then you come back here raring to go. We've got a big year ahead of us."

Jesse shook his hand and turned to go.

"And while you're there, you be sure to have dinner at Ernie's. I haven't been to San Francisco in years, but I remember that restaurant fondly."

"I'll do that, Herman," Jesse said, then left the office.

When he got home, Jenny and Carey were standing on the front porch, shivering, talking to another woman. He climbed the front stairs.

"Jesse, have you met Margery Twomy?" Jenny asked.

Jesse smiled and shook the woman's hand. "I've seen you at church, Margery. I believe Carey is staying with you while we're on our honeymoon."

"That's right," she replied. "I've just come to get Carey now."

"But she's coming to San Francisco with us for the weekend," Jesse said. "She'll be back Sunday night."

Jenny spoke up. "Jesse, I'm afraid that's not going to be possible. The school is having a special science workshop for Carey's class this weekend and next, and attendance is mandatory."

Jesse's heart was pounding against his ribs. "Well, surely a weekend away wouldn't hurt," he said.

"It's all right, Jesse," Carey said. "I have to stay and go to the workshop. Maybe we can go to San Francisco another time."

He looked down at the little girl. She didn't seem in the least upset about the sudden change in plans. "Whatever you say, honey."

When Margery Twomy had left with Carey, Jesse took Jenny inside and put his arms around her. "I'm sorry," he said, holding her away from him, pointing at the ceiling and tapping his ear. "I know you were looking forward to showing her San Francisco."

"It's all right," she said. "We'll have a family vacation next year and take her there." She laid her head against his shoulder and sobbed silently.

"Well," he said, "If we're going to make that plane, we'd better get our luggage in the car and get going."

All the way to Spokane, he kept glancing in the rearview mirror. Sometimes a car was there, sometimes it wasn't.

42

Jesse spent half an hour going through the suite at the Ritz-Carlton, looking for bugs, and he didn't find a thing. Apparently, Jack Gene Cold-water's arm was not long enough to reach inside a San Francisco hotel suite. He came back into the sitting room, where Jenny was curled up on a sofa, watching CNN on television.

"It's clean," he said, and sat down next to her. "We can talk."

"You understand that I can't leave without Carey," she said quietly.

"Of course I do."

"I was so excited about going abroad, but I'm excited about being in San Francisco, too. Can we see *everything*?"

"We sure can." He picked up a phone, called the concierge and asked him to book a table at Ernie's for the following evening. "Herman Muller rec-ommended it," he told Jenny.

"I never thought of Herman as a restaurant

critic," she said, laughing. "What are you getting me into?"

"It's a famous restaurant, an old San Francisco favorite." He found a room service menu, and they ordered a late dinner.

"Have you ever been to San Francisco before?" she asked.

"Once, for a conference six or seven years ago. Mostly, it consisted of getting drunk with a lot of other agents."

Her eyes widened. "You were some kind of agent?"

"I'm sorry, I shouldn't have said that. You'll be a lot safer if you don't know any more than you do."

"Jesse, we're married now," she said firmly, "and I'm entitled to know everything. I've certainly told you everything about me."

Jesse sighed and leaned back on the sofa. "All right, I guess it's time. You're not going to like some of this; I hope it doesn't make a difference to you."

"You just tell me."

"For a start, my name is Jesse, but not Barron; it's Warden."

"Like a prison warden?"

"Like that. I'm a minister's son."

"Uh, oh; you know what they say about the minister's boy."

"And they're not far wrong. Oh, I started out as the straightest arrow you ever saw; then I became a cop for the federal government, and being a cop has a way of getting you bent."

"How did you get bent?"

"I stole some money."

"A lot of money?"

"Yes, some tens of thousands of dollars."

"Why?"

He told her about Beth and her illness, and about Carrie.

"So the story about the wife and three daughters—"

"Was a cover; it was somebody else whose name I took. But Beth and Carrie were real, and they're gone."

"I'm so sorry, my darling," she said, running her fingers along his cheek, then kissing him. "That's more trouble than anybody should ever have in a lifetime. Where's Carrie now?"

"She was adopted when I went to prison, and I probably won't ever know where she is."

Jenny put her arms around him and held him close. "I know how I would feel if I were separated from Carey," she said, "so I know how you feel. Do you think there's any hope of ever finding her?"

"I'd like to think so, but I have to be realistic. That's why I was prepared to leave the country without her. Adoption agencies are a tough nut to crack, and I'm hardly in any position to try."

"Why not?"

"There's a lot more that I haven't told you. I went to prison."

"For stealing the money?"

"No, they never found out about that. It was drug money that we'd confiscated; I just swept it under the rug, and no record was ever made of it."

"Why did you go to prison?"

"I was convicted of killing my partner and stealing a great deal more money, but I was innocent on both charges."

"Then why were you convicted?"

"Because someone in my agency was determined that I would be. It was set up so that I would never have a chance, and, of course, I didn't. Somebody else wanted the money, and he was willing to kill my partner to get it."

"How long were you in prison?"

"Fourteen months."

"So short a time for such serious charges?"

"The man I used to work for and another agent, a friend, got me out, because they wanted something done."

"What did they want done?"

"Jack Gene Coldwater."

"They sent you to St. Clair alone to arrest Jack Gene?"

"To find out enough about him so that they could arrest him. I'm not a cop anymore, just a spy."

"Does Jack Gene suspect?"

"No, but Kurt Ruger does. Not that he knows anything, he just suspects I'm not quite right."

"Can he hurt you?"

"Not so far. There was a nasty incident earlier today, but Pat Casey and Jack Gene took my side."

"What happened that was so nasty?"

"Do you know a man named George Little?"

"Yes, and he's pretty nasty, too."

"I killed him this afternoon."

She stared at him. "He wasn't *that* nasty."

"He caught me making a telephone call to my contact in Washington. I was up on the mountain behind the plant, and I found an opportunity to push him into a deep ravine."

"My God," she said, putting a hand to her face. "There must have been some other way to handle the situation."

"There was another way: I could have gone up to Jack Gene's house at gunpoint with George Little, and I'd be dead by now."

She put her arms around him again. "In that case, I'm glad you did what you did. And if you have to do it again, you go ahead."

The doorbell rang, and Jesse let the waiter into the room. They had a quiet dinner by candlelight, not talking much.

As they were finishing the wine, Jenny said, "Everything has changed, hasn't it? Nothing will ever be the same."

"You're right," he replied.

She raised her glass. "To nothing ever being the same again," she said.

They touched glasses and drank. In bed they didn't make love; instead, they lay in each other's arms until they fell asleep.

43

On their first day in San Francisco they walked. Jesse wanted to know if he was still being followed, and walking was the best way. They walked from the Ritz-Carlton to Union Square, and Jenny went shopping.

She had never seen anything like it; there were Sak's Fifth Avenue, Macy's, Neiman Marcus and the Ralph Lauren shop, all within a few steps of each other. With his first ten-thousand-dollar payment from Coldwater in his pocket, Jesse made her shop. After all, he thought, they wouldn't be abandoning their luggage at the hotel to sneak out of the country.

Jesse watched constantly for a tail, checking reflections in shop windows, never looking behind him, and it wasn't long before he found his man. He didn't recognize this one; he was tough-looking, better than six feet, more than two hundred pounds, close to Jesse's own size. He was very good at his work, Jesse thought.

They had lunch in a pub, then shopped some

more. Finally, when they were ready to drop, they took the cable car up Powell Street and walked a block or two to the hotel, lugging many packages and shopping bags.

At Ernie's that night they were treated as old friends, given a secluded table and served to within an inch of their lives.

"I've never seen such a beautiful room," Jenny gushed, waving at the mahogany paneling and the fresh flowers. "How much is this costing?"

"It's not costing us a dime," Jesse replied, smiling. "It's all on Jack Gene, one way or another. We can take some comfort in that."

The following morning, Jesse rented a car and they drove north, over the Golden Gate Bridge, through Marin County and up into the wine country. They followed the road up the Napa Valley and found an Italian restaurant, Tre Vigne, for lunch. It was an unusually warm day for the time of year, and they asked for a table in the garden, which they had to themselves.

They ordered pasta and a good bottle of Napa chardonnay and had a leisurely lunch. As they were finishing, there was a sudden scraping of chairs, and men in suits occupied the tables on either side of them. Then, another man in a suit pulled a chair up to their table and sat down.

"May I join you?" he asked, somewhat tardily.

"Hello, Kip," Jesse said.

"Hello, Jesse. And may I be introduced?"

"Jenny, this is Kip; Kip, this is Jenny."

"I'm very pleased to meet you, Jenny," Kip said. "I wonder if you would be kind enough to go to the ladies' room? Mr. Smith over there will guide you." He nodded toward a man at the next table.

"It's all right, go ahead," Jesse said.

Jenny got up and left.

"Well, Jesse," Kip said, "what brings you to this part of the country?"

"I'm on my honeymoon," Jesse replied.

"I thought I told you not to travel without . . . What did you say?"

"I said I'm on my honeymoon."

Kip's mouth fell open. "You got *married?*"

"That's what you do, right before a honeymoon."

"Are you completely crazy?"

"Kip, I thought you'd be pleased; it's excellent cover."

Kip stared at him a moment, then smiled. "You're right, it is excellent cover; I'm pleased. I mean, congratulations. I never thought you'd go this far, Jess."

"She was my landlady from the beginning. It didn't take us long to fall in love."

"You're a lucky man, Jess—so far."

"Why so far?"

"What happens if this all goes wrong? What are you going to do with a wife?"

"Having a wife is good motivation to keep things from going wrong, isn't it?"

Kip shook his head: "I'm flabbergasted, I have to admit it."

"Kip, stop being flabbergasted and tell me what you're doing here, intruding on my honeymoon."

"You were spotted on Friday night at the airport. Remember a guy named Hennessy, from the South Florida Task Force?"

"Vaguely."

"He called Dan Barker, and Barker called me. Barker was *not* happy. He thought you were planning to skip the country."

"You can put his mind at rest. We're here for the week, and we're going back next Sunday."

"How do I know that without keeping a tail on you?"

"Jenny has a daughter; she was supposed to come with us, but at the last minute she was required at a weekend school project."

"So Coldwater is keeping you on a short leash?"

"That's about it. He knows Jenny wouldn't go anywhere without her daughter."

"Jesse, if you're going to go bouncing off like this, maybe I'd better put somebody else in St. Clair to keep an eye on you."

"You got somebody you want immediately dead?" Jesse asked. "Or is it just that you want me immediately dead?"

"We're a little slicker than that."

"Kip, listen to me. You reached into the gutter and you picked just about the only guy in the world who could waltz into that town and do what I've done. Two guys had already vaporized, remember? You send somebody else in there now, you'll not only kill him, you'll kill me. I'm your only shot at wrapping up this crowd, and you'd better not fuck with me, do you understand?"

Kip nodded. "I understand, Jess; I was just pulling your chain a little. After all, Barker's been pulling mine."

"You tell Barker that if these people tumble to me and start asking me questions under, shall we say, duress, I'll give *him* to them. One dark night they'll snatch him off some Georgetown street corner and disembowel him. They're like that."

"I'll mention it."

"Tell me, when you decided to put a team on me, did it occur to you that Coldwater might have been in there ahead of you with his own team?"

"That's the first thing we checked for. Remember, we spotted your tail in New York."

"Another thing: I was on to the tail yesterday, practically as soon as we left the hotel. If I find somebody else behind me during my honeymoon, I'll drag him into an alley and break his arms, and I mean it."

Kip held out his hands. "Jesse, Jesse, there's no need to get riled. You did something you weren't supposed to, and you got caught. Don't repeat the experience."

Jesse nodded. "Now, since I have no information to impart to you that I didn't impart in our conversation on Friday, I'd like you and your merry band of flatfeet to be gone before my wife returns to the table."

Kip stood up and gestured to the others. "Sorry

for the intrusion. I'll give Barker your message."
He turned to go.

"Kip?"

Kip looked back. "Yeah?"

"How's the new baby doing?"

"Just great."

"I'm glad. Give him my best."

"Thanks." And he was gone.

Jenny came back to the table. "What was that all about?" she demanded.

"Kip is the guy who sprung me from the joint."

"Joint?"

"Prison."

"And he's who you're working for?"

"He's my contact."

"What did he want?"

"He wanted to be sure we weren't skipping the country. Seems a colleague of his recognized me at the airport the other night, and there was a general panic that I was about to bolt."

"What if we had been bolting?"

"It wouldn't have worked. I'm going to have to give bolting some additional thought."

44

Jesse and Jenny arrived home late on Sunday evening, exhausted and happy from their time together and, especially, their time away from St. Clair. As they climbed the front steps with their bags Jesse was again feeling the strain of being someone else, and he was filled with dread to see an envelope pinned to the front door. He ripped it open and read the note.

Meeting tomorrow morning at eight sharp at J.G.'s.

Casey

Here we go again, he thought.

Jesse was normally at his desk by eight, and he had to call Herman Muller and beg an hour or two. When he arrived at Coldwater's house there were half a dozen cars and pickup trucks parked in the forecourt, and when he was let into Jack Gene's study there were as many men there. He took a few steps into the room and froze. Sitting in a chair beside the fireplace was perhaps the one person in the world he least wished to see at that moment. His presence meant that Jesse was, from this moment, effectively a dead man, that perhaps the only thing between him and death was torture.

Charley Bottoms rose from his chair at the sight of Jesse, and his gaze bored into him from across the room. He was dressed in neat sports clothes, a contrast to the jeans and leather he had worn in Atlanta Federal Prison. Long sleeves covered the prison tattoos, and he seemed, if anything, more massive than when Jesse had last seen him in the punishment cell at Atlanta.

"Good morning, Jesse," Coldwater boomed. "I want you to meet some colleagues."

Jesse's mind went nearly numb as he was introduced and shook hands with four strangers, and finally, he snapped back to reality as Charley Bottoms took his hand.

"And this is Charley Bottoms, who heads a clan of the Aryan Nation about a hundred miles north of here."

"Pleased to meet you, Jesse," Bottoms said, holding on to his hand for a moment.

"Good to see you, Charley," Jesse replied automatically.

"Let's all have a seat and talk for a minute, then we'll take a tour of the top of the mountain," Coldwater said. Everyone sat down, and Coldwater continued. "Most of us have met before in passing, at least, but it seemed to me that we have enough in common that we might do some good for each other. Yesterday afternoon, after your arrival, you saw the town, some of the local businesses and the Wood Products plant, which Jesse here takes a hand in running. We expect to be in control of that business in the near future, and that will consolidate our control of the town. In a few minutes I'm going to show you something that might surprise you, and I hope that what you have seen and will see here will give you some ideas about how to gather power in your own communities."

Coldwater droned on about how much everyone had in common, while Jesse fought the urge to throw up on the beautiful oriental rug at his feet. What was Bottoms waiting for? Did he want to get Jack Gene alone before he blew the whistle? Jesse looked around. There were only two ways out of the room: Casey sat between him and the door, and if he should throw himself through the windows he had at least a fifty-foot drop. He was sweating now, and he didn't want to call attention to himself by mopping his brow.

"Is it warm in here, Jesse?" Coldwater said suddenly. He got up, opened a window and sat down again.

"Thank you, sir," Jesse said, taking a deep breath.

Coldwater talked about cooperation and togetherness for another ten minutes, then he rose. "We'll have to take more than one car, it seems; you two can ride with me, Pat, you take Bob, there, and Jesse, Charley can ride with you." Coldwater retrieved a roll of blueprints from the bookcase, then the men filed out of the house and went to their respective cars. Coldwater drove off, leading the way.

Bottoms got into Jesse's truck and slammed the door. He pointed at the dashboard and mouthed, "Is it bugged?"

"No," Jesse replied. "I've been over it."

"Well," Bottoms said, "I guess I gave you a jolt, huh? I mean, I think I scared the shit out of you."

Jesse glanced across at the big man. "That's a fair statement, I guess."

"I wanted to warn you earlier, but you were out of town until last night, I hear."

Jesse nearly drove off the road. "You knew I was here?"

Bottoms laughed. "Haven't you figured it out yet?"

"Charley, what the fuck is going on?"

"Well, a couple of days after Barker sprung you, he sprung me. I'm supposed to keep an eye on you, make sure you're not so unhappy you'd fly the coop, or so happy you'd change sides."

"I should have known Barker would have a backup in place. It's like him to be that cautious."

"Backup is not far wrong. The deal was, I'd come up to Idaho, where a couple of old acquaintances had established the Nation up north, and get in good with them. Then, if they popped you, I'd be in place to step in. And, of course, I would burn the whole bunch in return for a free pardon."

"Let me get this straight," Jesse said. "You were willing to turn in your biker buddies to save your own ass?"

"Damn straight," Bottoms said. "I never met anybody on a bike, or on foot, come to that, whose ass was as valuable to me as my own. I never even liked most of 'em. Fuck 'em, is what I say, if it gets me a fresh start."

"You been dealing with Kip Fuller?"

"Right."

"I told the son of a bitch not to send anybody else in here. Is he *trying* to get me burned?"

"I doubt it. I think Barker insisted."

Suddenly, Jesse was delighted to see Charley Bottoms. "Well, I'll tell you, Charley, you aren't going to believe what you're about to see, but I want you to remember every fucking detail of it and report everything to Kip and Barker. They wouldn't take my word for it."

"Sure thing, pal. You know, I always wondered what would have happened if you and me had gone toe to toe in the yard. Didn't you?"

"Never crossed my mind."

"Well, you got out just in time, buddy; I'd have smeared you across the pavement real good."

"You know, Charley, it might have been interesting. Up until the time we met in solitary, I had just been trying to stay alive. But I think that after our chat, I would have started killing people, and you would have been first in line."

Bottoms grinned. "I like you, Jesse; I always did. You always handled yourself real good in the yard; took out some guys I'd have thought would have stomped you into the ground. I'd have hated to kill you, but I'd have done it the minute you set foot out of that cell. I'm glad our present circumstances don't require me to do that."

"That's sweet of you, Charley," Jesse replied.

"I never saw anybody I couldn't take in about a minute," Bottoms mused, "except maybe Coldwater."

"Coldwater scares you, does he?"

"You heard the stories about him in Nam?"

"Nope."

"Shit, he'd go out in the jungle and hunt Slopes with nothing but a knife; they say he killed more people in silent combat than anybody in any service, including the marines and the CIA. And now he turns up in Idaho with all that hair, talking like a preacher. I bet if you looked at him cross-eyed he'd tear your throat out with his hands without even blinking."

"You might keep that in mind, seeing that you're doing what you're doing here," Jesse said. He drove through the gates, then pulled up on the mountain top and parked the truck.

Bottoms stepped down and looked around him. "What we got here, summer camp?"

"Stick around, Charley," Jesse said. "Your eyes are about to be opened."

They stood around a conference table in Coldwater's underground office, following him as he took them through the blueprints of the installation. Jesse, as he had been doing for the past hour, snapped photographs with his Zippo lighter/camera whenever he had the opportunity. He took the opportunity to look closely around Coldwater's quarters, too, and he saw something he'd seen before: a bookcase that held spines only, and, unlike the one that hid the safe back at Coldwater's house, the false front was narrower and went nearly all the way to the ceiling.

"Jack Gene," somebody interrupted, "I don't see why you've stored gasoline instead of diesel in your underground tanks. Twenty-five thousand gallons of gas could make this place awful hot."

"That's an easy one," Jack Gene replied. "First of all, the gasoline is in super-hardened tanks, no closer than fifty feet to the surface; second, in the last ditch, gasoline can make a powerful weapon, even if only in Molotov cocktails. And we've got flamethrowers we can use, if we have to."

"I see your point," the man said.

"Well, that's all, gentlemen," Coldwater said, rolling up the plans. "Let's go back to the house for some brunch. He handed the rolled-up blueprints to Jesse. "Hang on to those for me." Then he led the way from his underground redoubt.

Back in the truck, Jesse dropped the blueprints behind the seat as he got in.

"Shit!" Bottoms breathed. "You ever seen anything like that?"

"No, and neither has anybody else. When are you talking to Kip again?"

"Soon as I get out of St. Clair."

"Tell him what you saw, will you? In the greatest possible detail?"

"You better believe it," Bottoms said.

Jesse drove back down the mountain toward Coldwater's house, feeling optimistic again. Maybe Bottoms's testimony would put some spine into Barker and get him moving. And Jesse now had one more opportunity to convince Washington.

45

Jesse went back to the office and spent the morning with Herman Muller, going over the production schedule on the New York plywood order. At lunchtime the plant emptied, and Muller, as usual, went into town for a hot lunch.

Jesse got Coldwater's blueprints from his truck and spread them out on his desk. He adjusted his gooseneck desk lamp for the best light and, one by one, photographed the pages with the Zippo camera. When he was done he went into Muller's private bathroom, got his telephone from his lunchbox and called Kip.

"What's up, buddy?" Kip asked

"Two things: first, Charley Bottoms showed up this morning and nearly caused me to clutch my chest and turn blue."

"Sorry about that; if you'd called in I could have warned you."

"Second, I've photographed a good chunk of Coldwater's fortifications and all of the blueprints."

"Holy shit! You really came through for me, Jesse!"

"You bet I did, buddy; now, how am I going to get the camera to you?"

"Got a pencil? I'll give you an address, and you can Federal Express it. Here we go, send it to John Withers, Nashua Building Supply, 1010 Parkway, College Park, Maryland." He added the zip code and phone number. "It's a drop I've set up. Can you get the camera off today?"

Jesse glanced through his glass wall toward the reception desk and the out box. "Yes, they haven't picked up yet today."

"Great, I'll look forward to your shots."

"Charley is my backup on this, Kip. Now you have all the evidence you need, right?"

"If all goes well, we'll be in there inside a week. I'll need a few days to plan and assemble a force."

"All right. The next time I talk to you, I want to hear that you're on your way."

"Over and out."

Jesse broke the connection, then went to the reception desk, found a FedEx form and envelope and addressed it as instructed. He inserted the envelope into a pile of a dozen waiting for pickup, then took the plans back to his truck. He spent the rest of his lunch hour eating a sandwich and leafing through the blueprints, and what he saw confirmed his suspicions about the bookcase in Coldwater's underground suite. When he got back to his desk, the phone was ringing.

"It's Jack Gene," a deep voice said. "What

happened to that roll of blueprints I asked you to carry?"

"Oh, I'm sorry, Pastor; they're in my truck; I forgot all about them. I'll run them by your house after work."

"Run them by my house now," Jack Gene said and hung up.

Jesse scribbled a note to Herman, then left the plant. He drove up to Coldwater's house, noting that the visiting cars had left, and rang the bell. Yet another beautiful young woman, this one pregnant, showed him to Coldwater's study. The room was empty.

"The pastor is on the phone in the kitchen," she said to Jesse. "He'll be with you in a few minutes." She left, closing the door behind her.

Jesse glanced at the telephone on the coffee table; a single red light glowed; Coldwater was on line one. Quickly he set the blueprints aside and went to the bookcase. He was surprised that the hinged false front yielded to only a slight tug; not even locked. Behind it sat a large red safe, a reproduction of a nineteenth-century model. Jesse had seen it offered in mail order catalogs. He knelt and put an ear to the safe, first glancing at the phone to be sure the red light was still on, then he slowly twirled the combination knob, listening to the tumblers. The mechanics of this safe had not changed for a hundred years, and Jesse believed he could open it in a couple of minutes.

He had once had a short course in safecracking from a snitch of his in Miami, an old-time thief who had turned to drug running for easier and bigger money, and he could open, he reckoned, about half of the safes he'd ever met. His snitch would have thought this one to be a piece of cake. Jesse looked at the telephone, and the light was out.

Quickly, he closed the cabinet and leaned on it, and one second later, Coldwater entered the room.

"There you are, Jesse," he said. "Take a seat; would you like some coffee?"

"Thank you, sir, yes," Jesse replied. He handed over the blueprints. "I'm sorry I took these with me; I just forgot they were in the truck."

"Don't worry about it," Coldwater said, lifting the telephone and pressing the intercom button, "I just don't want them out of the house. Bring us coffee for two," he said into the phone.

The two men settled into chairs before the fireplace, and Coldwater gazed sleepily at him. "What did you think of Charley Bottoms?" he asked.

"Big fellow," Jesse replied. "I wouldn't want him mad at me."

"Quite right," Coldwater said, smiling. "Did you think he was bright?"

"I didn't have much of a chance to form an impression," Jesse said. "Is he important to you?"

"He could be; any of those men here this morning could be, in the right circumstances. They and their followers have a lot of combat experience among them."

"Are you anticipating combat?"

"I've learned to anticipate every eventuality," Coldwater replied. "I'm always ready for anything." The coffee arrived, and Coldwater poured for them.

"This is a beautiful house," Jesse said, looking around. "Did you build it?"

"I did, and I designed it, too. Tell me, have you spotted the safe yet?"

"I beg your pardon?" Jesse said. His heart was beating faster now. Maybe Coldwater did have some sort of weird sixth sense.

"There's a safe somewhere in this room. Can you find it?"

Jesse looked around. "Behind a picture?"

"Nothing as obvious as that. Come on, you're a builder; where would you hide it?"

"May I look around?"

"Go right ahead."

Jesse walked slowly around the room, pretending to search, and he saw something he hadn't noticed before; there was another false bookcase that matched the one in Coldwater's underground study. He kept moving, then stopped in front of the bookcase that hid the safe. He fingered a book spine, determined it to be fake, then ran his fingers along the shelf. It opened easily.

"Well done," Coldwater said. "Do you know you're the first person to find it in under a minute? Pat Casey, as good as he is, took nearly ten."

"I guess Pat has never built a bookcase," Jesse said, sitting down again and picking up his coffee.

"You know anything about finance, Jesse?" Coldwater asked out of the blue.

"Just that part of it that pertains to running a small business. I've never been in the stock market or had any investment more complicated than a CD."

"Pity," Coldwater said. He seemed suddenly discouraged. "I've begun to think that Kurt Ruger, as talented as he is, as long as he's been with me, might no longer be the right man for his job."

"He certainly seems very competent," Jesse said.

"Yes, but suspicious to the point of paranoia. That's a good trait, up to a point, but Kurt went past the point a long time ago, and he's beginning to make a nuisance of himself. You saw the way he behaved over George Little's death."

"Well, yes; I did find that surprising. Flabbergasting might be a better word."

"Yes, flabbergasting. Pat Casey was furious with him." He looked up. "Jesse, is there anything you want?"

"How do you mean?"

"Anything. Anything that you don't already have, I mean."

"Not at the moment. I'm very content with my lot."

"If there's anything you ever want, you come to me," Coldwater said. "Doesn't matter how difficult it might be. You just come to me, and it's yours."

"Why, thank you, Pastor," Jesse said. "I'm very grateful."

"Well, you'd better get back to work," he said. "Anything to report on Wood Products?"

"Well, no sir; I haven't spent a great deal of time there since we talked about it."

"Of course not; you let me know when you have something."

They shook hands, and Jesse left. Driving back to the plant, he reflected on how he might get his hands on that safe. When the feds launched their raid, he had to get to that safe before anybody else.

46

Jesse waited until the end of the week before he called Kip. It was hard to wait, and he had grown very tense. He was having a hard time sleeping, and when he did his dreams were confusing and disturbing. He was always back in New York, walking down Fifth Avenue, window shopping, and what he saw had an awful effect on him. He would wake up, shaking and bathed in sweat, and not be able to remember what he had dreamed. His appetite diminished and he didn't feel well. Herman Muller had commented on how pale he looked.

On Friday at lunchtime, when the office was empty, he called Washington. He no longer felt comfortable doing this on the mountain, so he did it from his desk, from where he could see anyone who came up the office stairs.

"This is Fuller."

"Kip, it's Jesse."

"Hi." He didn't sound happy about the call.

"What's going on? What was the reaction to the photographs?"

"Well, the shots weren't what we hoped they'd be; all we could see was hallways and boxes; hard to tell what was in the boxes."

"I did what you asked with the equipment you gave me."

"I know, Jesse, and it's not your fault."

"Haven't you heard from Charley Bottoms?"

"Yeah, but Barker—"

"Barker what?"

"Barker is getting paranoid about this, I think. He seems to believe that you and Charley are somehow colluding to make an ass of him."

"What about the shots of the blueprints?"

"The shots are a little washed out. The camera was loaded with a special, low-light film, and you lit the plans too brightly when you photographed them."

"All I used was a desk lamp."

"It was too much; you'd have been better off just using ambient light."

"Listen to me, Kip: our deal was that I would get evidence to indict Coldwater and his partners. I've done that; I've provided you with both testimony and documentary evidence, and Charley's testimony confirms it. Now I'm at the end of my tether, and you're going to have to move your ass if you want my testimony in court."

Kip ignored this. "Let me ask you, since you know the territory, how many men are we going to need, and how should we come in?"

Jesse thought for a minute. "First of all, the best

cops in the world are not going to be enough; you're going to need soldiers, and I don't mean the Idaho National Guard. I would get the attorney general to go to the president and request crack troops, trained in urban tactics, street fighting."

"That's not going to be easy," Kip replied.

"You're going to have to do a lot of things simultaneously; you're going to have to put troop-carrying choppers on top of that mountain, establish a perimeter and hold it, to keep Coldwater and his people from getting into that underground system. Unless you can do that right off, a siege situation will develop and you'll look like idiots.

"Simultaneously, you're going to have to take Coldwater, Casey and Ruger; otherwise they'll rally their followers, and you'll have a pitched battle on your hands. Cut off the head of the snake, and the rest will be easier.

"Third, you're going to have to seal off the town to prevent anyone from getting in. Coldwater now has alliances with other groups, like the one that Charley Bottoms is in, and they might well come to his aid. Also, you can't let any of Coldwater's people get out. The nasty part of this is that, even if you capture the mountain and arrest Coldwater and his principal aides, you're going to have to round up the rest of the church congregation from wherever they are, and they may fight on an individual basis."

"How many people are we talking about?"

"Judging from what I've seen at the church, I'd estimate somewhere between five hundred and a thousand men, and three or four times that many women and children. They seem to have a lot of kids."

"Will the women fight?"

"My guess—and it's only a guess—is that Coldwater doesn't invest enough confidence in women to train them, and that you'll have to deal mostly with men and boys. I'd count on being opposed by teenagers with assault rifles, if I were you."

"What you're saying, essentially, is that, no matter how we do this, it's going to be a mess."

"I think you have a choice between a mess and a godawful, mind-boggling tragedy that could shake this country to its roots, that could make the attorney general, the president and the military look like bumbling idiots who can't be trusted to keep order. I think that if you screw this up you have the chance of having the biggest pitched battle in this country since the Civil War."

Kip was silent for a long moment. "We're going to need armor, aren't we?" he asked finally.

"You're going to need it, but how the hell will you get it here without alerting Coldwater? If you fill up the roads of northern Idaho with tanks and armored personnel carriers, it'll be on radio and television a long time before they can get here, and Coldwater is going to be ready. Your best bet is choppers, a lot of them, and enough men to mop up the town on a house-to-house basis."

"Is there an airport?"

"Yes. I've seen a sign pointing to it, but I've never been out there."

"You better take a look at it and get back to me."

"That's a good idea; I'll do it."

"How many troops are we talking about?"

"What was it they called Field Marshal Montgomery in World War Two? Something like Martini Monty, because he wouldn't attack unless he had a six-to-one advantage. I think you'll need that, if you fail to cut off the head of the serpent first."

"So we're talking five, six thousand men with full field gear, assault weapons, flak jackets, the works."

"I think you better bring in heavy weapons, too, in case Coldwater makes it to his fortress. You'll want to be at least as well armed as he is."

"Nothing like this has ever happened in the history of this country," Kip said, sounding disconsolate. "At least, not since the Civil War, as you pointed out. American troops carrying out a full-scale assault on an American town? It's insane."

"Maybe so, but comparatively speaking, it's even more insane to do nothing, not to mention negligent. Something else, Kip, and I hate to bring this up: you'd better be ready for casualties. This could be bloody, so you'd better have both the medics and the PR people on alert to handle the dead and wounded and to break it to the public."

"Barker wants to round up a thousand federal agents from the FBI, from the U.S. marshals, from Alcohol, Firearms and Tobacco and the Treasury Department and send them in there on the ground, in APCs, with bullhorns, telling everybody to surrender."

"You tell Barker for me that, if he does that,

he's going to lose half of them, and the other half will have to run, if they're not surrounded. *Then* he'll have to bring in the military to pull it out of the fire, and he'll have to destroy this town to win."

"I don't know if he's going to buy your recommendation."

"Then, Kip, you have to go over his head; you have to go outside the Justice Department, if necessary, straight to the White House."

"If I do that, they'll hang me out to dry, my career will be over, and I'll have a wife and two kids that I can't support."

"If you don't do it, Kip, the press will hang the whole thing on you and Barker. After all, you're the official contact with Bottoms and me. When this is over, and the president appoints a commission to investigate why such a huge tragedy occurred, you'll not only be hung out to dry, you might end up in prison, and where will your family be then?" Jesse was trying hard to scare Kip to death; he had the feeling that if he didn't, nothing was going to happen. He played his last card. "You tell Barker I'm going to give him fourteen days to act, and in force. If he doesn't, I'm getting out, and if I'm arrested by your people I'll see the whole business on the front page of the *New York Times* and the *Washington Post*. I'll write a book about it; I'll sell it for a TV movie; and I'll never *ever* shut up. Do I make myself clear?"

"Jesse, don't even think about doing that."

"I've already thought about it, Kip, and as God is my witness, I'll do it. Your only other choice is to get me a presidential pardon *now*, and let me and my family get out of here. That'll shut me up."

"Call me Monday."

Jesse had a desperate thought. "Wait a minute, Kip."

"Yeah?"

"I want to come to Washington and make a presentation to your people, the military and somebody from the White House."

"That's crazy, Jess; an escaped convict standing up in front of that kind of meeting? What kind of credibility would you have?"

"The credibility of an eyewitness who knows what he's talking about."

"How would you get out of town without Coldwater knowing about it?"

"This drop of yours that I sent the camera to—is that a real building supply company?"

"Yes, and a big one, out in College Park."

"Do this: call St. Clair Wood Products, ask them for their fax number, then fax Herman Muller a request for a presentation by a salesman. Say that you're looking for a major new source of plywood and chipboard, and you'd heard good things about his company. Tell him your need is urgent, and you want to see somebody right away; he'll send me. Coldwater will know about it, but it won't worry him, because I did the same thing in New York."

"I'll do what I can, Jess, but I can't promise. Barker will have to approve this, and I think it's unlikely. If Muller gets the fax, then you'll know you're on. I won't contact you again, just go directly to Nashua Building Supply, 1010 Parkway, in College Park, and ask for John Withers; he'll take it from there."

"Just remember that I might be followed."

"I'll plan for that."

"Something else, Kip; call somebody at the National Security Agency and get some satellite shots of the St. Clair area; they'll help me make my case, and they'll help you when you go in."

"I'll see about that."

"Thanks, Kip."

"Thank me when I make it work." Kip hung up.

47

On Sunday afternoon after lunch, Jenny was helping Carey with some homework. "I think I'll take a drive," Jesse said to her. "Will you join me?"

"We've got work to do here," Jenny said. "You go ahead."

Jesse got into the truck, drove to the center of town and set the odometer of his truck at zero. He drove east, past Wood Products for another mile, and turned right at the sign for St. Clair County Airport. He noted that the road was paved and broad, and after a couple of minutes he came to the airfield. An asphalt strip stretched out in both directions; there were some small T-hangars and one large hangar with an office shed attached and a fuel truck parked alongside. The doors to the large hangar were open, and Jesse saw someone working under the cowling of a Cessna single-engine airplane. He drove toward the hangar, and, as he approached, he saw that the man was Pat Casey.

Jesse got out of the truck. "Hey, Pat."

"Hey there, Jesse, what brings you out this way?"

"Just went for a Sunday drive, and I saw the sign. First time I've been out here."

"I'm out here every chance I get," Casey said. "Nothing I love better than flying."

"Pretty nice setup," Jesse said, pointing toward the runway. "What is it, about thirty-five hundred feet?"

"Forty-five hundred. You can get a corporate jet in here, no problem. You ever done any flying?"

"Yeah, I had about thirty hours in a Cessna 172 back in my hometown. That was seven, eight years ago. I soloed and did the required cross-country stuff, but never got my license." This was true, but it had been in Miami.

"I'm just finishing up on a little light maintenance here, cleaning the plugs. Want to do a little aerial sightseeing?"

"Sure, love to."

"Give me five minutes."

Jesse moved his truck so that Casey could get his airplane out of the hangar, and, when the police chief had finished his work, helped him roll the Cessna out onto the apron.

"Want to fly left seat?" Casey asked.

Jesse grinned. "That depends on if you can land it from the right seat, should you have to."

"I can. Hop in the left side, there."

Jesse got in, adjusted his seat and fastened his seatbelt; Casey climbed in beside him, cleared a double handful of charts and books off the copilot's seat, dumped them on the backseat and handed Jesse a headset. "Nice panel," Jesse said. "A lot better than the old 172 I learned in."

"Yeah, I got rid of the original avionics and put in a whole new panel last year. All King stuff, except for the GPS—that's from Trimble."

"That's Global Positioning System?" Jesse knew more about it than he let on.

"Right. It's satellite based and accurate to within about a hundred feet, I think. Wonderful navaid. All you have to do is enter the three-letter identifier of any airport, press this button twice, then set the course into the course deviation indicator right in front of you. Switch on the autopilot, and it'll fly you straight there." Casey produced a laminated sheet of paper. "I've already done a preflight inspection, so I'll read you the cockpit checklist; it'll all come back to you."

Jesse was surprised that it did come back. Soon they were taxiing to the end of the runway.

"This is a 182, which is larger and heavier on the controls than your 172 trainer, but not all that different. I'll work the radios for you." Casey announced their intention to take off on the local frequency. "Okay, let's go; set the trim in the green and put in fifteen degrees of flaps, that's the first notch; throttle all the way in."

Jesse slowly shoved in the throttle, and the airplane began to move down the runway. There was no wind, and the takeoff was uneventful. Jesse got the flaps up.

"Climb to four thousand feet," Casey said. "The

airport elevation is three thousand, so that'll put us a thousand feet above ground level."

Jesse did as he was told, then leveled off at four thousand feet.

"Okay, reduce power to, let's see, about twenty-three inches of manifold pressure and twenty-three hundred rpm. Good, now I'll lean the engine, and we're in business. Turn left to two-seven-zero, and hold your altitude."

Jesse made the turn without losing any altitude.

"Want to see St. Clair from above?"

"Sure."

"See the church steeple there? Head for that."

Jesse picked out the steeple rising above the trees, then saw the mountaintop just behind it. He headed for the church, then continued straight on toward the mountain.

"Look, there's Jack Gene's place," Casey said. "Head over there."

Jesse turned the airplane slightly, and soon the snowy swath of Coldwater's garden hove into view.

"There's Jack Gene in the garden," Casey said, smiling. "Let's do a low pass over his house. Drop down a couple hundred feet, and when you get over the house, make a thirty-degree turn to three-six-zero."

Jesse pushed forward slightly on the yoke and the airplane began a descent and picked up airspeed. He could see the figure in the garden now; he was sitting on a bench and seemed to be holding a book.

"Here we go, start your turn," Casey said.

Jesse looked at the attitude indicator and picked out the thirty-degree mark, then rolled the airplane to the right.

"You're losing altitude," Casey warned.

Jesse hauled back on the yoke and the airplane began to climb again.

"Now roll out level for a minute and then turn left to two-seven-zero."

Jesse leveled the wings momentarily, then turned left. As he rolled out again on the westerly heading, he looked to his left and saw that he was level with the mountaintop and only about three hundred yards away from it. Then he saw something else: around fifty feet down from the mountaintop there was an opening in the brush, and, set into the mountainside, a large round opening with a grate over it.

"Let's circumnavigate the mountain, now," Casey said. "Just fly right around it, and we'll head back to the airport."

Jesse continued around the mountain, and he saw two more of the grates. Somebody came running out of one of the small buildings on top and trained binoculars on the airplane.

Casey took the copilot's yoke and wagged the wings. "They know my airplane," he said. "Anybody else would get a stinger up his ass, flying this close to the mountain."

Jesse continued around the mountain and, on the town side, which was sheer cliffs, he saw two more grates.

"Now fly a heading of zero-niner-zero until

you see the field. That'll put you on a downwind for runway two-seven."

The field appeared after a couple of minutes, and Jesse, following Casey's instructions, entered a right downwind for the runway, descending slowly, while Casey announced their intentions over the radio. Jesse turned base, then turned onto the final approach.

"You're a little high," Casey said. "Reduce power a good bit. That's right, now she'll fly you right down to the threshold."

Jesse pulled back on the throttle, and the airplane settled toward the end of the runway.

"Start your flare, now, and reduce power even more. You want an airspeed of seventy knots over the numbers. Here we go, flare some more, now."

Jesse hauled back on the yoke, the stall horn went off, and the airplane struck the runway solidly. "Sorry about that, Pat."

"That was just a nice firm landing," Casey said, laughing. "You just fell about the last five feet."

Jesse taxied back to the hangar, and Casey showed him the shutdown procedure.

"Pat, that was a real treat; thank you."

"You did real good, Jesse; you must have had a pretty good instructor."

"Fellow by the name of Floyd; a real old-timer with about ten thousand hours."

"Those guys are the best. I've got my instructor's ticket; you want to start working on your license again? Cost you eighty bucks an hour for the aircraft and fuel; I'm free."

"That's a terrific offer, Pat; I'd really like that."

"Next Sunday, same time?"

"You bet."

"I'll get you the instruction book and a new logbook."

"Can I borrow your pilot's operating handbook until next week? I'd like to read up on the operating speeds and all that."

"Good idea." Casey reached into the cockpit and handed him a thick notebook.

"Thanks, see you next Sunday," Jesse said.

"Hey, Jimmy!" Casey called to a man near the fuel truck. "Top her off, will you? Just the right tank."

Jesse got back into his truck and drove off. He checked the speedometer for distance, then drove home. He'd learned a lot more than he'd expected to on a Sunday afternoon.

That night, Jesse had the dream again. He was walking down Fifth Avenue in New York, and he saw the little girl he had taken for his own Carrie. He had decided it wasn't Carrie, and this was where the dream had stopped. Only this time it continued. It was if they were all in slow motion. The woman bent over and pointed to something in the shop, as Jesse watched through the window, and she seemed terribly familiar. Then she straightened up, and Jesse could see for the first time that, even under the overcoat, the woman was pregnant. He jerked awake, this time with the scene fixed in his mind. Then he remembered something Kip had said, about how he would take care of his family if he lost his job.

Jesse sat very still, hardly daring to breathe, lest the dream should leave him. Machinery in his mind turned, like the tumblers in a safe, and the combination clicked.

Doors swung open. He fell back on the pillow, exhausted from his insight.

48

The fax arrived on Tuesday morning. Jesse saw it spat from the machine, and he resisted walking over there. The secretary took the document from the machine, glanced at it and took it into Herman Muller's office.

Muller read the letter, then read it again, then picked up the phone and dialed a number. He spoke for some minutes, nodding a lot, then hung up and walked into Jesse's office.

"Jesse, I've had a fax from a company in Maryland that's looking for a new supplier. I called the fellow—Withers, his name is—and it looks like he's hot to trot. You think you could fly east the next day or two and make the same presentation to him you made to the folks in New York?"

"I'd be glad to, Herman."

Muller handed him the fax. "Here's the letter; you work it out with Withers about when you'll meet." He went back to his office.

Jesse went out to the receptionist. "Agnes, could you check on a flight schedule for me tomorrow from Spokane to Washington D.C. National Airport?"

"Sure, Jesse. You're becoming the real jet-setter, aren't you?"

"That's right; I'm meeting Elizabeth Taylor there."

When Jesse had the schedule on his desk he picked up the phone, called Nashua Building Supply and asked for John Withers.

"Mr. Withers, this is Jesse Barron at St. Clair Wood Products. My boss, Herman Muller, said you'd like to get together and talk about plywood and chipboard."

"That's right, Mr. Barron," Withers said, "and we're kind of in a hurry. When do you think you could get to College Park?"

"You're right near Washington, aren't you?"

"Yep. Just north of there. I could meet you at National Airport."

"Tell you what; I'm looking at a schedule that would get me into Washington early tomorrow evening. How about we meet at your office the following morning."

"Ten o'clock sharp?"

"That's fine with me. Your address is on your letterhead."

"Right, any map of the area will show you where we are. We're not far from the University of Maryland."

"If I get lost I'll call you."

"See you Thursday morning," Withers said.

* * *

Jesse stayed late at the office, working at the computer. He wrote a document of some twenty pages, then printed out half a dozen copies. He put each copy into a Federal Express envelope, made some phone calls to information in New York, Washington, Los Angeles, Atlanta, Miami and Seattle, then filled out the FedEx forms and inserted one into the plastic holder of each envelope. He put them into his briefcase, locked up the office and went home.

At dawn the next morning they were driving toward Spokane.

"We can talk," Jesse said. "I've been over this truck with a fine-toothed comb and it's not bugged."

"Why am I driving you to the airport?" Jenny asked.

"If anybody asks, your car doesn't have four-wheel drive, and you wanted the pickup to use if it snows. It's supposed to snow."

"Okay, I understand. What are all these envelopes on the front seat between us?"

"They're Federal Express packages. I'm going to call you when I get to my hotel, and again before I leave the hotel the next morning. I'll just ask how you're doing and if you and Carey are okay; innocuous stuff like that. Don't talk about anything important. After that, if I fail to call you every twelve hours, or if I say the words, 'I love you very dearly,' on the phone, I want you to go straight to the Federal Express substation in town and hand them these packages. They're already addressed and the cost will be billed to Wood Products' account."

"Why do you want me to do this?"

Jesse told her, at length, what he was planning.

She didn't say anything for a long time, then she sighed. "Are you sure there's no other way to do it?"

"I can't think of another one."

"All right, that's good enough for me. I'll get Carey ready. This is what I'll tell her." She spelled out a story.

"I like that; it should do the job."

"When will we leave St. Clair?"

"As soon as I possibly can after I get back. A lot depends on what happens while I'm gone."

"What if this doesn't work? What if it all goes wrong and you can't come back?"

"If that happens, if you don't hear from me during any twelve-hour period, I want you to drive the truck into your garage, and crawl underneath it. There's a safe welded to the chassis; it'll be covered with mud and ice, so you'll have to clean it off before you can open it." He told her the combination and asked her to repeat it to him. "Good, now don't forget it; repeat it to yourself a lot.

"Inside the safe are several things: there are passports for you and Carey; there is a little over fifty thousand dollars in cash; and there is a pistol. I want you to take Carey, and, in the dead of night, take some clothes, get into the truck and drive to Seattle. Find a downtown parking garage and leave the truck there, then find a travel agent. There are nonstop flights from Seattle to Tokyo; make two reservations and pay for them in cash. Then go to a bank; buy ten thousand dollars in traveler's checks, keep a couple of thousand in cash, then buy a cashier's check with the remainder of the money. Go to the airport, get on the plane and fly to Tokyo. When you arrive there, don't leave the airport; buy two tickets on the next flight to Hong Kong, then make room reservations at the Peninsular Hotel for seven nights. When you get to Hong Kong, check in, get some sleep and do some sightseeing. If I am still free, I'll meet you in Hong Kong within the week or I'll call you with other instructions. If you haven't heard from me in a week, fly to Sydney, Australia, and check into the Harbour Hotel.

"An old friend of mine tends bar in the hotel; his name is Arthur Simpson, but everybody calls him Bluey. Call or see him once a week; I'll be in touch with him. If he tells you I'm in prison, then it's time to forget about me, because I'll be there a long time. Bluey will help you get work papers and find a job and a place to live. Start a new life."

"Without you?"

"If I'm free, I'll be with you eventually; if I'm not, I won't be, and either way, Bluey will hear about it. Your passports are real, so you don't have to worry about that; you can renew them at the embassy when they expire. After a year or two, it should be safe to come back to this country, if that's what you want. I'd feel better if you stayed in Australia."

"What's the gun in the safe for?"

"That's to use on anybody who tries to keep you from leaving St. Clair. If Pat Casey or any of his people follows you and tries to take you back, shoot him where he stands. I take it you know how to fire a pistol?"

"Everybody in St. Clair knows how; we learned as children."

"If you can get out of town, even if you have to kill somebody doing it, I don't think they'll send out a police alert for you; you have too much of a story to tell, and if you are arrested, don't hesitate to tell it. The money will buy you a lawyer, and you won't be convicted for shooting somebody who tried to make a prisoner of you. And remember, throw the gun into the nearest trash can before you go into the airport."

Jesse pulled up at the airport curbside check-in. He switched off the engine and turned to her. "Jenny, you're a strong person; I know you can do this, all of it."

"I can if you want me to," she said.

"It's the best I can do for you." He took her in his arms and held her for a moment, telling her that he loved her, then he got out of the truck. "I hope I'll be back," he said, then he turned and walked into the terminal.

49

Jesse arrived at Washington National at seven in the evening. In the gift shop he bought a book of large-scale maps of Washington and its suburbs, then rented a car and drove into the city. He checked into the Watergate Hotel, then phoned Jenny.

"Hi, I made it safely."

"Glad to hear it; everything all right?"

"Everything's fine; my appointment's at ten in the morning. If we finish by noon or so, I can make a three o'clock airplane home. I'll call you and let you know what plane I'm on."

"I'll meet you in Spokane."

"Did it snow?"

"Yes, and it's still snowing; we've had eight or nine inches, and they say we'll have a foot."

"I'm glad you kept the pickup, then. Well, I'd better get a bite to eat and some sleep; I'll talk to you tomorrow."

"I love you."

"You, too; say goodnight to Carey for me."

He hung up, then ordered dinner from room service. While he waited for it to arrive, he picked up a Washington phone directory, but could not find what he wanted. He had more luck with the information operator.

He studied his maps for a few minutes, then went downstairs and asked for his car. He forced himself to drive slowly, normally, not to get excited. He drove into northwest Washington and found Argyle Terrace, driving slowly until he spotted the house number. He drove to the end of the block, turned around, drove back down the street and parked a couple of houses away. His view was good. He could see the whole front of the house and one side, and it appeared that the kitchen was on the back corner. The lights were on there, and he could see a woman moving about, probably cleaning up after dinner.

When he had seen enough, he drove back to the Watergate and tried to watch a movie on television, but he couldn't concentrate. He switched it off and lay in the bed, planning the next day to the nth degree, rehearsing his actions. It was past two when he finally fell asleep.

He found Nashua Building Supply with no difficulty, across the road from the university, as Withers had said. It did not seem that he had been followed. He parked in front and went into the huge, hangarlike building. He was shown to an office constructed in the rear of the building and was greeted by John Withers, who shook his hand and closed the office door behind him.

"This way," Withers said, leading him to another door, which opened to the outside at the rear of the building.

A plain sedan was waiting, with only a driver inside. Jesse recognized him as the man who had followed him in San Francisco.

"We've only got a two-minute drive," the man said. "Kip has arranged for a room at the university. Get your head down."

Jesse was led into a red brick building and down a hallway to a room where another man in a suit stood guard. The man rapped on the door, and Kip Fuller stepped out into the hallway.

"Come over here a minute," Kip said, drawing Jesse away from the other two men. "There are some things I have to say to you before we go into that room."

"Shoot," Jesse replied.

"First of all, the people in there are Barker; an assistant attorney general with responsibility for oversight of Justice Department law enforcement agencies, reporting directly to the AG; an army brigadier general who oversees all unconventional warfare units for the Pentagon; and a bird colonel, who is a military adviser to the National Security Council, and who has the ear of the president. Does that sound like who you wanted?"

"It certainly does."

"Now listen; I have not reported your threat of 'move in two weeks or exposure' to Barker, and it's extremely important that you make no threats while you are in that room. These people are here to listen to you make your case, and they're your best chance of getting this done the way you want it done."

"I understand."

"Okay, follow me. By the way, I won't be making any introductions; they'll think you don't know who they are."

"Right." Jesse followed Kip into the room. The seats were arranged on steeply pitched tiers, and each desk had its own lamp. The shades were drawn and the room was lit by those lamps and by floodlights that illuminated the blackboard area, where satellite photographs of St. Clair and the surrounding area were mounted. The photographs that Jesse had himself taken were there, too, and he guessed that they had been computer enhanced. He followed Kip to the lectern.

"Gentlemen," Kip said, halting their conversation, "I'd like to introduce Jesse Warden. Jesse, why don't you begin at the beginning; explain who you are and how you came to be in St. Clair."

"Good morning, gentlemen," Jesse said, taking a deep breath and trying to calm a sudden attack of stage fright. "My name, as Mr. Fuller has said, is Jesse Warden. I was formerly an agent of the Drug Enforcement Agency, attached to the South Florida Task Force and specializing in undercover work. My commander at that time was Mr. Barker, and Mr. Fuller was my colleague in the office.

"Just over two years ago, I was arrested and charged with the theft of half a million dollars from the office evidence locker and the murder of my partner, whose body was found in the trunk of my car, along with the money."

There was the slightest stirring among his audience.

"I was innocent of both charges, but I was convicted of the murder of a federal official and theft of government property; I was given a life sentence and incarcerated in the Atlanta Federal Penitentiary. After serving fourteen months there I was released in the custody of Mr. Barker and Mr. Fuller and offered a presidential pardon, if I would assist in the conviction of the head of a religious cult and his two chief aides, who were rumored to be amassing large numbers of weapons and other materiel in a small town in the Idaho panhandle."

Barker was glowering at him; apparently, he had not expected any mention of the pardon.

Jesse took the group step by step through his infiltration of the First Church of the Aryan Universe, and finally, through a complete description of what he had seen in Coldwater's underground fortifications. His audience maintained a dead silence until he had finished, and the silence continued for another half a minute thereafter.

Finally, the man who Jesse assumed to be the assistant AG spoke. "Mr. Warden, have you determined what Coldwater's intentions are?"

"No, sir, I haven't, and I have the feeling that I won't know until it's too late to do anything about it. All I can tell you is that he's planning something that might make things so hot for him and his followers that he would have to retreat underground."

"Do you think Coldwater is insane?"

"I have no qualifications in that sphere; I can only give you my personal impression of the man. There are times when I think he's nutty as a fruitcake, but he is always very self-possessed and seems to always know exactly what he is doing. I think he certainly has very pronounced megalomaniacal tendencies, but I'm not sure whether that qualifies as insanity."

"Do you think he is fully capable of using this . . . facility he has built?"

"I have the very strong impression that he is determined to do so. Whether it will be in a day or a year, I cannot tell you."

The man who Jesse thought was the brigadier general spoke up. "For a start, why can't a detachment of federal officers in plain clothes simply drive up to Coldwater's house and arrest him?"

Jesse suppressed a wild laugh. "Sir, that would be about as easy as driving through the White House gates and arresting the president of the United States. The very first thing that must be done is to take the mountaintop and the reinforced facilities there, so that Coldwater cannot bring his people inside and button it down tight."

"I'd be interested in hearing how you think that could be done," the general said. "I mean, after seeing these satshots of the place, I'd really like your suggestions."

"I'm not a military man, sir, but if it were up to me I'd go at it in three ways: first, I'd infiltrate a large armed contingent at night three or four miles north of the mountain and have them approach it on foot and scale the sides; second, I'd send a large truck or two, filled with troops and disguised in some way, right up the road to the top and try ramming the gates; third, I'd send helicopters, armed with armor-penetrating weapons to attack the smaller structures on top, and follow immediately with many troop-carrying choppers. There are, of course, drawbacks to each of these methods."

"And what are the drawbacks?" the general asked.

"First, it would not surprise me to learn that Coldwater has placed some sort of sensors in the woods to the north to pick up anyone on foot, and I know that there are machine-gun emplacements on all sides for the purposes of repelling infantry; second, I think the chances of trucks getting up the road undetected and breaking open the gates are no better than fifty-fifty; and third, I had a look at the top of the mountain in a light airplane last Sunday, and I was told that there were stinger missiles in place that would take out any approaching aircraft. You're likely to lose some choppers."

Jesse turned back to the satellite photographs. "I think, also, that in any first strike, you should take the police station, here, which is the security center; the telephone company, here; and I think you should cut the high voltage power line that brings in the town's electricity from the north, or get the power company to. That would do a lot to cut or, at least, confuse their communications with Coldwater and his with his people."

"You know," the general said, "if this were a proper war, I would just bombard that place with heavy artillery until there was nothing left standing, then walk in."

"I think you can see that that is impossible in this situation," Jesse said.

"Yes, I can see that," the general said wearily.

Jesse spoke up again, pointing to the photographs. "Coldwater lives here, Casey here and Ruger here. If you can knock out power, security and telephones simultaneously with capturing Coldwater, Casey and Ruger, your battle would be over, except for the mopping up. That, of course, could be nasty."

"It's all going to be nasty," the general said quietly.

There were other questions for nearly an hour, then the meeting broke up. The general approached the lectern and stuck out his hand. "You're a brave man," he said. "I'm glad I'm not in your shoes." He turned to Barker. "Dan, we'll get back to you first thing in the morning with some kind of rough plan."

Barker nodded and shook the general's hand. "Look forward to hearing from you."

The three visitors left, and Barker motioned for Jesse to take a seat. "I've got some questions for you, Jesse."

"All right," Jesse said. "Let's make it quick; I've got a three o'clock flight from Dulles Airport to make."

"When did you first meet Charley Bottoms?" Barker asked.

Jesse saw where this was going. "I saw him around the yard on those rare occasions when I wasn't in solitary," he said. "I never spoke to him until the day Kip came to get me out. He came to my punishment cell and said he wanted me to join up with the Aryan Nation crowd in the joint, said they'd protect me from the other cons. He offered to beat me to death if I turned him down."

"And when did you next see him?" Barker asked.

"Last week, when he turned up at a meeting at Coldwater's house. We drove up to the top of the mountain together, and he told me you'd sprung him right after me. That's the sum total of our contact."

Kip spoke up. "I've spoken with Bottoms about this, and he confirms everything Jesse has said." He turned toward Jesse. "I know this wasn't part of our deal, but do you think you could take out Coldwater prior to our going in?"

"The chances of my getting at him and staying alive would be slim," Jesse said. "And you're right, that's not part of my deal. What I want to know, Kip, Dan, is are you going to stick by our deal?"

Barker glowered at him again. "You'll get the pardon when we've cleaned out this nest of maniacs, and not before. And I'll expect you to do whatever you're told to do when we go in."

Before Jesse could speak, Kip held out a warning hand. "Not now, Jess; we'll talk about it later."

Jesse shook Kip's hand, then, ignoring Barker, went back to his car and drove south. But he didn't head for Dulles Airport, or, for that matter, for National.

50

Jesse drove slowly down Argyle Terrace, then back again, casing the house. In daylight he could see a fenced backyard behind the place, and as he watched, a woman passed through the kitchen and out the back door.

He quickly parked the car and walked to the front door. Glancing up and down the street, he pretended to ring the doorbell, then turned the knob; the door was unlocked. He walked into a large entrance hall and looked around; somewhere a television set was on. He turned left and walked through the dining room and into the kitchen. A coffee pot sat on a warmer, and he poured himself a cup and sat down at the kitchen table. He could hear voices from out back. A soap opera was on television; he hated the music that played constantly during the programs. It was good coffee.

After a few minutes, he heard a foot scrape on the back steps, and she walked into the kitchen.

"Hello, Arlene," he said.

She froze, staring at him, saying nothing.

"It's Jesse Warden," he said. "I'm sorry I don't look quite the same as I did in my Miami days."

Her shoulders relaxed, but her face remained wary. "Why are you here?" she asked, glancing at the wall phone.

"We'll call Kip in a few minutes," he said soothingly. "Now pour yourself a cup of coffee and have a seat. Let's talk."

She ignored the coffee but sat down at the table.

"It's been a while," he said. "What, two and a half, three years?"

"About that," she managed to whisper. "Why are you here, Jesse?"

"I want to see her. I want you to call her in from the backyard, tell her there's a friend here. After we've visited for a few minutes, we'll call Kip, then I'll leave."

She didn't move.

"You've nothing to fear from me, Arlene; I'm not here to hurt you. Call her from the door, please; don't go out into the yard."

Reluctantly, she rose and opened the back door. "Carrie, please come inside; you have a visitor."

"An old friend," Jesse said.

"It's an old friend, Carrie."

Jesse was suddenly filled with panic. She wouldn't know him, would scream at the sight of his battered face.

The little girl came into the kitchen, her cheeks red with the cold, her eyes bright. "Who is it, Aunt Arlene?" she asked. Then she saw Jesse.

"Hello, Rabbit," he said. Only he had ever called her that.

She blinked, staring at him. "Are you my daddy?" she asked, finally.

"I sure am," Jesse said. "And I'm so very glad to see you."

She came closer to him, gazing into his face. "You look different," she said.

"I know; I had an accident, but I'm fine now."

Suddenly, she rushed at him, threw her arms around him, laughing. "Oh, Daddy!" she cried. "Aunt Arlene and Uncle Kip told me you had gone to heaven."

"They were wrong," he whispered into her ear. "I'm right here with you, my Rabbit." He held her back and looked at her. "You've grown so; you're a big girl, now."

"I'm going to be six next month," she said.

"I know, sweetheart, and I'm going to get you a wonderful present. Six is a very important birthday; you'll be going to school in the fall."

"Where's Mommy?" she asked. "They said she was in heaven, too."

"She is in heaven, sweetheart, but she looks down on you, and she knows what a wonderful little girl you are." He was having trouble maintaining his composure; his throat was tightening up.

"I have a new little cousin," Carrie said. "He's in the backyard in the stroller. Would you like to see him?"

"I would in just a minute, Rabbit. Why don't

you go and make sure he's all right, and Aunt Arlene and I will be out in a few minutes."

She gave him a big kiss on the cheek. "Don't be long," she said, then ran out the back door.

"Jesse, I want you to understand," Arlene said. "We never set out to steal Carrie from you; we thought you would spend the rest of your life in prison. We couldn't bear the thought of Carrie being put up for adoption; Kip and I both thought it was better that you didn't know where she was."

"I believe you, Arlene," Jesse said. "But you understand, things are different now."

"Are they so very different, Jesse? Kip hasn't told me in any detail what you're doing, but it was my distinct impression that your life is constantly in danger. Do you think you're ready to make a home for Carrie?"

"Arlene, my life was constantly in danger when I was working undercover in Miami, and yes, I think I'm ready to make a home for Carrie. I've remarried, and she'll have a sister."

"I don't know how to argue with you," she said. "Carrie has missed you so much. She still talks about you all the time."

"Thanks for telling me that," Jesse replied. "Now, I don't have much time, and I'd better call Kip." He went to the wall phone and dialed the office number.

"She would never call us Mommy and Daddy," Arlene said quietly, and a tear ran down her cheek.

"This is Fuller," Kip said.

"Kip, it's Jesse."

"Did you miss your plane?"

"I'm afraid so; I had another stop to make."

"Another stop?"

"I'm at your house."

Kip made a sort of strangling noise before he could speak. "Jesse, if you lay a hand on any of them, I swear I'll have you back in jail today."

"Kip, Kip; there's no need for that. Everything is going to be all right."

"What do you want, Jesse?"

"It's very simple; I want my little girl."

"Jesse, you can't; we've adopted her, and it's all perfectly legal."

"Kip, take a couple of deep breaths, and listen to me."

"Let me speak to Arlene."

Jesse looked at the phone and saw a speaker button; he pressed it. "Arlene is right here," he said.

Arlene stepped closer to the phone. "I'm here, Kip; we're all right. He's seen Carrie; she knew him."

"I'm sorry he's put you through this, honey," Kip said.

Jesse spoke up. "I'm going to try to make this as easy for everybody as I can, Kip. I'm going to explain this to you and Arlene, so please listen."

"I'm listening," Kip said.

"And Kip, it would be a very grave error, bad for everybody, if you called the police."

"I haven't called anybody, Jesse; tell me what you want."

"This is how it's going to be: Carrie and I are

going to leave the house in just a minute. Everything is going to be calm and orderly, and there won't be any fuss."

"Jesse, you can't do this," Kip said. "You'll put her in very serious danger."

"No, I won't do that, believe me, Kip; she'll be very safe with me and her new mother."

"Oh, God," Kip moaned.

"Arlene is taking this better than you are; now settle down and listen to me."

"I'm listening."

"First of all, I'm very grateful to both of you for taking such good care of Carrie. Arlene has explained your reasons for not telling me, and I accept them. Because I'm grateful, I'm going to try and forget that you knew Barker framed me—"

"Jesse, I couldn't prove it."

"Kip, listen to me. Barker was the only one who could have done it; you knew that, and Barker knows you know; that's why he's letting you run this show. I know you felt badly about it, and that's why you got me out of prison."

"I had no evidence, Jesse. If I had, I'd have nailed him."

"I believe you, Kip."

Arlene spoke up. "I'm going upstairs and pack some things for Carrie." She left the room.

"Daddy!" Carrie called from the backyard. "Come and see the baby!"

Jesse cracked the door. "I'll be there in just a minute, Rabbit!" He picked up the telephone receiver. "Kip, listen very carefully, because this is the last time you and I are going to discuss Carrie. She's coming with me, now, and you're going to think up something to tell the neighbors—the adoption went wrong, something like that."

"Jesse, you can't go on the run with Carrie," Kip moaned.

"I'm not going on the run," Jesse said. "I'm going back to St. Clair with Carrie, and now I'm going to explain to you why you aren't going to do the slightest thing to stop me or get her back."

"I'm listening."

"You remember the threat I made to Barker?"

"Yes."

"I'm withdrawing that; I'm going back to St. Clair and help you nail Coldwater, even though that exceeds our agreement. But if you make the slightest difficulty for me with regard to Carrie, I'll blow the whole thing sky high. I've already made arrangements to do that, unless I periodically make certain phone calls. If, for any reason, I'm unable to make those calls, half the newspapers in the country will receive a certain information packet containing irrefutable proof of what you're up to. If you make a move on me, Coldwater will immediately know everything, and you know what that means."

"I know," Kip said weakly.

"Even if you take Coldwater cleanly and shut down his operation, you still won't want the papers to know about me, Kip. You'd never be able to explain to the press why you had a convicted murderer released from prison, unless you exonerated me, and Barker can't let you do that, because he knows he'd go down. Do you understand me?"

"I understand."

"There's more than your career at stake, here, Kip; there's your life. If you make a move on me or Carrie, I'll find you, and I'll kill you, and you know I can do it."

"I know, Jesse."

"You still have a chance to be a hero in the department, Kip; arrange for Justice to forget about me, and I'll help you be a hero."

"I'll do as you say, Jesse."

"When this is over, my family and I are going to disappear."

"I'll get you in the witness protection program," Kip said.

"I don't want that; I'll make my own life, but you and the federal government are going to have to forget I ever existed."

"I'll see to it," Kip said.

"I want my fingerprint and criminal records destroyed."

"I'll do it."

"I don't want any problems from Barker."

"I can handle Barker."

"If he gives you a hard time about me, tell him I'll kill him, too. He understands that sort of threat."

"Barker won't be a problem; I won't let him."

Arlene came back into the room carrying a small suitcase and a teddy bear.

"Goodbye, Kip; I'll call you from St. Clair."

"Goodbye, Jess; don't let anything happen to Carrie."

"She'll be fine, I promise you."

Arlene set Carrie's things on the kitchen table. "She won't go anywhere without the bear," she said.

Jesse nodded. He'd given her the bear when she was no more than an infant. He stepped out the kitchen door and walked to where Carrie was waiting with the baby.

"Isn't he beautiful?" Carrie said.

Jesse knelt next to the stroller. "He certainly is," he said. "And do you know something? You've got more than a new cousin; you've got a new sister."

Carrie's eyes widened. "I have? Where is she?"

"You're coming home with me, and I'll tell you all about her on the way," Jesse said, scooping up his daughter in his arms.

In the kitchen he gave her the teddy bear, picked up her suitcase and turned to Arlene Fuller. "Thank you," he said, then he walked out of the house with his daughter.

51

Jesse sweated National airport, even though he
had told Kip he was leaving from Dulles. He
turned in his rent-a-car and, with Carrie in tow,
went to the airline counter and bought her a one-
way ticket to Spokane, all the while sweeping the
area with his eyes. The ticket bought, he went to
a phone and called Jenny.

"Hi, everything's fine; I'm making the plane
all right."

"Good, I'll meet you in Spokane."

"How's Carey?"

"She's just fine, and she's looking forward
to . . . seeing you. No problems at all?"

"Not a one; I think I sold some major plywood
this morning."

"See you tonight."

Jesse had a few minutes before the flight, so he
made a tour of the airport shops with Carrie,
checking each window for the reflection of a tail.
By the time they reached their gate, Jesse's heart
was pounding. The boarding call asked for people

with small children first, so he was able to sit on the plane and scan the face of each person who passed them. Any one of half a dozen business-men fit the type he was looking for, but none of them showed the slightest interest in a man and a little girl.

Carrie was asleep before the airplane left the ground, and as soon as the seatbelt sign went off, Jesse ordered a double bourbon. He needed it. He stroked the little head on a pillow in his lap and tried not to think of the future. For the next few days he must live entirely in the present and not be distracted by dreams of yet another new life.

Halfway home, Carrie woke up. She stared into her father's eyes. "Where have you been?" she asked. "If you weren't in heaven, why didn't you come get me?"

"Rabbit, believe me, I came the first minute I could. When Uncle Kip and Aunt Arlene took you to Washington, they didn't tell me, so I had to look for you for a real long time."

"Oh," she said.

"Were they nice to you?"

"Oh, yes; they gave me lots of toys and things, but I wouldn't call Aunt Arlene mommy, and she didn't like that."

"You did the right thing, sweetheart," he said. "Now I have some wonderful news for you."

"Oh, tell me, tell me!"

"You remember I told you I had found you a sister?"

"Yes, where is she?"

"We're going to a town called St. Clair, and she's waiting for you there. It'll be real late when we get home, and she'll be asleep, but you'll meet her in the morning."

"Is her mommy in heaven, too?"

"No, her mommy is meeting us at the airport, and I think you're going to love her a lot. She's going to be your new mommy."

Carrie's eyes widened. "I didn't know you could have two mommies."

"When your first mommy goes to heaven, then your daddy can find you a new mommy."

"And you found me a new one?"

"I sure did, and she's wonderful."

"What's her name?"

"Her name is Jenny."

"Do I have to call her mommy?"

"Not unless you want to. It would make her very happy if you did, though."

"Did you and Jenny get married?"

"Yes, we did."

"Well, I guess she's my new mommy, then, isn't she?"

"Yes, she is."

"And I won't live with Aunt Arlene and Uncle Kip anymore?"

"No, you'll live with your new family."

"Will I ever see Aunt Arlene and Uncle Kip again?"

"Maybe, but not for a long, long time."

"Will it make them sad?"

"Yes, they'll miss you a lot, but they have the new baby to love."

"That's true," Carrie said, nodding gravely. "They won't be all by themselves." Soon she was asleep again.

Jesse carried the little girl, still sleeping, off the airplane, and Jenny was at the gate to meet them.

"I'll introduce you to your new daughter," he said, "if she ever wakes up."

"Plenty of time for that," Jenny said. "What have you told her?"

"I've told her about you and Carey."

"What are we going to do about the names? They sound just alike."

"I haven't a clue."

When they had left the airport and were driving toward St. Clair Jesse asked, "What did you tell Carey about us?"

"I've told her that you had a daughter by your first marriage. She immediately asked if all your daughters weren't killed in the car wreck, but I told her one of them wasn't in the car with you, and she had been living with friends in another town until you were ready to bring her to St. Clair."

"Do you think she'll tell anyone at school?"

"I've told her it's a big secret for the time being, and when she asked me why, I told her that was a secret, too. She seemed to accept that."

"Do you think she'll turn us in at school?"

"The school has warped some of Carey's attitudes, and we're going to have to work to help her get over that. But she and I have a bond that the school hasn't been able to penetrate, and if she tells me she'll keep the secret, then she will. You can depend on that."

Jesse hoped she was right.

They arrived at home in St. Clair after two in the morning, and Jesse carried the luggage into the house first, making sure they were not being watched.

They tucked Carrie into bed, and then Jesse spent another two hours going over the whole house, looking for bugs. It was after four when he finally went to bed.

"Did you find anything?" Jenny asked.

"There were two: one in the living room and one in the kitchen. I've disabled the one in the kitchen, so be sure and keep Carrie out of the living room when I'm away from the house."

Jenny snuggled up close. "She's a beautiful child. I'm going to love her, I know it."

"And she's going to love you," Jesse said.

52

Jesse arrived at the office the following morning to find a fax from Nashua Building Supply waiting, placing a large order for plywood. It was good cover, and he was grateful to Kip for that. He waited until everyone had left for lunch before calling Kip.

"How's Carrie?" Kip asked immediately, and there was pain in his voice.

"She's very well. She slept through most of the flight and all of the ride from the airport. She met her new mother and sister this morning, and she seemed very happy with them. But I don't want to talk about Carrie again."

Kip was suddenly all business. "All right. What's up?"

"You remember how you got the Zippo camera to me?"

"Yes."

"Can the same man deliver another package to me?"

"Sure; what do you want?"

"A list of things; got a pencil?"

"Shoot."

"I want a pound of plastic explosive and half a dozen detonators and timers, and an explosives mat about four feet square."

"What are you going to do with all that?"

"You're just going to have to trust me, Kip."

"All right, what else?"

"A couple of hand grenades; something incendiary. I also want a light machine gun and half a dozen clips of ammunition. And I want some night goggles, the lightest you can find."

"When do you need it?"

"Tomorrow night."

"I think I can do that. Where do you want it delivered?"

"On the road going east from St. Clair, just beyond the Wood Products plant, there's a bridge over a creek. Have him use duct tape to fix the package in the supports under the bridge. Tell him to make sure it can't be seen, except from underneath. Tell him after he makes the delivery to fix a twelve-inch strip of duct tape to the northwest end of the bridge, so that it can be easily seen from the road, as a signal that the goods are there."

"I'll get right on it. You sure you don't want to tell me what's going on?"

"I'm sure; do you have a date for your entry into St. Clair yet?"

"The army delivered a preliminary plan this morning, and we're still going over it. My best guess would be that the earliest possible time would be seven days; the latest, ten days."

"I'm going to try to make it easier for them," Jesse said.

"I'll tell them."

"I'll try to call you every day from now until you go in," Jesse said. "It's critically important that I know exactly what the plan is and when it begins. I can't be of any help to you unless I know that."

"I'll see that you're fully briefed. Do you think you could make a meet with somebody to go over the details?"

Jesse thought for a minute. "I doubt it; it could be too dangerous at this stage of the game. I'll think about it, though, and let you know."

"As you wish; I just want you to know everything we know."

"Thanks, but we'll probably have to do it on the phone." He said goodbye and broke the connection, and not a moment too soon. An instant after he had concealed the phone in his lunchbox, Pat Casey appeared in the reception room, carrying a red zippered briefcase.

Jesse left his office and greeted the police chief.

"Hear you've been out of town," Casey said.

"Just overnight; we had a call from a big building supply company in Maryland who'd heard about us, so I went out there and made my pitch. Come on in the office." He led Casey inside, closed the door and handed him the fax from Nashua. "Here's the result."

"Hey, good going," Casey said. "Jack Gene will be pleased to hear it. You making any progress on getting into Muller's computer ledgers?"

"Not yet, but I've hardly been in the office since we discussed it. I think the best way is for me just to ask Muller if I can see the books."

"Is there no other way?"

"His computer password is in his head; I don't know how else to get it."

"Use your own judgment, then; all he can say is no."

"The other way is to try to figure out what the password is, but that's a real long shot."

"I agree. I'll leave it in your hands," Casey replied. He held up the red briefcase. "Oh, here's why I dropped by; it's your flight training materials."

Jesse accepted the case, opened it and shook out its contents on his desk. There were a large red-covered instruction book, a logbook, a book of sample test questions and a manual flight computer. He had seen them all when he had taken his first lessons years before.

"I'd like you to read the first four chapters before our lesson on Sunday," Casey said. "Since you've already been through most of the course once, we should be able to move fast."

"Okay, I'll start on it tonight."

"By the way, you remember the group Jack Gene had visiting last week?"

"That fellow Bottoms and the others?"

"Right; he's having them back next Wednesday for another meeting, plus a few others representing other groups in the Northwest. He'd like you to be there."

"What time?"

"There's a dinner at seven that evening, followed by an important business meeting. Jack Gene's going to be making a big pitch to sell them some weapons. We've got good sources, and we can make an outstanding profit."

"I'll be there."

Casey got up. "I'll see you Sunday afternoon at two."

"I'll be there, too."

When Casey had gone, Jesse looked at his watch. In ten minutes, people would be back from lunch. He got out the phone and called Kip again.

"You forget something?" Kip asked.

"No, I just heard something. You're going to have to go in next Wednesday night."

"Jesus, Jesse, today's Friday."

"You said you might be able to do it in seven days; that gives you six."

"Why Wednesday night?"

"Because there are going to be a bunch of people here from other white supremacist groups to hear a weapons sales pitch from Coldwater. I'll be a witness to the meeting, so you can bag them all for arms dealing. Casey and Ruger will no doubt be there, too."

"Well, that's a terrific idea; I'll bring it up with the planning group and push them to make it."

"You do that; I've got to hang up before somebody comes in. Oh, and you can give your man until Sunday night to deliver my package."

"The extra time will help. See you."

Jesse put the phone away. He had a lot to do before next Wednesday.

53

Saturday was Jesse's first whole day with Carrie in more than two years, and he relished every moment of it. The two little girls took to each other immediately, and both reacted soberly when the rules of Carrie's stay—that she remain inside and out of the living room at all times and that Carey tell no one of her presence—were explained to them. Jesse spent nearly every minute of the day with the two girls, and after supper, when it was time for bed, he tucked them both into their beds in Carey's room.

He kissed Jenny, then sat down in an easy chair in the living room and began to study. Before he went to bed at 2 A.M. he had read not just the four chapters that Casey had assigned, but the entire flight manual.

Jesse arrived at St. Clair Airport half an hour early for his flying lesson. He nodded to the fuel attendant, then took a stroll around the big hangar, peering through the windows of small airplanes.

Pat Casey's Cessna 182 was parked in the premier position in the hangar; no aircraft had to be moved in order to get the Cessna out onto the apron. He noted that two huge sliding doors secured the hangar, and he paid particular attention to a combination padlock hanging open on its hasp. Whoever had set the combination into the lock had done it the easy way; 1234 opened the lock.

Next, Jesse strolled into the little flight office and looked around. A large map of the United States hung on one wall, and Jesse spent several minutes locating St. Clair and measuring distances to various other airports. He looked, too, at a rack of air charts on a counter, picked up one and noted which charts covered which areas of the country. Finally, he found an airport directory and flipped through it, making mental notes. Then he saw Casey's patrol car coming and stepped out of the building to meet the chief of police.

"How you doing, Jesse?" Casey asked.

"Fine, and looking forward to my lesson."

"Great, but first we do ground school."

"Of course."

Casey sat down on an old sofa in the flight office and motioned Jesse to join him. He then took his pupil methodically through the first four chapters of the flight manual, asking and answering questions as he went. When he was satisfied that Jesse was familiar with the material, he got up and headed for the hangar.

"Let's do a preflight inspection," Casey said. He opened the airplane door with a key, got out a fuel tester, then led Jesse around the airplane, following a checklist. When he was satisfied that the airplane was flightworthy and the two men had pushed the airplane out onto the apron, he handed Jesse the key. "Okay, hop into the left seat, and let's get going."

Soon they were in the air. Casey instructed Jesse to head a few miles south of town, then climb to six thousand feet. "We're going to be performing some maneuvers, and we want plenty of altitude," he explained.

While Jesse flew, he took in the landscape surrounding the airport. The principal obstruction was the mountain that rose above the town, and that was to the west of the airport, plus the low mountains to the north. Anyone taking off from St. Clair could fly in a southerly direction and easily avoid obstacles while climbing.

Casey had him perform shallow and steep turns, then do some stalls. Jesse found his old experience coming back to him, and he performed well. On one occasion, Casey reached forward and pulled the red mixture knob all the way out. The engine died.

"Okay, what are you going to do?" Casey asked.

"Find a place to land the damned thing, I guess," Jesse replied.

"First, establish eighty-eight knots of airspeed—that's your best gliding range. Good, now where you going to put it?"

Jesse looked around, then pointed. "There's a straight stretch of road."

"Yeah, and it's also got a straight stretch of telephone poles right alongside it. Telephone wires are a no-no."

The airplane had lost a thousand feet of altitude when Jesse spotted a green pasture. "How about over there?"

"Head for it, and we'll take a look," Casey said.

Jesse pointed the airplane at the field, and, keeping his airspeed steady, allowed the machine to descend. He had lined up for the field and was down to six hundred feet of altitude when he saw the cattle.

Casey pushed in the mixture control and the engine leapt to life. "Better get out of here," he said. "Both you and the cows are hamburger. You're dead." He laughed. "Got to watch out for everything in an emergency landing. Let's go home; you're tired, or you wouldn't have made that mistake. Know where the airport is?"

"Afraid not," Jesse said. "All this maneuvering has confused me."

"Put the identifier into the GPS," Casey said, pointing at the instrument. "That'll give you a heading."

Following Casey's instructions, Jesse dialed in the correct identifier, pressed a button twice, and a heading popped onto the little screen. "There it is; we're six and a half miles out, and the heading is three-three-zero."

"Exactly right. Now engage the autopilot. First, put the arrow on the instrument in front of you on three-three-zero, then press the alt and nav buttons, then the on button."

Jesse did as he was told, and he felt the autopilot take charge of the airplane.

"Now the autopilot will maintain our present altitude, and it will navigate us directly to the airport."

"How do you find out an airport's identifier?" Jesse asked.

Casey reached between the seats and held up a little book. "This has all the information about every airport in the West. Or, you can simply enter the name of the city into the GPS, and it will give you the identifier. Simple, huh?"

"Dead simple." Jesse saw the field ahead. "Pat, what's the range of this airplane?"

"About six hundred and fifty miles at maximum cruise in a no-wind situation. Of course, you almost never get a no-wind situation. Generally, the winds are westerly—higher at high altitudes and lower at lower ones, but you can get an anomaly in the weather and get the opposite. The airspeed indicator gives you your speed through the air, once you've set in your altitude and the temperature, and the GPS gives you your actual speed over the ground. It also give you your ETA at your current ground speed. Over there on your left is the fuel flow computer, which gives you the hours and minutes of flight time available on the fuel you have remaining; it's accurate to within a gallon. You compare the flight time remaining on the fuel flow computer to the ETA on the GPS. Allow yourself an hour's fuel for safety, and you know at any moment if you have enough fuel to reach the airport."

"And what sort of cruise speed do you get?"

"Standard is about a hundred and forty knots, but I've got a lot of speed equipment—fancy wheel skirts, aileron gap seals, etcetera, so I get closer to one fifty-five."

Jesse nodded and flew over the field to get a look at the windsock. He selected a runway and turned downwind. Soon, they were pushing the airplane back into the hangar.

"Top her off," Casey called to the fuel attendant. Then he shook Jesse's hand. "You did good. We'll have you a private license in a couple of months."

"Thanks for your time, Pat. Next Sunday?"

"For sure." Casey got into his car and drove away.

Jesse went into the flight office and bought some charts and an airport directory.

As soon as the girls were in bed, he went to work. He spread out the charts on the dining room table and began measuring distances to various destinations.

54

Jesse pored over the charts until midnight, then he began reading the pilot's operating handbook for the Cessna 182. He concentrated on the airplane's systems, then memorized the operating speeds for takeoff and landing and for the stall speeds. He read up on the avionics, aircraft icing and emergency procedures. By two o'clock his eyes were burning. He put down the book and got into his coat.

He drove once around the town, as if he were simply an insomniac out for a wee-hours drive. All was quiet. He parked in an alley, as he had done before, and walked to the courthouse. The locks were easier this time, and inside half an hour he had entered the county clerk's office and forged a birth certificate for Carrie.

As he walked back toward the truck the waxing moon came from behind the clouds and lit the streets as if it were daylight. Jesse crossed the street to stay in the shadows and, at that moment, he saw the police car.

It was driving slowly up the street toward him, swinging its spotlight back and forth from one side of the street to the other, checking the store-fronts. Jesse flattened himself against a building, feeling terribly exposed; if he ducked into a door-way, he would be illuminated when the light hit the front door of the shop. He stood, frozen, wait-ing to be seen, trying to make up a story to ex-plain his presence on the street in the middle of the night.

The spotlight hit the front of a shop across the street, then swung to the other side. As it moved, it caught Jesse full in the face, momentarily blind-ing him. It paused on the shop's front door next to him, then moved on down the street. After a few seconds, the police car turned right and disap-peared around the corner. Jesse couldn't move for a moment. He had been fully visible to the driver, but he apparently hadn't been seen. He sprinted for his truck.

He gave the police car another minute to move on, then he started the truck and headed east from town. He passed Wood Products and came to the bridge over the creek. A foot-long length of duct tape was stuck to the railing on the opposite side of the road. He pulled the truck off the road and into the woods, then walked back to the side of the road. He looked in both directions, then sprinted across the road and down the embank-ment, snatching the strip of duct tape from the railing as he went.

His flashlight found the bundle, taped securely in a corner of the bridge supports. He used his pocket knife to cut it free, then stripped off the remaining bits of tape and stuck them in his pocket. Back at road level, he knelt behind the bridge railing and waited for an eighteen-wheeler to roar past, then ran for his truck.

Back at home, he took the bundle into the kitchen and ripped away the plastic covering with his knife. Inside he found a canvas backpack, and inside that were all the items he had requested, plus one more. There was a typewritten note taped to it: "You *must* wear this wire to the meeting," it read. "The tape will be crucial to our court case." He ripped up the note and flushed it down the garbage disposal. The recorder was small, he'd give them that. If he wore it in some clever place, a body search might even miss it.

He put the materials back into the backpack, took it out to the garage and concealed it under a stack of firewood. Then he got under the truck, opened the safe and stashed Carrie's birth certificate with the passports.

As he climbed the stairs to bed, he thought carefully about his plan. He had nearly everything he wanted now; the remainder of his needs he would find at Wood Products.

On Monday morning, Jesse rapped on Herman Muller's office door, and Muller waved him in.

"Morning, Jesse."

"Morning, Herman; have you got a minute?"

"Sure I have. Sit you down."

Jesse sat. "Herman, I think I've got a pretty good grip on how the plant runs now, and I seem to have a little time on my hands. I just wondered if you could use a hand at the bookkeeping."

Muller regarded him for a moment, then smiled. "Jesse, you put your finger on the thing I hate doing most around here. My wife kept the books until she died; fortunately, she got the computer system up and running before she passed, and she taught me to run it. I guess it's time I taught you."

"I'll be glad to learn," Jesse said.

"Pull your chair around here and look over my shoulder," Muller said, switching on the computer. "You start from the main menu and press B for books, then it will ask you for your password. The password is Tommy."

Jesse spent most of the morning following Muller through the program; it really was very straightforward. When everybody left for lunch, Jesse went to the computer, entered the password and asked the program to print out a balance sheet for the previous year. It took less than a minute to do so.

He put the statement into his pocket, found his coat and went down to the parking lot, then he drove into town and parked in front of the bank.

"I'd like to see Kurt Ruger," he told the secretary. Then he looked up to see Ruger waving him into his office.

"What can I do for you, Jesse?" Ruger asked, and his tone was cool. "You want to borrow some money?"

"Thanks, Kurt, but I'm here to do something for you." He produced the balance sheet, unfolded it and handed it over.

Ruger read the document, then smiled, the first time Jesse had ever seen him do so. "Well, I'll be damned," he said. "The old goat is doing even better than we thought!"

"This year ought to be a lot better," Jesse said. "I've developed two new plywood outlets in the East, and I think those will lead to more."

"Yeah, Casey told me about the order from Maryland. That and the New York order, on top of the usual business, ought to keep the plant humming for the better part of the year."

"That it will," Jesse said.

"How'd you do it? How'd you get the computer password?"

"I just asked. I offered to help with the bookkeeping, and Herman jumped at it; said he hated doing it himself."

Ruger stood up and offered his hand. "Jesse, I've underestimated you, and I've been suspicious of you over nothing. I want to apologize."

Jesse shook the man's hand. "Don't mention it," he said. "Is there anything else you want from Herman's books?"

"If you could get me a temporary balance sheet for this year so far, that would help," Ruger said.

"I can do that; I'll drop it by tonight on the way home."

Ruger smiled again. "We'll own that business before the month is out," he said.

Jesse left the bank and went back to his truck. Before the month is out, he mused, you'll be in the joint. Or in hell.

55

At lunchtime on Tuesday, Jesse made what he was sure would be his last call to Kip Fuller.

"Kip, it's Jesse. What's happening?"

"Jess, we need another day."

Jesse felt anger replace the dread. "Well, you can't have it."

"Listen to me, Jess; we're going to do it the way you wanted; the army is sending in a battalion of Rangers, the best they've got. But they need a little more time to get things in place."

"Well, they can't have it. They're just going to have to get their asses in gear and get it done very early on Thursday morning." He looked at his watch. "That's thirty-odd hours, and they'd better not be late."

"Let me tell you the plan; it's very close to what you suggested."

"Okay, tell me."

"The Rangers are being transported in a fleet of trucks—everything from a UPS van to eighteen-wheelers."

"That's good, I like that."

"At one A.M. on Friday morning they're going to simultaneously hit the police station and the telephone exchange. Ten minutes later, a specially reinforced truck carrying a heavy load of ballast is going to crash the gate at the top of the mountain; follow-up vehicles will discharge a company of Rangers, and at the same time, electric power will be cut to the whole town. This is very close to what you wanted."

"It is, and it sounds right."

"The Rangers will then take the weapons emplacements outside the main fortification, and when they've secured the ground-to-air missiles, the choppers will come in and put another two companies on the mountaintop.

"Right behind the troops at the main gate will be three heavy-duty swat teams of specially trained U.S. marshals; they'll hit the homes of Coldwater, Casey and Ruger at the very moment that the truck crashes the gates.

"Headquarters will be in another specially equipped eighteen-wheeler; when they get word that the big three are in custody and that the Rangers are on the mountaintop, they'll send in four C-130 aircraft, each of which will hold an armored personnel carrier and a complement of troops. Your airport at St. Clair has a forty-five hundred foot strip, and there's a thousand-foot grass overrun, winter-hard, at one end of the runway. That's enough for the C-130s. At the same time, other troops will arrive in unmarked cars and begin a door-to-door sweep of the whole town. We've arranged the biggest federal search warrant in history; it's good for the whole county. We reckon that by dawn the town will be ours, and we're counting on minimum casualties."

"Kip, I think your plan is good. But it has to happen Thursday morning."

"Jess—"

"Kip, shut up and listen to me. Tell them to hit at three A.M., not one. These people are likely to still be awake at one. I've got a shot at keeping Coldwater and his people out of the fortifications; if it hasn't happened by three A.M. it won't happen, and they'll have to take their chances on a security leak that could give Coldwater some warning. You better pray I make it."

"I don't understand—what's the big deal about another day?"

"The deal is, I can't last another twenty-four hours. I've hardly slept at all since Sunday, and I'm starting to come unglued."

"Come on, Jess, you're tougher than that."

"Kip, I don't have anything left, and that's the truth. I've planned for tomorrow night, and tomorrow night it is. Can this phone reach you at that time?"

"Yes, I can use call-forwarding to route your call to the headquarters truck."

"Is there any way for you to find my position by backtracking the telephone?"

"No, we can only tell what cellular service area you're in, and all of the area in the Idaho panhandle is in the same service area. We'll have to depend on position reports from you."

"I understand. Remember, now, hit the police and telephone buildings at three A.M., and not a minute before. I'm going to have a shot at paving the way for you, but I can't promise anything, so don't expect it." He hung up before Kip could reply.

He hadn't lied about his condition; he was a wreck, and he was going to have to get some sleep tonight, or he'd never make it.

56

Wednesday. Jesse suffered through the day, stopping work now and then to do his yoga breathing exercises, the only thing that seemed to help him relax. At the end of the day, he pretended to still be working while he waited impatiently for everyone to leave. When he was finally alone in the plant he went downstairs to the machine shop, found a canvas tool bag and started to select equipment. He wasn't sure what he'd need, but he chose a six-pound sledge, a couple of cold chisels, wire cutters, pliers, some screwdrivers, a thick roll of duct tape and a pair of short bolt cutters. Finally, he unplugged a heavy-duty, half-inch, battery-operated drill from its charger and dropped that into the bag, along with a spare battery. The bag wouldn't hold any more, so what he had would have to be enough.

He drove home, forcing himself to obey the speed limit, and parked the truck in the garage, then he dug out his bag of equipment from Kip and tucked it behind the seat of the truck, along with the tool bag. He crawled under the truck, opened the safe and extracted the contents. He put the pistol and spare clips into the canvas backpack and took the money, the passports and the miniature tape recorder into the house. Jenny was feeding the girls an early supper, as planned.

"Hey, everybody," he said, trying to sound jovial. He sat at the table and drank a glass of milk while they finished their dinner, and, when the girls had been tucked into bed, protesting, he took Jenny back downstairs to the kitchen.

"All right," he said, "time for final plans." He went to the sink, took a plastic tool box from underneath it and emptied out the tools, then he removed the money from its brown paper bag and packed it into the tool box. "That's a little over fifty thousand dollars," he said. "Pack some sandwiches around it."

"What's going to happen tonight?" she asked.

"I'm going to a dinner meeting at Jack Gene's house, and I'm going to record the proceedings; what I get there should be enough to put everybody present away for a long time."

"Do you want us to wait here?"

"No. I want you to pack one bag for each of us, and put them into the trunk of your car, along with the toolbox and some blankets, and at two A.M. I want you to take the girls and drive out to the St. Clair airport."

"Are we going to fly out of here?"

"Just listen. Be sure and have some story ready, in case you're stopped by a patrol car. There's a big hangar next to the flight office, and it has a combination lock; the combination is 1234. I want you to unlock the hanger and, just inside the door, along with several other airplanes, you'll find a Cessna—that's an airplane with high wings, the kind you can walk under—and the number on the side of it is N123TF. Got that?"

"N123TF," she repeated, "and the combination for the lock is 1234. That's all very simple."

"The airplane will be unlocked; there's a rear door to the luggage compartment on the left-hand side, and I want you to put all the luggage and the toolbox in there, then I want you to put the two girls in the back seat of the airplane with a couple of blankets. Then you drive your car into the woods, where it can't be seen from the airport, go back to the hangar, close the doors from the inside, get into the airplane and wait for me."

"Jesse, can you fly an airplane?"

"Sort of. Now listen; if I'm not there by three-fifteen, I want you to put everybody back into the car, drive back to the main road, turn east and then, as soon as you can, head south toward Salt Lake City. There, do what you were to do in Seattle the last time we planned this: get most of the money converted to traveler's checks and a cashier's check; make a reservation for Tokyo, this time through Los Angeles. Here are your passports and Carrie's birth certificate; you can talk her through with that.

"After Tokyo, it's the Peninsular Hotel in Hong Kong for a week, then to Sydney and the Harbour Hotel, ask for Bluey at the bar."

"I remember all that."

"I'll join you if I can. If I can't, take care of yourself and the girls; make them happy."

She reached across the table and squeezed his hand.

"I'll most likely make it to the airport, but if not, look for me in Hong Kong."

While Jenny was upstairs packing, Jesse took off his shirt and dropped his pants. It wasn't the first time he'd worn a wire. Using the special tape provided with the wire, he taped the recorder to the inside of his left thigh, high up, next to his testicles. In his experience, most men didn't like groping other men's crotches, even in a search. He plugged in the microphone wire, then ran it between his legs and up between his buttocks to his waist, anchoring the wire there with tape. He then ran it up his back, taping as far as he could reach, then again at his shoulder. He ran it down his left arm, applying patches of tape as he went, then he attached the microphone to the wire and taped it securely to the inside of his wrist, a couple of inches above his watchband. A switch on the tiny microphone would allow him to start the recorder; after that, it would record whenever it picked up someone's voice.

He got dressed again, swung his left arm around and walked around the kitchen to be sure he had free movement. The microphone wire was very thin, and he didn't want to put any strain on it. He went upstairs, got his dark brown sheepskin coat, a pair of hiking boots and some thick socks, then came back down to the kitchen. Jenny joined him there.

"You're sure you understand everything?" he asked.

She nodded.

Jesse looked at his watch; quarter to seven; time to go. He took Jenny in his arms, hugged her, kissed her; he tried to keep it light; didn't want it to seem like goodbye, although God knew it might very well be.

"I love you," he said.

"I love you," she replied.

He got into his coat, tucked the sheepskin jacket and the boots under his arm and left the house.

57

Jesse arrived precisely on time and was shown into Coldwater's study by one of Jack Gene's young women.

"The pastor will be with you shortly," she said. "Please make yourself at home."

As soon as she was gone, Jesse went to the false bookcase at the end of the room and tugged at it. The facade gave way to reveal a door, securely locked, and it was made of steel. Jesse rapped on it sharply with a knuckle; at least a quarter-inch thick, and there was an echo from behind it. He closed the bookcase and quickly found a chair.

Coldwater entered the room, followed by Pat Casey and Kurt Ruger, and at that moment the doorbell rang. "Ah, here they are," Coldwater said. "Good evening, Jesse."

"Good evening, Pastor," Jesse replied, rising. He nervously checked his necktie.

A moment later a group of men were shown into the room, led by Charley Bottoms, who winked at Jesse.

Don't *do* that, Jesse said to himself. He counted eight men as he was introduced; some, like Bottoms, had been in the last visiting group, but two were new. Jesse recognized one of them as the Reverend John Packard, a Seattle minister who specialized in racial and anti-Semitic epithets; he had often been on the news.

The young woman who had admitted them entered the room, opened a concealed wet bar and began offering drinks. Jesse accepted a bourbon, but he drank little of it.

"Gentlemen," Coldwater said to the room at large, "I hope you'll forgive the inconvenience, but in the interests of security, it will be necessary for each of you to be, ah, looked at more closely. Not you, Reverend, of course."

There was grumbling, but each man submitted to an expert search by Pat Casey and Kurt Ruger.

"Pastor," the reverend said, "I hope you won't take offense, but your crowd will have to be looked at, too."

"No offense taken," Coldwater replied. "Go right ahead."

"Charley, will you do the honors?" the reverend said.

"Sure thing, Preacher," Bottoms said. "You fellows mind unbuttoning your shirts?" He quickly patted down Casey and Ruger, then turned to Jesse. "You're next, pal."

Jesse's back was to the fire, but he still held his breath while Bottoms ran his hands over his body. If Charley wasn't on the feds' team, he would find out about it now. Charley found the wire running up his back. He turned to Packard. "They're clean, Reverend."

Jesse started breathing again.

"What did you fellows fly down in?" Coldwater asked the Reverend Packard.

"I got a King Air," the reverend replied. "I fly it myself; we made it in no time flat."

"I fly a rather old Commanche, myself," Coldwater said. "You like our little airport?"

"Real nice," Packard replied.

Charley Bottoms took a large swig of whiskey and announced, "I came in a Chevrolet. You guys are doing awful good for yourselves."

The Reverend Packard laughed heartily at this.

Jesse thought about the King Air out at the airport—a twin-engined turboprop. It flew a lot faster than the Cessna he was planning on leaving in, but he knew nothing about flying twins, and he wasn't going to start learning tonight.

The conversation grew louder as the alcohol circulated, and then they were called in to dinner. Jesse aimed at a seat near the middle of the table, on Coldwater's right. There were twelve of them at the long table, and he wanted to be able to record as many of them as possible. From the middle of the table, he thought, the recorder might manage it.

Dinner was served, and Coldwater waxed eloquent about the wines, while Jesse ate and drank little.

"Jesse," Coldwater said suddenly, "you're not drinking my wine; what's the matter?"

Jesse placed a hand on his belly. "Some kind of bug, I think; my stomach's a little unsettled."

"Can we get you something for it?" Coldwater asked solicitously.

"Thank you, no; I think I'll be fine, if I take it easy."

"Sure you wouldn't like to go and lie down for a few minutes?"

This was a tempting possibility, but Jesse had to record the conversation in this room.

"Really, I'll be fine," he said.

"As you wish," Coldwater said. "Let me know if you take a turn for the worse."

"Thank you, sir; I'll do that."

Dessert and coffee were served, and a large decanter of brandy was placed on the table. Kurt Ruger, who was sitting near the opposite end of the table from Coldwater, got up and left the room.

Coldwater poured himself a brandy and passed the decanter. Jesse took none. Ruger came back into the room, but, instead of sitting down again, he leaned against the wall at that end of the table, his hands behind him.

When everyone had been served brandy, Coldwater tapped on the edge of his glass with a knife; the crowd grew quiet. "Before we proceed with our presentation," he said, "there is a little security matter we must deal with." The room was deadly quiet now.

Jesse pretended to scratch his forearm, while switching on the recorder. Wait a minute, he thought; did he say security?

Coldwater continued. "It seems a member of our party has not been entirely candid with us. When he was a prisoner in the Atlanta Federal Penitentiary, he seems to have been led astray."

Jesse's breath grew short. He was a long way from the door, and he didn't like the way Kurt Ruger was standing, with his hands behind him. In order to get out of the room, he'd have to go through Ruger at one end or Coldwater at the other. He stared down at the table. A trickle of fear ran through his bowels.

"Tell us, my friend," Coldwater said, staring down the table, "Just what did you do to get put into prison?"

Jesse swallowed hard and tried to take a deep breath. He would have to keep this as close to the truth as possible. He opened his mouth to speak.

"I was in for armed robbery and second degree murder," a voice said.

Jesse looked up. Charley Bottoms had spoken; Charley was sitting at the foot of the table.

"And what was your sentence?" Coldwater asked.

Jesse discovered that he had been holding his breath. He let it out in a rush. Across the table, Pat Casey glanced sharply at him, but Coldwater didn't seem to notice.

"I got twenty-five to life," Charley said. He was beginning to look ill at ease.

"Which means you would ordinarily serve, let's see, twelve and a half years?" Coldwater asked.

Charley said nothing.

"And how long did you serve, Mr. Bottoms?"

"Three years and two months."

"Three years and two months," Coldwater repeated. "Your behavior inside must have been *awfully* good."

Charley shrugged. "I got lucky, I guess."

"I guess you did, Mr. Bottoms. Out in three years and two months. What luck!"

Jesse placed his hands on the dining table, the more to get the microphone out in front of him.

"I'm going to ask you just once, Mr. Bottoms," Coldwater said. "Who got you out, and why?"

Charley continued to play dumb, which turned out to be a big mistake. He shrugged. "The parole board."

Coldwater looked up at Ruger. "Kurt, please escort Mr. Bottoms downstairs and put the question to him a little more firmly."

Ruger pushed himself off the wall and put an automatic pistol to the back of Charley's head. "Easy, now, Bottoms; let's not put your brains on the table."

"Jesse," Coldwater said.

Jesse's head jerked around toward Coldwater. "Yes, sir?"

"Give Kurt a hand." He reached inside his jacket, produced a 9mm automatic and handed it to Jesse.

Jesse took the gun. The evening was not going at all the way he had planned. He stood up and followed Charley and Ruger out of the dining room. They entered the kitchen; two young women were washing dishes at a double sink; they looked up then quickly down again.

"Jesse, open the cellar door," Ruger said.

Jesse looked around and spotted the door; he opened it and stood back.

"Right down the stairs," Ruger said to Bottoms. "Come on down, Jesse." He switched on a light.

Jesse followed the two men down the stairs. As they walked down, Jesse considered his position, and he didn't like it at all.

"Right over there," Ruger said, shoving Charley.

Jesse saw a heavy wooden chair, and it was bolted to the floor.

"There's some cord attached to the back of the chair; tie his hands behind him."

Jesse followed Ruger's instructions, but he didn't tie Charley's hands too tightly.

Ruger tucked his pistol into his belt, picked up a length of pipe from the floor, then squared off before Charley Bottoms. "I know you're not going to answer my questions right away," he said, "so why don't we just skip that part." He struck Bottoms across the face with the pipe.

The sound was like a football being kicked, Jesse thought.

Ruger turned away for a moment, as if to take a deep breath. Charley Bottoms turned toward Jesse, his face bloody, and silently mouthed, "Shoot me."

Jesse looked away. If he helped Charley he'd give himself away, and they'd both be shot. Charley had just told him, in effect, that he expected to be killed and that Jesse should save himself.

58

Ruger had been at it for half an hour, and Charley Bottoms was no longer recognizable. He was alive, though, and occasionally, he spat out some blood.

Jesse stood, the gun dangling at his side, and tried not to watch. Ruger drew the pipe back again, and as he did, the door at the top of the stairs opened, and Ruger and Jesse both turned to look. Coldwater's feet appeared on the stairs, and at that moment, Charley's right hand shot out. He grabbed the pistol from Ruger's belt and fired two rounds into his tormentor's head. Then, without hesitating, he flipped the gun around, got his thumb on the trigger and stuck the barrel into his mouth.

Jesse's shot went off simultaneously with Charley's. Charley lurched backwards and sideways, leaving blood and brains on the wall behind him. Without thinking, Jesse fired a second shot into the body.

Just as Jesse's knees buckled, Coldwater reached

out and took the pistol from him, and he sagged into Pat Casey's arms.

Jesse sat on the sofa in Coldwater's study, his face in his hands.

"Feeling better?" Coldwater asked.

"I should have been faster," Jesse said.

"I saw it all; you couldn't have done better," Coldwater replied. "He might have gotten me."

Pat Casey handed Jesse a damp face cloth. "Here," he said, "maybe this will help."

"Poor Jesse," Coldwater said. "And you weren't feeling well to begin with. Why don't you stretch out on the sofa for a while? I have a business negotiation to complete." He turned to Casey. "Pat, see that the mess downstairs gets cleaned up."

"Right," Casey replied, then left the room.

"Are you really better?" Coldwater asked, concern in his voice.

"Thank you, sir," Jesse muttered. "I'll be all right in a minute."

Coldwater clapped a hand on his shoulder. "You stay here; I'll check on you later." He left the room, closing the door behind him.

Jesse gave them fifteen seconds by his watch before he moved, then he got up, went to the bookcase and moved back the facade, exposing the safe. He put an ear to it and starting moving the tumblers. He couldn't hear well enough, so he went to the bar, got an empty glass, pressed it against the steel, put his ear to the glass and tried again. Better. He glanced at his watch.

Forty minutes later, the safe door opened; it

had been harder than he had thought it would be. The bottom of the safe was full of papers, he didn't much care what, and the top shelf was lined with dozens of neatly banded stacks of hundred-dollar bills.

Jesse looked around the room, and his eyes fell on a large, wicker wastebasket with a plastic liner. Jesse ripped out the liner, emptied the trash back into the basket and began raking the money into the bag. He hesitated for a moment, then he packed the papers at the bottom of the safe into the bag, as well. He closed the safe door, twirled the knob and shut the bookcase facade, then he took the corners of the plastic bag and tied them into a secure knot.

There were voices from the front hall. Jesse looked around for a hiding place for the bag and didn't see one. He ran to the windows, pushed one up and stuck the bag outside. He swung it a couple of times, then let go, tossing it in the direction of the road. The door behind him opened.

"Feeling better?" Coldwater boomed.

"Yes, thank you, sir; I was just letting in some fresh air. How did your meeting go?"

"A great success, I'd say." Coldwater poured himself a brandy from the bar and one for Jesse, as well. "This ought to make you feel a little better, and close that window, will you? It's freezing in here."

Jesse closed the window and accepted the brandy. He took a good-sized swig, then sat down.

"Jesse," Coldwater said, "I'd like you to take on some of Kurt's duties."

Jesse looked at him, surprised. The man had just seen his old friend and partner murdered. He moved his glass to his left hand, and scratched his arm with his right, made sure the recorder was going.

"That's very flattering, sir. I'm afraid I don't know much about finance."

"You're a highly intelligent and quick-witted man, though, and that's my need at the moment, now that Kurt is gone. Pity about Kurt; good fellow." He didn't sound grief-stricken.

"Yes, sir."

"Your first assignment is to take Wood Products away from Herman Muller; do it any way you can; Kurt showed me that balance sheet you got him, and let me tell you, that company is a plum."

"I think I can handle that," Jesse replied.

"As soon as you do, you're going to become president of the bank," Coldwater said. "No need to know anything about banking; I know more than enough about that. But I need my own man in there."

"Thank you, sir," Jesse said, trying to sound brighter. Then he thought, what the hell, last chance to find out. "Pastor—"

"Call me Jack Gene; you've earned the right."

"Thank you. Jack Gene, I don't really have any grasp of what's going on here. I mean, what's the bunker for?"

Coldwater laughed aloud. "I suppose you must have thought I was mad," he said. "Well, I'm not. It's a very fine weapons store, isn't it?"

"It's all about weapons, then?"

Coldwater grinned. "You really are very bright, Jesse. If I was going to deal in weapons on any sort of scale, I had to have a secure storage site, didn't I?"

"But why all this religion business? Why found a church?"

"Think about it, Jesse; nobody can build something as big as what's inside the mountain without one hell of a lot of people knowing about it. With the church, I got to control the people who knew about it; the people who, in fact, built it, saving me millions of dollars in the process. Of course, I've enjoyed taking over and running this little town; that was fun. But it was all to protect the weapons business."

"And controlling the town meant that nobody asked questions about all the trucks that were bringing in and taking out the stuff?"

"Exactly. And there were a *lot* of trucks. We deal worldwide, you know—not just to people like those yokels who just left. Mind you, I've equipped just about every bunch of nutters in the western half of the United States of America, and some in the East, too. The profits have been mindboggling. I have bank accounts in every safe haven in the world—Zurich, the Caymans, Singapore—so does Pat; so does Kurt, for that matter. After I've moved some of the money, I'll see that you get the numbers to his accounts. It wouldn't be fair to give you everything Kurt had earned, would it? I'll take half, give Pat a quarter, and you can have the rest. That number will approach ten million dollars."

Jesse blinked. "Thank you, sir. I must say, I'm

a little surprised that Kurt would let you have the numbers to his bank accounts."

"Why not? I opened them for him and put the money into them. Casey's, too."

"So, if something happened to Pat—"

Coldwater smiled broadly. "Now you don't think I'd let anything happen to Pat? Couldn't get along without him."

Jesse thought, You're fucking well getting along without Ruger all right, aren't you?

"You're going to become as indispensable as Pat, Jesse, don't you worry. Listen, if you don't want to go abroad when this is over, I'll give you Muller's business. If you feel you *must* work, you can stay in St. Clair and play with that."

"When is it going to be over?" Jesse asked.

"Well, it's winding down already, isn't it? I mean, Charley Bottoms is the third federal agent we've had in here in the past year and a half. *Somebody* must suspect *something*." He chuckled.

"Doesn't that worry you?" Jesse asked.

"Not in the least; the feds are very slow to catch on to anything, and I control the local law completely. No, I've got another year, at the very least, before I move on to greener pastures."

"Well, it all sounds very exciting," Jesse said.

"More exciting that you can imagine," Coldwater replied, then his eyes lit up. "Maybe I should show you just how exciting." He pointed toward the bookcase. "Remember my safe? There's a million and a half dollars, cash, in there. It's yours." He made to get up.

Jesse threw up a hand. "Please, Jack Gene,

please. You don't have to do that. I trust you completely."

Coldwater paused, half out of his chair. "You're sure?"

"Absolutely," Jesse said.

Coldwater grinned. "I trust you, too, Jesse; you were different from the beginning. You knew what was in your interests, but you didn't buy the religion, ever, did you?"

"I can't say that I did."

"The sheep," Coldwater said contemptuously of his congregation. "It has always astonished me the number of seemingly normal human beings who will follow, even lay down their lives for, any man who shows them some leadership. Did I tell you about the abortion clinics?"

"No."

"We've razed a good number of clinics in the Northwest, for no other reason than to get the congregation excited about something, and, not to mention, to incriminate a fair number of them."

"Why abortion clinics?"

"Oh, they're very fashionable among the faithful, you know, and they're also wonderfully easy pickings. They attract big headlines, too, and lots of TV time. The faithful like to know that their good works are not going unnoticed."

Coldwater put down his glass and massaged his temples. "Well, I'm a little tired; such a big evening. I think I'll turn in." He got to his feet.

Jesse rose with him. "I could use a good night's sleep, myself," he said.

Coldwater put an arm around Jesse and walked

him to the front hall, then helped him into his coat. "Tell you what, why don't you come to lunch tomorrow? We'll break bread, drink a fine bottle of wine and talk about the future."

"I'd like that, Jack Gene," Jesse said, shaking the man's hand.

Coldwater suddenly embraced Jesse. "We're going a long way together," he said. Then he stood in the door and watched Jesse walk toward his truck.

"Not as far as you think," Jesse muttered to himself.

59

Jesse drove slowly down the long driveway, and, at the road, he stopped. He switched off the headlights, reached into the backpack behind the seat and extracted the night goggles. He slipped them on, then, instead of heading down toward town, he turned right and drove slowly up the mountain a few yards. He had no trouble seeing the road.

Coldwater's house was nearly at the top of the mountain; only one thing lay in the fifty yards between the house and the gates. When he was nearly at the top, he turned right, down the dirt road, and a minute later stopped at the firing range. He got out and looked up. A hundred feet above the earthen bank that received the bullets, he saw what he wanted. The full moon came out from behind the clouds for a moment, and in the bright light the goggles were almost too much.

He changed his shoes and got into his warm jacket, then retrieved the backpack and the tool bag from the truck and checked his equipment.

He stuck the pistol into his belt and the spare clips into his pocket, then slipped on the backpack, slung the tool bag over one shoulder and the machine gun, an Uzi, over the other and started climbing the mountain.

It was tough going with only one free hand and so much gear, but he made it in twenty minutes. He sat down beside the ventilator grate and rested for a few minutes. He checked his watch; just after midnight; he had plenty of time, he hoped.

He stood up and, through the night goggles, examined the grating. It was much like a storm sewer grating, just as thick, but round and about three feet across. There was a noise from above him, and Jesse flattened himself against the mountainside, swiveling his head up and around. On the cliff twenty feet above him stood a man holding an assault rifle. He struck a match, lit a cigarette and tossed the match down the steep incline. It landed at Jesse's feet.

Jesse stood, frozen, until the man moved on. He waited another half minute, then looked at the grate again. It was secured by two large bolts, and the heads were not slotted. He considered using a chisel on them, but that would be noisy; same with the electric drill. Finally, he went into the backpack and came out with the plastic explosive. He got out his pocket knife and cut a large chunk from the main piece; he carefully divided it, then shaped and packed it around the four bolts. It took another few minutes to wire all four charges to one timer, then he took the explosives mat out of the backpack and spread it over the grating. He taped it in place with some duct tape, and then he was ready.

But there was the matter of the guard above. Jesse put down the Uzi and very carefully, foot by foot, scaled the steep incline. He got a toehold just below the top, then stuck his head up and looked around. There were two of them, it seemed, and they were standing next to a shed nearly a hundred yards away, leaning on their weapons and smoking. Jesse thanked heaven for the night goggles. He turned around and slid the twenty feet down to the ledge where he had been working; he took hold of the timer and set it for thirty seconds, then quickly worked his way along the ledge away from the grating. He stopped, turned his head away and held his breath.

There was a muffled *whump*, and the explosives mat flew off and down the mountain. Quickly, he made his way back to the grating; it was hanging by one bolt. He tossed all his equipment into the pipe, climbed in and pulled the grating back into place. He sat that way, holding the grating, for half a minute before he heard the voices.

"What the fuck was that?" one man said.

"I didn't hear anything."

"You were farting, that's why."

"Maybe that's what you heard."

"Naw, I heard a kind of, I don't know, a—"

"It was probably an eighteen-wheeler backfiring down on the road."

"No, it was more like a—"

"Well, everything seems to be all right, doesn't it?"

"Yeah, I guess so."

"You can log the noise, if you want to, but I'm not going to say I heard it."

"Well, fuck you, then."

The voices faded away.

Jesse waited for them to go, then gently let the grating hang on the one bolt again. He turned and, pushing his equipment ahead of him, started down the tunnel on his hands and knees.

There was so little ambient light in the pipe that not even the goggles were of much use, so he pulled them down around his neck and switched on a small flashlight. Holding the light in his mouth, he moved on down the tunnel until he came to another obstacle.

This one was nothing more that a piece of chain-link fencing that had been cut to size and welded to the steel pipe; he wouldn't need explosives for this. He got out the bolt cutters and snipped his way through.

He was well inside the mountain now, and his next obstacle was a fan that nearly filled the tunnel. Suddenly, it came on, and there was a roar as air began to rush down the pipe. He got out his wire cutters, found the power cord and cut it. The fan slowly came to a halt. It took him half an hour to get the blade off and dismantle enough of the frame to get through. There was one last ventilator grate, but this one was of thin aluminum, and he was able to kick it out. He peered out into a long hallway; he was a good eight feet above the floor; about every fourth ceiling light was on.

He lowered his equipment to the floor, then jumped down, squatted and listened. It seemed unlikely that anyone was inside this place late at night, but he wanted to be sure.

Hearing nothing, he thought about his position and decided he must be in the north hallway on the first, highest, level. Then he remembered what was up the hall toward the main entrance. Leaving his tools where they lay he trotted up the hallway, turned a corner and opened a door. A small room was stacked to the ceiling with crates marked "ammunition: recoilless rifle." He tried a couple more doors, checking labels until he found a single crate, marked "C-4 Plastique." Perfect. The box held at least twenty pounds of the stuff. He got it open and took out two brick-sized blocks, wired a detonator to it and looked at his watch; one-twenty. He set the timer for one hour and forty minutes; it would go off at exactly 3:00 A.M. He took the crate and went back to where his tools lay, then he sat down and remembered what he could of the layout from his previous visits and from the plans.

By two-thirty, he had set more Plastique in half a dozen ammunition caches all over the complex. That would have been enough to keep anyone from using the facility any time soon, but it didn't satisfy him. There was one more job to do. He picked up his gear and ran down to the generator room on the second level.

The door was locked, and he had no time to pick the lock. He got out the drill and went straight through the cylinder. Inside the room were two enormous generators; his guess was that one of them was enough to light the facility; the other was a backup. Above them, built into the mountain were two hardened twenty-five-thousand-gallon gasoline storage tanks. Thank God they were on the north side of the mountain, away from the town, he thought. His Plastique might not punch through the tanks, but there was another, simpler and more effective way to deal with it. He set his equipment on a workbench, got out the bolt cutters and stepped behind the machinery; using his flashlight, he located the two armored fuel lines; the bolt cutters made quick work of both of them. He turned two taps, and gasoline began to pour onto the floor, he guessed at the rate of about twenty gallons a minute from each line.

He picked up his gear and got out of there. He was soaked up to the knees with gasoline.

Early on, he had decided not to go out the way he came in. The tunnel was too close to the gasoline tanks, and if he made some miscalculation, and the place went up while he was still in the tunnel, he would be fired from it like the human cannonball at the circus—that, or the mountain would simply collapse on top of him. There was a better way out, he was sure of it.

He charged down the steps to the lower level and ran toward the rear of the structure, toward Jack Gene Coldwater's offices. He realized that the hallways were all slightly inclined, and he could hear gasoline pouring down the steps behind him. He checked his watch; two forty-seven; thirteen minutes left. He didn't like the number.

He ran through the suite of offices outside Coldwater's and came to a stout set of doors, locked. He hadn't counted on this, and he didn't want to take the time to drill. He put on the night goggles for protection, aimed the Uzi at the lock and emptied a clip into it. The wood was splintered, but nothing had budged. He inserted another clip and tried again. Still holding. The final clip did it; the lock fell from its casing, and the doors swung open.

Jesse went straight to the false bookcase and moved it back; he found a steel door identical to the one in Coldwater's study. He heard a trickling noise and looked down; gasoline was streaming into the room. Too late to use the Plastique; not the Uzi, either, even if he had had the ammunition. The lock was brass, though; it shouldn't make sparks.

He got out the drill and started on the cylinder. It was tougher, though, than the lock to the generator room, and the drill began to falter. He looked at his watch. Six minutes to go. He dug in the tool bag for the spare battery for the drill, found it, ejected the old one and snapped in the new one. The drill came to life again. Half a minute later, the cylinder gave. He put down the drill and rammed the door with his shoulder. Apart from bruising his shoulder, nothing happened.

Jesse picked up the sledge and went to work on the door. Finally, it gave. Two minutes to go. He placed the remainder of his Plastique on the floor, put the two incendiary grenades next to it and set the timer, then he grabbed his flashlight, the drill and the sledge and ran through the doorway, pulling the steel door shut behind him. The tunnel sloped downward steadily, and there were no steps, so he could run quickly. He stopped thinking about the time, he just went as fast as he could. He had covered what seemed like about a hundred yards when the tunnel suddenly turned ninety degrees to the left and came to an end. The steel door was in front of him.

Forgetting about the noise, forgetting about everything, he dropped the sledge and, holding the flashlight in his mouth, put the drill to the lock and leaned on it. The bit skidded off the lock and hit the steel door with a clang. He started over. This time the bit seated, and he was boring away the brass. He put all his weight and strength against the drill, desperate to get through, and, a moment later, the drill and the cylinder came out the other side.

He picked up the sledge and began wildly banging at the lock. He hit it six times, then eight; on the tenth blow the door gave, pushing the false bookcase before it. He stepped through and found himself in Jack Gene Coldwater's study.

"*I made it!!!*" he screamed at the ceiling.

"You made what?" Coldwater's voice answered.

Jesse opened his eyes and found Coldwater and Pat Casey staring at him; both were holding guns.

"Well, Jesse, I wondered what all the racket was," Coldwater said. He motioned Jesse to move away from the tunnel door. "That escape route was meant for me; I never expected anyone else to use it. Tell me, what are you escaping from?"

Jesse stared at the man, mute. The pistol was still in his belt, but he could never fire it in time.

"I think it's time you told me who you really are," Coldwater said. He sounded very disappointed.

Jesse found his voice. "I'm the heat, Jack Gene, and you're burnt."

Coldwater raised his pistol and pointed it at Jesse's head. "Then you'll have to join your colleague, Mr. Bottoms," he said. He thumbed the hammer back.

Then, from somewhere deep inside the mountain, came a deep rumble, and the floor underneath them shook.

Casey was the first to speak. "What the fuck was that?" he asked.

Coldwater looked at Jesse questioningly, and, as he opened his mouth to speak, there was a loud roar, and the room shook like a baby's rattle. Beams crashed to the floor, and dust filled the air.

All three men were thrown to the floor, but Jesse was the first to his feet. He did the only thing he could do—never mind that they were fifty feet above the ground—he ran hard toward the windows at the end of the room and dove headlong through the glass.

60

Jesse thought as he fell. Fifty feet. He couldn't survive that in one piece. Then he hit the tree. It rose a good thirty feet out of the ground, leafless, in its winter mode. Jesse, upside down, grabbed at branches, trying desperately to slow his fall. He tumbled, hit larger branches, held on to smaller ones, and suddenly, he was on his back in three feet of accumulated snow, wondering what had happened to him. A gunshot cleared his mind of fog. He rolled over and, clawing at the snow, got to his feet and ran toward the road, pulling the night goggles on as he floundered forward.

There were more gunshots and the soft "plop" that came when one struck the snow, but they obviously couldn't see him; they were just hoping for a strike. Jesse's mind was on something else, anyway; somewhere around here was a plastic bag with a million and a half dollars in it, and he was going to find it if he had to go through a gunfight to do it.

His pistol, amazingly enough, was still in his belt, and he drew it, just in case, to give himself the extra half-second. He stopped and looked around, and there it was, stuck into the snow like a bottle of champagne in a wine bucket. He snatched up the plastic bag and headed for the road. Then he stopped. He heard the front door of the house open and footsteps on the plowed driveway. Coldwater and Casey were in pursuit on foot.

They would think he was headed down the mountain, so he climbed a retaining wall of snow-covered boulders, ran across the drive and headed up the mountain, struggling through the snow. It was only twenty or thirty yards, he knew, even if it seemed like a thousand.

He made the clearing, and the truck was still there; he was afraid the mountain might have fallen on it. Then the vehicle became easy to see, because the sky was filled with light. He hit the snow, flat on his face and waited for the shock wave. When it came, it rocked the truck so much that he feared it would turn over. That explosion had been the gas tanks, he was sure, but they were on the north side of the mountain, thank God.

He got to his feet, got into the truck, turned it around and headed for the road. When he got there he turned off the engine and coasted down the mountain. Lesser explosions were going off, now, but they were increasingly behind him. Then, ahead, he saw a man in the road. It was Coldwater, and he was in a marksman's crouch, aiming a pistol at the driver's side of the truck.

Jesse ducked just as the windshield went white. He was driving from memory, now, trying to stay in the road. He heard Coldwater shout an obscenity as the truck passed him, then Jesse shoved the truck into gear and gave the engine a rolling start. No need to be quiet now.

He stuck his head up for one second and punched frantically at the windshield, breaking out a hole that let him see, and just in time to make a sharp curve. As he did so, a round through the rear window sprayed him with broken glass. Jesse floored the accelerator and concentrated on his driving. At least two more shots struck the cab of the truck, and then he seemed to be in the clear. He passed the church and turned right, and as he did, he was greeted with an improbable sight. Two vehicles passed him going the other way, one a milk truck, the other an eighteen-wheel Mayflower moving van. He had already done their job for them, and he was glad he hadn't met them on the mountain road.

He came to an intersection and turned left, missing a Federal Express truck by inches. There was a soldier at the wheel. Checking the rearview mirror, he saw lots of headlights in the town behind him.

Two minutes later he turned onto the airport road. His hands were nearly frozen to the wheel since there wasn't much windshield to keep out the frigid night air. The moon came out, and he could see the outline of the big hangar ahead of him, with the Reverend Packard's King Air parked next to it. He had to get out of this airport before C-130s starting landing on it.

He screeched to a halt next to the hangar, grabbed the plastic bag, got out of the truck and kicked open the flimsy door of the flight office. He vaulted over the counter and played his flashlight on a board festooned with airplane keys, looking for the right one. He found it, then ran out of the office and toward the hangar. He shoved open first one big door, then the other, then the idea of a possible pursuit occurred to him. He pulled the pistol from his belt, and, taking careful aim, shot out the nosewheel tire of the King Air.

"Jesse?" Jenny's voice called.

"I'm here, sweetheart! Stay in the airplane!"

He ran around to the pilot's door, tossed the plastic bag into the airplane and leapt in, slamming the door behind him.

"What's that?" Jenny asked.

"A new life," he replied. "I'll explain later."

He stuck the key into the ignition and groped between the seats for the checklist. Oh, the hell with it, he could remember enough to start it. He shoved the mixture and propeller control forward, flipped on the master switch, and began priming the carburetor. As he did, he looked up and saw, a mile away, a car's headlights; they were coming toward them at a high rate of speed.

Jesse turned the ignition key and prayed that the engine wasn't too cold to start. It caught, and after running roughly for a few seconds, revved smoothly.

No time for warmups, runups or checklists. Jesse shoved the throttle halfway in, and the airplane roared out of the hangar. Who could be in the car, he wondered; Coldwater and Casey couldn't have eluded the invading forces so easily. Could they? He stood on the right brake so hard that the airplane nearly spun back in the direction from which it had come.

The car was moving directly toward the airplane now, and if Jesse tried to taxi to the runway he would collide with it. Instead, he pointed the nose of the plane down the narrow taxiway and shoved the throttle to the firewall. The airplane began to pick up speed. Airplanes don't have rearview mirrors, so Jesse couldn't tell where the car was; instead of worrying about it, he flipped in the first notch of flaps and watched the airspeed indicator. He could fly at sixty knots.

Forty, then fifty, then the needle crept to fifty-five. Jesse was aware that headlights behind him were lighting his way. At sixty, he yanked back on the yoke, and the little airplane leapt into the air. As it did so, a car roared underneath it. Somebody had tried to ram him from behind.

He couldn't see the car now, because he was climbing too steeply. His airspeed was falling, and he pushed the yoke forward to let it rise again. As soon as he had eighty knots, he turned right ninety degrees; never mind waiting for the usual five hundred feet. He wondered if they were shooting at him, if they would somehow cripple the airplane.

He pushed the nose of the airplane down again, wanting to gain speed and put as much distance between him and the airport as possible. Trees rushed past him in the moonlight, fifty feet below, his recent reconnoitering made him feel safe, knowing that there were no high obstacles immediately to the south.

The GPS was still set to the St. Clair airport, so he could watch his distance increase on its screen. At five miles out, still at a hundred feet, he started to climb. He grabbed a headset from between the seats and handed one to Jenny.

"Are you and the girls all right?" he asked.

She pointed at the back seat. "I gave them each some bourbon in tea," she said.

Jesse looked back. The two little girls were sound asleep under a blanket. He went back to flying the airplane, establishing a cruise climb speed. When the climb was stabilized, he turned to the GPS and dialed in SLC, for Salt Lake City.

Jenny watched him do it. "How far is it to Salt Lake City?" she asked.

"Four hundred and eighteen miles," he said, pointing to the GPS.

"How long will it take us?"

"About three hours and a half, if there's no headwind. When we level off, the GPS will tell us exactly."

He continued climbing. His course was east of south now, so he needed an odd-numbered altitude, plus five hundred feet. He decided on eleven thousand five hundred, for the moment. Later, he'd have to climb to thirteen thousand five hundred, in order to clear the mountains south of St. Clair.

As he climbed, he made a ninety-degree right turn; it would take him off course, but he wanted to look back at the town.

As the airplane came around, he pointed toward St. Clair. "Look at that," he said.

The two of them stared at the conflagration atop the mountain. Occasionally a shell would cut an arc into the air, like a Roman candle.

"What is it?" Jenny asked.

"It's the end of Jack Gene Coldwater," Jesse replied, with some satisfaction. He turned the airplane back on course and dug behind the seat for a chart. Now he had to navigate them to Salt Lake City without coming to a sudden stop against a mountain.

61

At dawn Jesse was yawning, trying to stay awake. He had expended so much adrenaline in the past few hours that he had precious little to get him through the remainder of the flight. He did an instrument scan to keep himself awake. They had a nice, twenty-knot quartering wind, he thought, since the ground speed on the GPS was that much faster than their airspeed, as shown on the gauge.

They were an hour out of Salt Lake City, and they had fuel for another two hours and twenty minutes of flight. They were in good shape. The only thing that worried him now was a thick layer of clouds about a thousand feet under them. He hoped that would break up before Salt Lake City, because he had no idea how to fly an instrument approach. He checked the back seat; the girls were still sound asleep.

Jenny stirred and opened her eyes. She was turned toward him, a blanket over her, and she pushed it away to have room to stretch.

"How are you feeling?" he asked.

"Okay, I think. I seem to have gotten some sleep." She reached over to kiss him on the neck.

As Jenny pulled back from him he smiled at her, and he saw her eyes widen. She put her headset on.

"What's the matter?" he asked.

She pointed past him. "Look," she said.

He swiveled in his seat and looked out the left side of the airplane. There, a mile and a half or two miles away, was a bright red shape.

"It's an airplane," Jenny said.

"You're right; I guess we're not alone up here, even at this hour of the day."

"What kind is it?" she asked, and she sounded worried.

Jesse squinted at the shape. "Low-winged, looks like a Piper." He looked back at her.

"Jack Gene has a Piper Commanche," she said. "And it's red."

Now the conversation about airplanes between Coldwater and the Reverend Packard came back to Jesse: Packard had the King Air, and Coldwater had said he owned a Commanche. Something else came back; in the big hangar at St. Clair, the airplane immediately behind the Cessna had been a red Piper. He looked back at the airplane, but the sun was now peeping above the clouds, and it blinded him.

Had the occupants of the Piper seen them? Certainly, the Cessna, given its position in relation to the sun, would be easy to see. Certainly, too, if Coldwater and Casey were in the Piper, they had figured out where he was going. Salt Lake City was certainly the logical airport, if the Cessna was heading south.

"It's Jack Gene, I know it," Jenny said. "What can we do?"

Jesse unfolded the chart in his lap. There were other airports he could head to, but they were smaller towns, without easy air connections to the coast. His eye fell on the southern tip of Nevada. Quickly, he picked up the airport directory and looked up Las Vegas. There were three airports; Las Vegas International, for scheduled service, North Las Vegas, which looked like the place where corporate jets might go, and one other: Henderson Sky Harbor. Sky Harbor was smaller than the other two, and a little farther from the city; its only services were fuel and rental cars. Jesse dialed the identifier, L15, into the GPS and pushed the button twice. They were three hundred and twenty-one miles from Sky Harbor, Las Vegas. He tuned the course into the autopilot, and the airplane turned right, then settled down on the new course. Jesse waited until the ground speed settled down, then checked the time to the airport. The new course did not take as much advantage from the wind: two hours and thirty-one minutes. He looked at the fuel computer for their remaining flying time: two hours and sixteen minutes.

"Oh, shit," Jesse muttered to himself.

"What did you say?"

"I said, we're going to Las Vegas," he said, reducing rpm's by a couple of hundred. He watched the fuel computer recalculate: they now had two hours and twenty minutes of flying time.

"Is everything all right?" Jenny asked.

"Everything's fine," Jesse lied. On their present heading they would cross one of the emptiest deserts in the United States, and Jesse didn't want to think about being on foot out there. He switched the GPS to its calculator mode; there was some sort of wind speed function in there somewhere; he was sure he had read about it. He found what he thought was the right function; he entered his true airspeed and heading, and the computer showed the winds to be twenty-three knots from 300 degrees. If the wind stayed where it was, they would run out of fuel eleven minutes from the airport; if the wind moved toward the west, ahead of them, they would run out of fuel over an empty desert; if the wind moved to the north, behind them, they might make the airport. Jesse decided to gamble.

He searched his memory for discussions with his first flying instructor about airplanes. What sort of range did a Piper Commanche have? As much as a Cessna 182? More? Less? Jesse prayed that it had less range.

As he thought about this, he looked out the right side of the airplane. There, a mile or so away and slightly behind them, sat the red Piper. Jesse pored over the chart again. There was an airport called Morman Mesa, fifty or seventy-five miles northeast of Las Vegas. If, when he reached Morman Mesa, the fuel computer and the GPS told him he still didn't have enough fuel for Las Vegas, he could land there.

But it was a small place, and it could be a dead end for him. He leafed through the airport directory until he found Morman Mesa: there was a two-thousand-foot dirt strip there, with fuel by prior arrangement, whatever that meant. Probably, you had to have an appointment with somebody. No rental cars. He did *not* want to land at Morman Mesa.

Jesse got the aircraft operator's manual out and read about fuel. The wings held thirty-eight gallons of usable fuel each, for a total of seventy-six. *Usable fuel.* There were another two gallons on each side that the FAA considered unusable, because it could not be depended upon, especially if the aircraft was maneuvering, as in a landing.

An hour and quarter passed. The red Piper remained a mile off their right wing. Slowly, tentatively, the wind swung to the north. Jesse recalculated the windspeed every five minutes. The Cessna's ground speed inched up six knots. A comparison of the GPS and the fuel computer showed forty-four minutes of flying time left and forty-two minutes of fuel. Morman Mesa was looming ahead, and if Jesse was going to land there he had to make the decision now. He looked over at the Piper. "You first," he said.

As if the pilot had heard him, the red airplane began a descent. Jesse laughed aloud. "He doesn't have the fuel for Las Vegas," he said to Jenny. "He has to land at a jerkwater airport and try to find somebody to sell him fuel. Once we're in Vegas, he'd need an army of cops to find us."

Jesse consulted the GPS and the fuel computer again. Either of them could be wrong, he knew; his first instructor had told him often enough *never* to rely entirely on electronic equipment. He had made his decision. Sky Harbor, Las Vegas, even if it had to be on unusable fuel.

With thirty minutes of flying time showing on the fuel computer a light began to flash. "Low fuel," it said, over and over. Jesse couldn't find a way to turn the thing off.

62

Fifty miles out of Las Vegas, Jesse tuned in the unicom frequency for the airport. "Sky Harbor Unicom," he said, "This is November one, two, three Tango Foxtrot. Do you read?" Nothing. He repeated the transmission until, twenty miles out, he got an answer.

"Aircraft calling Sky Harbor," a voice with a thick foreign accent said.

"Sky Harbor, this is November one, two, three Tango Foxtrot. My name is Smith; I'm landing in fifteen minutes; can you arrange a rent-a-car for me?"

"Sure thing, Mr. Smith," the voice said. "The active runway is three-six."

Jenny had not noticed the blinking "low fuel" light, and Jesse saw no need to mention it to her. He began to get ready for his landing. He had descended to thirty-five hundred feet and reduced power when he spotted the airport at twelve o'clock. His instruments said he had four minutes to the airport and three minutes of fuel. He was approaching from the north, so in order to land on runway three-six he would have to fly around the airport and turn back to the north. The hell with runway three-six, he thought. I'm approaching from the north, and I'm going straight in to one-eight. He got on the radio. "Sky Harbor traffic, Sky Harbor traffic, this is November one, two, three, Tango Foxtrot. I am short of fuel, and I am straight in for runway one-eight."

A voice came back, "Tango Foxtrot, this is Whiskey Romeo; the active runway is three-six, and I'm already on base."

Jesse had the runway in sight now. "Whiskey Romeo and all Sky Harbor traffic, Tango Foxtrot is on a three-mile final for three-six and short of fuel. I say again, short of fuel. I'm landing on one-eight, so get the hell out of my way."

There was a brief silence. "This is Whiskey Romeo; one-eight is all yours."

Over the runway numbers, Jesse began to breathe normally again. He taxied toward a row of tied-down airplanes and spotted a space between two other Cessnas. Camouflage, he thought. He turned into the space and stopped. As he reached for the mixture control to stop the engine, it stopped itself. The airplane was out of fuel.

"Okay, everybody, out of the airplane!" he cried.

Jenny woke the girls and, carrying their luggage, they walked to the terminal. Jesse kept a particularly tight grip on the plastic bag.

He persuaded the man at the counter to accept a five hundred-dollar cash deposit in lieu of a credit card, and a hundred-dollar bill for himself, in lieu of a driver's license. Jesse explained that he had left his wallet at home.

The car was filthy; it appeared never to have been washed, the ashtrays were full and it had eighty thousand miles on the speedometer, but Jesse loved it. No one would give it a second glance. On the drive into town, a happy thought occurred to him: they were in the one city in the United States where no one would bat an eye at the sight of large numbers of one-hundred-dollar bills.

They drove down the main drag, blinking in the desert sunlight and agog at all the neon. Jesse picked the biggest, gaudiest hotel he could see and pulled into the driveway.

"Checking in, sir?" a doorman asked.

"You bet." Jesse handed him the keys. "Take everything in the trunk, please." The man began removing their bags. "I'll carry this one," Jesse said, taking the plastic bag from him. As they were about to enter the hotel, there was a huge roar behind them. They turned and stood, transfixed, as a man-made volcano erupted before their eyes. "Only in America," Jesse said to the sleepy girls.

Jesse presented himself at the front desk. "I'd like a two-bedroom suite, something very nice," he said to the desk clerk.

The young man typed a few strokes on his computer keyboard. "I'm afraid we don't have anything at all, sir," he said, eyeing the rough-looking man in the sheepskin coat with the hillbilly accent.

Jesse placed the plastic bag on the counter, counted out ten banded stacks of hundred-dollar bills and stacked them on the counter. "And I'd like a hundred one-thousand-dollar chips," he said.

A sharp-eyed older man in an expensive suit practically elbowed the clerk out of the way. "Good morning, Mr. . . . ?"

"Churchill," Jesse said. "W. S. Churchill."

The man scribbled out a receipt for Jesse's money, then hit a bell on the desk. A bellhop materialized. "Take the Churchill family up to the Frank Sinatra suite," he said to the man, then turned back to Jesse. "Your accommodations and all your food and drink will be compliments of the house, Mr. Churchill. May I send your chips up to your suite?"

"Thank you, yes," Jesse said. They followed the bellman toward the elevators.

Jenny tugged at Jesse's sleeve. "Did that man mean everything is *free?*"

"Sweetheart, when you can afford to buy it, you often don't have to," Jesse replied.

"I don't understand this place at all," Jenny muttered as they got onto the elevator.

The following morning, they breakfasted *en famille* on their rooftop terrace. The living room was filled with boxes and tissue paper and luggage from their shopping, and there were one hundred and twelve one-thousand-dollar chips on the coffee table. Jesse had been down nineteen thousand dollars at one point, but he had come out ahead.

Jesse was transfixed by the *New York Times*. The story began on page one and was continued inside on two full pages. The explosion at St. Clair was being compared to Mount St. Helens. Troops were in charge of the town, hundreds of people were being questioned at the church and, in spite of sporadic gunfights, casualties were light, and there had been only two deaths, the guards on the mountaintop. Jack Gene Coldwater and his principal lieutenants were presumed dead in the explosion. He'd have to do something about that.

Jesse got up from the table and found the plastic bag. He emptied all the money into a new plastic briefcase, then took the papers from Coldwater's safe and spread them out on the coffee table. Jesse became short of breath. The documents were bank statements from all over the world, and, at a rough calculation, the balances totaled something over fifty million dollars in Coldwater's accounts alone. Letters from the various banks contained the secret numbers for all the accounts—Coldwater, Casey and Ruger's.

It occurred to Jesse that he was now rich beyond his wildest dreams. If he wanted that. He thought about it for a while, then he put the documents in an envelope, along with the recorder he had worn, and scribbled an address. He picked up the phone and asked the hotel manager to come to his suite.

When the doorbell rang he cinched his new

silk robe around his waist and went to answer it. The manager stood at the door. "Good morning, Mr. Churchill. You wished to see me?"

"Yes, please come in," Jesse replied.

The man removed an envelope from his breast pocket. "Incidentally, here are the air tickets to Los Angeles you requested."

"Thank you." Jesse had made Tokyo reservations from Los Angeles in their new name at a travel agent's. "Please have a seat." The two men sat in chairs on opposite sides of the coffee table.

"What else can I do for you, Mr. Churchill?" the manager asked.

Jesse set a plastic briefcase on the coffee table beside his chips. "I have a hundred and twelve thousand dollars in chips to cash in, and inside this case is another one million, four hundred thousand dollars in cash, all quite legal, I assure you. I probably shouldn't be carrying around this much cash, and I would like your advice as to what sorts of negotiable instruments I could exchange it for."

"Will you be traveling abroad?" the man asked.

"Possibly."

"I would suggest either gold certificates or bearer bonds," the manager said. "Either can be negotiated at any large bank in the world in a matter of hours, and I could arrange either for you by lunchtime."

Jesse scooped the chips into a large ashtray and handed them to the manager, along with the briefcase. "A million and a half in bearer bonds will do very nicely," he said. "I'm sure there will be some fees and commissions involved; the extra twelve thousand in chips should cover that."

"Oh, much more than cover it," the manager said.

"See that anything left over goes to your favorite charity," Jesse said.

"Thank you, sir," the man said, writing out a receipt for the funds. "Will there be anything else?"

Jesse held out his parking check. "Would you see that this rent-a-car is returned to Sky Harbor airport as soon as possible. There's a five-hundred-dollar cash deposit there; that can go to charity, too. And may we have your limousine for the airport at two o'clock?"

"Of course."

"One other thing." He handed the manager the large envelope containing Coldwater's banking documents. "I want to send a friend this package, and I don't want him to know where it came from; sort of a little joke."

"I understand," the manager said. "Perhaps I could forward it through our New York office."

"Excellent. Could you Federal Express it to them and have them take it to a FedEx office there and resend it?"

"Of course." The manager looked at the envelope and repeated the address. "Mr. Kipling Fuller, Nashua Building Products, 1010 Parkway, College Park, Maryland."

"That's it. And I think that's all you can do for me."

The manager stood. "May I say what a great

pleasure it has been having you and your family as guests in our hotel? We hope you'll come back soon and often."

"Thank you very much. You may be sure that when we are in Las Vegas we will always stay with you."

At two o'clock, the Churchill family departed the hotel in the longest limousine Jesse had ever seen, even in Miami. Outside the terminal, Jesse dropped a paper bag containing his pistol in a trash can. The luggage was checked at the curb and the skycap handed Jesse his baggage tickets.

"Gate three, sir; you have thirty-five minutes before your flight."

Jesse gave the man twenty dollars and followed his family to the departure lounge. He had been there for ten minutes when a uniformed airline employee approached.

"Excuse me, Mr. Churchill, there's a problem with a piece of your luggage; could you follow me, please?"

"What sort of problem?" Jesse asked.

"They didn't say, but it should only take a moment."

Jesse turned to Jenny. "I'll be right back, but in any case, you get on that plane, you hear?" He handed her the briefcase containing the bearer bonds. "Take care of this."

She nodded.

Jesse got up and followed the man across the lounge and down a flight of stairs. "Down at the end, there," the man said, pausing at the bottom of the stairs and pointing at a door a hundred feet away.

"Thanks," Jesse said. He walked through the area, where baggage was being moved to and from airplanes, then came to a door marked, "M. Quentin, Baggage Manager."

Jesse stepped into the office. A man seated at a desk looked up.

"Hello, Jesse," Coldwater said.

63

The door slammed behind Jesse, and he turned to see Pat Casey standing behind him. He noted that both Casey and Coldwater's pistols were equipped with silencers. When the time came they wouldn't have to worry about noise.

"You are a very great disappointment to me, Jesse," Coldwater said sadly.

"Jack Gene," Casey said, "why don't you just off him and get it over with?" He walked carefully around Jesse and stood in front of him as Coldwater came from behind the desk.

"He can't do that just yet, Pat," Jesse said. "He doesn't know what I've done with his banking documents; yours, too."

Casey turned to Coldwater. "What is he talking about?"

"Let me explain, Pat," Jesse said. "When I opened Jack Gene's safe and took the money, I took all the banking documents, too. They included the numbers to all the secret accounts, Jack Gene's, Kurt's and yours. You understand, don't you, Pat, that anybody with the account numbers has access to the accounts?"

Casey looked alarmed. "Jack Gene—"

"Shut up, Pat," Coldwater said. "Now Jesse, I'm prepared to do a deal; you give me the documents and you can keep the cash from the safe. That's enough for a fresh start somewhere, isn't it?"

Jesse managed a smile. "Not as fresh a start as with the sixty or seventy million in all those banks," he said. "What's the matter, Jack Gene, didn't you memorize the account numbers?" He turned to Casey. "You didn't think you would live to spend all that money, did you, Pat? Jack Gene had your account numbers, after all. He had Kurt's, too. He never planned on letting you keep it."

Casey stopped looking at Jesse and turned to Coldwater. "Listen to me, Jack Gene—"

Coldwater looked annoyed; he turned slightly and shot Casey once, in the forehead. Casey spun around and fell across a stack of suitcases, and his pistol landed at Jesse's feet. Jesse started to reach down for it, but Coldwater was too quick.

"No," Coldwater said, training his gun on Jesse. "You couldn't pick it up fast enough, believe me. Now think about it, Jesse, and you'll do the right thing."

"You mean, just hand over the documents and go on my merry way with your million and a half in cash?" Jesse reckoned his flight was boarding now. Time was short. "Could I trust you to do that, Jack Gene?"

"All I want is the documents, Jesse."

"Sure, Jack Gene. After I've just watched you execute your oldest and dearest friend? Why would you want to be so nice to me?" He had to get closer to Coldwater, or get Coldwater closer to him. He watched Coldwater thumb back the hammer on the pistol. "That's unnecessary, Jack Gene; that model is double action, after all."

"Jesse, you're wasting our time; we both have planes to catch."

"Come on, Jack Gene; there's a nationwide APB out for you already; you wouldn't even get through airport security."

"Nobody's looking for my Comanche," Coldwater said, "and I've got the range for Mexico."

He was right, Jesse thought. In any case, Coldwater had more time to waste than he did. "Well, I guess you're in something of a quandary, Jack Gene. If you shoot me, you'll never get the documents and the money. You'll be right back where you started, twenty years ago. On the other hand, if you put down the gun, then that would make me feel that we could trust each other. I mean, the million and a half is already in a bank abroad; you couldn't take it away from me."

Coldwater gazed at him. "You have a point, Jesse." He kicked Casey's pistol away, then tossed his own onto the desk behind him. "All right, where are the documents?"

"At this moment," Jesse said, "they're in the hands of a task force in the Justice Department, the same people that took your town last night." Jesse shifted his weight slightly and turned a shoulder toward Coldwater. "So, you see, you've never going to get your hands on a single dollar of that money. You're going to be a fugitive for the rest of your life, however short a time that may be."

Coldwater looked stunned and that quickly changed to anger. "You idiot," he said. "Do you think I need a weapon to kill you?"

"Yes," Jesse said. "You do."

Coldwater's fingers darted toward Jesse's eyes, but Jesse was ready. He caught the thrust on his left forearm, and, as hard as he could, he rammed his fist into Coldwater's throat. Coldwater grabbed at his neck with both hands, staggering backward toward the desk. Jesse kicked with his left foot and swept the bigger man's legs from under him.

Coldwater lay gasping for air, his eyes wide. Jesse moved gingerly around him, pushed the desk out of the way and retrieved Casey's pistol.

"You have a minute or so before you lose consciousness," Jesse said to Coldwater. "And a little while after that before you expire. I learned about that from somebody in prison who tried to do it to me."

Coldwater's hands slipped away from his throat, but he continued to stare at Jesse.

"Of course, that kind of death would point to a third party," he said, "and I don't want anybody looking for me." He brought the pistol up. "This is for Jenny," he said, then fired a single shot into Coldwater's throat.

Jesse quickly removed the two men's wallets,

then rearranged the bodies, wiped his fingerprints from the pistol and placed it in Coldwater's hand. A murder-suicide was the best he could manage on short notice. When everything looked right, he cracked the door to the office and looked around. He found a "do-not-disturb" sign hanging on the inside doorknob, transferred it to the outside and closed the door behind him.

He found Jenny where he had left her, and a voice was announcing final boarding for their flight. "Sorry to be so long," he said, picking up the brief-case. "Let's get aboard." He walked them toward the boarding gate, then, as they passed the ticket agent, he tugged at Jenny's elbow. "You take your seats; I'll be right with you."

"Jesse—" she said, alarmed.

"I'll be there in two minutes, I promise."

Reluctantly, she herded the girls down the gangway.

Jesse stepped a few paces aside and took the portable phone from his pocket. He dialed the number of the Justice Department in Washington. When the operator answered he said, "This is Dan Barker; patch me through to Kip Fuller, with the task force in Idaho."

There was a short delay, then a ringing.

"This is Fuller," he said. "This better be important."

"You busy, Kip?" he asked.

"Jesse! Where the hell are you?"

"I'm gone, Kip; I just wanted to say goodbye and to do you a favor or two."

"A favor? What are you talking about?"

"First of all, I've sent you a little package, care of Nashua, in College Park. I think you'll enjoy the contents."

"What is it?"

"Don't be impatient, Kip. Let me speak to Barker."

There was some mumbling, then Dan Barker came on the line. "Jesse?"

"Listen carefully, Dan. I can still blow you out of the water by releasing everything to the papers. I might even be able to get the investigation into my partner's death reopened. Do you understand me?" This was a bluff.

There was silence for a moment, then Barker folded. "Yes, I understand you."

"Good. Unless I read in the *New York Times* within ninety days that you've resigned from the Justice Department, I'll release everything. I have only to make a phone call. Do you understand me?"

"Yes," Barker said.

"Good; you have ninety days to think about it. Now put Kip back on the line."

"I'm here, Jesse," Kip said. "What was that all about?"

"Barker is considering early retirement."

"Listen, we found Ruger's body, along with Charley Bottoms'. What happened?"

"The recorder is in the package; it will explain everything."

"What about Coldwater and Casey? Where are they?"

"Don't worry, they'll turn up. But believe me, they're not going to be a problem."

"Jesse, I can get you the pardon now; no problem."

"You hang on to it for me, Kip, in case I ever need it."

"If that's what you want."

"Tell Barker I'll be watching the papers, and take care of yourself."

Jesse broke the connection. He wiped the phone clean of fingerprints and dropped it in a trash receptacle, along with Coldwater and Casey's wallets, then he boarded the airplane.

Epilogue

Akaroa, South Island, New Zealand,
Four Months Later

Jesse stopped into the village post office for his mail. Along with the usual utility bills and advertising circulars there was a letter from the home secretary's office in Wellington.

"Morning, Mr. Warren," the postmistress said. "Lovely day."

"Getting a bit chilly, though," he replied.

"Winter's coming."

Winter came in June in this country. "Suppose you're right."

"Think you'll like us as well in winter?"

"Seems an awfully nice place. I thought I'd look at some property." The postmistress was the local real estate broker, too.

"Glad to show you some; there's a very pretty place down on the point; bit pricey, though."

"I've got to run up to Christchurch today. Maybe we could look at it tomorrow."

"Glad to show it to you."

Jesse stepped out onto the porch of the post office. Behind him he heard the postmistress speak to another customer.

"That's Mr. Warren," she said. "American writer; pretty well known in the states, I hear. Been here for a couple of months, now; looks like he might stay."

Jesse opened the letter from the home secretary and read it. He, his wife, and his two daughters had been granted permanent residence status in New Zealand. Jesse smiled, put the letter into his pocket, got into the car and headed for Christchurch. It was his habit to drive up there once a week.

In the public library at Christchurch he read through the most recent copies of the *New York Times*. They were always at least a month old. On the national news page he found what he was looking for:

NEW APPOINTMENT AT JUSTICE

The White House press office announced today that Kipling Fuller has been named Assistant Attorney General for Law Enforcement. Fuller, who has been given credit by insiders for masterminding the successful raid on the Aryan Universe cult in Idaho, had been Deputy Assistant Attorney General, in charge of the department's special task force on dangerous cults, following the resignation of Daniel Barker, who retired last month.

The piece went on to recount Kip's background in law enforcement and his leading of the raid. Then, further down the page, Jesse saw something he had not expected.

DEATH AT ATLANTA PRISON

The Justice Department announced today that Jesse Warden, a former DEA agent who was serving a long sentence for the murder of another agent, died yesterday in the hospital of Atlanta Federal Prison, of injuries received in a fight with another prisoner in the exercise yard. Warden left no survivors.

Jesse closed the newspaper and returned it to the stacks. Well, he thought, it was almost as good as a presidential pardon.

He got into his car and drove back toward Akaroa. If he hurried, he would be in time for lunch.

Santa Fe, New Mexico, October 31, 1993

Acknowledgments

I am grateful to my editor, HarperCollins Vice President and Associate Publisher Gladys Justin Carr, and to her staff for their hard work in the editing and preparation of this book; to all the other people at HarperCollins who have worked for the book's success; to my agent, Morton Janklow, his principle associate, Anne Sibbald, and their colleagues at Janklow & Nesbit, who have been so important to my career; and to my wife, Chris, for her help, understanding, and love.

Author's Note

I am happy to hear from readers, but you should know that if you write to me in care of my publisher, three to six months will pass before I receive your letter, and when it finally arrives it will be one among many, and I will not be able to reply.

However, if you have access to the Internet, you may visit my website at *www.stuartwoods.com*, where there is a button for sending me e-mail. So far, I have been able to reply to all of my e-mail, and I will continue to try to do so.

If you send me an e-mail and do not receive a reply, it is because you are among an alarming number of people who have entered their e-mail address incorrectly in their mail software. I have many of my replies returned as undeliverable.

Remember: e-mail, reply; snail mail, no reply.

When you e-mail, please do not send attachments, as I *never* open these. They can take twenty minutes to download, and they often contain viruses.

Please do not place me on your mailing lists for funny stories, prayers, political causes, charitable fund-raising, petitions, or sentimental claptrap. I get enough of that from people I already know. Generally speaking, when I get e-mail addressed to a large number of people, I immediately delete it without reading it.

Please do not send me your ideas for a book, as I have a policy of writing only what I myself invent. If you send me story ideas, I will immediately delete them without reading them. If you have a good idea for a book, write it yourself, but I will not be able to advise you on how to get it published. Buy a copy of *Writer's Market* at any bookstore; that will tell you how.

Anyone with a request concerning events or appearances may e-mail it to me or send it to: Publicity Department, Penguin Group (USA) Inc., 375 Hudson Street, New York, NY 10014.

Those ambitious folk who wish to buy film, dramatic, or television rights to my books should contact Matthew Snyder, Creative Artists Agency, 2000 Avenue of the Stars, Los Angeles, CA 90067.

Those who wish to make offers for rights of a literary nature should contact Anne Sibbald, Janklow & Nesbit, 445 Park Avenue, New York, NY 10022. (Note: This is not an invitation for you to send her your manuscript or to solicit her to be your agent.)

If you want to know if I will be signing books in your city, please visit my website, *www.stuart woods.com*, where the tour schedule will be published a month or so in advance. If you wish me to do a book signing in your locality, ask your favorite bookseller to contact his Penguin representative or the Penguin publicity department with the request.

If you find typographical or editorial errors in my book and feel an irresistible urge to tell someone, please write to David Highfill at HarperCollins Publishers, 10 East 53rd Street, New York, NY 10022. Do not e-mail your discoveries to me, as I will already have learned about them from others.

A list of my published works appears in the front of this book and on my website. All the novels are still in print in paperback and can be found at or ordered from any bookstore. If you wish to obtain hardcover copies of earlier novels or of the two nonfiction books, a good used-book store or one of the online bookstores can help you find them. Otherwise, you will have to go to a great many garage sales.